Scrabble Weather

Montana Rising

Book 2

LeeAnn Bonds

Whithersoever Books
Saipan, CNMI

For Zack

you're always my next adventure...

CONTENTS

Your Free Book Is Waiting

When Marla's drug-riddled, chaotic life puts her beautiful little girl in danger, it takes every ounce of courage Marla has in her to make a heartbreaking sacrifice.

Read the story of the fateful day when Kit and Montana Rising's daughter, Marla, leaves 11-year old Noelle with the Risings and disappears from all their lives for years…

The game board that inspired this Scrabble Thread story.

Each of the words played in this game appears somewhere in the
story Monti is writing, the chapters of which are included in
alternate chapters in this book.

In the Air

The roar filling the cabin changed tenor in that distinct way that meant they had left the ground, and Monti let out her breath. Seven hours. A short layover in Denver in the middle, but in seven hours they would touch down in Orlando, collect their baggage and hug Monti's waiting parents.

And Marla. They'd see Marla for the first time in eight years. But first they had to get through the flight. Monti sneaked a sideways glance at Kit. He looked okay so far, "so far" being about sixteen minutes in the luxurious leather first class recliner. She smiled to herself as she realized he was exploring all the bells and whistles of his seat's accoutrements with studied nonchalance.

Neither of them had ever before, in sixty-something years, flown first class. But Monti had insisted this time. The bare thought of Kit's long limbs and deteriorating spine crumpled into the pressurized sardine can that was coach seating made her cringe. It would be disastrous. They could afford this.

Monti turned to check on their granddaughter across the aisle. Noelle was exploring her accommodations too, but with wide eyes, appreciating the luxury and no doubt eagerly anticipating a sweet seven hours of pampering.

No anxiety pinched the young woman's face but it would again soon, Monti knew. Noelle hadn't slept well for days, worry over the reunion with her estranged mother compounding the grief of having lost her home and all her possessions in the house fire.

A stewardess—flight attendant—Monti corrected herself, stopped at her seat. "Good morning, ma'am. My name is Teri. May I bring

1

you a cup of coffee or another beverage?" She offered Monti a menu printed on thick, textured card.

"Oh yes, coffee please," Monti said. "Cream and sugar?"

"Of course, ma'am," Teri said, her eyes crinkling as she smiled.

She must be forty-three or four. Monti tried to imagine working in the confined spaces of an airplane, on her feet all day responding to the whims and complaints of anxious travelers, into her forties. She hoped Teri enjoyed her chosen profession. It made Monti tired just to think about it.

"G!" Noelle stage-whispered at her, waving her phone and waggling her beautifully shaped eyebrows. "Scrabble?"

"Sure, sweetie. Give me a minute." Monti tugged her purse out from under the seat and found her phone.

"Did you see this?" Kit said, holding a newspaper toward her.

"Hmm?" She looked from it to him. "When would I see the newspaper…you just bought it at the airport, Kit."

"Mike Rutherford's wife is divorcing him."

"Oh." Monti sank back. "That's rotten. No second chances for him, huh?"

"Hmph. I'm sure he's far beyond second. But no, she's not going to stick with him through this rough stretch."

"But rough stretches are when it really counts!" Monti said, feeling ridiculously outraged at Valerie's formal abandonment of her husband.

She'd never even met the woman, or Mike for that matter. But even though Mike was Blaine's father and Blaine had wreaked havoc in their lives, and even though Mike himself, driving drunk and without a license, had crashed into an old lady and hurt her terribly, Monti tried not to wish for bad things to happen to either of them. Her face went hot at these unlovely thoughts.

"Are you going to call him when we get back?" she asked.

"I guess so." Kit shifted in his seat.

Uh-oh. "You all right?" She asked.

"Yes, I'm fine," he bit out. "Don't start that already, Monti, or it's going to be a really long flight."

Stung, Monti turned back to her phone. She found the Scrabble game just as the flight attendant arrived with Monti's coffee in a ceramic cup and saucer, with a tiny basket of cream and sugar and a real spoon. "Thank you, Teri," Monti said.

"You're welcome," she said, as she set a cup in front of Noelle. "Anything else I can get for you ladies? Sir?"

"No, thank you," Kit said. "Where are you from, Teri? I hear a remnant of the deep south in your voice, don't I?"

"Yes, sir, I'm originally from Georgia."

"Oh, so you're headed almost home on this trip."

"Well, no sir, Georgia hasn't been home for a very long time. I live in Seattle now." She cleared her throat. "Are you folks from Florida?"

"No," Kit said. "My wife's parents live there, and our daughter is…also there. We're going to see them."

"Very nice," Teri said with a professional smile. "Well, enjoy the flight and y'all let me know if you need anything at all." She blushed at her conscious slip into the twang of her youth and moved on down the narrow aisle.

"Monti," Kit said, his voice low.

She slid her eyes sideways at him.

"Sorry," he said, his cheeks red.

She reached out and squeezed his hand. "You want in on the Scrabble game?" she asked.

"No, no, you girls battle it out. I'm going to finish the newspaper and then try for some sleep." He shifted again and settled back, flicking and folding the paper into a readable arrangement. Monti noticed the tight lines around his eyes and mouth. He was in endurance mode already.

She tried not to think about it and opened the Scrabble app on her phone. Noelle was a good match for her, and she relished practicing with her granddaughter when Kit wasn't available. Kit groused about this being unfair, but she knew she needed all the practice she could get if she was ever going to win anything like half their games together.

Would Marla play Scrabble with them? They used to play when Marla and Stephen were teens, the four of them. But that was light years ago. She had no idea what Marla was like now. No idea whether Marla even had the luxury of things she liked to do, or hobbies, or favorite books.

Monti's heart clenched at the thought of how much damage her daughter had done to herself. Would they be able to weather it? She prayed it would not destroy their family when Marla came home.

She looked forward to talking with her mother, asking if she'd gained any insights in the short time Marla had been with them since getting out of rehab. Her mother would tell it to her straight. And she had good instincts about people. Monti would make it a point to get alone with her soon as possible after they arrived.

Her phone pinged as Noelle's first play appeared on the board. Monti hadn't even looked at her digital tiles yet. She'd better get busy.

Anniversary

Nora leaned against a giant tree and pulled off her shoe. She had another rock. "Hang on, Logan," she called. He turned, frowned, and hiked back to her.

"Do you need help? Careful, that's a cedar. You don't want to get a cedar sliver in your hand, it'll fester."

She stood back from the tree and examined her hand. "Why do you know that?" She sighed and sat on a handy boulder to knock the rock out of her old tennis shoe. "I should have worn better shoes." She glanced at him waiting for the *I told you so,* but he smiled.

"It's all right Nora-ne-Nelson," he said, using the nickname he'd coined for her when he read their wedding announcement in the paper. "Maybe we can duct tape around the tops so rocks can't get in."

She rolled her eyes. "The Wiz of Sticky rides again! Is there any problem in the world you think can't be solved by a judicious application of duct tape?"

"It might actually work," he said.

"Well, maybe. Tell you what, hon. If I get two more rocks in my shoe, we'll give it a shot."

"I brought the Hello Kitty duct tape...I'm just saying."

She laughed as he pulled her up, and after she redid her ponytail and pulled it through the back of her pink baseball cap, they stepped back onto the trail. The warm August sun found its way to the forest floor here and there in bars of spangled light. Their feet crunched through the pine needles on the path.

Nora shifted her pack, breathed in the rich cedar-and-moss

scented air and followed her husband of 364 days, deliciously cute in his faded *Hike for Hospice* T-shirt and nerdy cargo shorts, pockets bulging. She admired his broad shoulders and the damp hair curling on his pink neck.

She couldn't quite remember how their first anniversary ended up as an overnight camping trip, but she was game to try it even though she'd never been a fan. She was a dyed-in-the-wool suburban girl, not having slept in a tent anywhere except her back yard since Girl Scout camp.

Twelve years old, she had been, enduring the bugs, the heat, and the sports activities with pronounced distaste, and flatly refusing to participate in the woodland hike. She'd sat in the cramped and cluttered camp director's office for the duration of that hike, in disgrace but profoundly relieved to not be wandering in the forest. It was hard to believe that was ten years ago!

Logan wasn't really an outdoorsman either, but his biology classes this semester included several sample-collecting treks into this bio-diverse forest. He wanted to show her his new skills and the gorgeous little Queen Lake. He'd been researching the Olympic National Park and planning like a maniac for weeks. And she was crazy in love with him, so camping it was.

Ahead of her Logan stopped. She moved up beside him.

"What is it?" she asked.

He was peering down an overgrown road curving away up the hillside. "It could be an old logging road…"

"Too narrow, I think," she said.

"Well, it's some kind of road. It must lead somewhere, right?"

"Yeah, so?"

"So, let's go see!" He looked at her with those big hazel eyes, sparkling with curiosity.

"Logan…"

"Oh, come on, just for a little ways."

"What if we get lost?" she said, her voice squeaking on the last word. "We don't have a map, right?"

"We don't need a map, hon, we have our phones," he said. He took his out and examined the face of it. "Oh," he said. "No bars. But hey, I have a compass and we won't go far, really. I just want to see what's up ahead. Maybe take a couple of pictures."

"Okay…okay, just for a little ways." Nikki tamped down the fear coiling in her belly. Logan wouldn't let anything happen to them. It was just a walk down a pretty trail. She needed to put her big girl panties on and act like a grown woman, not a scared little girl.

Logan grinned from ear to ear, shifted his pack and beckoned her forward with his entire body. He didn't notice her discomfort, for which she was grateful. He didn't need to know what a wimp she was and to what depths her childhood fear still tormented her.

They had only walked about 10 yards when Logan's boot made a hollow clomp as he stepped onto a sheet of plywood in the trail. It spanned a muddy gully gouged through the path. Eye bolts stuck out of one edge of the plywood. Curious, Nora said, "Logan, pick it up."

"What?"

"The plywood. There are eye bolts in it. It used to be a sign or something."

Logan stepped backwards off the plywood and wedged his fingers under one edge. It resisted being lifted and made a bizarre sucking sound as it let loose of the mud beneath it. Nora grabbed a stick and scraped away the goo still clinging to it. "No Entry," she read. She raised an eyebrow and looked at her husband. "No Entry," she said again.

"It's not saying that anymore," he said. "The sign has been re-purposed and is now just here to increase the safety of people walking on this trail."

Nora narrowed her eyes at him. She looked around. There were posts on either side of the trail with remnants of chain still dangling from them. Obviously the sign hadn't moved far from its original home. She pointed silently at the posts.

"Yeah? Same deal. They took the sign down, Nora. Honest, it's fine to keep going. Do you see any no trespassing signs on any trees?"

Nora felt frustration rising. His logical mind was so hard to argue with. And she knew her objections rose from fear. She consciously relaxed and made herself give in. "Okay Logan," she said. "But it's on you if we get lost and arrested and taken to a dungeon and tortured and excommunicated and deported."

Logan laughed. "You're hilarious, Nora-ne-Nelson," he said and kissed her between the eyes.

Fifty yards later Nora had another stinkin' rock in her shoe! "Logan!" she called. He wasn't that far ahead but a roaring sound had been getting steadily louder, and her shout sounded tiny. He didn't hear her. No way was she going to let him out of her sight. She jogged up the trail limping with each step as the rock pressed into her heel. "Logan!"

Logan stopped. She moved up beside him. They were at the edge of a roaring creek. A cool breeze saturated with spray caressed them. But her eyes widened and she looked up at her husband. There was no bridge. They were standing on one end of a huge log laid across the rushing water. A huge *wet* log, dark and slick with moss. And rot.

"You've got to be kidding me," she shouted at him above the roar. "No freaking way!"

"It's safe," he shouted back. "Look at the footprints." He gestured at the overlapping prints, recently made, covering the top of the log. The fear in her stomach uncoiled and spat at her. What was the matter with her? She was with Logan now. Everything was fine.

"Never give up, never turn back," Logan quipped.

She rolled her eyes. No fair using a line on her that she always used on him. This was different.

"I'll go first," Logan said. "I'll make sure it's safe." He looked at her to see if she would buy into that. She gritted her teeth and nodded. Logan walked out to the middle of the log, over the center of the crashing creek. He did a little leprechaun jig to show it was safe, which made her smile.

Then a shot rang out, making them both jump. Logan's big backpack pulled him off balance and he fell, wide eyes locked on hers and arms cartwheeling, into the rushing water. Nora screamed. Had he fallen or had someone shot him? She darted out to the center of the log, dropped to her hands and knees and scanned the water below the log.

Logan surfaced, his eyes bulging and terrified. "Nora!" He spluttered. He reached for her outstretched arm, but the current carried him away downstream, smashing him against rocks and logs protruding from the violent water.

Nora, sobbing uncontrollably, hurried to the far bank and left the path to follow his progress along the shore, scrambling through thickets, wincing as blackberry thorns tore at her, crashing into trees, crying out as tree branches knocked her cap away and whipped into her eyes, falling again and again as she watched him and not the ground in front of her.

She lost him once, twice. Each time she spotted him again her heart lurched with relief. She gasped as Logan smashed up against a tangle of logs and roots, grabbed a leafy branch and held on with white knuckles. The creek was wider here, shallower and quieter. Nora struggled to free herself from her backpack, slid down the gravelly bank and waded out to him. She stumbled and fell against him sobbing with relief.

Logan, gasping for breath and gritting his teeth, gripped Nora's shoulders and pushed her away from him. "Nora," he gasped. "Get off…"

"What?" She said. "What's wrong? Are you okay?" She scooted back and looked him over. She followed his movement as he reached down to grip his submerged right leg. Her world went wobbly. Logan's leg was so, so very broken.

On the Ground

"Please return your seat backs and tray tables to the upright and locked position," crackled over the speaker, waking Monti from a light sleep. She set about pulling herself together.

She had enjoyed the flight, eating a reasonably decent meal on real plates, receiving solicitous care from the attendants offering drinks and warm washcloths and blankets and entertainment and whatever else you could possibly want, apparently.

But Kit's suffering blunted her enjoyment. He was still sleeping now, having eventually given in to the need for medication. He would be groggy when she woke him. And grouchy. The sooner they got on the ground the better. She sent up a plea for grace and reached over to tug at his sleeve.

Fifteen minutes later the three of them maneuvered up the aisle and clomped down the jet-way. They paused for a moment when they got inside the terminal while Kit snapped open his brand-new collapsible cane.

Monti wasn't too familiar with the Orlando Sanford airport, having only visited her parents a few times since they had left the mission field and settled in Florida. Kit pointed out the baggage claim sign and they joined the flow in that direction. Monti walked quickly, eager to see her parents again.

She spied her dad first, head and shoulders taller than most people. Her mother, a bright bird, flitted about her towering tree of a husband. When she saw Monti, she waved with her whole body and smiled her 5000-kilowatt smile. Monti's eyes filled. As aggravating as her mother could sometimes be, Monti loved her deeply. She had missed them both more than she'd realized.

She scanned the people around her folks but didn't see anyone who might be Marla. Was she here?

As soon as they reached her parents her mother wrapped her in a fierce hug. "Montana Eloise Rising!" she said. "Let me look at you."

When she pulled back Monti looked the question into her mom's eyes.

Her mom shook her head. "She didn't come, sweetie," she said. "She tried, but she just couldn't do it."

Monti's dad left off hugging Noelle and reached for Monti to pull her in close. "You'll see her soon enough, Monti," he said. "She's doing okay, don't you worry."

Monti put her arms around her dad and hugged him tight. "Hi Dad," she said, her throat tight.

Her dad leaned down to her ear and said, "Kit looks like he's hurting pretty bad, what can we do to help?"

Monti turned to look at Kit. He was about done. She went to him. "Kit? What do you need?" She slipped her hand into his.

"I guess I need another of those damn pills," Kit said, his voice low. "How far is the drive to your folks' again?"

"About an hour," she said. "Would it be better to go straight there? Or stop at a restaurant first maybe?"

"I don't guess it's going to make a lot of difference at this point. Let's see what your folks want to do."

After a few minutes the group reached a consensus. They would stop at a Hardee's about fifteen minutes away, eat a sausage biscuit and catch up a little, then head home.

They collected their bags and hauled them to the Housels' van, a lime green 15-passenger monstrosity with "Life Begins at the End of Your Comfort Zone" painted on the side in almost straight letters. Its steering wheel was the size of a wagon wheel. A chair lift replaced the side doors on one side, and a cardboard box of snacks held a place of honor in the front passenger seat.

"Corn Nuts, Jody?" Kit asked as he collapsed his cane and laid it on the console between the front seats.

"Hmm? Oh, those Lost Boys are wild for Corn Nuts," her mom said. "I can't keep them in stock. I finally ordered two cases from the grocer to give myself a little breathing room." She took the box from

Kit and plunked it into the back acreage of the van somewhere.

"So you're still working with the Sudanese refugees?"

"Oh yes, we love those young men. Those four are keeping us from getting old, aren't they, Bob?"

"Yes indeedy. Until we keel over trying to keep up with them. Everyone buckled in?" Bob asked, peering back at them in the wide rear-view mirror. Kit had climbed in to ride shotgun, Monti sat next to her mom, and Noelle slid into the row behind them. Bob found his way out of the parking garage and into the traffic on Airline Avenue.

"Mom, you're wearing hearing aids!"

Jody touched her ear self-consciously. "Yes, I finally gave in. They're so expensive, I didn't want to spend the money. But I have to say, it's lovely to hear what's going on and not always have to ask Bob to repeat everything."

"I bet he likes that, too," Monti said.

"You have no idea," her mom agreed, rolling her eyes.

Monti shifted to face her mother. "How's Marla, Mom?" she asked.

Her mom tilted her head, intensifying her resemblance to a fluffy little bird, and reached over the back of their seat to grab Noelle's hand. "She is so looking forward to seeing you all. But it might not seem like it straightaway. She's been through a lot, and it's taken its toll. It breaks my heart."

Monti glanced at Noelle, who was trying not to cry. The knot in Monti's stomach undid itself and tied itself in a fancier tangle. "Do you think rehab did what it was supposed to do?" Monti asked. "Is she...is she clean and sober?"

"I think she is," her mom said. "She's very quiet, and humbled. Embarrassed I think, but beginning to open up a little to your dad and me. We love her just the same as we used to, you see, and I think she's starting to believe that."

"That's good. That's good," Monti said, letting out a deep sigh. "We want her to come home with us, but I admit we're scared. And with our temporary living quarters, there isn't much room. Could get pretty stressful."

"Have you thought about her birthday?"

"Not much, to be honest. We'll just have got back home on the 14th, so dinner out for her birthday the next day, I guess?"

Her mom nodded. "I think that's a good enough plan for now. You don't want to go overboard right away."

"Right. Save the going overboard for later..." Monti grimaced at her mother, who just grinned at her and patted her cheek.

"How's the new house coming?" she asked. "Did you bring pictures?"

"Of the fire?"

"Well, no. I don't guess you took pictures of that, but of the lot. What it looked like after the fire. And you know, any progress since then."

"Kit actually has taken quite a few pictures. He started the next day, so we do have the sodden heap to show you," Monti said. "We're starting from scratch. They let us pick through the heap after they decided it was safe, but we didn't find much worth salvaging. So they bulldozed it flat and we have a clean slate for rebuilding."

"But the good thing is," Noelle said quietly, glancing at the men who were deep in conversation, "we're going to do the new house all on one floor. We're putting in ramps and handrails and wheelchair accessibility all through the house. You know, planning ahead."

Jody bit her lower lip. "Yes, I can see that will be a good thing for Kit." She took hold of Monti's hand. "Oh, but Monti, that breaks my heart too."

Monti squeezed her mom's hand. "Mine too, Mom. We do what we have to do, right? This is going to be a really good thing, so we can stay where we are in the town we love, and Kit can have his independence far longer than otherwise."

"And here we are," her dad announced, pulling into the Hardee's parking lot. They piled out of the van. Monti went to Kit's door, surreptitiously offering her shoulder to steady him as he climbed down. They exchanged a look and Monti was surprised to see gratitude in his eyes and not irritation.

He grasped her shoulder and stepped down out of the van. He

was reaching back in for his cane when his grip on her shoulder tightened fiercely, making her cry out as the pressure forced her down and Kit collapsed to the pavement on top of her.

In the River

"Oh my God, Logan!" She couldn't process what she was seeing. The dreadful syllables 'com-pound-frac-ture' banged repeatedly through her head like hammer blows. Just below the knee, Logan's leg bent in a bad, bad direction. A point of shattered shin bone tented the skin, just shy of breaking through. She gulped, forcing back vomit. She tore her eyes away and looked at Logan's face. His eyes were clenched shut, his face white and rigid with pain. She didn't know what to do. But she was already shivering from the icy water.

"Logan, sweetheart," she said. "Logan, I think we have to get you out of the water," she said into his ear, still having to talk louder than the noise of the creek.

He opened his eyes and looked at her. She could see him forcing himself to understand what she was saying. He gave her a curt nod. Nora tugged at his backpack straps, and after a few seconds he started helping her to free him from the pack. That was the easy part. That would probably be the easiest part of anything they did for the foreseeable future. Now what?

She needed to get him loose from the snarl of roots and branches. She tugged at his right arm, pulling him toward her. He leaned toward her compliantly, until the movement shifted his shattered leg. He let loose a scream that shook Nora to the bone. She wept heaving sobs for his torment but didn't let herself give into it. She had to get him out of the freezing cold creek.

"I'm sorry, I'm sorry Logan," she cried. "I have to do this!" She got her hands underneath his shoulders and pulled him away from the mass of downed trees as he howled in pain.

Once they were free of that she pulled him backwards toward the bank an inch at a time. Logan screamed almost nonstop, clamping down on it when he could, gritting his teeth, but the screams burst out again and again as Nora dragged his leg across the creek bed.

She stumbled as they reached the bank and sat suddenly on the graveled slope. She peered up the slope to the forest floor. How on earth was she going to get him up the bank? She was gasping for breath already, her muscles quivering from unaccustomed exertion. She couldn't believe how cold the water was, burning her skin. Logan was shivering too and crying.

She bent her head to his and cried with him. *Oh God, what are we going to do? I can't do this!*

Rope.

Nora lifted her head. Rope? Did they have rope with them? "Logan," she said, jiggling his shoulder. "Do we have rope?" Where had that thought come from?

"Yes," he said through blue lips and clenched teeth. "In my pack."

Of course he had packed rope. He had a list of everything they could need for camping and emergencies and who knows what else, and had meticulously checked off each item as he stowed it in his or her pack.

"I'm going to go find it," she said, "to help us get you out of the water."

He nodded. She squirmed out from under him and laid him gently back onto the creek bank. Then she waded back out to the mess of roots where Logan's pack was snagged. It took her a couple of minutes to untangle it and pull it free. She was astonished at how much heavier it was than hers. Of course, it *was* soaking wet. She couldn't lift it. She dragged it, tripping and stumbling through the water to Logan, where she stopped to rest and push the wet hair out of her eyes, breathing hard.

She laid the pack against the bank, got under it and pushed it up the slope, slipping and scrambling for footing, until she heaved it up onto the level ground above.

She fell against the bank, catching her breath. She glanced down at Logan, several feet below her. "You okay, Logan?" What a stupid question. He was as not-okay as it was possible to be.

He raised a hand to her and let it flop back down.

She scrambled up to the level ground, shrugged her own backpack off, grabbed Logan's pack and unzipped the main compartment. She froze as a dime sized beam of light shone through a hole in the pack onto the contents.

There were two holes…she slid her finger through one and imagined a trajectory. Then she carefully packaged that thought, compressed it into a tiny lump and pushed it into a dark corner at the back of her mind.

Nora shivered and dug around until a neon green hank of nylon rope surfaced. She grabbed a jacket and a towel too, and slid back down the bank to Logan, where she made herself look at his leg again. Should she try to splint it before moving him again?

"Logan," she said, teeth chattering. He turned his head toward her. "Logan, should I try to…stabilize your leg before we move you again?" He stared at her, uncomprehending. She was going to have to make this decision on her own, somehow.

Wait…rope. That was the thought put into her head. Rope meant moving him. So she would do that first, and hope it was the right thing. Besides, they were going to freeze to death if they stayed in this icy water long enough for her to figure out how to splint a compound fracture.

She worked steadily, threading the rope under her inert husband's arms, padding it with the towel and jacket. Knotting the rope behind him, she left the two long ends trailing. She had no idea if this was right, but it looked vaguely like the rescue situations she'd seen in a movie or two. Who knew she should have paid more attention to mountain climbing disaster movies!

"Okay, I'm going back up to the top and find a tree to use." Logan didn't respond. Her heart pounded and the writhing fear in her stomach somehow roared in her ears louder than the creek. She'd better hurry.

She grabbed the rope and scrambled back to the top, wishing for gloves. Wishing for a ladder. Wishing for espresso and a shower and a weekend at a spa and to be sleeping and wake up from this horrible nightmare.

She stood, every muscle on fire, with the rope in her hand. A convenient tree at least a foot in diameter stood ready to help. She walked around it with the rope and got ready to pull.

"Are you ready, Logan?" she yelled. "I'm going to pull you up the bank now!" No response. She shot up a prayer for strength and pulled.

At first she thought he must be caught on something because she pulled with all her might and nothing moved at all. But just as she was about to cave, she felt movement!

She set her feet again and pulled harder. A small shift, and another—she was doing it! She re-gripped the rope further up and heaved again, then glanced back. She couldn't see him yet, but it was working.

She put her whole body into a prolonged pull, stepping with tiny steps back from the tree as Logan moved up the bank.

Then Logan screamed and she nearly let go the rope. What had happened? He continued screaming—but she couldn't let go or she'd have to start over and there was no way she'd be able to do that. She gripped the rope harder, shocked to see red smears on the green nylon where her hands had been. She pulled with everything she had, glancing back again and again, until she saw his head appear, then shoulders, and then the pulling was suddenly easier.

He was on the forest floor.

She pulled until his feet were up, then let go the rope and fell on her rump, stopping herself just in time from catching herself on her hands. She didn't dare look at them. They were burning with pain and she wanted to see, but that would be a bad idea.

She turned and shuffled over to Logan on her knees. His screams had quieted to crying again. "I got you," she said, kissing his forehead. "I got you, Logan."

She started to loosen the rope from around him, ignoring the pain in her hands, working gently. She glanced down at his leg and instantly understood the screams. The fear slithered out of her stomach, up her throat and choked her.

A tip of splintered bone now protruded through Logan's skin.

Ambulance

Monti's chin hit the rough pavement of the parking lot. *What just happened?*

"Grandma?" Noelle said, her voice squeaky with panic. "Grandpa, are you okay?"

Kit lay heavily on Monti and she worked to get out from under him, bloodying her hands and knees on the oily asphalt. A sharp pain shot up her back as she twisted free and knelt over him. His eyes were closed, but he was breathing. "Kit!" She jiggled his shoulder. "Kit! Come on honey, talk to me."

Kit grimaced and grabbed her hand. "I'm okay," he said.

"You are not!" Monti said.

Bob had turned back toward them from the door of Hardee's. "Jody call 911," he yelled into the restaurant. He jogged back to the van, reached in and produced a towel which he rolled up and put under Kit's head.

"Noelle honey, keep an eye out for cars pulling into the parking lot." He squatted down next to Kit. "What's going on, son?" he asked.

"No idea," Kit said. "I'm on the ground, not sure why."

"You fell, or collapsed or something, as you were getting out of the van," Monti said. "Did you black out?"

Jody hurried toward them with two husky men in EMT uniforms behind her. "Bob, look who was having lunch at Hardee's!"

One of the men, pink and blond and not much over 20 years old, made a quick detour to their ambulance and fetched a medical kit. His partner, an older man with chocolate skin and compassionate eyes, checked Kit's vitals and began asking him questions. Between the two of them they examined him from head to toe.

19

Monti backed off to give them room to work and stood rigid in Noelle's embrace, hardly able to breathe.

"Grandma, your hands! Oh, and your poor chin!" Noelle said. "Let's go in and wash them. You need a Band-Aid or two or three."

"No, maybe in a little bit." She moved to get a better look at what they were doing to Kit.

Jody, ever watchful over her peeps, caught this exchange and extracted a first-aid kit from the vast interior of the van. Bob brought a chair from the Hardee's dining room and pushed Monti down into it. Jody cleaned and bandaged her daughter's scraped face, hands and knees. Monti was oblivious.

People stared out the windows, and a chubby man with a "Manager" name tag stepped one foot out the door. "Anything I can do to help, folks?"

Bob said, "Thank you sir, I think these gentlemen are doing what's needed."

"Allrighty then," he said, and disappeared back inside.

The blond EMT jogged back around the corner of the restaurant to their vehicle and came back pushing a gurney. Monti stood up. "What's happening?"

"Ma'am, he needs to go to the hospital to get checked out more thoroughly," the older man said. "He's stable and in no immediate danger, but he needs to be examined by a doctor. You can ride along with him."

Monti nodded. Her family piled back into the van in silence while Monti walked alongside Kit, holding his hand as they rolled him to the ambulance. A young lady in a Hardee's apron dashed out and handed the blond EMT a paper sack. "The rest of your lunch, sir, and a couple extra sandwiches," she said, and dashed back to her work.

"Well ain't that nice," he said, and nestled the sack at the foot of the gurney.

They did all the mechanical things with the gurney's under-structure and slid Kit into the back of the ambulance. The young EMT helped Monti in before jogging around to the driver's seat.

Monti sat on a vinyl bench seat against the wall. She took in the acrid disinfectant smell and the tightly packed, combo RV/emergency room/airplane fuselage look of the space in a daze while the older EMT opened and closed cabinets, ripped open Velcro, snapped things shut, checked gauges and made notes on a clipboard. Monti lost her balance as the ambulance started up and braced herself on the bench.

"Monti," Kit said. She focused on him and leaned in. "I'm okay," he said.

"We're in an ambulance, Kit. We wouldn't be in an ambulance if you were okay," she said.

"The EMT said he thinks it might have been a TIA."

"TIA. Temporary insanity action, timeline inversion area, terrible icky… aardvark," she said, gripping one trembling hand with the other.

"Monti, you're yammering. TIA is transient ischemic attack, I think that's right. A mini stroke. No permanent damage."

"Okay, that's not really making me feel better." She looked up as the older EMT sat down across from her.

He smiled at her and said, "I have a few more questions for you folks."

He and Kit talked for the rest of the drive. Monti spiraled off into her internal fears, terrified of what might happen. Terrified of losing him. She barely formed that thought and tears threatened to choke her. She dove deep to find the Rock and ask for peace and courage to face whatever it is they would have to face.

By degrees the terror eased off, and when she was again able to focus on what they were saying, they were no longer discussing Kit's medical history. The EMT was talking about his walk with God and the strength that gave him to do this difficult work.

"I was deeply grateful for the medical personnel after my injuries in Kuwait," Kit said. "They did outstanding work that saved my life and gave me back to my family, and I still ask God to bless them every day."

The man nodded in understanding. "Don't worry, sir, we're gonna take good care of you today too, so you can get back to your family."

Monti wished fervently that she could feel the calm confidence that these men exuded instead of the shaky faith and brain-sucking fear that rose up if she didn't keep tamping it down. It would back off surely, once she had more information. There were too many unknowns. She needed to research TIAs. In fact, she wanted to do that right now, but couldn't quite bring herself to pull her phone out of her pocket and consult Google on the matter.

You would think after losing a son, and almost losing her husband in the war and her daughter to drugs, and then weathering the house fire, that her faith would be a little more robust by now. But every new test seemed to knock her back almost to square one, panicking about how she was going to get through it and wondering where God was in this mess. Sometimes it made her wonder whether she really believed at all.

But when she considered any other foundation for her life, any other way to live at all, she couldn't stand it after about 3 1/2 seconds. She knew in the depths of her soul Who she belonged to. Now, if she could behave like one of his children for the rest of the day, that would be a noble accomplishment.

The ambulance slowed, turned, and pulled up to the emergency room entrance. Monti took a deep breath and thought of "girding up her loins" as she took the hand of the EMT and descended from the ambulance.

First Aid

Nora shivered as Logan lay clenching his teeth with his eyes squeezed shut. She had to get help. She had to call 911, if there was service here. Where was her phone? She fought off the buzz of panic and concentrated on that question.

It was in the special padded device pocket in Logan's pack. She gingerly turned the pack over using her arms, unzipped the pocket with the tips of her damaged fingers, and pulled out her phone. She sank back onto her heels. It was as dripping wet as she was. She tried turning it on—nothing.

Where was Logan's phone? It had a waterproof case! He usually kept it in his back pocket. She shuffled around him on her knees and wriggled her hand under him, wincing with pain. There it still was, amazingly! She bit her lip as she struggled to get a grip on it and work it loose from his pocket without jostling him. There!

But her triumph evaporated when she saw the smashed screen and bent frame. It was destroyed.

What was she going to do now?

First aid kit.

Nora startled, and then choked out a bitter laugh. First aid? She needed second aid. She needed one-thousandth aid. But she would look in the pack and see if there was a first-aid kit.

Every muscle in her body screamed for her to lie down and be still. Instead, not wanting to touch her shredded palms to the ground she shuffled back around to Logan's pack. She stuffed both ruined phones in the padded pocket and zipped them in. She found first a bottle of water, opened it and took a swig. It slid sweet as nectar down her throat. She stretched one arm out to Logan, scooting closer until she could reach him.

"Water, Logan," she said. "Take a drink, sweetheart."

He let her dribble some water into his mouth and then took the bottle from her and drank deeply.

"Maybe not too much right away," she said pulling the bottle away from his lips, though she wasn't sure why. Wasn't that what people said in the movies? "I'll hold onto this for you, okay? You can have some more in a minute." Logan nodded and she kissed his dirty face.

She dragged herself upright to sit in front of the pack and resumed digging through it, flinching whenever her palms brushed against a rough surface. She pulled out a red, soft-sided nylon case. The white cross printed on its side told her she'd hit pay dirt. She ripped open the Velcro straps with a couple of non-shredded fingertips and unfolded the kit on the ground in front of her. Wow. It kept unfolding and unfolding, emergency treasures tucked into each little pocket.

But what did she need? She picked up a packet of capsules. "For severe pain. Take two with water." Well, Logan needed that, for sure. She started the trek back to her husband, stopped, and snagged a strap of the first aid kit. No use going back and forth a hundred more times. She dragged it behind her and positioned it near Logan.

"Logan, I found some Tylenol or something." She tore open the packet, opened the water again and helped him down the capsules with a swallow of water. "Good. That should help you, honey." Though she didn't see how anything in a packet in a first aid kit could put a dent in the pain he must be enduring.

She returned to examining the kit. Iodine? She read the tiny text on the miniature bottle and nodded. Gauze bandages. Tape. Antibiotic ointment.

She arranged her chosen supplies next to Logan's thigh. First she dumped the rest of the bottle of water over the horrible blood-stained abomination poking out of his leg, shuddering as she did so. Logan didn't react.

Then she dribbled all of the bottle of iodine on and around the wound, staining his skin and bone yellow-brown.

She tore open the packet of antibiotic ointment. Could she put this on without hurting him? She glanced at him again, and then squeezed a worm of ointment out of the packet, letting it drop onto the tip of bone, swiveling her wrist to make a swirl, like poisonous frosting a nightmare cupcake. She pressed the packet again, and squeezed every last bit of the ointment out onto the bone and the torn edges of skin.

Logan uttered a guttural moan, sending shards of ice through the bottom of her stomach. She had never heard him moan before. And she didn't ever want to hear him moan again. She shook herself. *Must finish.*

Nora tore open several paper packets and pulled out gauze bandages. She lay the small snowy squares over the exposed bone. They stuck to the ointment and stayed where she put them. Then she unfolded two big gauze bandages like handkerchiefs and layered them carefully over the whole mess, taping down the edges as gently as possible. She examined her handiwork. It would have to do. She wadded up all the packaging and stuffed it down into his pack.

Smoothing Logan's damp hair away from his eyes, she kissed his temple. His eyes were closed again, and he seemed to be resting okay. Maybe the medicine was taking the edge off.

Nora pulled the first aid kit open yet again. A big pocket held a thick tablet-style paperback: *US Army Survival Manual.* Her heart raced at that. She could read directions, couldn't she?

She set it beside her and rummaged in the kit again until she found another packet of ointment and bandages for her hands. She smeared and wrapped one hand and then the other, relieved to have some protection for her damaged palms during whatever she was going to have to do next.

She picked up the survival manual again and found the table of contents. Psychology of Survival...A Look at Stress...maybe she'd read that later. Down to chapter 4, Bone and Joint Injury. She flipped to page 27 and read:

"There are basically two types of fractures: open and closed. With an

open (or compound) fracture, the bone protrudes through the skin and complicates the actual fracture with an open wound. After setting the fracture, treat the wound as any other open wound."

So she'd already done things in the wrong order. She scanned down to find out how to set the fracture, and the words began to swim in front of her eyes. It overwhelmed her. Improvised traction splint. V-notch of a tree...follow the guidelines for immobilization...guidelines for splinting... Where were all these guidelines?

How could she ever do this? Her hands throbbed and she was so, so tired. She let the manual slide to the ground and put her head down on her knees.

"Aleph bet vet...," she sang quietly, beginning the singsong Hebrew alphabet song she'd learned with her tutoring student last year. "Gimmel dalet hey..." It had become a mantra to her, its foreignness sharpening her focus and bringing her calm when she was stressed. She sang the soothing syllables, phrase after phrase. "Samech, ayin pe fe." She breathed deeply, straightened her back, and by the time she reached "Shin, sin, tav," she was ready to do the next thing.

She picked up the manual again. Tucked into the book were two yellowed sheets of paper stapled together. She slid the creased and grimy pages out and unfolded them. *Directions How to Build a Travois* stared up at her, along with crude line drawings and instructions in odd, error-filled English.

She turned it over. Where had Logan found this? She remembered the word *travois* from somewhere. An old schoolbook about Native Americans, maybe? Except the picture here showed not a horse, but a person pulling the triangular frame of poles.

She sat back. It was exactly what they needed. She couldn't set his leg. When she imagined trying it, all she got was Logan screaming in unending pain, and her pathetic, hysterical, inevitable failure. She had to get him to someone who could help them. She read the instructions from beginning to end, and then again. She might actually be able to make one of these to move Logan to...where?

She pushed that thought aside for the moment while she

pondered the next problem. She would need an ax or something, and she *knew* Logan didn't have an ax! Nora dropped the pages and leaned over to look in Logan's pack.

A shot cracked the air and she jumped, cowering as adrenaline surged through her and the sound bounced around in the trees. She peered into the woods around them, having no idea which direction the sound had come from. She couldn't see far. The light seemed dimmer...how much daylight did they have left? She glanced at Logan—his eyes were still closed.

Shelter.

The command in her head would not be ignored. Shelter. Like a tent? They didn't have a tent, Logan had reserved a cabin for them somewhere.

Another shot zinged through the forest and she froze—but it was far away. At least, she thought it was further away than the last one. Maybe she had a little time. And what were they shooting at anyway? Were they hunters? Bad guys?

Never mind, she had to do the next thing. Shelter, apparently. She dug through Logan's pack, certain there was no tent, not sure what she was looking for, until her hand closed around a handle. She pulled out a miniature hatchet in a black nylon sheath.

Unbelievable. He *did* pack an ax. She didn't even know they owned an ax, or hatchet, or whatever. What was the difference between an ax and a hatchet anyway? She would look it up. Someday.

Embroidered on the sheath was the word Gerber...like the baby food company? Well, it *was* a baby hatchet. Heavy, though.

Okay, hatchet...she peered into the pack again and something shiny caught her eye. She pulled out a Ziploc bag containing several silver mylar emergency blankets, each compactly folded into the size of a deck of cards. She recognized them from the space suit costume she'd cobbled together one Halloween without anyone's help, using three or four of these dollar store 'space blankets' and a roll of duct tape.

Hey! Logan said he'd packed the Hello Kitty duct tape. She raked through the contents of his pack, wincing as pointy bits poked her hands, until she came up with the roll.

"Look at that, Logan, I'm going to build you a space suit. Or a tent. Or something." She picked up the Survival Manual again and found the section on Shelters. She skimmed past all the instructions involving ponchos and parachutes, but read the 'field-expedient' section carefully. She sat and thought for a couple of minutes, forming an idea, planning it out.

She would chop a few branches from nearby trees and make kind of a shelter around Logan. She would spread an emergency blanket or two over that and tape them in place. There was nothing in the manual about mylar, but the book was old. Maybe mylar hadn't been invented yet when they wrote it. She'd use another couple of the shiny sheets as actual blankets for them.

Nora unsheathed the baby hatchet and tucked the cover in her jeans pocket. After checking that Logan still slept, she went to look for some branches that she could reach.

About fifty feet away she found a tree with branches almost down to the ground. She selected one, positioned herself and swung hard, whacking into a branch (not the one she was aiming at) and sending searing pain through both hands. She gasped, blew out a couple of hard breaths, and forced herself to try again.

By the time she'd mangled three or four boughs so badly that they fell off the tree, blood was seeping through her bandages and her stomach was rumbling. She sheathed the hatchet and tucked it into her waistband. Gathering her branches, she dragged them back toward Logan, tripping over roots in the failing light. She'd better hurry.

A mournful howl stopped her cold and a scream fought to escape from behind her clenched teeth as she fell and curled into a terrified ball on the ground.

Hospital

Noelle sat with her great-grandparents in the hospital cafeteria. She scooted her chair closer to the worn Formica table and wrinkled her nose at the floor cleaner vs. overcooked veggies smell permeating the room.

They all sipped coffee. Noelle and Jody had sweet, frothy cappuccino-like concoctions dispensed from a fading but functional cup-at-a-time machine. Bob's black brew made him grimace with each swallow, but he kept swallowing.

"Why are you drinking that if it's so horrible?" Jody said.

"I've had worse," he muttered.

Jody shook her head and leaned toward Noelle. "What he really means is he paid $1.75 for it and there's no way he's gonna let that money go to waste."

She patted Noelle's knee. "Are you ready for us to call your mom? She'll be expecting us to show up at home pretty soon. I need to let her know what's happening and make sure she doesn't panic about her dad. But do you want to talk to her on the phone? Or do you want to wait until we get home?"

Noelle hesitated. "GG, I think I want to wait. Is that okay? I need to see her face when I talk with her, if that makes any sense."

"Of course it makes sense, honey," Jody said, patting her knee again. "This isn't going to be easy, any of it. We'll just take it slow." She stood up. "Okay, I'll go find a quiet spot and call her. Then we can think about something to eat. Maybe you can investigate the menu for items that look marginally edible?"

Noelle laughed. "I will GG."

***

Monti walked into the cafeteria to find her father and Noelle standing in front of a black felt board with push-in letters. They were arguing the relative reliability of chicken à la king versus beef stroganoff versus a can't-go-wrong chef salad, with the gravity of homeowners choosing new siding. Monti cleared her throat.

"G!" Noelle turned and hugged her. "How's G?"

"Sleeping," she answered. "Where's Mom?"

"Calling Mom," Noelle said. She reddened. "I wasn't ready to talk to her."

Monti pulled her granddaughter in close. "That's okay, Nellie. There'll be plenty of time. Looks like we'll be in Florida for a little longer than we planned. In fact, Dad," she said over Noelle's head. "Do you have plans for Christmas?"

Bob shifted his attention from the tray-filling options to Monti's question. "Ah...we do, but what they are is eluding me at the moment."

"What's eluding you, Bob?" Jody asked. She still held her phone. A vertical line between her eyes marred her usually sunny face.

"Our Christmas plans," he said.

The line disappeared as Jody smiled at Monti. "Are you staying for Christmas?"

Monti nodded. "If that's okay. The young man who says he's Kit's doctor but looks more like he's in costume for his high school play, says he doesn't want Kit to fly for ten days. And by then it will be the twenty-first, and I don't know that we'd be able to get a flight home that close to Christmas."

"So it was a TIA then," Jody said.

"Yes, but the tests they did..." Monti rubbed her eyes with her fingers, squeezing away the tears forming there. She looked at her parents. "They got a fresh picture of how badly his spine is deteriorating. We hadn't had any imaging done back home for a year or so."

Noelle hugged her tighter. "Not good?"

"Not good," Monti agreed. "Kit was just getting to the point where he could use the cane without it ruining his day. This doctor put the word *wheelchair* out there, and Kit didn't take it well."

"Oh, honey," her mom said.

"Kit is set on a second opinion, by which he means Charlie Eastman, but the doctor showed us the films and it was pretty obvious even to me. I don't think he's going to hear what he wants to hear from Charlie." Monti's parents and Noelle surrounded her and they held each other close.

The tension in her shoulders was softening just a bit when someone said "People? Can we do the hug therapy somewhere else, please?" They all turned to see who had spoken. A muscled man in scrubs and a meticulous goatee glared at them, arms crossed.

"There's no need to be rude, young man," Jody said. "You might try the time-honored phrase 'excuse me'." Monti and Noelle moved back to the table, and Bob guided Jody away from the offender. "People, indeed. I'd like to talk to his mother." Bob shushed her.

When Jody sat down Monti asked her, "Did you get a hold of Marla?"

The line between Jody's eyes reappeared. "I did. She sounded...off. I'm a little worried about her."

"Off?" Monti said. "What do you mean 'off'?"

"Oh, nothing I can put my finger on. Maybe she was sleepy. She didn't know what time it was, and she didn't really want to talk."

Bob said, "We should get home as soon as we can. It might be better if she's not by herself."

"I can't leave Kit," Monti said. "But you guys go. We'll get a cab. I agree, if she doesn't sound right, then you should go be with her." Monti took Noelle's hand in both of hers. "What about you sweetheart, you want to go with the Great-Grands?" Noelle stiffened and her eyes widened. "You don't have to, you can stay here with me," Monti assured her. "Like I said, we're going to be here for a few days. There's no rush."

Noelle relaxed, but tears stood in her eyes. "I want you to be there with me, Grandma," she whispered.

Monti nodded. "No problem," she said firmly. "You stay with your grandpa and me for now, and my folks will give us a call when they figure out what's up with your mom, right?"

She looked at them to confirm. They nodded, their compassion for their great-granddaughter painted across their faces, making Monti's heart spasm with love for them.

"Mrs. Rising?"

Monti turned. A young nurse in a pony tail and apricot scrubs held a clipboard. "Yes?"

"Dr. Porter wants you to come back to Mr. Rising's room, please."

"What's happened?"

"I'm not sure ma'am, but he said you should come right now."

Monti looked at her family for a moment, then followed the girl out the door.

Wolf

She was lost! Mommy and Daddy were away on the boat and Uncle Jimmy would never ever find her and the wolf would pounce on her and rip out her throat and turn her into a werewolf and Annie wouldn't want to be her BFF anymore...she moaned, rocking herself in her tight ball on the ground, face grinding into the sticks and pine needles, inhaling dust and grit as she drew in breath for another sob.

This started her coughing and broke the spell of ancient terror as she was forced to sit up and catch her breath between coughing jags. When they subsided she took stock. She was alone in the forest. In the chill almost-dark. With a wolf. But she was not four years old. And no, actually, she was not alone.

The wolf howled again. She cringed...but instantly a blanket of peace settled over her, dispelling the cold and her fear and infusing her with courage. She sat up tall. Listened.

"Abba?"

Go on, child.

She stood immediately, trembling in awe...wanting to stay and understand what was happening but knowing she had been commanded and must go, back to Logan, back to do the next hard thing.

She looked around, picked up her fallen hatchet and the cut boughs, and hurried back to where her grievously injured husband lay, needing her as she had never yet needed him.

She carried out her plan, first carefully stashing the hatchet in her pack. She arranged the boughs as she had envisioned, using the tree Logan was lying under as a pillar to support the structure. Even as she heard the howl again she kept on, unfolding the mylar sheets and draping them over the boughs. She used up the whole roll of Hello Kitty duct tape securing them.

She retrieved both packs and the first aid kit and leaned them against the tree. She untied their sleeping bags from the pack frames and rolled hers out next to him, on the side away from his mangled leg. It would be impossible to get him into his sleeping bag, so instead she lifted his head and flattened his bag into a pillow for him. She tucked the last shiny blanket over his still-sleeping form, avoiding his leg.

Her stomach rumbled insistently. It was dark. She was exhausted. A fourth shot—or third? Or fifth? —ricocheted through the forest and she flinched. Maybe the shooter was hunting the wolf. More power to him.

She contemplated looking through the packs again for a flashlight, or a granola bar. Or her hairbrush, she thought, pulling out her hair band and dragging her fingers through the tangles in her hair. Instead she opened her sleeping bag and lay down. She looked at Logan's dirty face, frowned at the deep furrow between his eyes where there hadn't been one this morning. She kissed him gently on the lips, listened to the mournful howls of the wolf for a moment, and sank into a miraculous, golden, unafraid sleep.

***

The flute soloist was doing a lovely job today. Her trills and runs floated like silk on a breeze. A second flautist joined in, not quite in tune with the first. Nora frowned. That couldn't be right.

A piercing squawk sounded right over her head and Nora sat up, suddenly wide awake. A bird flapped away in a burst of noise. When she realized where she was, she groaned and tried to lie back down but her hair had caught in the branches of the shelter she'd made.

She'd made a shelter!

Travois.

She froze, her bandaged hands deep in the tangled hair above her head. She waited, holding her breath.

Travois.

Yes! She let out her breath, relaxing. It was undoubtedly going to be horrible, but she would not be doing this day alone.

She looked down at Logan, whose waxy skin and sweat-beaded forehead drained away her confidence. She couldn't force her eyes down the length of his leg. She yanked at her hair until it pulled loose from the branches and knelt down to feel his cheek. He opened his eyes.

"Hi Nora-ne-Nelson," he whispered.

"Hi love. How's things?"

Logan groaned and shut his eyes for a long moment. "Did you hear the wolves?"

Nora gulped. "Yes. Yes I did." She pushed the memory of them back into the corner of her mind where she'd crammed them last night. "How's your leg, sweetheart?"

"Not too good. Got any more of those pills?"

"Let me look," she said, and grabbed the first aid kit. She rifled its pockets thoroughly, twice. No pills of any kind. She frowned. "There aren't any, Logan," she said. He groaned again. "But we have water, and granola bars." She opened her pack and pulled out another bottle of water and several granola bars, as well as a fat chocolate bar in a purple and gold wrapper "Hey! My favorite! Thanks, Logan."

"Your favorite what?" he rolled his head toward her.

"Cadbury's Fruit and Nut," she said.

"What?" he frowned at her. "I didn't..." He gasped. He must have moved wrong, because his whole body convulsed with pain and he uttered that guttural moan that raised goosebumps on Nora's arms. She clasped his hand.

"Hold on, Logan, hold on." She fumbled for the bottle of water, took a long swig and wrapped Logan's hand around it. "Here's the water, and an excellent granola bar," she said, setting a couple on his stomach. "No high-fructose corn syrup or anything. Just the good stuff." She paused to kiss the vein throbbing at his temple and whispered, "I have to make a travois now."

She scrambled to her feet, stuffed a granola bar in her pocket and after a moment's hesitation, broke the Cadbury's in half. She lay one half on Logan's stomach, popped a fat square in her mouth and put the rest in her vest pocket. Cadbury's for breakfast beat even the most excellent granola bars in her book.

"I won't be far," she said around the chocolate. "I have to go down to the creek and get some poles." This source of raw materials had just come to her in a flash of brilliance, "So if you need me, yell."

"What?" Confusion fought with pain on Logan's face.

She leaned down and smoothed damp hair away from his eyes. "It's gonna be okay, Logan. We're not alone. I love you like crazy, I'll be right back." She blinked back tears he didn't need to see, snatched the hatchet from her pack and crunched through the deep layer of dry pine needles and frilly Douglas Fir cones to the creek bank. Looking out over the burbling water, she spied several straight, slender trees in the tangle not far from the bank.

Now all she had to do was get down there, whack off enough branches to free three of the trees, haul them up the bank, tie them together per the directions on the mysterious how-to sheet, make some sort of flat surface on the top for Logan to rest on, and find a way to get him onto it without killing him.

Then load him on the travois, and then…her mind stalled, refusing to move in that direction, because there was no more plan after that. Her shoulders slumped as yesterday's exhaustion threatened an early return. She wanted to sit down and cry.

But she couldn't. She couldn't sit down, and she couldn't cry, and she couldn't think about that right now. Right now she had work to do.

Impatient Patient

Monti stepped off the elevator behind her apricot guide and was led to the nurse's station. The teen-aged doctor...*no, I have to stop that.* Dr. Porter looked up from a chart and said, "Mrs. Rising? Please step in here a moment." He gestured to a tiny waiting room.

Monti's heart thumped. A private consultation without Kit didn't bode well.

"Mrs. Rising," he started when they were both seated.

"Please call me Monti," she said.

"Very well. Monti," he started again. "Uh...I see you've injured your face and hands."

"Yes, when Kit fell." She waved that away. "What is it you need to talk with me about?"

"Ah, yes. Your husband is insisting that we discharge him."

"Oh, excellent!"

"No, ma'am, not excellent." The doctor shook his head, looking more than ever like an inexperienced high school actor.

"Why not? Is there a problem?"

"Well yes, there are several more tests we want to run. And we'd like to keep him overnight for observation."

"I see." Monti thought fast. Kit would already have asked this doctor all manner of questions before putting his foot down on being discharged, so Porter must not have a very convincing argument. "Are these additional tests critical? I mean, is he in danger if he doesn't have them?"

"No ma'am, not immediately."

"What do you mean, not immediately? Is he, or isn't he in danger if he doesn't have the additional tests?"

The doctor frowned. "The initial test results were encouraging," he said. "We don't think he's high risk for a stroke, or even another TIA. So he's not in immediate danger. But the tests will tell—"

"The tests can wait, in other words, until we get home?" she asked, and raised an eyebrow at him.

He hesitated, then caved. "Yes, technically they can wait. But—" He raised a finger at her and said, "But we want to keep him overnight—"

"Why?"

"—for observation."

Monti folded her hands on her lap. "Young man, will you kindly stop talking to me as if I'm a brainless cardboard 'family member of patient' or however you're labeling me in your head and think carefully about the next thing you say? I would like to know the reason—the life-protecting, medically critical reason—why my husband needs to spend a night twisting and turning on a horrible hospital bed, being subjected to frequent interruptions to whatever brief bits of sleep he might manage to get? Why is this necessary? What could you possibly observe that's so important that this sweet, strong, long-suffering man needs to be put through more pain and humiliation than he's already enduring all day long, every single day?"

The doctor blinked at her. He inhaled and opened his mouth. He shut it again. He cocked his head. "Humiliation?"

"Yes, humiliation!" Monti said. "He's a retired Army officer, doctor. He's capable and intelligent. He commands, he makes things happen. You're beginning to know what that's like, aren't you?"

The young man nodded, blushing, which made Monti decide he might be all right after all.

"Kit is trying very hard to accept the continuing deterioration of his body, but it's not easy." She stopped and put her hands on her knees.

"We are deeply grateful for the blessings of modern medical care. But you must admit it comes with a heavy dose of humiliation. Gaping gowns, disgusting food, shuffle to the bathroom, pee in a cup, did you have a bowel movement, wake up for vital signs every two hours, et cetera ad nauseum.

"So unless there is a critically important reason for him to stay overnight, let him out of here so he—so we—can deal with this new development at home, with our family."

She sat back and looked him in the eye. "I promise Kit will go see his doctor when we get back to Idaho, and will have whatever tests you recommend, and will follow his doctor's instructions.

"Besides, you can't keep him from leaving if he wants to, trust me on that."

The young doctor sat silent for a moment, presumably processing Monti's rant. He opened Kit's chart, examined each page, returned to the front page and scribbled for a bit, then closed the chart again and stood. "Mrs. Rising, pardon me, Monti...I'm going to recommend your husband be discharged today."

Monti started doing an internal happy dance with fist pumps, but he interrupted her.

"As long as he takes the medication I'm prescribing, and checks back with us every two or three days until you leave."

That slowed her inner dance a little, but it still felt like a victory. Outwardly she practiced her mature, calm, reasonable face. "Thank you so much, Dr. Porter." She stood, too. "I'll make sure he comes back to see you at whatever intervals you want. Is there anything else?"

"No," he said, his tone and his shoulders expressing unaccustomed defeat. "No," he said, making another note and scribbling out a prescription. He tore it off the pad and handed it to her. "You're all set."

She inclined her head in farewell and went to find Kit, marveling at what she'd just done.

Inexplicables

I can do all things through Christ who strengthens me.

Nora inhaled deeply, breathed out through her mouth. Clamping the hatchet under her arm, she adjusted the grimy, bloodstained bandages on her hands, smoothing and tucking them into some semblance of 'tidy.' She sat down, gripped the hatchet tightly and stepped off the edge of the steep riverbank.

She slid, flailing her arms to keep her balance, and landed with a splash at the bottom. She gasped as the icy water chomped at her ankles. She rolled over and squinted back up the slope. Had she really dragged Logan up that bank all by herself?

All by myself as opposed to what? Some friendly tribe of loggers who happened to be in the neighborhood? She leaned her head on her hands. So. She had done that yesterday (*only yesterday?*) without any loggers. Today she would chop trees (without any loggers) and build a travois.

She pushed herself to her feet, got her bearings and waded over to the tangle of trees and roots and—ugh! Dead things! Nora averted her eyes from the scraggly mass of sodden fur wedged into the snarl of plant matter, one ambiguous little clawed foot sticking up into the air. Whatever it had been, she didn't want to investigate.

She selected a suitable travois pole. "Aleph bet vet...," she sang. Whack! "Gimmel dalet hey..." Whack! She winced as the hatchet handle broke open the raw places on her palms. Whack! She sang, whack! And prayed, whack! And bled and cried, and one by one she hacked three poles loose from the mass and leaned them against the bank.

Two shots cracked through the forest while she was working and she barely noticed. When she was finished she fell back against the slope to catch her breath.

I am so thirsty. I am so wet, and dirty, and sweaty, and I'm bleeding and scared and I hurt all over. And my Logan is...oh God, oh God help us.

She gave in to the tears then and cried hard, deep wracking sobs until she couldn't cry anymore. Finally she wiped her eyes and her nose with the bottom of her sopping wet, filthy, pink *'You Can't Overdose on Music'* T-shirt, and took several calming breaths.

Time to do the next thing.

She pushed heavily away from the bank, brushing the pine needles and duff from her hair and arms. A movement caught her eye and she froze. She slid her eyes sideways to the far bank of the creek and gulped.

A huge buck stood gazing at her, his gigantic antlers a majestic crown above his head. They looked velvety, could that be right? He flared his nostrils and stamped one foot and an electric shiver coursed through Nora. She held her breath. He held her gaze for a long moment before dipping his head and making a graceful leaping turn back into the forest. He disappeared and she was left staring at nothing.

Nora blinked, turned, and grabbed one of the poles. She experimented with grip for a moment, and started up the bank. She felt like she could carry all the poles at once and run up the slope. Her fatigue had disappeared with the deer and she buzzed with energy. Before she knew it she had wrangled the first pole to the top and levered it onto the level forest floor. She slid back down for the second, and then the third. She clambered up to the top and stood amazed at what she'd somehow done.

"Nora?"

She turned to Logan, went to him and knelt to kiss him. "Hey, honey, how you doing?"

"Nora, I've been thinking." He pulled at one of her stray, tangled curls.

"Yeah? About what?"

"This anniversary has to go on our List of Worsts."

Nora laughed. "Oh, yeah, definitely," she agreed. Their List of

Worsts included terrible movies, disgusting restaurants, observed (lack of) parenting skills, coma-inducing professors, and groaner jokes...so far. "This will be hard to beat, for sure," she said.

"Nowhere to go but up," Logan said, rolling his head to the side and micro-adjusting his leg.

She watched him, wincing at his pain. "Logan, I saw the most beautiful deer."

"Yeah?"

"Yeah. A buck with huge antlers, across the creek. He looked right at me. It kinda, I don't know, energized me. It was weird." She shook her head, watching for his reaction. "I'd been so exhausted, and scared and crying and everything, but then after I saw him I just hauled those poles up the creek bank like they were chopsticks."

"Huh," Logan said, reserving judgment as he often did. His scientific mind and his generous heart prevented him discounting others' experiences without firm data to the contrary. "I'd love to see him."

She nodded again. She wanted to tell him about the voice in her head, too, but she couldn't form the words. They sat silent a moment. "How's your leg?"

He made a face. "A dull roar. A very loud dull roar," he said. "And not all that dull, honestly. I'm thirsty though, and my stomach is rumbling."

Nora's eyes widened. "Wow, I was really thirsty too, but I'm not now."

He raised an eyebrow at her.

"I know, I told you it was weird." She opened a pack and started rummaging through it. "Here's a bottle of water." She counted, "Two, three, four bottles of water left." She handed one to him. "Now, grinds." She dug through and pulled out a packet of mixed dried fruit and a couple more granola bars. Then she remembered the candy bar in her pocket.

"Hey Logan, thanks for the Cadbury's," she said, pulling it out. It was only a little worse for wear, a bit melty and squished.

"Nora, I did not buy that."

"What? You must have, I didn't. I've been really good—I haven't bought one for a month or so." She looked at him. "Maybe it was in the cupboard?"

He shook his head. "I didn't pack it."

"Well you packed all the food…" she trailed off. "Weird."

"And where did you find this?" He held up the travois instructions.

She stared at him. "It was in the Army Survival Manual," she said, "tucked in between the pages."

"Army manual?" Logan's eyebrows rose into his curly hair. "You mean the booklet in the first aid kit?"

She shook her head and pulled the pack open. "It was in the first aid kit, but I wouldn't call it a booklet." She pulled out the worn yellow manual and handed it to Logan.

He held it in both hands, idly flipping through the pages. He scrunched his eyes in that way that meant he was deep in thought, untangling a problem. "Someone got a hold of our packs," he said. He focused on Nora. "We stopped at Bill and Connie's to give her the key so she could feed Mendel. Maybe Bill snuck this stuff in my pack?"

"And the chocolate in mine?" she said. "Why would he do that? I mean, we hardly know him…unless Connie put him up to it."

They fell silent, each thinking through the oddness of this. "But you put stuff in there too," she said, "that I didn't know we had. Or rather, I didn't know we had funds in the budget to buy…" She didn't want to argue about money, for heaven's sake. But she held the hatchet in front of her to gauge his reaction. She was not surprised when his eyes went wide.

"Nora. No. I did not buy that. I bought a little curled up wire saw…did you find that?"

"No, Logan, I found this. In your pack."

"I can't believe Bill would give us that. That's gotta be like $30 or something. Their budget's just as tight as ours."

Nora dragged both packs to her. "Let's take everything out and see what else is in here."

She made a pile of extra clothes, towels, toiletries, a journal.

Water, food, flashlights…all the stuff they'd carefully selected and packed. She made a separate, smaller, mystifying pile of things they hadn't.

They both stared at these items. The half-eaten candy bar. The travois instructions. The Army survival manual. The hatchet. An old Swiss Army knife, ("It's not mine," Logan insisted) and a drawstring muslin bag full of a mix of aromatic herbs, their various leaves and buds still recognizable as parts. Even the first aid kit. "That is so not the five dollar one I bought," Logan said.

"I don't understand," Nora said.

Logan, who had propped himself up on his elbows to examine Nora's piles, grimaced and lay back. "I don't either. Are you sure there's no more of those pills in that first-aid kit?"

Nora shook herself and pulled the inexplicable first-aid kit to her. "I don't think so, but I'll look again." She went through it thoroughly, intermittently glancing at Logan's ashen face and increasingly rigid jaw. "I'm sorry, Logan, there's nothing."

She went to him, kissed his damp forehead. Swallowing her tears, she said, "I'm building the travois now, and I'm going to get you out of here, to somewhere we can get help."

He was not hearing her now, lost in the resurging pain. She plucked the neon green rope from the "known items" pile and the travois instructions and pocketknife from the "inexplicables", and turned to the poles she'd cut.

Abba, help me. I've never built anything more complicated than a sandwich.

Sprung

She poked her head into Room 414. Kit lay on the bed, eyes closed, a frail and faded version of his true self. Her gut clenched. He looked old. She turned away from the door as tears threatened, leaned on the wall in the hallway to catch her breath and pull herself together.

A passing nurse stopped. "Are you okay, ma'am?"

Monti nodded, tried a smile. She waved the woman away. The nurse looked uncertain, but turned to go on her way, glancing back before she rounded the corner.

Monti dabbed her eyes, firmed up the smile, drew in a deep breath and went in. She sat on the chair at Kit's bedside and put her hand on his.

He turned to her. "Hey, lover," he said.

His rich baritone sent a shiver to her toes. He didn't *sound* frail and faded. Her smile deepened and she said, "Hey yourself."

He scanned her face, turned her hand over and frowned at the bandages. "I'm sorry I banged you up, Monti."

"Nonsense. How much sense does it make to apologize for things that happen while you're unconscious?" she said, and kissed his cheek. "I'm fine, love."

"What am I missing?"

"Oh, not much," Monti said. "You want the good news or the bad news?"

"You know me," he said.

"Right. Bad news first. Nothing really bad, just…Mom talked to Marla and thought she sounded 'off.' They're headed home now to see what's up."

"And Noelle?"

"Is staying with us for now. She's not ready to see Marla without us by her side."

He nodded and adjusted his shoulders. "Good. We'll face her together." He looked at her. "And the good news?"

"We can go face her anytime you like. I got the doc to discharge you today."

"That's my girl. Thanks, Monti." He adjusted his pillow and bent his knees. "He had a lot of energy and I was just too tired to argue with him beyond saying 'no'."

"You're welcome, but it was completely selfish. I don't like to sleep alone, you know." She stood up and looked around for his clothes. "You ready to get dressed? Let's blow this pop stand."

Monti closed the door and they set about transforming Kit from hospital patient to retired colonel on vacation. They were making a last survey of the room for personal items when Noelle knocked. Monti opened the door. "Hi, sweetheart. Have the great-grands left?"

"Yep. How come you're dressed, Grandpa?"

"I'm sprung," he said. "Your grandmother batted her eyes at the jailer and got my sentence commuted."

"It's more like probation," Monti said. "We have to stop at the pharmacy and pick up some," she scrunched her eyes at the prescription, "aspirin? Kit, it looks like he wrote you a prescription for aspirin!"

"Makes sense, they already gave me a dose." Kit took the prescription from her, read it and shrugged. "Sure enough. Regular old aspirin. No need to go to the pharmacy for that."

"And I promised you'd come back for follow-up appointments every other day or so while we're here. And I'm going to make sure you do, too."

"Hmph. I guess that's a small price to pay for freedom." Kit gestured for Noelle to come sit by him on the bed. "What say, young lady, shall we go see your mother?" He put his arm around her and kissed her head.

Noelle shrugged closer to her grandfather and leaned her head on his shoulder. "Yes, I think so. It can't be any scarier than today has already been," she said. She wrapped her arms around herself. "I need a cat to hug."

Kit laughed but Monti startled. "Oh! That reminds me, I'd better call Austin. He's going to be cat-sitting for longer than he signed up for."

"Better do that before we enter the maelstrom," Kit said. "Not that your mother is a maelstrom, Noelle..."

"But she very well could be," Monti said. She pulled out her phone and dialed Idaho.

"Austin? Monti Rising here. We've had a complication." She explained the events of the day and finished with, "He's not allowed to fly for ten days, and by then flights will be impossible. Would you be able to stay with Gulliver for that extra time?"

She listened. "I know. Yes, after Christmas. Will that be okay?" Monti's face contracted in sympathy. "Oh, no..." She dropped her head into her hand and listened for a good while. "Oh Austin, I'm so sorry. But yes, please have Warren join you at the apartment, it's no problem at all. Gulliver will love having extra staff." She nodded, "Yes, please don't worry, Austin. It will work out. They're all grownups, after all. Okay, I'll call you when we have a firm arrival date. Thank you."

Monti ended the call and looked at her family with dismay. "They have maelstroms in Idaho, too."

"What happened, G?"

Monti shook her head, having a hard time believing it. "Austin's dad has been arrested, his aunts and uncles are on the warpath, his mom and step-dad, Brad, are lawyering up, and Austin and Warren are stuck in the middle of it."

"Arrested for what?" Kit asked.

"Assault. He punched Brad, and Brad pressed charges," Monti said. "I guess he mouthed off at the judge too, and now has to come up with $5,000 bail."

"He's digging a hole..." Kit said, shaking his head.

"Yes, and his siblings are apparently helping with the shoveling. They threatened Austin's mom and Brad, the judge warned them to back off, and they're having a hard time doing that."

"Wow. Our little maelstrom is looking pretty tame in

comparison."

"No kidding," Monti agreed. "Since Warren is 17 he's allowed to stay with Austin, so he can just join the party at our apartment until the trouble blows over or until we get home."

"That works for me," Kit said.

"Oh, and Austin noticed that Gulliver smells like smoke," Monti said.

"That's so weird," Noelle said. "I gave him, like, three baths. The smell is just as strong as the first day."

"I guess that's going to remain one of the several mysteries of that day," Kit said.

Their conversation trailed off. They looked at each other. Monti straightened the items left on the nightstand. Noelle redid her ponytail. Kit watched them. "It's no good, girls," he finally said, and slapped both hands on his thighs. "What say we go storm chasing?"

Travois

Nora struggled with the knot as she straddled the crossed poles. She knew a basic lashing technique and even a timber hitch, random bits of information permanently lodged in her brain from visits with her grandfather, who was always building or fixing something. But this rope was slippery and a little stiff, and her shredded hands made everything ten times more difficult.

She finally got the strands to push through where she wanted and pulled them tight. She straightened, stretched her back and examined her handiwork. It would probably not make the cover of Boy's Life, but she thought it was sturdy enough.

The next part was going to be just as hard. The only thing she could think of in the way of a flat surface for Logan to lie on was their brand-new sleeping bags. Thanks to the existence of the inexplicable pocket knife, she planned to cut little holes in them for rope to go through, stack them, and tie them to the poles kind of like a hammock.

But first she needed a break. And a drink of water. She walked over to their bower, her steps crunching on the crackly forest floor. Logan's eyes were closed. She hoped he was sleeping, and she tried to be silent as she leaned down and extracted a bottle of water from the known items pile.

"Hey, Nora-ne-Nelson," Logan said, his voice a hoarse whisper.

Nora lowered herself to the ground. "Hey sweetheart."

"Your hands are bleeding," he said, the new furrow deepening.

She tucked her hands between her knees. "It doesn't matter. I have antibiotic ointment on them."

"What are you doing?" he asked.

"Taking a break. From building the travois, remember?"

"Oh, right. I thought maybe I dreamed that." He looked at her, awe on his pasty face. "Wait. You know how to build a travois?"

She giggled, which seemed incredibly inappropriate, but she couldn't help it. "No, silly. You gave me—I mean someone put the instructions in your pack, in the Army manual, remember?"

He shook his head, staring at her.

"Don't worry, Logan. Really, it'll be okay. When we get out of here I'll explain all the weird parts. I mean I'll tell them to you. I can't explain them. But I have now truly and actually built a travois frame, and I only need to...," she trailed off, alarmed at Logan's face. He was staring at something...she turned to see.

There stood the magnificent buck, not twenty feet from them. Logan grabbed her bandaged hand and squeezed it. They gazed at the beautiful creature, taking in his majestic velvet-clad antlers, the skin twitching on his tawny flanks, his flaring nostrils and his liquid brown eyes. He stared back at them for a moment, chuffed imperiously and stepped slowly away through the sunlit forest.

"That was him," Nora whispered.

"I figured," Logan whispered back. He smiled at her. "I felt it."

"What?"

"The energy," he said, blushing at the incredibly unscientific statement he'd just made. "Like a...like being recharged."

"Exactly!" Nora said, standing up. "That's it! I have to go finish the travois now, Hon. Will you be okay?"

"Yeah," he said, a look of wonder on his face. "Yeah, I will. My leg still hurts, but it's like it hurts someone else."

"Huh?"

"Never mind, Nora. You go, I'll be okay." He waved her off.

She leaned down to kiss him and turned to go. Then she remembered she needed the sleeping bags. "These are never going to be the same, I'm afraid," she said as she collected them, and waggled the pocketknife at him.

Nora, brimming with energy, set to ruining the sleeping bags. The pocketknife made ragged tears rather than clean holes. But the holes went clear through all the layers, which was all that mattered. She spread the bags out over the travois frame, threaded lengths of rope through the holes, pulled everything as taut as she could and tied knots everywhere.

She stood back to admire her work, then decided admiration was not really in order. It was a mess. Hopefully it would support Logan's weight and not fall apart on the way to…to where? She had no idea.

But first things first. Nora pulled the band out of her hair, finger-combed it as well as she could, hampered by raveling gauze bandages, and gathered it all in the band again. Now, to see if she could drive the travois. She stepped into the apex of the joined poles, squatted and grabbed a pole on each side. *Ouch!* She stopped to smooth off a sharp bit on the right side.

She adjusted her grip again and maneuvered the travois around to drag it in the direction of their shelter. It caught on a surface root. On a rock. On a fallen branch. But she got it pulled the few yards to Logan, stepped out of the frame and did a victory dance, glancing at Logan to see his response.

Dang it! He was asleep again. She dropped to her knees beside him, frowning. He was so…still. She hesitated, then shook his shoulder gently. "Logan?" His head rolled to the side, sending adrenaline shooting through her. "Logan?" she insisted, shaking him harder.

No response.

Meeting Marla

Their taxi pulled up in front of the Housels' miniature home. Kit paid the driver, who looked to be about eighty, while Monti and Noelle stepped out into the blazing heat and looked around.

"I forgot how small it was," Noelle said.

"It is teeny," Monti agreed. "I can't imagine how we're all going to fit in there."

"Wasn't that the original plan?" Noelle asked.

"Yes, but that was for a long weekend. Now it's going to be for a very hot, long, week plus. And Christmas."

Kit and the cabbie came around with their bags. The men shook hands and the driver saluted Kit before climbing back into his cab.

"He's a decorated Vietnam Vet," Kit said as the car pulled away. "Wounded at the Battle of Kham Duc."

"He survived his wounds, that's great. Let's go see if we can survive the Battle of Prodigal Daughter."

"I thought she was a maelstrom," Kit said. "Are we mixing our metaphors, Monti?"

She rolled her eyes and grabbed her carry-on bag.

The front door opened, and Bob stepped out onto the porch step and closed the door behind him.

"A report from the front lines," Monti said.

"Or the eye of the storm," Kit said. He rounded up the remaining bags as Bob joined them at the curb.

Monti's dad kissed her and Noelle's cheeks while they waited for an update. "I think we're okay," he said.

Monti let out a sigh and felt her knees wobble with relief.

"She's napping in the guest room. That's where she's been staying. She told us the anti-anxiety meds make her really sleepy, and Jody looked it up online to confirm." He nodded. "It washes. It just sounded more pronounced over the phone than in person, so it spooked us."

Bob took a suitcase from Kit and they all moved up the sidewalk. "The online info said the sleepiness should eventually decrease as she gets used to the medicine."

"Anti-anxiety meds," Monti said. "There's a lot behind those words."

Kit opened the door and held it for them. "Yep. More than we'll find out today, I'm sure." A welcome blast of cold air washed over them as they set their bags down in the tiny entryway.

Jody bustled out from the hallway and kissed everyone. "Let's get you settled," she said quietly. "We can stash the luggage in our bedroom for now, and then firm up where everyone's going to sleep later." They nodded and maneuvered around each other silently until all the bags were deposited in the Housels' bedroom.

They gathered in the living room, a space separated from the kitchen by a bar-height counter complete with stools. Jody added a pitcher of sweet tea and a bucket of ice to a tray of tall glasses. Soon they were sitting together knee-to-knee on the sofa and chairs, sipping their tea, just like on every other visit. Except for the tension in the air.

Monti felt like they really were in the eye of a storm, not daring to relax, breathing in the thick air, watching the weird light and waiting for the second half to hit. "Definitely the storm metaphor," she said.

"What?" Jody said.

"Uh...sorry, I didn't realize I said that out loud," Monti said.

"We were vacillating between storm and battle metaphors earlier, anticipating our reunion with Marla," Kit explained.

"It's been pretty calm so far for us," Jody assured them. "She thanked us for collecting her from the rehab clinic, and fitted herself into our routines with no problem." Jody patted Monti's knee. "I think it'll be fine."

"Okay, calm before the storm, then." Monti looked up to see confusion on her mother's face. "I was thinking eye of the storm, but if there hasn't been any..."

"Why does there have to be a storm?" Bob said, also looking confused.

"I'm afraid I started that, sir," Kit said. "I suggested that Marla could be a maelstrom..."

"And we all know it doesn't take much more encouragement than that for Monti to go...I was going to say *storming off*..." Jody said, grinning sheepishly.

"Who's going storming off?"

All heads turned to see Marla scrubbing her sleepy eyes with a balled-up fist, just like she did when she was four years old.

Into the Woods

She grabbed his hand. His arm was completely limp. "Wake up, Logan! Wake up now!"

No, no, no, no, no! This couldn't be happening. He was okay just a few minutes ago. Was he breathing?

She lay her head on his chest. His heart beat was strong and slow. She fell against him, limp with relief. Yes, she could feel him inhale...exhale. Nora sat up. But why wouldn't he wake up?

What should she do? They were almost out of light. Should they spend another night here and head out in the morning? Or go now, into the night? She grabbed her head, pulling her hair. She had to think!

She couldn't wake him, so she needed to get help. There was no help here, so she had to take him to...somewhere else. As soon as possible, because without help he might die and her mind reeled away from that with a dizziness that took her breath away. She forced herself to finish her train of thought. 'As soon as possible' meant leave now, dark or no dark.

She set to work positioning the travois beside Logan. Then she ever so gently lifted, rolled, and shifted him onto the travois. He never made a sound, and she realized it was a mercy he was unconscious. Everything she'd just done would have caused him unbearable pain, and she might not have been able to force herself to do it.

She lashed Logan to the travois with the last of the rope and stood up to stretch her aching back. She caught a movement from the corner of her eye and whirled around in a panic.

The buck had returned. He stood gazing at her calmly, waiting.

Waiting?

He chuffed and stamped one hoof. She got the message, and she had no doubt it *was* a message.

Time to go.

Nora looked around their campsite, and quickly threw everything into the two packs. She tore the mylar off the branches and crumpled them up with a cascading crushing sound, picked up two water bottles, and crammed all that into a pack, too. *Leave only footprints.*

Satisfied she had tidied everything from the clearing but the hacked branches, Nora gently placed the smaller pack—there wasn't room for the larger one—on the travois next to Logan and draped his arm over it to hold it in place. Then she hefted the larger pack, staggering under its weight, and fumbled with the waist belt clip and shoulder strap adjustments until it felt bearable.

Stepping into the front triangle where the poles joined, she paused to smooth out the bandages on her hands, got a good grip on the poles, and lifted. Her center of gravity was off, that was going to be tricky. She swiveled around to check Logan, but he hadn't stirred. She turned back to face the buck, and he dipped his head and did that step-whirl thing to head back into the black forest. She followed.

This was totally crazy. Her trail guide was a deer high-stepping through the forest on undetectable trails to some unknown deer destination. But it felt right, and it wasn't like she knew which direction to go on her own, anyway.

The travois continually bumped and caught on roots and rocks that she couldn't see, jerking Logan around horribly. Nora grew deeply thankful for his oblivion. He could never have borne it.

Thank you, Abba, for letting me see how something as terrifying as Logan being unconscious is working together for our good right now. I wish I knew what your immediate purpose is, but I'm trusting you. And the trail guide you sent.

Nora was surprised to feel this gratitude well up in her, and examined it in a detached way. She *was* grateful.

Logan was terribly hurt, but he was alive. They hadn't been shot.

Come to think of it, she hadn't even heard a single shot for...how long now? She shook her head. *No idea.* They were together. It wasn't raining. Some unknown benefactor had given them gifts to help them in their crisis. And a wild animal was clearly guiding her through the forest, how incredible was that? As horrific as the situation was, it could have been far, far worse.

The light had absolutely gone. She tripped again and again in the inky dark, but didn't fall. The buck stayed close enough that she could see him, though he never looked back at her. Occasionally he paused to nibble a lichen or the end of a cedar branch, but he always stepped out again before she bumped into him.

The forest filled the night with hoots and creaks, sighs and skitterings. Nora jumped when a low animal whine creased the dark on her left, but she didn't panic, and the buck took no notice so she hurried to stay with him. A rich loamy smell tickled her nose, a spicy cedar aroma wafted by elusively, and the pungency of damp decay lay beneath it all. She didn't remember noticing these smells and sounds when she was little.

But this was nothing like her childhood memories of the forest at night. She wasn't terrified, for one thing, though how that could be she didn't know. She wasn't four years old. She wasn't alone. She was not lost. Or wait, actually she was lost but someone was guiding her. Someone, really? She shook her head.

Well, maybe it was Someone, with a capital S. No, nothing like that long-ago nightmare at all. Much better, amazingly, even with Logan's dire situation.

Nora didn't know how long they walked. She just kept putting one foot in front of the other, shifting the weight of the pack on her burning shoulders, correcting her balance when her ankle turned on a rock or her toe caught a root, carefully keeping the hind end of the buck in sight just ahead of her. She stopped turning to check on Logan, because she really couldn't see him. But she kept listening, and he never made a sound to add to the night's low cacophony.

Eventually, of course, it seemed like she'd always been tripping through the deep woods in the middle of the night, following a magical deer, carrying a pack far too heavy for her, and pulling a travois that cut into her ruined hands. She just kept going, because what else was there to do?

She tripped again, very badly, and went to the ground, her hands screaming at the contact with the rough surface. She clenched her teeth to stifle a cry of pain. She stood back up slowly, finding her balance, and brushed the litter off her bandages. She hefted the travois and took one step before she froze.

The buck was gone.

Mom

Noelle stiffened at the sound of her mother's voice, then consciously forced herself to relax. She checked her face—was she frowning? She didn't think so, but decided to make a smile if she could.

She couldn't really, so she settled for keeping her bottom lip from trembling.

Her mom shuffled over to the group and sat cross-legged on the rug. Great-grandma poured her a glass of tea and she accepted it without a word.

Mom's hair was a wreck. Messy from sleeping, sure, but it was like straw, kind of broken and stiff, and was dyed at least three different colors rather than the black she remembered. It was even a weird rusty purple in places.

Noelle examined her face, trying not to stare but drinking in the sight of the mother she hadn't seen in eight years, trying to match how she looked with the memory from when she was eleven and Mom had left her with G & G.

Deep furrows ran between her eyes and down her cheeks. Sunken circles like bruises gave her eyes an exhausted look. Her eyebrows had been plucked into non-existence. A thick scar she didn't recognize bisected her right eyebrow, and her skin was splotched and coarse. Noelle felt tears start in her eyes as she remembered the smooth, flawless cheek she used to stroke when they snuggled together.

Mom looked at her and she quickly averted her eyes. Grandma must have noticed because she said, "Do you feel better after your nap, sweetheart?"

"Yeah, sure," Mom said. Then she shook her head. "But no, not really. I'm sorry, I'm really out of it. I had a wicked bad headache this morning, and the meds…" she trailed off. Noelle looked up to find her mom's eyes locked onto her, a hunger in them that looked soul-deep.

"Marla," Grandpa said.

But her mom ignored him, unfolded her legs and moved on her hands and knees the three feet to the chair where Noelle sat. She reached out, wrapped her arms around Noelle's waist and hugged her fiercely.

Noelle burst into tears. She lay her hands on her mother's broken hair and stroked it. Her heart was going to explode. She slid off the chair, hugged her mom and cried so hard she couldn't breathe.

When Noelle finally caught her breath and could stop sobbing, she opened her eyes and saw Grandma, her own eyes wet, holding a box of tissues out to her. She laughed and took two or three tissues. Her mom let loose of her. She had been crying, too. Grandma kept bumping the tissue box against Mom's shoulder until she noticed and took a tissue to blow her nose.

Everyone still sat around them, concern pinching their faces, and she could swear she felt physical waves of love flowing silently out of them toward her and her mom.

"I'm okay," she said.

"Me too," Mom said.

"That's good," Grandpa said. "Phase one successful."

"Are phases in the storm metaphor or the battle metaphor?" Grandma asked.

"What?" Mom said.

"Never mind, Marla," Grandpa said. "She's just being Monti. We'll explain later." He stood and offered her his hand. "Why don't you sit on the sofa here, I need to find a firmer chair." She took his hand and he pulled her up and into a tentative hug. "It's good to see you, daughter," he said, and kissed her cheek.

Mom just nodded, looking like she was going to start crying again. Grandma stood too, pulled Noelle up and turned it into a group hug. Then the great-grands got in on it too, and Noelle could hardly breathe.

But it was good, so *so* good, to have everybody together again.

Almost everybody. She couldn't remember why she'd been so scared and stressed out.

Dark

Now she *was* alone. Aside from Logan, who was no help, and Someone, who was now not being any help either.

Terror ramped up in her, pushing her toward the edge of nothing good. Her breaths came ragged and shallow, sweat poured from her face and trickled down her back. Her heart pounded like it needed out of her rib cage as bad as she needed out of these woods.

Nora nearly dropped the travois but forced herself to set it down gently on the trail. If there was a trail. What should she do? Should she call out? She felt her throat close up at the thought. Even though she hadn't heard any shots this night, she was loathe to start yelling into the darkness for whoever to hear.

She stepped gingerly out of the frame, and peered around, with absolutely zero effect because she couldn't see her hands in front of her face. How had she seen the deer?

She shook her head. *Focus, Nora!* What were her options?

Leave Logan and look for the buck. *Not happening.*

Yell for help? *Ditto.*

Sit down and wait for daylight. How long would that be? She pushed the light button on her watch. 2 a.m. There must be at least three hours before dawn. Too long. She would have a complete meltdown before then.

Light—she needed light. They had flashlights, didn't they? Of course they must, but she'd no idea where they'd ended up when she threw everything from the known and inexplicable piles back into the packs. She would just have to dig until she found them.

Nora shrugged the big pack off her shoulders, but started her search in the small pack, figuring there'd be less digging overall if she found it there. She lifted Logan's arm with care and tugged the bag out from its resting place.

She opened it and patted the contents, then shoved her hands, wincing with the pain, down into the depths, finding clothing and crinkly food packets, the Army manual and balls of socks, but no flashlight.

With a sigh, she snugged the drawstring opening tight again and eased the pack back under Logan's arm. She got right down to his face and listened. His breathing was even. She lay her hand on his forehead. It was smooth and dry. She kissed it, her lips lingering on his warm skin, closing her eyes and willing herself not to cry.

"I love you, baby," she whispered. Then she felt for the big pack behind her and unclipped the fasteners. After rummaging shoulder deep in the bag, she felt a thrill when her hand closed around a cool metal cylinder.

Score.

She pulled it out, and took a few seconds working up the courage to turn it on and reveal her surroundings. She clicked on the power, leveled the light beam and began to swing it in a slow 360 degree circle.

Firs and pines, closely packed and impenetrable. A huge boulder disguised with mosses and ferns growing from every craggy crevice. The faint trail they had just traveled. Firs and cedars, trunks further apart but clogged with giant ferns and service berry trees....there! In front of the travois, in the direction they had been walking, there was an opening in the dense foliage.

Nora stepped carefully to the opening and shone the light on the ground out in front of her. It was a clearing, at least. She raised the light higher and swept from left to right. Not a large clearing, though. Wait! She moved the light back to the left.

Was that...a house?

Nora snapped off the light. She waited for her eyes to adjust to the absolute dark, noticed she was breathing hard, and deliberately slowed it down. *Aleph bet vet...gimmel dalet hey....*

But after a full minute, the dark remained unrelieved by any light at all from the house, which Nora began to disbelieve in. Panic clawed up from her stomach, and she snapped the light back on.

At the far side of the clearing, not fifty feet away, there stood an ancient stone house. It was small, just twenty feet or so across, with an oversized double-door in the center sheltered by a roofed archway, and a window on either side.

A wild profusion of growth that looked nearly like a garden lay like a moat between the clearing and the house, and a path led through it to the door. Mosses blurred the outlines of the structure, and made it hard to see but for the wide windows reflecting the flashlight's beam. Shutters flanked each window, standing guard, ready to close and render the house invisible.

Nora moved the light to the left and right. No sign of any road, or even a trail. Towering trees crowded the house, leaning in far above to protect it. She swung the beam up, found a wide chimney, and further up was shocked to see that the house backed right up into a steep mountainside, whose height was a mystery hidden by the trees and the night.

They were on the remote edge of the back of nowhere, and there was no evidence of a road in any direction. It wasn't a tumbledown ruin. The glass in the windows wasn't broken, and even looked clean and polished.

Perhaps an eccentric, rich hermit? Nora sized up the small clearing. She didn't think there was enough room to set a helicopter down here, and there was no other way to get here other than trekking through the dense forest. It didn't make sense.

How could this house be here?

She was starting to disbelieve in the house again, despite what her eyes were telling her, when a light flared in the right-hand window.

She froze for a moment, then fumbled with the flashlight and turned it off. She stumbled back to Logan and spun to gaze across the clearing. The right window was suffused with a warm glow, and as she watched a light flared in the other window, growing until the house fairly blazed with light.

Then the door opened, and someone stepped out.

Houseless at Housels

Monti pulled away from the group hug, wiping her eyes and looking for a tissue for her nose before it got out of control.

Jody said, "Well! We never did get our Hardee's biscuit, or any food at the hospital, though I think that was a providential escape. Who's hungry?"

The 'hug therapy' broke up with a few last squeezes, and Kit raised his hand. "I could eat," he said, and the others agreed.

Marla said, "Can I help you, Grandma?"

"Oh, why don't you all visit, sweetie, and Bob and I will throw something together." She fluttered off to the kitchen, four feet away, and Bob followed.

"Okay, Grandma," Marla said. She slid her hands into her back pockets and turned back toward her folks. She hesitated, then took Noelle's hand in hers. "How're things, daughter?"

"Oh, good," Noelle said. "I mean, aside from the fire, you know."

"She's in honors classes at school," Monti said. "The fire got her laptop, which set her back a little, but her teachers have been good about making alternate arrangements for her to finish her semester's projects."

"I've never seen a house fire," Marla said.

"And you don't want to!" Monti was firm. "It was horrible. And I'm so sorry you won't get to come home to your familiar place."

"It's okay, Mom. I didn't live there long, really. Just a couple years. I'm used to moving around, like, from birth, remember?"

"Well, that's good because we might have to do a little of that again before the bungalow is rebuilt. I can't see us staying in the apartment we're in now for very long."

"Too small?"

"Yes, it's pretty snug, and it's furnished with somebody's broken down 1970's castoffs. But mostly it's so noisy! Lots of college students. They don't exactly keep the hours we do."

Marla laughed. "You sound like an old lady, Mom!"

"Hmph. Well I guess I am an old lady, sort of."

"Sort of old, or sort of a lady?" Kit put in.

"Oh hush," she said, and swiped at him. "But don't worry, Marla, we have a room for you that will do until we find a better spot. A realtor at church is keeping an eye out for a bigger place for us. It could be a year until we're back home."

"We brought the initial drawings for the new house, if you want to take a look later," Kit said.

Jody asked from the kitchen, "Do they have any idea what started the fire?"

"Oh gosh," Monti said. "That's such a complicated story. And we're nowhere near 'the end' yet."

"They haven't even definitely decided if it was accidental or arson," Kit said with a fierce scowl.

Jody stopped chopping. "Arson?"

"It may not have been," Monti said quickly. "But you know all the...incidents...we've had over the last few weeks, involving our guest's ex-boyfriend..."

"But I thought he was in jail!" Jody was all fluffed up and furious, like the irate little bluebird in the famous photo.

"He was. He is," Kit said. "But unfortunately he was only the sidekick of a shadier character. A man who was definitely involved in some of the incidents, and we're now thinking he was pushing Blaine on to greater violence."

"But why?" Jody asked.

"Drugs, what else," Monti said, then reddened as she slid her eyes to Marla. "Oh honey, I'm sorry. That was..."

"It's okay, Mom," Marla said. "I think it's clear that drugs have wreaked havoc in my life, and I'm sure they're doing the same for those guys."

An awkward silence fell over the room, broken when Jodi resumed chopping vegetables. Finally Marla spoke again. "So, Dad, if it was arson, what happens next?"

Kit shifted in his chair. "It probably won't make a lot of difference on the ground," he said. "They tell me arrests are only made in about 10% of fires deemed to be arson-related, and few of those cases go to court. It's apparently very difficult to pin even obvious arson on a particular person."

Bob started setting out TV trays in the living room, as there wasn't enough room at the tiny table for everyone. The Housels tended to have their get-togethers out at the community picnic lawn. Jody set a big bowl of salad on the bar, along with dressings, a platter of croissants, and the pitcher refilled with sweet tea.

"Okay, what have I forgotten?" she asked.

Bob returned to the kitchen. "Salad bowls and forks? Just a suggestion," he said.

"Oh, bother," Jody said, and rummaged about until she had enough for everyone, and a stack of cloth napkins. "There. I think we're ready. Just come on and fill your plates here, family." They all fetched their food, moving cautiously around each other in the limited space, careful not to knock elbows or upset plates. Finally everyone settled in a seat, with Monti and Marla ending up at the table.

"Let's pray, huh?" Bob said. "Father, we're so grateful. We have our family together at last. Thank you for that long-awaited answer to many prayers. And thank you for putting medical care right where we needed it today. Thank you even for the extended visit we get to have with our family, instead of the weekend we originally planned. Thank you for sometimes allowing us to see how all things work together for good, for those who love you and are called according to your purposes. And thank you for providing for our needs, including this supper. In the name of Jesus, Amen."

Hearty 'amens' echoed around the room and everyone dug in. Forks clinked in bowls for a few minutes as everyone discovered they hadn't eaten in several hours.

"Marla, what about letting your folks have the guest room, and you and Noelle camp out in the living room?" Jody said.

"Sure, Grandma, that'll work," Marla answered. "I have my

sleeping bag Noelle can use. If you have a blanket and a pillow, I'll be fine."

"Oh, we can do a little better than that," Jody said. "The futon love seat will pull out flat for you, Marla, and we have a cot for Noelle. Bob aired it out and repaired a little three-corner tear, so that's all ready to go. There won't be much walking around room, but I don't think we have any sleepwalkers, do we?"

"Not me," Marla said, and laughed.

After they finished eating, Monti touched Kit's shoulder and said quietly, "Lover, do you want to lie down for a few minutes?"

"Actually, I think I'm about ready to turn in for the night. It's been a long day." He put his hand over hers. "But first I'll just help Bob get things set up while you girls clear away supper."

Monti nodded, and she went to help her mom clean up the supper things while her dad brought in the cot and bedding, and pointed out where everything needed to go for their close-quarters sleeping arrangements to work.

Marla and Noelle set up the Lilliputian living room for a sleepover, while Kit helped Bob shove the desk in the office against the closet and unfold the sofa sleeper. Marla had been sleeping on it in its sofa configuration, but that wouldn't do for the two of them.

"The mattress is pretty good on this thing," Bob assured Kit. "And we have a gel topper for it, hang on—oh shoot, it's in the closet." He wiped his forehead and shook his head. "We'll have to move the table again, won't take but a minute."

"How about we do that tomorrow, Bob?" Kit said. "I appreciate it, but I'm beat. This'll be fine for tonight."

"Sure, son. It's been quite a day. You feeling all right?" Kit was leaning heavily on his cane and Bob frowned as he noticed.

"I wouldn't want to tackle any new projects just now, but I'll be right as rain in the morning, thanks, Bob."

"Of course. There's a stack of towels in the bathroom. You might want to duck in there now before the ladies start heading that direction. Plenty of hot water," he said.

"Thanks Bob, I think I will," Kit said. "Tomorrow I'd be grateful for your input on our new bungalow plans."

"Oh sure, I'd love to take a look," he said. He put a hand on Kit's shoulder. "It's good to see Marla safe and sound, isn't it?"

"She's a sight for sore eyes, and that's the truth," Kit said. "We can hardly believe she's real. Monti's about to burst with hope. And anxiety. And Nellie's all over the map. But I think she handled seeing her mom really well. Tears notwithstanding."

"She sure did. She's a trooper. Can't even imagine what the next few days are going to be like. I'm glad we get to be part of your reunion. Good night, son," he said, and gripped Kit's shoulder for a moment before stepping out and closing the door behind him.

Barnabas

It was too dark to see the person clearly, but he—Nora was reasonably sure it was a man—held a lantern aloft in one hand and gripped a cane with the other. He leaned heavily on the cane as he took slow steps toward them across the clearing. The lantern revealed a detail or two with each swing as he drew nearer. A trim white beard. A leather vest. Thick canvas work pants. Deep wrinkles. Laugh lines.

"How do you, young miss?" he said when he stopped ten feet from Nora. "Why are you in these deep woods in the far hours o' the night?"

"H-hello, sir," Nora said. "I—we were hiking and...Logan got hurt and...we need help." She choked out the words and 'help' became a sob. She fell to her knees, suddenly exhausted beyond endurance. "Please help us," she pleaded.

The old man lifted the lantern higher and moved to see behind Nora. "Mercy!" he said, the word infused with wonder. "I do believe it's the broken boy." He looked more closely at Logan, sweeping the lantern slowly over him, and then returned to Nora. "Now, now," he said, and placed a gentle hand on her head. "Never fear, all will be well."

Peace flowed from his hand into her body. Peace like she had felt in the woods. She raised her wet eyes and gazed up at him. "Abba?"

"No, child, no. Naught but a bondslave." He patted her head, then hung his cane on his arm and stooped to grip her elbow and help her to her feet. "Come, let us bring your dear one to the house, and then we shall begin to set things aright."

The exhaustion backed off a millimeter, and after checking that Logan still did not stir, Nora found she could step one more time into the frame of the travois and lift it.

The man walked beside her with the lantern, showing the way a step or two in front of her stumbling feet, using the cane to point out a hummock here, a rock there to avoid. They crossed the clearing in silence until they reached an arch built of fat cedar poles guarding the door, the covered area paved with huge flagstones. The man hung the lantern on a hook embedded in the wall.

"Welcome to Hart's Burden," he said. "Now, off with thy burden, child." He helped her lower her pack to the ground. Then he slid the smaller pack from the travois and set them both on the floor just inside the open door. Nora watched in a daze.

He opened the other door. "Come in now, and let me help you with that," he said, and gripped one side of the front of the travois with a strong hand. Nora grabbed the other side and they dragged it into a capacious foyer and down a wide hallway. He stopped at a polished cedar door standing ajar.

"Let it down," he said. "Now, we must loose your broken young man from the conveyance, for 'twill not fit through this doorway," the man said, and stooped again to examine Nora's knots. "Hmm." He straightened, rummaged in his pocket, and pulled out a folding knife.

Before Nora could think to be afraid, he made short work of all the knots with a few slices of the knife. Back it went into his pocket. "We shall lift him free from the frame sideways, shall we? You take the bottom."

Nora nodded, and after the man positioned himself carefully, they tugged the sleeping bags off the travois. He shoved the frame out of their way. Now Logan lay on the hall floor.

"Now join me up here, young miss. You take that corner and I'll take this. We'll have to drag him in."

She obeyed, lifted her corner of the stacked, ruined sleeping bags, and walked with him into what she could only think of as a bedchamber. She was instantly captivated by the charm of the low, wide four poster bed, shelves of books, and much more waiting to be discovered, but she had to focus. Her arms trembled as they reached the bed and positioned Logan parallel to it.

"Give me a moment," the old man said. He hooked his cane on the frame of the bed, moved to Logan's feet and braced himself with his weak leg against the bed. "I'll need you to take the top end, my apologies," he said. "Otherwise, I shan't have the bed for a brace. On three, then," the old man said, "And we'll lift him onto the bed." Nora nodded. "One, two, three."

They swung and lifted in unison like an experienced team and deposited Logan gently on the bed. Then Nora stumbled and fell onto a soft rug next to the bed. She had no more strength at all, and rested her head on the side of the bed, unable even to consider trying to get to her feet again.

"Well done, my dear," the man said, retrieving his cane. "Let me help you to this chair," he nodded toward a deep armchair near the bed, "and then you can rest while I fetch you some tea."

As he practically carried her to the chair, she protested. "But Logan..."

"Never fear, child," he said. "Everything in order." He lifted one of her hands and grunted as he appraised the filthy bandages wrapped round them. He released her hand, lifted her feet and used his cane to scoot a footstool under them. He briefly examined Logan, still unmoving, before leaving the room without another word.

Nora leaned her head back. Surely she had not sat in a chair for years. She could stay in this one forever. She closed her eyes, just for a moment, and next thing she knew a...a tea trolley? A tea trolley rolled into the room, pushed by her host, who was using it like a walker.

He poured tea into a china cup for her, added cream and a couple of lumps (actual lumps!) of sugar, and handed it to her on its saucer, with a spoon.

She stared at the cup in her hands, remembering the Victorian tea place she'd gone to last year with some friends, dressed to the nines for High Tea and feeling like a little girl playing dress up. The fragrant steamed wafted to her nose, and she returned to the present, stirred her tea and lifted it to her lips for a sip. She closed her eyes and inhaled deeply.

What was this stuff? She took a deep drink, half draining the cup. It was amazing! Not Lipton, that was for sure. She drank the rest in two swallows.

"There is plenty more," the old man said, not even looking at her. He was at the bed, with Logan's head in one hand, trickling a liquid into his mouth.

"What are you doing?" she asked, setting the tea cup on a small table next to her and leaning toward the bed. "What's that?"

"'Tis the herbs you brought, my dear. They will ease his pain when he wakes, and help him heal quickly."

"Herbs? I didn't bring any herbs!" Nora said.

"In your pack, child," the man said patiently.

"You got into our packs?" she asked before she could stop herself. "I'm sorry, that was rude." She felt her cheeks redden. "You're helping us, I appreciate that. But I didn't..."

Then she remembered, in the pile of inexplicables, a drawstring bag of fragrant dried plants, which she had labeled in her mind as potpourri, which seemed totally stupid now. "But, how did you know they were there?" she asked.

"In good time, child," the man said, still trickling the brew into Logan's mouth. "Have another cup of tea. You'll need it for what we must do next."

"What we must...?" she said faintly. A chill shot through Nora from heart to toes. She didn't want to do any more hard things. She was totally done doing hard things. "What do we have to do?" she asked.

But she knew the answer. She shuddered, and decided another cup of tea would be good. She fetched her cup from the table and fixed another cup of tea.

"Um, sir, what's your name?" She couldn't very well call him 'the old man.'

"I am Barnabas," he said. He peered round at her and asked, "And you?"

"My name's Nora," she said, "and he's Logan, my husband." She frowned. "You called him 'the broken boy'."

The man...Barnabas...nodded, and said, "I did. Time enough tomorrow for that." He lay Logan's head back on the pillow. "There." He turned to the tea trolley. "Now I'll just have a cup, too, and then we'll be ready."

Nora didn't think she'd be equal to the next thing no matter how many cups of tea any of them had, but she just swallowed hard and took another sip. They sat silently for a few minutes, Nora in her chair and Barnabas perched on the edge of the bed, finishing their tea.

Nora looked around. She had never seen a room like this. It looked like something out of a story book, the kind with British children and fairy godmothers and goblins, and handsome young boys who saved the day and the princess and the kingdom all at once. Tall bookcases full of leather-bound volumes with gold lettered-spines stood against two walls.

A dressing table, all curves and flourishes, held aloft a huge oval mirror on two ornate arms. Carved over every side, with miniature drawers and shelves on three stepped tiers above the dresser's top, her mom would have called it a dust-catcher. But not a speck of dust or a single smudge marred the shiny wood.

Barnabas stood before her, offering to take her cup. "Are you ready, my dear?"

She shook her head. "No," she whispered, and tears trickled down her cheeks.

Dreams and Clouds

Gulliver was hiding again, and towering flames surrounded her while she searched everywhere. She found him in the linen closet, of course. She dragged him out of there, his claws buried deep in her grandmother's quilt, and scrabbled to the front door with him and the quilt clamped to her chest, barely making it out to toss him into Noelle's arms before the house collapsed behind her in a gigantic whoomph.

Monti woke gasping for breath.

She lay listening to her heartbeat slowly return to normal. She had had this dream, or a variation of it, three or four times since the fire on the first of December. She hoped it wasn't going to continue like this. She hoped Noelle wasn't having similar dreams. She wondered what was going on in Kit's head about it.

She rolled over and saw he was still sleeping. *What time is it anyway? Does it smell like smoke in here?*

Monti rolled back over and swung her legs down to the cool tile floor. *I've got to get a grip.* She gingerly touched the scabbed over scrapes on her knees and chin, eased out of the bed, drew on her robe and tiptoed to the door. She stopped with her hand on the knob. *Wait. If I go out there, I'll wake up the girls…Unless it's time to get up anyway?* Her internal clock, never too reliable, was seriously off-kilter after the transcontinental flight yesterday.

She padded over to the table where she'd left her watch and earrings, found her watch and pushed the button to light the display. Except she accidentally pushed the button to change the settings and was immediately lost in loops and layers of menus. A frustrated *Aargh!* escaped through her clenched teeth.

"Monti?"

"Oh rats, sorry sweetheart," she said softly. "I didn't mean to wake you."

"What are you doing?"

"I'm just trying to see what time it is. I had another fire dream and…I don't think I can sleep anymore."

Kit squinted at his watch, which he wore 24/7, which would've driven her nuts. "It's 3:45 a.m. Come back to bed."

She sighed. She couldn't go to the kitchen and make a cup of tea without waking the girls up. She'd have to get past them to get to the screened porch. She couldn't sneak to her office and write, because it was over 2000 miles away and oh, yes…had burned to the ground, computer, legal pads, pens and all. She slipped off her robe and threw it on the end of the bed.

"I guess I don't have many options for larking about."

"It's not time for larks yet. Dawn is hours away. You'd just be lurking about."

"Ha ha." She climbed back in and accepted his silent invitation to lay her head on his shoulder.

"You okay with the dream?" Kit asked.

"Yeah. This time I rescued Gulliver and Grandma's quilt." Without warning she burst into tears, aching suddenly with the unbearable loss of that quilt and everything else. A lifetime's worth of carefully considered keepsakes, kept back from all the moving sales and yearly shedding of extra stuff. Just one thing to remember her grandmother by. Her mother's crystal salad bowl. One childhood souvenir from each of the places she'd lived. The map of their honeymoon trek to Texas. The photo albums. The beautiful Craftsman furniture they'd collected over the years. All the wardrobe finds she and Noelle had picked out together. On and on, she could recite the list of losses for days.

Kit held her, kissed her hair, waited it out. She hadn't thought much about what he'd lost. Those aquariums and their occupants. The small online fish-fanciers business he had almost offhandedly built, not making a big deal of it. It was something he could do no matter how his body deteriorated in the coming years. It had just been building momentum and now it was gone. His books. His own keepsakes, though he was far more ruthless than she about shedding the excess.

"You lost the packet of letters from your dad," she said, barely able to form the words through the tears still choking her throat.

"Not entirely," he said.

"What?" She raised herself onto one elbow. "What do you mean, 'not entirely'?"

"I scanned them into the computer a year or so ago," he said.

"You did? You never told me."

He shrugged. "I was just puttering, testing the idea. I scanned lots of things in."

"Photos?" Monti didn't dare to hope.

"Sure," he said. "Remember the stack of Yellowstone vacation pictures you left on my desk? Those are in the cloud."

"They are?" Monti was dumbfounded. "What else? What about the albums?"

"Not all of them, sorry Monti. It was tricky peeling them out of the plastic cover sheets, and lots of them were completely stuck to the page. But I got some. We can look at them tomorrow…today…if you want. I'm sure your folks won't mind, and we can give them access, too."

"Kit Rising, you're an amazing man. How come you didn't tell me after the fire?"

"I honestly didn't think of it. There was a lot to deal with. It just hadn't risen to the top yet." He pulled her closer. "I'm sorry, love. I didn't think how it might help you to know that not everything was gone beyond recovery."

"Well, I forgive you, since you made the recovery possible in the first place." She flopped back down on the bed, feeling as if an elephant had decided to shift off her chest and go lay elsewhere for a bit. "That is so excellent. You get a thousand gold points."

"Gold points, huh? Are those different from regular points?"

"Of course. Way better." She rolled toward him. "I love you like crazy, you know."

"Mm-hmm. Can we go back to sleep now?"

"Oh, I doubt it!" she said. "Now I'm too excited."

"Well just snuggle down here and try to relax for a minute," Kit said. "You never know."

"Yeah right," Monti said, but snuggled down anyway. In seconds she was snoring.

Bones

"Now, now," Barnabas said. "It always seems impossible until it's done, as Madiba used to say." He took her cup and set it on the tray, then offered her his hand. "Now you can wash while I prepare Logan."

Barnabas opened another cedar door in the fourth wall of the room. "Take the bandages off your hands, we'll treat your injuries as soon as we have seen to Logan. Return as soon as you can, his injury must be attended to without further delay." She nodded and went through the door.

The scent of lavender made her inhale deeply. She looked around and wished she was not exhausted and in a hurry to help set her husband's horribly broken leg. The huge clawfoot tub called to her, enticing her with the charm of a long soak.

Maybe later. She turned on the water at the sink and glanced in the mirror. Her mouth fell open—she looked as if she'd been snatched up in a tornado, then dragged through a war zone. Her hair was a five-star disaster. Tangled knots held dirt and leaves, sticks and at least one bug! She clawed the bug out and shuddered. She finger combed a little but got her fingers stuck in the snarls. She tried bending over and shaking her head. A flurry of foreign objects scattered onto the glossy tile floor. She clamped her hand over her mouth—how would she clean that up?

Never mind that now. She put her hair back its band. She quickly unwound the tattered gauze strips from her hands and dropped them in a wastepaper basket next to the sink.

After adjusting the temperature, she thoroughly rinsed her face and hands with hot water. A bar of lavender soap, even though it stung her torn hands, made the second round of scrubbing deeply refreshing as she sudsed clear up to her elbows.

She rinsed the soap and about a pound of dirt and half her exhaustion down the sink. Still, she hesitated to touch the thick white towel—she was nowhere near clean yet. She patted her hands tentatively on the towel and decided she could air dry.

Nothing for it now, she had to do this.

Back in Logan's room, Barnabas had opened little cupboards built into the tea trolley. She hadn't noticed them before, and they were filled with medical supplies. *How odd.*

He had cut away Logan's pant leg, laid out towels under his mangled leg and washed him. He was just finishing irrigating the wound, flushing out dirt and forest that had managed to get in despite Nora's best efforts.

Nora's stomach churned at the sight, but she forced herself to focus on Logan's injury. The glistening point of protruding bone was horrible beyond enduring. The wound was angry, swollen, and draining ugliness. It must be infected by now. His foot was gray, that was wrong! She gulped and stepped to the man's side.

"What can I do?"

"We must move quickly," he said. "He will not sleep much longer. Get up onto the bed and lay across his chest."

"But I'm so dirty!" she protested, while nevertheless hurrying to obey.

"No matter," Barnabas said. "You must hold him down, while I set his poor leg."

"Yes, all right," Nora said, though her eyes filled with tears and she started shaking. "Like this?" They were really going to do this.

"Yes, dear. Here we go." Barnabas gripped Logan's foot and gave a controlled but tremendous heave, and the bone squelched back into the leg with a sound from a nightmare. Logan uttered a deep groan and Nora jumped.

"He's waking up!" she said. "Can I get off him?"

"One moment, let me be sure," Barnabas said. He examined the wound closely and appeared satisfied the bone was set properly. "Now, Nora dear, you may climb down."

"Logan, hon, I'm here," she said, brushing his hair away from his eyes.

He flopped his head over toward her, groaning again and frowning deeply.

She smoothed the furrow between his eyes. "You're safe now, sweetheart," she said. "We have help."

She watched as Barnabas slathered a thick green salve over the wound and covered it with gauze. At his direction she lifted Logan's leg so Barnabas could wrap the bandaging. It looked so much better, Nora could hardly believe it.

"Sit in the chair, dear," he said. He gestured for her to hold her hands out. He coated her wounds with the same salve he had used on Logan, and expertly re-bandaged both her hands in just a couple of minutes. She could already feel the throbbing pain beginning to back off.

"You stay with him now. I need to fashion a splint," he said. He gestured toward the tea tray, now set on the little table. "As he wakes, persuade him to take the tea, it also has a measure of the healing herbs in it. You have some more too, dear." The teapot now hid under a quilted cozy, like her grandma had. He must have refilled the pot while she washed up.

"Thank you," she said, tears choking her voice. "Thank you so much, for everything." She wanted to hug Barnabas, but he didn't seem quite the hugging type and she couldn't bring herself to do it.

He nodded. "You're quite welcome, child. Only what was needed, after all." He turned the tea trolley round, pushed it out the door and left Logan and Nora together.

Nora turned back to her husband. She took his hand and kissed it.

"Nnorra?" Logan said, with effort. "Where are we?"

"I don't know, love, only we're in a stone house set into the side of a mountain." She nodded toward the door. "That was Barnabas. He set your leg and bandaged it up."

Logan peered down his nose toward his leg, but couldn't lift his head enough to see it. He fell back. "Hurts."

"I know, sweetheart. Barnabas said you should drink some of this tea, and it will help." She pulled the cozy off the pot and poured him a cup. "He mixed in some of the herbs from that bag in our inexplicables pile."

"Wha…?"

"Never mind, just have a sip of this," she said, and supported his head while he drank, unresisting. She kept at it until he had drained the cup, then she poured another for him and one for herself.

She noticed a small plate on the tea tray, covered with a linen napkin embroidered in cabbage roses, and peeked underneath it. A pile of unprepossessing rectangles sat stacked there, each bearing rows of fork pricks on its top. Shortbread? She chose one and took a tentative bite.

It was shortbread, as she'd hoped! But the most marvelous shortbread, leaving Walker's in the dust, and Walker's was her very favorite. The morsel dissolved in her mouth and she bit off another chunk. "Mmmmmmmmm!"

"What?" Logan rubbed his eyes and frowned at her.

"You have to try this," she said, bringing a piece to him. "It's the best shortbread ever!"

"Nnnot really a fan, Nora," he said, pushing her offering gently away.

"I know, I know, but trust me," she said, insisting. His power to resist anything was low at the moment and he didn't fight her further. He sighed, took the cookie from her and nibbled a tiny edge off it. After a second, bigger bite, his eyebrows rose and he popped the rest in his mouth. "Ivv der more?" he asked around the mouthful.

Nora laughed and moved the tea tray from the table to the edge of the low bed. She nudged him to lean forward and stacked two pillows behind him.

"Comfy?"

"Amazingly, yes," he said, spewing only a few shortbread crumbs with the 's'. He was becoming more alert with each passing moment.

She sat in the armchair next to the bed, and they proceeded to drink every drop of tea in the pot, with every drop of milk and most of the sugar, and eat every last bit of shortbread on the plate. Nora was just tidying up the stray crumbs when Barnabas knocked on the open door, carrying a bundle of what must be materials to splint Logan's leg.

"Ah, you're awake, young man, I'm glad to see it."

"We ate all your shortbread," Nora blurted out, suddenly unsure if they'd been meant to share with him.

"Oh, very good, very good," he said.

"It was the best shortbread I've ever had," Nora said, a wistful note in her voice.

"I'll give you the recipe, shall I?" he asked, and moved to the bed to examine Logan. "How are you feeling?"

"Like I might survive," Logan said. "I'm not being flippant, sir. I mean there have been moments in the last…" He failed to figure out how long they'd been in the forest. "Since I fell, when I thought for sure I was going to die in the woods."

Nora gripped his hand as tears flooded her eyes.

"Nora was doing everything she could, and I was sometimes aware of that, but it just seemed impossible." He squeezed her hand back, then wiped away her tears with his thumb. "You've been amazing, Nora-ne-Nelson."

"Not really," she said. "I had no idea what to do. But…" and here she paused, her cheeks heating up. *This would sound crazy.*

She whispered, "Abba helped me. And things kept happening, with the packs and the deer, and…I don't understand it at all."

She looked to Barnabas, who did not appear to think she was crazy. He merely nodded, and took Logan's pulse, probed his neck with gentle fingers, and laid the back of his hand on his forehead.

"All in good time, children," he said. "There is no great mystery. Or rather, it is a great mystery, but we can address that in the morning. Now let's get this splint on, and then I think that will be quite enough for one day." Barnabas positioned a long, white cupped piece of plastic next to Logan's leg.

"Is that PVC?" Logan asked, the scientist in him intrigued by this improvisation.

"Yes. 'Tis not an ideal solution, but a splint will do until a proper cast can be had." Barnabas said. "If one turns out to be needed." He gently lifted Logan's leg and scooted the half-pipe under it. "It will, however, require plenary cooperation from the patient," he continued, peering from under his eyebrows at Logan, whose jaw had gone rigid. "You mustn't move the leg any more than is absolutely necessary."

"Yes, sir, I understand," Logan said, only a slight tremble in his voice revealing how much the movement had hurt. They watched Barnabas adjust the splint and wrap it, with what looked like strips of bedsheets, above and below the fracture. With a separate strip, he completed the wrap over the break.

"That way we can unwrap just this bit to check the wound, and make sure it's healing well."

"I see," Logan said. "Makes sense."

"And there we are," Barnabas said, straightening. He collected the leftover bandaging, tucking his scissors into the bundle and the bundle under his left arm.

He handed Nora a small tin and a white paper packet. "Here is more salve, and fresh bandages for your hands. You'll need to change them again after your bath," he said. "And do not neglect to apply the salve." He gave her a stern look and she nodded. "Now since you have a devoted nurse at your side, Logan, I shall leave her to attend to your comfort before you sleep. There is a bedpan in the night table there. Can the two of you manage that?"

Nora blinked. "Sure, sure," she said. "No problem, we'll manage." She felt her cheeks flame at the sudden mentioning of such a personal matter. Never had she imagined needing to help Logan in this way.

"Very good," Barnabas said, smiling at her. "And then what you both need is sleep. Nora dear, for tonight you can sleep in the next chamber just through the bath. Tomorrow, if you wish, we can move a cot into this room for you."

Nora nodded, suddenly yearning for a bed even more than a bath. But she would have to bathe before she could even think about lying on clean sheets. The sooner, the better. She pulled herself to her feet.

"And tomorrow," Logan said, "can we ask you who might have

been shooting at us?"

Barnabas looked at him sharply. "Shooting? What do you mean?"

"It was a gunshot that startled Logan and made him fall into the creek," Nora explained. "And we heard several more shots over the next day and night."

Barnabas scowled, and looked not remotely huggable. Nora was glad *she* had not been shooting in his woods.

"Yes," he rumbled. "We'll talk about this tomorrow, also." He took a moment to clear his brow and put that thought aside. "Meanwhile, children, if you need me in the night, Nora can find me further down the hall, first turn to the right, at the end of the corridor."

Nora screwed up her courage and took his hand in both of hers. "Thank you, Barnabas."

He patted her hands and his eyes shone from the mesh of crinkles that formed when he smiled. "Good night, my dear." He retrieved his cane from the bed frame and left them then. They stared at the closed door, then at each other, not quite believing he'd been real.

"A bedpan, huh?" Logan said, scrunching his face. "Bummer for you, Nora."

"No pun intended, I assume," she shot back.

"Assume? Really?"

"I didn't even do that one on purpose, Logan," she said, rolling her eyes at him.

"But really, Nora, can you grab that? I drank a lot of tea," he said, his tone sobering. She was going to have to help him with this most basic function, and he was going to have to get used to her doing so.

"Sure honey," she said, opening the indicated cupboard. "Good practice for when we're broken down ancient people."

"Yeah, we'll practice while I'm a broken-down young person," he said. "We'll get good at it."

"And then hopefully not have to practice again for several decades," she said, giving him an exhausted smile. They fumbled and blushed and figured it out. Afterward Nora held the pan carefully and opened the door to the bath. "Do you want me to wash your face for you? Never mind, I'll get a washcloth and be right back."

"It can wait, Nora."

"No way. I know how filthy I am and you're even dirtier, like someone dragged you through the forest or something. It'll make you feel a tiny bit better. One sec." She carried the bedpan gingerly to the toilet, emptied and rinsed it. She found a thick stack of washcloths and wet one with hot water. As she wrung it out she looked in the mirror and forced herself to look herself straight in the eyes. She deliberately unwrapped the tiny package tucked in the back of her mind.

When she got back to Logan, she was going to have to tell him about the bullet hole.

A Short Drive

The aroma of coffee, faint but irresistible, called to Monti, making her flare her nostrils and inhale deeply. *Caffeine awaited.* She turned to tell Kit, but he was gone. She lifted her head to check the door. Daylight leaked in at the bottom edge. Time to get up and join the party!

She threw back the covers and threw on her robe, remembering halfway through with a thrill that brought a giggle bubbling up from her belly, that Kit had saved their pictures. Some of their pictures. She couldn't wait to find out which ones, how many…

She stopped off in the bathroom for the briefest of ablutions, hearing voices from the kitchen, hating the thought that she was not part of the conversation. She tweaked her hair into a vague approximation of yesterday's spikiness and called it good.

"Monti, honey!" Her mother smiled and opened her arms for a hug.

"Good morning, Mom. What did I miss?"

"About seven and a half minutes of everyone waiting for the coffee to be ready," Kit said. "I think they had you in mind when they coined the term FOMO, Monti." It was his turn to draw her in for a good morning hug.

"FOMO?" Bob said, eyebrows asking for illumination.

"Fear of missing out, Bob, remember?" Jody said. "It was in that crossword the other day and we Googled it."

"Well, Jody, I can't remember every single thing we Google, that's for sure," he said. "I don't know how we endured wallowing in the depths of ignorance before we had Google at our beck and call 24/7."

"We had an encyclopedia set," Kit said. "Though I don't

remember looking things up in that a half-dozen times a day. We could have, I suppose."

"You couldn't take the 20-volume set with you and read it while driving down the road," Monti pointed out.

"You shouldn't be looking things up while you're driving down the road," Jody said, scandalized.

"No, Mom, riding down the road, I meant, while someone else is driving."

"What on earth are you guys talking about?" Marla asked. She draped herself over the end of the counter, bleary-eyed, her hair in a vague approximation of yesterday's mess without any tweaking.

"Your mother's personality disorders," Kit said. "As usual."

Monti left Kit to go hug Marla. "Hey, baby girl," she said. "You have no idea how exquisitely wonderful it is to give you a hug in the morning."

"Yeah, it's good, huh," Marla agreed, a half-smile turning up one corner of her mouth.

Monti peered over Marla's shoulder at her granddaughter. "Nellie's the last one sleeping, there's a shocker."

"We talked for a while," Marla said, "until she couldn't keep her eyes open."

"Yeah?"

Marla nodded, but didn't elaborate. She had never been a 'sharer,' which made it even tougher to help her through her tough times.

The waiting coffee mugs clinked together softly on the bar as Jody straightened them and began pouring the java. The intensified aroma elicited movement from the far corner of the living room, a good nine or ten feet away, and Noelle sat up.

"Coffee?" she said, extracting herself from her covers and heading their way.

"Marla, was 'coffee' actually Noelle's first word when she was a baby?" Kit asked, deadpan. "It's so often her first word now, that we have to wonder."

"Oh, Grandpa," Noelle said, "don't tease me first thing."

"Right, wait until after…um…your first cup of coffee?"

"Yes, please," she said, leaning into him and yawning hugely. "Pardon me." Jody pushed a full mug toward her, and Noelle gussied it up.

"Dad, can we borrow your laptop?" Monti said. "Kit told me he put some of our pictures in the cloud over the past year or two, so we haven't lost all of them."

"Oh, marvelous," Jody said. "Kit, you're a keeper. Let's keep him, shall we?"

"I want to see, too!" Noelle said. "Did you get all my school pictures?"

"I don't remember what I got and what I didn't," Kit said. "Don't get your hopes up, there are bound to be disappointments. We'll just take a look. After breakfast, maybe?"

"Oh yes, breakfast," Jody said. "Bob and I thought maybe we'd take you all to Hunter's. That sound okay?"

"Well, Mom, I think it's a well-established sacred tradition by now, so sure. It'll take me a few minutes to get ready." Bob was already dressed in his trademark khakis and short-sleeved plaid shirt, and Kit looked like he'd been up for hours, but the ladies were still in various states of early morning disarray.

They absorbed the rest of Caffeine Dose #1 in silence, then set about getting ready for the day. The ladies shared the mirror and sink while Kit and Bob poured another cup and dove into the digital world to locate Kit's photos. Finally the girls were ready, and they all climbed into the behemoth green van.

Monti, used to Idaho's elbow room, soon found herself impatient with the closely packed traffic. "Where are all these people going?" she asked.

"To breakfast, maybe," Kit answered. "In a hurry, Monti?"

"I just can't believe all these cars! Is it always like this? It would drive me nuts."

"Well that would be a short drive, anyway," Bob said. Monti stuck her tongue out at him.

"Florida has the third most vehicles on the roads, after Texas and California," he added, unflustered, checking the rear-view mirror, moving smoothly ahead as traffic would allow. "Nothing one can fix by getting annoyed." Monti rolled her eyes.

"Marla, why don't you tell your mom what you told us the other day, about your plans?" Jody put in.

"Oh, well it's nothing fancy," she said. Her cheeks flushed and she didn't continue.

"You have plans, sweetheart? We want to hear them!" Monti said.

"It's just an idea," Marla said. "Just...when I was in New Mexico at a, like, a half-way house, some guys started a bike repair thing. And renting them. I mean they'd repair your bike, or rent you one. One of the older guys was a genius at it, and he taught me the basics, of repair I mean. I kind of have a knack for it," she said, blushing more deeply.

"You always could put things back together," Kit said. "Even when you were tiny. Barbies and toy cars and..."

"And the box fan one time," Monti added, "After Stephen barreled into it running through the house."

Marla nodded.

"Go on," Monti said. "You were learning bike repair."

"Yeah, well, we'd pick up broken-down bikes here and there and clean and fix them up. We collected a whole stash of bikes in a storage unit, ready to deliver to people who wanted to rent them. One of the guys even put up a website and we were getting hits..." She trailed off.

"And what happened?" Monti said.

Marla sighed. "It fell apart," she said, shaking her head. "Like everything did, eventually, in those days. They couldn't keep off...they couldn't stay away from the drugs and it all fell apart." She sighed. "Me too. I fell apart, too. Again."

The silence in the van grew until you could hear the click-click, click-click of the turn signal as Bob navigated through the traffic.

Monti put an arm around her daughter. "But you're in one piece now," she said. "And you're home, if you want to come home, and we can help you stay in one piece."

Marla slowly raised her arms and wound them around Monti's neck, and buried her face in her mom's neck. Monti pulled her in close. She felt Marla's shoulders shudder with silent sobs.

She looked over Marla and met Kit's eyes, her own shining with tears. He closed his eyes briefly, and smiled his 'it'll be okay' smile at her. Monti patted her daughter's back until she quieted, then laughed as a box of tissues appeared at her elbow. Jody was on duty, as always. Marla sat up at the laugh, and smiled at the tissues.

"You guys and your tissues," she said. "Do we own stock in Puffs, by any chance?" She pulled out a couple and set to repairing the damage. Noelle reached over her shoulder and grabbed one too, causing Marla to look her way.

"Are you okay, honey?" she asked Noelle.

"Sure, Mom," she said. "I pretty much always cry when someone else is crying."

"So does your Grandma," Kit said.

"I do not!" Monti was indignant while she rummaged around in her brain for ready examples of her *not* crying when someone else was crying. "Okay, well that might be true," she admitted.

"No kidding," Kit said almost under his breath, but smiling at her with sparkling eyes so she could hardly hold it against him.

"Really?" Marla asked. "I thought I was weird…and don't even go there, Dad. Whenever anybody cries for any reason, I'm right there bawling too. Now I understand."

"That your weirdness runs deep in the female side of the family…" Kit said.

"Gallops," Bob put in offhandedly, palming the big steering wheel with smooth expertise like a trucker as he turned into the restaurant parking lot.

"Now boys," Jody said, dabbing at her own damp eyes. "We'll start talking about your idiosyncrasies next and then we'll be late for breakfast. And possibly dinner."

"Ouch," Kit said.

"Don't dish it if you can't take it, love," Monti said, and blew him a kiss.

Bob parked, shut off the motor and turned to look at his passengers. "Everyone reasonably reassembled after the waterworks?" he asked. "No rush."

The ladies checked each others' mascara and shortly agreed they were ready.

"Coffee," Noelle said.

"Coming right up," Bob said as they began disembarking.

Monti hurried to be at Kit's door when it opened. Their eyes met and she held her breath as he leaned on her to make the climb down. He reached back in for his cane, snapped it open, and she let out her breath. He leaned down to kiss her cheek. "Thanks, lover," he said. "Quit worrying about me."

Monti rolled her eyes. "Right away, sir," she said. "As soon as I figure out how."

She strolled into the restaurant arm in arm with Kit, smiling at all the people she loved best in the world, minus the one she still missed terribly, though with not so fierce a pain as she used to.

She had her baby girl back, and that was enough for one day.

Berries, Bears, and Bullet Holes

Nora collected the clean bedpan, the hot washcloth, and a towel. But when she stepped back into Logan's room, he was fast asleep.

The bullet hole revelation would have to wait until morning. Washing his face could wait as well, she decided. He needed rest far more than a clean face, and she didn't want to risk waking him.

She tiptoed to the bed and laid the towel in the chair, set the bedpan on it and the washcloth on that. She leaned over her exhausted, broken husband and kissed him softly on the forehead. "Goodnight, love," she whispered.

She examined him. Under the grime, his color was better. The new pain lines on his face had eased. He looked...comfortable, and she knew he hadn't been within light years of comfortable since he'd toppled into the creek. *Thank you, Abba, for comfort.*

She tiptoed to the door and pulled it nearly closed as she stepped back into the adjoining bathroom. Now she could finally get clean and go to bed. Where was her pack? Probably still in the entryway. She opened the door to her room, flipped a switch on the wall and caught her breath as warm light flooded the small bedroom.

The room was spare. But every detail of the few items in it was perfect. The narrow bed sat high on a white metal frame painted with roses. A thick down comforter peeked out from beneath a hand-stitched quilt in every shade of pink, red, and green imaginable. A thick, forest green rag rug lay next to the bed.

The shelves of the single pale oak bookcase sheltered an orderly but varied collection of leather-bound books. On each shelf the row of books stopped a respectful distance from a delicate blown glass object. A tiny grand piano on the right end of one shelf. A high-topped boot on the left end of the next. A ladies' hat. A long-haired cat. Nora could not focus on the fine points of the figurines, her eyes were so tired.

A long row of white-painted, curved wrought iron hooks marched along one wall, and a shell-pink silky robe hung from the hook at this end. She caressed the shimmery fabric. A simple white dressing table with a mirror and a matching upholstered stool completed the room's furnishings. She could totally live in this room.

Bath. No matter what time it was, Nora needed a bath before she could bury herself in that wonderful bed. And her teeth, she decided as she ran her tongue over the fuzziness in her mouth. She had to brush her teeth.

She opened the door into the hall and peered toward the front door. Both packs still slumped there. She went to hers and slung it over her shoulder, wincing at the sore muscles that were bound to be way worse tomorrow. Or was it tomorrow already? She had no idea.

Back in the bathroom she ran piping hot water into the tub. Spying a jar of lavender bath salts on a stand beside the tub, she dumped in a generous handful. Fragrant steam enveloped her as she undressed, sending a gentle wave of wellbeing through her as she inhaled. Shampoo and soap waited on the rack across the tub, with a thick white washcloth and a loofah. She could've been at a fancy spa. Nora slid into the water, closed her eyes and smiled. This was really, really good.

She didn't know how long she soaked before she got down to the business of washing the forest litter out of her hair, made difficult by her soaking wet bandages catching in the snarls. But when she finally got her hair clean and rinsed smooth, she felt immensely better.

She scrubbed herself from head to toe and brushed her teeth. She would have loved to soak a bit more, but the water was disgusting now, so she sighed, pulled the plug and stood up. She wasn't as bone-weary when she stepped out of the tub as when she'd stepped in, but she was sleepy. Very sleepy.

She toweled dry and wrapped herself in the pink robe, promising herself she'd wipe out the tub tomorrow. She fought to keep her eyes open as she smoothed a thick coat of salve on the gouges in her hands and re-wrapped them haphazardly in fresh bandages. It was good enough for tonight.

She peeked into Logan's room. He was sleeping peacefully. She'd leave both doors open in case he needed her during the night.

Thanking Abba again for this safe haven, she turned off the bathroom light and returned to her chamber. She thanked him for rescuing them, for providing help for Logan, for magical backpacks and the majestic deer and a kind soul to take them in. She prayed as she pulled a clean t-shirt from her pack to sleep in, and tears of gratitude, exhaustion, hope and fear made winding paths down her clean cheeks as she climbed into the bed.

She was hopeful. But fear still scraped at the inside of her stomach. Because they weren't home yet, not by a long shot. And Nora tried to push away an uneasy feeling that she'd not yet reached the end of her hard times in the dark forest.

***

Nora rose slowly out of a dream...tea and scones with her grandmother, who wore buttoned up boots and a wide brimmed, feather trimmed hat, and who kept pulling additional scones out of a bedraggled backpack. Her grandma had died ten or twelve years ago, and she'd favored sweatshirts and tennies over feathered hats. But Nora could practically taste the scones. And smell them...

She opened her eyes. Was it morning already? There were no windows in her room, she just noticed. Of course, the house must be mostly dug back into the mountain. How weird! She hadn't thought twice about that last night, but now it struck her as bizarre. Like a prepper's bomb shelter or something.

She slid her feet down to the floor, taking a moment to dig her toes into the thick rag rug, and examine her bandaged hands. She shook her head. She must have been really tired last night—the bandages looked like a three-year-old had done the job. But her hands didn't hurt. At all. Wild. She found her watch over on the dressing table. Seven o'clock! She'd better go check on Logan.

She threw on the last clean clothes from her pack, winced as she tugged the comb through her hair, tangled from going to bed with it wet. She pulled it back into an elastic band. Her eyes fell on a rainbow heap of ribbons in a crystal bowl on the dressing table, and on impulse she plucked a bright green grosgrain out and tied it around her pony tail.

She stopped in the bathroom to splash water on her face, trying not to get the gauze bandages too wet as she did so. The bathroom was a mess. Where had all those sticks and leaves come from? She'd have to get back here and tidy it up, but Logan first.

She opened his door and peeked in wearing a sunny smile for him.

His bed was empty. She went in and looked around, but there was nowhere for him to go except the bathroom and she was just there. And besides, he couldn't get out of bed by himself. Her stomach did a mean flutter kick. She frowned it into submission, turned around and opened the hall door.

When she stepped into the hall, she again thought of scones, and when she inhaled she added bacon and coffee to her mental picture. She followed the aromas, and soon heard voices.

She stepped into the open kitchen at the front of the house, and Logan said, "Nora!" with his own sunny smile for her.

She went to him. "Logan. How are you, sweetheart?" She leaned down to kiss him.

"It's amazing, Nora-ne-Nelson," he said. "Barnabas found this cool chair in one of his back rooms, but I really don't think I'm going to need it for long."

Logan sat in an antique wicker wheelchair with elaborate separate foot supports and three wheels. He spun around in a slow circle, showing it off to her.

"It's beautiful," she said. "Your leg...it isn't hurting you?" she asked.

"It is, a little," he admitted. "But nothing like..." his face contorted as he tried to express his thought. "Nothing like yesterday. It feels like just a minor injury compared to yesterday, although Barnabas says I shouldn't put weight on it for another couple of days."

"Couple of days!" Nora didn't think that could be right. "Shouldn't it be a couple of weeks? Or more? Logan, the bone was...it was sticking out of your leg!" Her throat constricted at the memory. "There's no way you can walk on it in a couple of days."

"Fret not, little one," Barnabas said. "Please be assured Logan is receiving good medical care, and will not be put at any risk whatsoever." He gestured to a chair at the table. "How are your hands this morning?"

"They feel great," she said, flexing them for him. "They don't hurt at all. What's that salve you have?" she asked.

Barnabas smiled and it transformed his face so that you could hardly look away from him. "The salve I make when I have a moment. I'll send a tin home with you, shall I? Have a seat, dear."

"Can I help you, Barnabas?"

"Yes, but not just now," he said. "We'll break our fast, shall we not?" A basket of scones and a dish of soft butter sat on the table, as well as a platter of bacon and a bowl of scrambled eggs. To these Barnabas added a huge bowl of the biggest blackberries she'd ever seen, and a pitcher of cream. "Help yourself to the coffee, Nora, unless you'd like tea." He scanned the table. "There we are, do you need anything else?"

Nora shook her head and after fetching some coffee, sat where he'd directed her. "It looks wonderful. Those berries are amazing."

"You might pick more today if you like," he said. "They grow abundantly in these woods."

"I could eat a horse," Logan said.

"Well, let's start with bacon and eggs, and see if that will suffice for now," Barnabas said with a straight face as he hooked his cane on the edge of the table and lowered himself into his chair. Logan and Nora both laughed and he just cocked an eyebrow at them.

Barnabas raised his eyes and his hands and by the time his guests realized he was praying he was half done. "Master, thank you for guiding these young ones safely to my door. Thank you for supplying their needs along the way, and for the gift of this food and this day. May our living of it give you pleasure."

Nora blinked and Logan said, "Amen." Then they fell to eating. The scones had that perfect initial crispness that gave way immediately to a buttery interior. Her eyes rolled back with pleasure.

"Mmmm!" she said. "These are magnificent. Are there currants in these?" She examined the broken edge of a scone, trying to identify the fruit morsel.

"No, they're dried huckleberries," Barnabas said. "Those also grow in these woods, but have already finished for this year. Farther up the mountain there may still be some on the bushes, if the bears haven't got them all."

Bears? Nora hadn't even thought of bears, but of course there would be… "We didn't see any bears," she said, her voice weak. "But we did hear wolves."

"Yes, the wolves are making themselves at home once again on the peninsula." Barnabas put the kettle back on the heat for another pot of tea. "And it's good no bears put themselves in your path. They can be aggressive this time of year, as they are needing to put on weight ahead of hibernation. Best to steer clear."

Nora's arms broke out in goosebumps. How do you steer clear of a bear? "I…I know you shouldn't run from a bear," she tried, then trailed off. She knew there was more to it than that, but whatever she'd learned at camp and in the scouts seemed to have been scoured from her brain, now that it might actually be useful knowledge.

"We don't need to worry about that now, right, Barnabas?" Logan asked. "We can get home without hiking back through the woods, can't we? I mean, there's a road, and taxis, or…" He seemed to think this unlikely as he was saying it, and stopped.

"There is a road, yes," Barnabas said, pouring hot water into the teapot. "But it is some distance away. And no taxis come out this far, I'm afraid."

Nora hurried to take the teapot from Barnabas and set it on the table. "Then how are we going to get back to our car?" she said, realizing afresh how very far they were from being out of the woods. She choked out a laugh at her unintended pun. "Logan can't really hike for a long while, even after he can put weight on his leg, right? What do we do?"

"There is much to do, child," Barnabas said, sitting again. "We should take it one day at a time, and do the work put before us as it is made clear."

That was a bit vague to suit Nora. She liked to have a plan. "So...what is the work we have to do?" she asked. "I know I left the bathroom a mess, and I was planning to clean that up. And I can help you with the kitchen." She gestured at the breakfast dishes on the table.

"Yes, yes, of course," Barnabas said. "But there is also the matter of the shots you heard."

Nora and Logan looked at him with wide eyes. The shots? What did that have to do with them? Nora suddenly remembered the bullet hole and felt the bottom drop from her stomach. It couldn't be...

"Barnabas," she said quickly, before she chickened out. "And Logan," she turned to her husband and gripped his hand. "I found a—a hole in Logan's pack," she said, swallowing hard. "I think it might be a bullet hole."

"What? Why didn't you tell me?" Logan said, his voice tight and frayed at the edges with panic, setting Nora's stomach roiling.

"When?" she protested. "When could I tell you, Logan?"

"Now, now," Barnabas put in, but his face bore a black scowl at the news. "Let us see the pack, yes?"

Nora nodded, and went to get it from the hall, but it wasn't there. She glanced at Logan and realized he had clean clothes on. Barnabas must have helped him. She sprinted down the hall to Logan's room and fetched the pack. She handed it to Barnabas and pointed out the holes in the top of the pack. They were not obvious in the black fabric, but easy to see once pointed out.

"Oh, my God," Logan breathed.

Birthday

That afternoon they pored over all the pictures Kit had saved online, scanned in many more that Bob and Jody kept in a row of chronologically organized albums, and mourned the loss of pictures everyone remembered but nobody had.

After supper Kit pulled the house plans out from his suitcase. He unrolled and spread them on the small dining table, and Jody kept them flat with a variety of paperweights. A scorpion encased in Lucite anchored one corner. A jade block engraved with an elephant held down another. A tiny Statue of Liberty lighted the way at one corner, and evidence of someone or other's brief kindergarten career as a clay artist crumbled gently on the last.

"The rebuild will be all on one floor," Kit said. "Four bedrooms still, or rather three and an office, so everything will have to be a little smaller."

"No garage?" Bob asked.

"Oh sure, detached, over here. It's healthier, they say, not to have your carbon monoxide mixing with your house air."

"It looks luxurious," Jody said.

"That's what I thought," Monti said, "but the insurance people say it's right in line with our coverage. And look at this, Mom." She pointed to her favorite feature of the floor plan. "It's got built-ins all through the house. Even more than we did have. Sitting alcove at the fireplace, book cases, even a built-in fireplace on the screen porch. Though Kit thinks he might like a grill better."

"There's room for everyone, too," Jody said. "Marla and Noelle right next door to each other, that's sweet."

"They practically have their own wing," Monti said. "And two sinks in their bathroom, which is never a bad thing."

"It'll all fit snugly on our lot," Kit said. "Ramp goes up this side, and we can do a covered walkway between here and the garage," he pointed.

"Fish tanks?" Bob asked.

"No, probably not," Kit said with a wry smile. "They were getting to be too much for me already."

"But you know, I think we might ask Austin and Warren about that, Kit," Monti said. "They have youth and muscle to spare, and they were fascinated with the tanks at Thanksgiving. I bet they'd love to work with you on that project."

"Huh. Maybe some new business partners?" Kit fell silent, and Monti could see the wheels turning as he thought of the possibilities.

"Who are Austin and Warren?" Jody wanted to know.

"Austin was in one of my classes last semester," Monti said. "He's had a rough go. Warren, too, that's his younger brother. Austin ended up in jail for a bit in November, but I think he's going to turn it around. I don't think he wants to go back there. Ever."

"Well, good." Jody said. "At some point you have to figure out how you're going to live your life. Jail is one way to learn how you don't want to do it, anyway."

"How soon can they start building?" Bob wanted to know.

"There are still some hoops to jump through," Kit said. "Another month or so, probably, before they break ground."

"We need to get settled in a place we can live for the next several months, and soon," Monti said. "I have to teach January 8, and Noelle has a heavy course load this semester. It's going to get really busy, really fast."

Kit put his arm around Marla, who hovered at the edge of the group, peering at the plans. "And you have projects of your own to develop, right daughter?"

Marla nodded and leaned into her dad. "I might need your help with that."

"Certainly. You let me know when you're ready and we'll put our heads together."

Monti loved Kit's low pressure support. He knew not to be too enthusiastic, or act like he was going to make things happen for her. She needed just what he was offering: a solid, reliable champion to provide encouragement and expertise if and when she wanted it. He had always had good instincts about how best to love and help Marla. If he hadn't been fighting for his own life when Stephen died, things might have gone better for her.

But there was no use dwelling on that. This was where they were, and God was working mightily in their situation. All would be well.

***

The following days flew by, though there was not much room to spread one's wings in the Housels' tiny apartment. They went with Bob and Jody to their small church, and met their Lost Boys. They were invited out to lunch, but begged off, as everyone felt the need for more cocooning with just the family yet, until things got to feel comfortable.

Marla and Noelle took to walking around the good-sized pond on the property. Everyone would be chatting and reminiscing, then Monti would notice that her girls were gone again. Sometimes they returned with red-rimmed eyes, other times they came in arm in arm, giggling.

Monti thought Marla looked younger with each passing day, as the deep furrows between her eyes eased, and the tension lines around her mouth melted away.

Kit borrowed the Housels' laptop several times. He went into research mode about TIAs and how not to have another one.

Monti kept him company when he dutifully returned to see the young doctor as they'd promised. Kit asked him a hundred questions, and Monti stumped him by asking about the rates of TIAs in those who've had a life-threatening injury. The young man promised to find out what he could before their next appointment.

The Scrabble board rarely made it back into its cupboard, because the next game was always happening soon. Kit against Bob, Bob against Monti, Monti against Jody. The girls played while the guys cooked dinner. The guys played while the girls batted clean up.

Occasionally they snagged Marla or Noelle to sit for a game.

Monti got in a long walk with Marla while Noelle played against Kit and the GG's. From dawn to far past dusk, old stories and older jokes salted the air with laughter. If Monti thought about it for too long, she felt her heart would burst from happiness.

There was also a fair amount of whispering, because Marla's birthday was coming right up on December 15. Jody and Monti took advantage of the girls' frequent walks and dashed out a couple of times to do a little stealth shopping at the mall down the road. Then on B-Day, they encouraged Noelle to finagle a longer-than-usual walk with her mom around the pond and grounds.

The instant they left, the four elders sprang into action and decorated the miniature maison from top to bottom and wall to wall with streamers, balloons, and even a ridiculous SpongeBob SquarePants pinata that Jody had carefully crammed into her bedroom closet for the last three days. It was only slightly dented when they pulled it out and strung it up in the screened porch.

Monti and Kit put together Marla's favorite dinner from childhood: spaghetti with giant meatballs, and whole string beans swimming in butter. A crusty loaf of garlic bread filled the apartment with mouth-watering garlicky goodness.

A tiramisu cheesecake from the boutique bakery hid in the fridge, awaiting its moment of glory. Monti couldn't believe they would need 43 candles. How was that possible? She and Jody decided that four jumbo-sized candles and three smaller ones would be less traumatic all around. These were stashed with a lighter under the duct tape in the junk drawer.

When it was all ready everyone flopped down in the living area and chatted quietly, alert for the sound of their girls crunching along the gravel path to the back door. Monti listened for giggling, but even when the crunching started, there were no accompanying voices.

She stepped into the screened porch. Marla and Noelle walked holding each other tightly, their heads bowed, shoulders slumped, feet nearly dragging. What had happened? She opened the screen door and met them on the path.

"Are you all right?" she asked. Her heart pounded. "Are you…what's up, girls?" Monti tried a smile, but her face wasn't buying it.

Marla and Noelle looked at her, their eyes streaming. Marla's face was ravaged by tears and years and grief, her eyes sunk in deep black hollows. Noelle's face was blanched, her eyes red and puffy.

"What, what?" Monti said, her arms fluttering helplessly, frantic to know the bad news or the worse news or whatever it was making them cry on her baby girl's birthday.

"Oh, Mom," Marla said. "I was just telling Noelle about her little sister."

Hart's Burden

Nora dropped into her chair, her knees weak with the renewed realization of how close Logan had come to being shot. Inches. Half an inch. She couldn't—that couldn't be thought about.

"Where were you when this happened?" Barnabas wanted to know.

"We were--well, I was--on a huge log over a creek," Logan said. "We'd gone off the main trail," here he shot a guilty look at Nora, "you know the Storm Ridge Trail?"

Barnabas set the pack down, went to a wall of built-in drawers and cupboards and rummaged in a wide, shallow drawer. He pulled out a rolled map and brought it to the big table. He began pushing dishes to the side and Nora leaped to help him.

They got the map unrolled and anchored at the edges with knives and the salt and pepper shakers. Barnabas slid a pair of reading glasses from his shirt pocket and peered through them at the closely figured details of the map. He found the trail Logan mentioned and followed a creek with his gnarled forefinger. He tapped the map. "Here, most likely," he said. He moved the salt shaker to mark that location and Nora put a spoon in its place on the edge of the map. "Now, where be that lodge…"

Barnabas studied the map, looking for something. "Year before last, a billionaire of some sort built a hunting lodge…though private resort would be a better description."

He plunked his finger onto a spot a couple of inches from the creek, perhaps a few miles on the ground. "Since then, a ridiculous number of hunting parties," he scowled at his guests, "emphasis on *parties*, have been roaming these woods, hunting in season and out, leaving their trash everywhere and raising the blood pressure of our Forest Service personnel and everyone else in the area."

"It's not hunting season now, is it?" Logan asked.

"No, it is not. But, be that as it may, our immediate need is to post a message to those who can help you two find your way back to your vehicle," Barnabas said.

"Post a message? You mean email?" Logan said. "Thanks, that'd be great. But, don't you have a phone?"

"No, Logan. No phone, and no email. People come here to...disconnect...from the world for a time." Barnabas said.

"Right," Logan said. "I can see that. Unplug, we call it. But, what about for emergencies?"

"Oh, one is careful, of course. But when something does go awry, it is amazing what one can do unassisted, if it becomes necessary." He peered at Logan from under his eyebrows. "But you children have telephones, do you not?" He removed his glasses and began to polish them with a capacious white handkerchief he unfolded from a back pocket.

"We did, yes," Nora said, her shoulders sagging. "But they were ruined in the creek. Mine is full of water and Logan's is smashed."

"Oh man, I just got that phone," Logan said. "Bummer." They mourned the loss of their cool phones for a minute. "Maybe we could try the bowl of rice trick on Nora's," Logan said.

"Pardon, I'm not following," Barnabas said.

"You know, putting the phone in a bowl of rice, uncooked, of course, overnight. Sometimes that dries it out enough to get it to work again." Logan frowned. "But it was in the creek for a while, right Nora?" She nodded. "And it's been over 24 hours. It might not work after that long. But we could give it a shot anyway."

"Hmm, rice. Ingenious idea," Barnabas said. "You are welcome to try it. I believe I have rice...somewhere. It's not something I eat often, but it does keep well, so I'm sure..." he stared off into hypothetical places where he might have rice stashed, seeming to discount one place, and brighten at the thought of another. "I'll check that cupboard," he pointed, "and if it's not there, I'll check the pantry.

"Meanwhile, a few miles from here is a post box, where the trail meets a dirt road," he said. "I very rarely use it—only if am in dire need—but Roland, who brings my supplies, checks it every two or three days. In case, as you say, there may have been an emergency."

Barnabas took a notebook from an open shelf, and opened it to a blank page. "Nora should be able to walk to the post box in two or three hours." He began jotting a note on the page.

"Nora? By herself?" Logan said, his hands gripping the armrests of the wheelchair, clearly not happy with that plan. Nora cringed at the thought of a solo hike and was grateful Logan had objected. "Can't we just wait until Roland delivers your supplies again and give him the message then?" Logan suggested.

"We could, though 'twill be nearly a month yet," Barnabas said. "He was here but two days ago."

"A month," Nora said. "Our friends would be crazy worried by then, not to mention our parents."

"Right. Dad will be demanding search parties way before then," Logan agreed.

"And you have to get your leg looked at, no offense, Barnabas."

"None taken," he murmured.

"Sure, but Nora, you can't hike through the woods alone." Deep concern for her etched grooves in his face.

"Pardon me," Barnabas said. "But your young wife has hiked, for all practical purposes, alone through the woods for many hours already. And in the dark of night." He let that sink in for a minute before adding, "We are speaking of a two or three hour walk in the bright morning, carrying no burden, and with a clear trail map to guide her. I have not the slightest doubt of her ability to accomplish the task."

"Plus two or three hours back, though, don't forget."

"Yes, that's true. Even so, she should be back well before dark."

Before dark. Nora's flesh went bumply and she shivered involuntarily. Though, as Barnabas had pointed out, she just had hiked through the forest in the dark. But somehow, having Logan with her, even if he couldn't protect her, had made all the difference. She knew she could never have done it otherwise. Plus, she hadn't known about the bears, and now she couldn't *un-know* about them.

"But that is not for today," Barnabas was saying. "Tomorrow will be soon enough, will it not, to prevent your family worrying overmuch? Today I believe you both need to rest." He closed the notebook with the pen still inside and slid it back onto the shelf. "You are free to explore the house if you like. There are some stairs that Logan won't manage, of course, but the main floor here is quite extensive." He gestured back into the depths of the mountain.

"Who built this place?" Logan asked, putting aside, she noticed, the question of her hiking to the post box.

"Ah, a good question," Barnabas said. "Without a simple answer. The details of its initial construction are lost to time. Some enterprising soul, or a fearful one, perhaps, built his little cabin backed up to the mountainside. Subsequent dwellers dug into the mountain itself, and down through the years succeeding tenants extended the interior this way and that, upwards and downwards. You'll see evidence of the work of different hands as you explore." He shook his head. "Sometimes I'm nearly certain I have not yet traveled all the corridors."

"How long have you lived here?" Nora asked. *And why?* She wanted to add.

"Oh, a good many years now," he said. "It is my hermitage, you might say. Though far too large to fit that humble designation, I suppose."

"Do you own the place?" Logan said.

"No, no, not at all," Barnabas said. "Naught but a bondslave."

He'd called himself that yesterday, but she couldn't bring herself to ask him to explain. It was such an odd thing to say. So then whose place was it? Nora wondered. The owner of the bondslave? Her American sensibilities recoiled at that thought. She shook her head. He made no sense. This place made no sense. But she was game to explore it if Logan was. The rooms she had seen so far were gorgeous.

"What do you think, Logan, want to go wandering?"

"Sure," he said. "We won't get lost, will we?" he asked Barnabas.

"Hmm, I suppose you might," he said, looking profoundly unconcerned about the possibility. "You perhaps should make some notes as you go regarding landmarks, so as to find them again as you wander back," he suggested.

Nora and Logan blinked at him.

"Notes. Right," Nora said. "I'll grab my Moleskin before we head out."

"Or in, rather," Logan said, eyes twinkling.

He really was feeling okay, then, if he was making jokes and ready to explore the house. She couldn't see how that made sense either, unless the herbs in that bag had properties she'd never heard of. But she would take it! She was not inspecting the gift horse, no she wasn't.

"Okay, in then," she smiled at him. "I'll wash the dishes, Barnabas, before we head in." It was the least she could do.

Barnabas inclined his head and said, "Why, thank you, young lady. You'll find some gloves under the sink, so you won't get your bandages wet. I shall locate the rice and then finish my note regarding the situation, in anticipation of your outing tomorrow." He gripped his cane and limped heavily down the hall to his— what—room? Suite? Wing?

"I'm gonna grab your phone, Nora," Logan said. "I can at least open it up and see what the damage is."

Nora nodded. "It's in the device pouch in your pack. Then if you do get it working it'll need charged, right?"

"Definitely by now. There have to be outlets, right?"

She looked around, but didn't see the usual 'above the counter' outlets in the kitchen. "I don't know. I don't see any here."

"Well, I'll look around," Logan said. He blew her a kiss and wheeled himself down the hall as if he'd been operating the chair for weeks.

Nora put the phone question out of her mind and focused on the task at hand. She found the gloves and eased them on over her bumpy bandages. It was a pleasure to wash the lovely dishes. The cream stoneware was edged with a pattern of grapevines. In the center of each piece villagers chatted over a wall, or milked a cow, or led a horse down a path.

She tidied the kitchen, peeking in cupboards and drawers more than was strictly necessary as she did, because every time she opened one, she was rewarded. Glimpses of sparkling crystal goblets, delicate china vases painted with Chinese maidens, linens embroidered in lush roses, a set of salt and pepper shakers carved from black wood in the shape of fat penguins.

Even the kitchen closet, in which she was searching for a broom to sweep up the crumbs, offered an exquisite fan shaped broom. It had a slightly kinked, slender tree trunk for a handle and a hand-woven top in which tiny shells on bright red threads were laced through the straws in an intricate design. She would have this hanging on her wall, but it was apparently meant for use, being the only broom in the closet. So she gave herself over to the pleasure of using such a beautiful object for its humble intended purpose.

Finally she was done. She found herself wishing this was her kitchen. If it was, she'd keep it sparkling 24/7. Her tiny, windowless kitchenette appeared in her mind, dingy and dim. But she felt inspired, now, to brighten it up somehow when they got home. She wiped her hands on a towel and went to find Logan.

Little Sister

"What?" Monti stuttered. "Little sister?" Her legs gave up and she sat down abruptly on a providential bench beside the path.

"Mom, it's hard to tell you," Marla said. "It's a bad story."

"Why do people keep telling me bad stories?" Monti muttered. Her eyes filled, her stomach churned in anticipation. "What happened?" she croaked out, and forced herself to look at Marla, taking in Noelle's pale, damp face as well.

Marla sat beside her and took her hand. "It's bad, Mom," she said again. She glanced at Noelle as if for support, took a deep breath, then pushed it all out in a rush. "When Derek left me the first time, when Noelle was two, I was pregnant. I had an abortion."

Monti slumped over on the bench, having known this was what it must be, but hating it fiercely. She pulled loose of Marla's hand, wrapped her arms around her and heaved great sobs as she held her tightly, grieving for her daughter. And her granddaughter. Both of her granddaughters. Marla wound her arms around her mother and patted her back. Noelle sat on her other side and leaned in.

The screen door opened and Jody peeked out. She took one look and hurried to them. "What?" she asked, searching Noelle's eyes for answers.

"I had a little sister," Noelle said, but even with her new hearing aids Jody could not hear the girl's whisper. She shook her head and leaned closer. Noelle put her hand on her great-grandmother's soft cheek and said right into her ear, "I had a little sister."

Jody's eyes went wide and her lower lip trembled. She put a hand out and gripped Noelle's shoulder to steady herself, because the bench was full. She closed her eyes for a long moment as her throat worked to keep down the cry trying to escape. She looked around at

111

the grounds, the trees darkening in the failing light, a thick damp settling over everything as the day abandoned them.

"Come on, Nellie," she said. "Let's get them inside."

Jody and Noelle fluttered around the bench, tugging at Monti, catching Marla's eye. Marla finally got the idea and helped Noelle pull Monti up. They guided her on either side as Jody held the screen door open, then the house door.

All four women stood blinking in the bright light of the living room, the brilliant colors of the streamers and balloons a watery blur as they each remembered what was supposed to be happening now.

Kit positioned his cane, pushed himself up and came to Monti's side immediately. "Monti?" He looked to the others for help as she clung to him, burying her face in his chest.

"I'm okay," she said. "It's okay, just..." She shook her head and looked up at her husband.

Kit got her over to the sofa, pushed her gently down and sat beside her. Marla and Noelle sat, too, and Bob hovered. Jody fetched the tissues and passed them around.

"I'm sorry," Marla said. "I didn't mean to ruin the party," she gestured at the decorations. Then she told her bad story.

"I didn't know what to do. I was alone. I was messed up and strung out. I didn't think I'd be welcome back home," she scrunched her eyes shut and swallowed tears. "I see now that was stupid." She opened her eyes and looked at them. "I know you would've taken me back with open arms," she said. "But I couldn't see it then."

After a silence broken only by sniffles and nose-blowing, Kit said, "What year? How old would she be?"

"She'd be just 17," Marla said. "The people at the clinic didn't do a due date or anything, of course, but I've thought it through a thousand times since then." She looked at Noelle. "She would have been born in June, just opposite Nellie and me on the calendar."

"Why do you say 'she'," Jody asked. "You can't have known..."

"No, no, I don't really know if it was a girl," Marla said. "I've just always thought of the baby as 'she.'" She stared out of the room into the past. "Anyway, then Derek came back. I didn't tell him. Things went from bad to worse after that, until he was killed."

The room fell silent again. Marla soldiered on. "I remember her birthday every year, right between Noelle's and mine, on June 12. I just picked a day," she said.

Kit cleared his throat. "Thank you for telling us, Marla," he said. "I know that was hard to do." He paused. "It *is* a bad story, but I think everyone in this room is certain we'll meet her one fine day, and that hope is a serious comfort, to me anyway."

"To me too," Jody said. "Especially since I'll probably get to meet her first."

"Mom," Monti said, further words failing her at her mother's macabre sense of humor, or whatever it was. "You see, Kit? What chance did I have with this role model?" Monti gestured at her mom and rolled her eyes.

"Uh, before we get to analyzing Mom's personality disorders again," Marla put in, "Sorry, Mom...it smells really good in here. Is it spaghetti and meatballs?"

"It is," Jody confirmed. "And garlic bread and salad and a special dessert."

"With candles, but not 43 candles," Monti said.

"Uh-huh. Well, can we eat?" Marla asked. "I'm starving."

This idea was enthusiastically received. First there was considerable tear dabbing, nose-blowing, tissue collecting, and face rinsing, but in short order the food was on everybody's plates, thanks were returned, and the party commenced, if on a significantly more subdued note than originally anticipated.

The spaghetti served as good comfort food, except for Bob, who failed to stop eating it before he was uncomfortable. "I've always had a weakness for pasta," he confessed.

"Bob, anyone who's eaten any meal with you besides breakfast knows that," Jody said.

"Where's the rule that says you can't have pasta for breakfast?" he said.

Jody rolled her eyes. "Regardless of who's going to polish off the leftovers first thing tomorrow morning, I'm ready for a break before the tiramisu cheesecake."

"You mean the *surprise* tiramisu cheesecake?" Monti said, with significant eyebrows.

"Oh, rats," Jody said, her shoulders slumping. "Well you know how I am with secrets. I hate them. And you all made me shop in secret and decorate in secret and cook in secret already. I used up all my secret-keeping for a while."

Marla laughed, "No worries, Grandma. I like a little anticipation." She leaned over the back of Jody's chair, hugged her neck and kissed her cheek. "I'm not too keen on secrets, myself. But I do love tiramisu cheesecake."

"Well, what about some Scrabble while we digest?" Monti grabbed Marla's hand and kissed it.

"We have too many," Jody protested.

"We could do Jankenpon to decide on who washes up?" Noelle suggested.

"Or we could all play, in teams," Monti said, "and wash up later."

"Or I could go sleep off the spaghetti and knock your field down to five players," Bob said.

"Oh Bob, don't be a party pooper," Jody said. "How about Jankenpon to decide teams of two?"

They all agreed, Bob with a sleepy nod, and Noelle got them organized to take advantage of the efficient and unchallengeable authority of rock-paper-scissors.

The second round was interrupted by Kit's phone ringing. He started to get the cane under him but Monti touched his arm and went to fetch it from the bedroom. She put it in his hand and kissed his forehead.

"Kit Rising," he said into the phone. "CJ, good to hear from you." He sat up a little straighter in his chair. "What's up?" He listened for a while, his face darkening into a black scowl. His left hand, still gripping the cane, grew white-knuckled. Monti hovered, watching him, her chest tightening. Everyone else gradually stopped what they were doing and waited, silent.

Kit grunted. "That's good, at least. And Jenny's okay?" He leaned the cane on the edge of the table, fiddling to find the balance point while he listened. "No, I can't travel until…we're heading home as soon as possible after Christmas. No, I'll tell you about it when we get back." The cane clattered to the floor and Monti jumped. "Yep. I appreciate you keeping us in the loop, CJ. You too, good night." He put the phone down and looked at Monti. She sat down and gripped her hands together on her lap.

"Stevie Jakes, remember, made bail a few days after the fire."

"Yes, yes. And?"

"The day we left, he failed to show for arraignment. And today, he attacked Jenny at the Cominskis'."

"He did not!" Monti said, and grabbed both sides of her head.

"Is Jenny—Grandpa, what about Jenny?" Noelle's voice failed her.

"Jenny and the baby are okay, they're pretty sure," Kit said. "Ray and Dot are with her at the ER now, getting her checked out. Ray came up from the basement to find Jenny on the sofa, Jakes on top of her, choking her. Ray hollered and Jakes came at him. Ray's banged up, but he happened to be bringing a 2x4 up from the basement, so Jakes got the worst of it. He's back in custody now."

"Where was Dot?"

"CJ didn't say. Not there, apparently."

Noelle wrapped her arms around Monti from behind and Monti held onto her tightly. "I thought it was over," Monti said, choking the words out.

"Jenny's the girl who was staying with you, right?" Jody asked, an empathetic rage reddening her cheeks. "Why did he go after her again?"

"Jakes and Blaine, Jenny's ex-boyfriend, are partners in crime. They're convinced Jenny overheard them scheming and then told the police what they were up to." Kit shook his head. "But she didn't. Nevertheless, this brilliant character can't get it through his thick skull that he's in deep trouble completely aside from anything Jenny knows, and he's dug his hole deeper with this attack."

"But he didn't burn your house down," Jody said, "If he didn't make bail until after?"

"Right," Kit agreed. "But I think Blaine and Jakes both are in over their heads with some really bad people. CJ thinks there's evidence of increased gang activity, and that a new group might be moving into the Coeur d'Alene area wanting to set up shop. Someone in that gang is likely responsible. But it could be a long time before we find out who, if we ever do."

Jody and Bob and Marla had a hundred questions, and the Risings filled them in. It was a relief to let it all out to sympathetic listeners, to be indignant and angry, to speculate unkindly about the intelligence level of the bad guys and to grieve for their family's losses. And to rage at Jakes' attack on Jenny and to exult in the bravery of their dear friend Ray.

Finally they were spent. They'd moved closer as the conversation went on, and were now huddled tightly together around the small table. At last Kit said, "Let's talk about something else, shall we? It's Marla's birthday and we seem to be having a hard time celebrating. But I for one am extremely grateful to have us all together, and the cheesecake has waited long enough."

That broke the spell and the ladies immediately set about fetching plates and napkins and candles and making a fresh pot of coffee. Inside of ten minutes they were singing Happy Birthday in three-part harmony and two-part dissonance, and Marla blew out the candles.

Bob offered heartfelt thanks to God for Marla's safe return to the family, and begged for wisdom and guidance in the Risings' ongoing situation back home, and even pleaded for the ne'er do wells to come to their senses and turn their lives over to Jesus, which eased Monti's guilty conscience a little for all the badmouthing they'd just done.

After the cheesecake was distributed, with two slices returned to the fridge for a post-birthday breakfast dessert, they relaxed into being together, and shut everything else—past, present, and future—out of the little house for a few hours.

Bob bailed first, and Kit turned in shortly after. Marla and Noelle volunteered for cleanup, and Marla wouldn't be dissuaded even though she was the birthday girl.

Monti was tempted to call it a day, too, but she didn't want to miss a single minute. "You want a game, Mom?" she asked.

"Oh, sure," Jody said. She never turned down a chance to play, whether it was Scrabble or gin rummy, badminton or volleyball, video games or freeze tag with a bunch of little ones, though she did draw the line at dodge ball these days. So they set up the board and were well into a lovely game when Monti couldn't stand it anymore.

"I have to text Dorothy," she said, and went to get her phone.

"Dorothy?" Jody asked, her eyebrows raised.

"That's Dot," Noelle said. She rinsed the last plate, dried her hands and went for her phone too. "I'm going to text Jenny, too."

The rest of the game was punctuated by reading aloud of texts from Dot and Jenny as they came in, interspersed with kibitzing from Noelle and Marla. They'd pulled chairs up to the table when they were done with the dishes.

The last of the cheesecake was eventually retrieved and shared around with the last of the coffee and the last of the tiles from the bag. The conversation with Dot had reassured Monti, and she was suffused with contentment, finding she could put the day's bad bits away from her a little distance, as something to think about tomorrow.

Jody won the game, but the board was intriguing, so Monti took a careful picture. TRAVOIS and TRIBE, LOGGERS and TANGLED and SECLUDED...she was thinking of story possibilities already.

Exploring

Nora found Logan in his room doing one of his absolute favorite things, messing about with books. He had a thick tome in each hand and was straining to examine the spines of the books on the top shelf.

"Careful, Logan. Not supposed to move that leg, right?" she kissed his offered lips. "Did you give up on the phone?"

"Hmm?" He pulled his focus back to the present with an effort. Offering a kiss could be done on autopilot, but answering a question occasionally required conscious attention. "No, I opened it up and put it on a towel. But I think it's a goner."

"Bummer. What about outlets?"

"I didn't find any yet. I got a bit distracted," he said.

"I can see that," she said, nudging him. "I wonder if this is a lending library?"

"Mm-hm," he said.

Nora shook her head. "I should clean up my mess in the bathroom before we go exploring."

"Okay, need help?" he said, but he had his head in the books again. She smiled to herself. That man and books. You could lose him for a whole morning in a big bookstore. A whole day if there was a coffee shop for on-site refueling. Not that she minded spending a day that way herself, not at all. They hadn't done that for a while. It was time for an all-day bookstore outing after they got back home.

It seemed like a month since they'd been home. Really, it was what, two days ago? A lifetime. She put the bathroom to rights, retrieving the broom from the kitchen closet to take care of the acre of forest undergrowth she'd accumulated on her body and transplanted to the bathroom floor. She didn't know what to do with her dirty towels and clothes, so she piled them by the door and made a mental note to ask Barnabas.

When she returned to Logan, he had stacked three books on the dresser, and was reading a fourth.

"What did you find?" she asked, walking up behind him and nuzzling the back of his neck, inhaling the undetectable but absolutely essential smell of him.

"Oh, Augustine," he said, leaning into her nuzzle. "The Happy Life. I haven't read this one."

"Hmm, a little light reading, huh?" Nora teased him. His reading tastes ran a fair bit deeper than hers. Give her a good post-apocalyptic dystopia and she was all set. "You ready to go exploring?"

"Sure, Nora-ne-Nelson," he said, and glanced around. She knew he was hunting for a bookmark. She joined in the hunt and her eyes widened as they fell on the prize. She reached over his shoulder and pulled a green glass jar from the top shelf, crowded with bookmarks of every description.

"Cool," Logan said, and selected a flattened brass stem with a miniature dragon dangling from the top. He lay the book on his nightstand, apparently intending to really and truly read it. "Where are we off to?"

"Dunno, I thought we'd just head into the mountain and see what we find. Though, if we find a laundry room, that'd be great."

"Right-o, looking for the laundry room, let's go!"

"I can't believe how chipper you are today. It was just yesterday, right? That you were unconscious from the pain of your broken leg?"

Logan looked at her, sobering down. "Yeah, Nora, it was. Can't stop thinking about that, actually. It's freaky, huh? If someone told me this story, I wouldn't believe it."

Nora laughed. "But we're both living it, so it can't be a dream. And I don't remember eating any mushrooms in the woods, do you?"

"No," he said, smiling and shaking his head. "Maybe it'll start to make more sense as we talk with Barnabas more. But meanwhile, yeah, let's look around."

They set off down the corridor, Logan working the wheels of his chair like an old pro, Nora walking beside him with a light hand on his shoulder. They passed the bathroom and Nora's room, and Nora tried the next door, which opened into a darkened room. She felt automatically for a light switch on the wall, which she found and then flipped on.

"Hey, Logan, the lights go on with switches, so doesn't it seem like there should be wall outlets, too?"

"You'd think," he agreed. The room was another bedroom for one person, with the addition of a cradle and a changing table. A hand-painted border of over-sized bright flowers grew up from the baseboard all the way around the room. But no outlets were revealed even when Nora checked behind the bed and nightstand.

"So how do these lamps work?" She pulled the chain on the bedside lamp and it lit up. Feeling around its base, she found no cord. "Batteries?"

Logan picked up the lamp and turned it over, but didn't find evidence of a battery enclosure. He began muttering about inductive coupling and resonance and non-radiative energy transfer. By the time he got to 'rectifying antenna' Nora's brain had completely glazed over.

"Logan," she said. "English?"

"Uh...wireless electricity," he said.

"Ya think?" she said, her hand on her hip. "How?" But she immediately put her hand out to stop an explanation. "Never mind. You lost me at electricity, anyway. Why do you know this stuff? This isn't medical bioengineering."

"No, it's not, but it's all connected, right? Power, life...your cells generate electricity, after all." He set the lamp down and turned his chair to look more closely at the rest of the room. "Some genius must have built this place, Nora. Or at least done some of the modifications. There's electricity built into this house, and that's still light years ahead of anything you can get from your local contractor."

"Hmm. So, charging my phone?"

"We'll have to ask Barnabas. But I bet there's a setup for wireless charging somewhere. If we can resurrect the phone in the first place."

They returned to the hall and headed for the next door. "I wonder what the rent would be on a tiny cabin with a thousand rooms out in the middle of nowhere, with wireless electricity and no road in sight," Nora said.

"Secluded paradise in the peaceful deep woods. Bigger on the inside," Logan said in a hokey salesman's voice.

"Oh, this is much more beautiful than the Tardis. And it doesn't make that awful noise."

"Yes, but you also can't time travel in it."

"How do you know that for sure?" Nora asked. "I don't think we've scratched the surface yet." She pointed to a brass plaque on the next door. "Oh! Laundry, yay!"

"Don't think I've ever heard you say that before."

"Ha, ha," she said, sticking her tongue out at him and opening the door. The large laundry room, painted a sunny yellow, featured a modern washer and dryer set and a cavernous linen closet, as well as an ironing station with clothes rods and baskets, and even a 5-lined clothesline set over a bed of gravel. A vintage embroidered bag of clothespins hung from the wooden support at one end.

"Weird," Nora said. "Why is there gravel? I guess for drainage? Weird in a house, though."

Logan rolled over to where she stood and stuck a hand out, waved it here and there.

"What?"

"A breeze, feel it?" He narrowed his eyes and searched for the source. He pointed up high on the ceiling. "Those look like regular heating vents," he said, "But that's not forced air heat. He's somehow got fresh air blowing through here."

"Well, you can't open the nonexistent windows, so that's a great solution for drying your clothes if you can figure out how to do it."

"Wild..." Logan muttered. He wheeled over beside the dryer and craned his neck to examine the back of the appliance—its cord was neatly coiled and duct taped to the metal. "Retrofitted. This place is totally wild. Let's go further." He wheeled around and back out into the hall, and they continued until they came to a four-way intersection.

"Barnabas' rooms must be down there," Nora said, peering down the corridor to the right. "Wonder what's to the left?"

"One way to find out," Logan said, and swiveled the wheelchair to port.

"Oh!" Nora said. "The floor changed." They had been walking on wide, silky smooth planks of some dark wood, black walnut perhaps, that made Nora want to take off her shoes and slide down the hall in her socks. But as they turned left, the floorboards gave way to flagstones.

"The air is cooler, too," Logan said. "I bet this wing is for storage." He rolled forward and sure enough, they found a gigantic pantry on one side of the hall, and a capacious dry storage room on the other, full of paper goods and cleaning supplies, various equipment and what must be spare parts for everything in the house.

"Who needs K-mart?" Nora said. "This is prepper central."

"If he only gets supplies in monthly, that'd be a long time with a broken toilet," Logan said. "Longer even, because his delivery guy would have to go buy the part and bring it back again."

Nora nodded, wandering through the sets of wide shelving. She turned to her husband. "Logan," she said. "What do you think about me hiking alone, out to the message box?"

He didn't answer right away, which she appreciated. Serious questions were worth carefully considered, thoughtfully worded answers in Logan's way of thinking, sweet man.

"Well, Nora, we're agreed, right, that we have to let our peeps know we're okay?" Nora nodded, while resisting the inevitable conclusion he was headed for.

"I can't go," he said, "I truly wish I could. And I know you wouldn't suggest Barnabas go with his cane and that limp."

"No, no of course not," she sighed. She plopped down on a two-step ladder sitting in the aisle and folded her arms on her knees. "I know I don't have a choice, but the idea terrifies me."

He took her hand and tilted his head. "No more peace, huh? Little girl lost is overshadowing everything?"

She let out a deep juddering breath. "Isn't that pitiful after all this time? I should get over it. And yesterday, I know Abba was helping me, helping us. It was powerful, that peace. Why can't I lay my hands on it now?"

He rubbed the back of her hand with his thumb. "Maybe because you don't really need it right now. Right now you operate on faith, and obedience. But think about what we've experienced so far. I'd bet my unbroken leg you'll be given what you need to do the thing, when it's time to do it, don't you think?" He squeezed her hand. "God is seldom early..."

"And never late," she finished. "Yep. Time to suck it up, huh. Never give up, never turn back."

"Baby, I know that's hard. Really, I get it."

"I know you do, Logan, and that's why I love you so much." Her throat tightened at the thought of how deeply she loved him.

"Sure, that and my incredible prowess as a fry cook," he said.

"Well of course, that goes without saying. Bacon and hash browns, what could be more essential to a girl's happiness?" She let one foot flop heavily to the floor and dragged herself upright off the stool. "As fascinating as this room is, I really had in mind hidden treasures, gigantic libraries, undergrounds gardens...you know, cool stuff."

"Underground gardens? You think Barnabas is using growlights..."

"No, silly," she pushed at his shoulder. "Let's go." She got behind him and wheeled him out of the room. The storage wing ended in a set of heavy oak double doors, but they were locked. So they turned around and made their way back to the intersection, and then headed left, deeper into the heart of the mountain.

Tree

"Monti, we're going to get a tree, do you want to come?"

"Hmm?" Monti responded.

"A tree, daughter, a Christmas tree," Jody repeated. "Kit is staying home, but your dad and the girls are going...Monti are you even hearing me?"

"Sure, Mom," Monti looked up from the laptop she'd commandeered from her dad first thing this morning. "Tree. Do I want one." She frowned. "Why do I want a tree?"

Jody rolled her eyes. "Never mind. I can see you'd have to be led around by the hand the entire time, because you're off in Storyland somewhere." She patted Monti's hand. "You stay here and write. Kit will take care of you and make sure you don't wander into traffic or anything, and we'll be back in an hour or two, okay?"

Monti nodded absently. Jody pecked her on the cheek, waved at Kit, picked up her list and led Bob and the Christmas tree entourage out the door.

"Bye, Mom," Marla said. Noelle gave her a kiss on the cheek, too. Monti waved at them, wondering vaguely where they were going and why. Then she noticed a stiffness in her neck and checked her watch. She'd been writing for two hours straight, no wonder. Time for a coffee break. Just then Kit walked up behind her and planted a very nice kiss on the nape of her neck.

"Mmm. I like yours best," she said.

"My what?" he asked, eyebrows waggling.

"Oh you know, kisses, everything," she said. "Coffee?"

"Just going to make a fresh pot. Marla and Bob drained it into travel cups on their way out."

"Yes, they all left...to go...?"

"You really are a space cadet, aren't you, lover," Kit said, dumping the wet grounds and measuring out fresh. "They went to buy a Christmas tree. Your mom invited you to go with."

"Oh. I was a bit distracted, right in the middle of a scene." She eased off the barstool and stretched her arms up high, then over sideways, various joints popping in protest. "I didn't mean to stay in one position so long."

"You're really biting into the new Scrabble story, huh?"

"Yep. It's flowing nicely. Please help me remember to keep backing it up onto this flash drive." She indicated a realistic plastic sushi serving disguising a thumb drive.

"I suppose you want to remember to take it home with us, too," he said.

"Yes, please."

"And/or, we could stash it in the cloud for you, so you don't have to remember all that."

"We could?" Monti was unsure.

"We could," he said.

"Okay, I'll let you be in charge of that. What're you up to today?"

"Research. I'm making a short list to talk over with Charlie, on the TIA thing." He pushed the 'go' button on the coffee maker and readied their cups. "And I've looked at cars a bit."

"Cars? Do we need a new car?"

"Not yet," he said. "But if...when," he ground the word out between his teeth, "when we need to load a wheelchair, well, the Baja isn't going to work for that."

Monti was floored. She blinked at him, her throat got thick and tears pricked. "No fun," she whispered.

"No fun," he agreed. "Gotta do what we gotta do, though, love. Better to plan ahead."

She nodded, but her lower lip trembled. She didn't want to think about it. She couldn't believe Kit was being so matter-of-fact about it. "How do you do that?" she choked out, and cleared her throat. "Do you promise to plan ahead for all my no-fun stuff, too?"

"Like losing the entire manuscript for a new story?" he grinned at her. "Sure, Monti, I'll take care of it."

"You know what I mean." She reached her hand over the bar and grabbed his. "Love you like crazy, Kit Rising."

"It's mutual," he said, squeezing her hand before letting go to fetch the cream from the fridge and pour their coffee.

They returned to their respective projects, Kit making do with Google on his phone, jotting notes in his pocket notebook, and Monti burning up the laptop. Before they knew it their family burst through the door, and an enticing oregano and garlic pizza aroma wafted through the laughing and talking. Monti saw with surprise that it was four in the afternoon! She had been lost in the woods for hours.

"You two look sleepy!" Jody declared.

"Not really," Monti said, "just in another world. That pizza smells great." Her stomach growled in agreement.

"Hit save, Monti?" Kit asked.

"Right, thanks!" Monti saved her story, and slid it onto the flash drive. "Into the cloud later?"

"Sure, love." Kit got to his feet. "What can I bring in from the car?"

"Oh, Bob's undoing the knots now, but I'm sure he could use a hand. And there are some bags," Jody added as she opened the door to the screened porch. "We're going to have to put the tree out here," she said. "There's not another inch of floor space anywhere."

"Wait!" Noelle blushed as everyone raised their eyebrows at her. "We need Christmas music!" she said. "We can't put up the tree without music."

"You're perfectly right, Nellie," Jody said, and changed trajectories. She found a local station playing carols with a reggae rhythm, and smiled. Monti and Marla shifted the porch furniture, stacking some chairs and pushing the table back.

"Just tell me where, Grandma. Want us to scoot these over?" Marla said.

"That's good right there," Jody said. She opened the storage closet off the side wall of the porch, pulled out the box of ornaments and handed them to Noelle. "I can't reach the stand, sweetie," she said to Marla. "Can you climb up and get it off that nail?"

Marla lifted down the red conical tree holder just as the men hauled in the tree. The fragrance of winter instantly permeated the tiny house; the smell of snow and hot cider, red cheeks and caroling, sleeping in and A Charlie Brown Christmas and It's a Wonderful Life. Monti couldn't fill her lungs deeply enough with the memory-soaked scent.

They performed all the ritual steps of leveling the bottom of the trunk, screwing it in the stand, deciding on the best side to face the room, and filling the stand with water. Monti thought it should all be accompanied by cheeks numb from the cold and a pile of snow-crusted boots thawing by the front door. But she had all her peeps in one house and happy together, and that was more than she'd dared even fantasize about a year ago.

She slid an arm around Kit. "Do you miss your folks at Christmas time?"

He leaned down and kissed her. "I have quite a few folks right here," he said. She nudged him. "Yes, I do," he admitted, "very much." After a moment he added, "But I don't know how we'd fit anyone else in here." She rolled her eyes at him, which was exactly the response he was going for.

"Mom," Monti said. "Do you remember that aluminum tree we had in Africa?"

"Oh sure, I loved that tree," Jody said. "You hardly had to water it at all. It finally fell to pieces a couple of moves ago."

"I remember reading somewhere that you should never put electric lights on those," Monti said. "You could electrocute someone."

"Really? Well, it's a good thing I didn't know that!" Jody said, "Or that could've been really dangerous!" Monti rolled her eyes again, and Jody continued. "But many years we didn't have electricity anyway, so it wasn't usually an issue, I guess. Now, do we want to decorate first or eat the pizza?"

'Pizza first' won unanimously. So they ate the pizza and then got down to the serious business of transforming the elders' miniature home into a semi-tropical Christmas wonderland.

Bob found the extension cord for the lights, which Marla and

Noelle strung with perfect teamwork. Then Jody plopped the plastic storage box of ornaments on the table. Although, ornaments might not be the first word to leap to most people's minds in association with the eccentric objects the Housels used for Christmas decorations.

There was the obligatory tinsel, and a diminishing collection of aging, fragile silver balls. But they'd collected trinkets from all the places they'd been stationed and visited, and many of these items had at some point been declared Christmas ornaments by fiat.

Monti was reasonably sure there were few other trees sporting an Oregon Ducks air freshener, but her parents had been hanging this increasingly bedraggled specimen on their tree since her brother, Oregon, was born.

An enameled tin mug with "MONTANA, Big Sky Country" had spent some time in the camping gear box before being promoted to Christmas tree service. A miniature red plush crab wearing a "Maryland" bandanna was balding in patches, but his alligator-clip claw still clamped onto a branch just fine. Florida contributed an actual Christmas ornament featuring Mickey and Minnie Mouse. It was so out of keeping with the otherwise offbeat theme that Monti thought someone must have given it to them.

The ornaments from overseas were more beautiful and even less Christmasy. A tiny tribal drum hung from a beaded loop. A cowrie shell bracelet slipped onto the end of a branch. A stylized conical doll had always disturbed Monti, reminding her of the Daleks on Dr. Who. But she had kept this to herself, and onto the tree it went every year.

Noelle lifted a Hot Wheels-sized airplane from the box. Its Army-green paint bore scuffs and scratches and its stickers were peeling off. She peered into the tiny cockpit at the tiny plastic pilot. Her eyes filled with tears and she moved to put it back in the box, but Marla put an arm around her from behind and gently took it from her hand.

"It's okay, baby girl," she said into Noelle's ear. Noelle turned around in her mom's arms and hugged her. "You don't need to worry about me," she said. "I'm good. I'm gonna stay good, I promise."

The elders stood quietly, warily touching their own memories of Stephen, testing the sharp points of the grief still lodged in their hearts like caltrops, primitive and brutal, able to cause pain no matter how old.

Kit gestured for the plane and Marla handed it to him. "We need a place of honor for our fallen soldier," he said.

"He never got to be a soldier, Dad," Marla said, a trace of the old bitterness in her choked voice.

"He did. He was just as much a soldier as anyone flying overseas. Every training accident makes future soldiers safer. He gave his life training for battle, to protect our ground troops and our country."

He tilted Marla's chin up and looked at her with gentle love. "He died doing work that mattered, and work that he loved, even if he only got to do it for a few months. I don't believe he would want you to still be distressed about that now."

Marla bit her lip, closed her eyes, and gave her dad a brief nod. "You're right, Dad. I've been working on that with the counselors. I...I still have a ways to go, I guess."

Kit drew his daughter and his granddaughter into his arms and kissed their cheeks. Then he walked straight-backed to the tree and hung the little plane by its red yarn loop high on the tree, pointed toward the sky.

It took a few minutes, but the family recovered almost all its Christmas cheer, and shared more memories of Christmases past, of family life in Rwanda and Nigeria, of travels far and wide.

As each object was taken from the box, it brought a story or memory to someone's mind. Sometimes the memories conflicted. By the time the last memory had been matched to the facts, or left to be resolved another year, and the last thread of tinsel had been draped over the last available inch of Douglas Fir bough, they'd gone through two pots of coffee, talked themselves hoarse, laughed 'til they cried and cried for real through half a box of tissues.

Kit checked his watch. "Folks, I don't know how this happened, but it's eleven o'clock," he said.

"Way past my bedtime!" Monti declared.

"Mine, too," Bob said, and his heavy eyelids bore witness. The ladies agreed, and in short order everything was tidied up, everyone was kissed and hugged, and 'good nights' transitioned into creaking mattresses and gentle snores.

Into the Mountain

The corridor that tunneled into the heart of the mountain disappeared in darkness far, far ahead. Logan and Nora passed corridors branching off at odd angles, but they stuck to the main hall.

They opened endless doors right and left, finding bedrooms, sitting rooms, and whole apartments with their own kitchens. A posh music room with a grand piano and a collection of ornate chairs on one side of the hall, was followed on the other by a tidy lab complete with Bunsen burners, test tubes, and glass cabinets full of standard sciency stuff.

They discovered a cavernous library. When they opened the door a palpable sense of ancient wisdom gave Nora goosebumps. A reading area welcomed them with deep leather sofas and Craftsman-style lamps, also wireless. A wide fireplace held a stack of logs ready to be lit. An elaborate screen, fashioned like a peacock with a wide fan of blue and green enameled feathers, stood proudly in front of the logs as if to say it was perfectly fine not to have a fire, too.

They wandered the book stacks in a daze for what seemed like hours, losing track of each other a couple of times. Finally they met again in the reading area, each carrying a pile of books. They set them on one of the tables and decided they'd come back later with a thermos of coffee to make up for the lack of a cafe. Nora slid the green ribbon off her pony tail and tied it around the doorknob, because the door was unmarked and they'd otherwise never find it again among so many.

"Why no plaque?" Nora wondered. "The laundry room was

marked, why not the library?"

"I'll add that to my growing list of questions," Logan said. "Reggie would say it's a secret library only visible to those with level twelve warlock powers or something."

"Which Reggie? That bi guy in our building?"

"No, the Reggie at McCormicks' party, who spent half an hour trying to make puns on the word 'trope'. Storm-troper, hung with an old trope, trope burns, the wandering trope-adour."

"Oh yeah, that guy. I actually thought 'hung with an old trope' was pretty good. But what does that have to do with level twelve powers?"

"Nothing. He's a gamer, and he's always throwing out these gaming-related phrases in conversation, and I never know what he's talking about." Logan wheeled his chair around in a slow circle.

"Well, maybe you should take up multi-player video games, sweetheart," Nora said, her voice as innocent as she could make it.

Logan snorted. "In a million years, maybe." Exactly the reaction she knew she would get. Logan peered down the corridor, searching the shadows. "Want to go further?"

"Coffee," Nora said. "Once the idea's in my head, it must be exorcised with the actual substance."

Logan nodded and they began retracing their journey back towards the front of the house. They walked in comfortable silence, Nora's hand once again on Logan's shoulder, as if they'd always traveled together in this manner, gentle wife walking beside her lanky, chair-bound husband.

As they neared the kitchen, a spicy aroma tickled their noses and set their stomachs rumbling. They unconsciously picked up their pace.

Barnabas turned as they came into the open kitchen. "Ah, there you are. Did you enjoy your exploration?"

"We did," Logan said. "We have a lot of questions…"

"Which I will do my best to answer," Barnabas said, and placed a tureen on the table. "But first, supper, what do you say?"

"Supper?" Nora looked at her watch. "Gosh, Logan, it's six

o'clock!"

Logan looked as shocked as Nora. "Wow, sorry Barnabas, we didn't mean to be gone the whole day."

"Oh, it's perfectly all right," he said, and pulled a pan of biscuits from the oven. "I remember when I first arrived, I could scarcely get any work done, the corridors drew me so irresistibly. Here, my dear, put these in this basket." He pointed out to Nora a breadbasket lined with a linen cloth. "Did you find the springs?"

"Springs?" Logan said. "I don't understand."

"Oh, excellent, we'll have a look after we eat, shall we? I haven't been down there in ever so long. It will do my leg good." He looked over the table and said, "Now, I think we're ready. Have a seat, children."

Nora raised her eyebrows at Logan and he shrugged. They'd find out what springs Barnabas was talking about after supper, apparently. During the meal, a thick beef stew, they asked him about the library. They were free to use it. Yes, even the fireplace. The laundry was also at their disposal.

"I'm not sure who devised the in-house breeze, though," he said. "Dr. Billings, perhaps? Or Flugge? My apologies, the early history of this house has not been thoroughly documented and there are significant gaps, especially concerning the more...esoteric modifications."

"No worries," Nora said, not having a clue what he was saying, but not wanting to trouble him about it.

Logan asked him about charging Nora's phone if he could get it working, and Barnabas said, "Yes, let me think. I know Nikola established a place for this function when he was here, but I never use it. A hermit, as a rule, does not avail himself of convenient communication devices, you understand. Therefore, please pardon me if I put you off while I try to remember where that is." He looked into the distance, as if traversing the map of the house in his mind. He shook his head, as if disappointed that an answer did not make itself immediately available.

"Nikola?" Logan asked, his voice a high squeak.

"Yes?" Barnabas said, his eyebrow cocked. "Children, this house has had hundreds of visitors over the years," Barnabas waved Logan's shock away. "Many of them left their mark on the place, some in quite substantial ways."

"Right," Logan croaked. Nora could tell he was hooked, and wouldn't easily be able to let these questions go. She hoped he'd get some answers before they left, or it would bug him forever.

Coffee appeared, and blackberry cobbler for dessert. Barnabas plopped big spoonfuls of thick, sweetened whipped cream on the cobbler, and Nora could've swooned with pleasure. "Barnabas, this is so delicious," she said. "I think I need this recipe, too."

Barnabas chuckled. "Certainly, dear. I can't remember the last time someone requested a recipe. It will quite go to my head."

"How long have you lived here?" Nora asked him again, hoping for something more enlightening than "a long while now."

"Oh. Well, I'll have to think about that for a moment. What year is it now?" They hesitated, wondering if he was serious, but apparently he was. Nora told him, and his eyes followed some private calculations on an invisible chalkboard. "I do believe it's twenty-eight years," he said, looking mildly surprised.

Nora gaped at him. "Longer than we've been alive," she said, and instantly regretted it. "Pardon me, that was rude."

"Oh, not at all, not at all, merely the truth, my dear girl." He smiled at them, no offense taken. "Others have come and gone during that time, of course, but I apparently have not yet completed the required work." An awkward silence grew until Barnabas said, "And where were you children raised?"

"I grew up on the other side of the mountains, in eastern Washington," Nora said, gesturing vaguely in some direction that might have been east. "But Logan…"

"I was born in Indiana, but we lived all over. Dad was always after a promotion, and that meant moving to where the next big opportunity was." Logan shrugged. "It was okay."

"What about you, Barnabas?" Nora ventured. "Where did you grow up?"

He chuckled. "We'll get out the map another time, shall we? To borrow Logan's summary, 'all over' might do for now." He got his cane in position and pulled himself to his feet. "Now, we must find swimming costumes for the both of you. Where would those be?" He began taking dishes to the sink, muttering to himself.

Logan and Nora shared another look. "Swimming costumes?" Nora said softly, scrunching up her nose. "Who says that?"

"And why do we need them, more to the point," Logan added just as quietly. "The springs, I guess, must be...hot springs?" He stacked their soup bowls.

"Well, that sounds yummy! But—in the house?" They shrugged at each other, and Nora hurried to finish clearing the table. The kitchen was tidied in no time, and then they followed Barnabas down the hall. He paused at one door, changed his mind with a shake of his head, then chose another.

"If I remember properly, there may be a trunk or drawer with what you need in here," he said as he opened the door. When he turned on the light, Nora was reminded of the costume wardrobe at school, if it had been combined with a sports equipment room. Parkas, hats and gloves, boots, skis and snowshoes awaited winter activities. A long rack of dresses, slacks, and shirts and blouses took up one wall, with a two-tiered shoe rack running the whole distance beneath it.

On another wall stood a built-in dresser holding at least a dozen drawers. Barnabas waved his hand toward it, and said, "You'll find something suitable in there, I believe. Change here, and I'll meet you at the crossroads." He cocked his head at them with a smile. "I mean the intersection of the hallways, of course. I'll just go to my rooms and put my trunks on." He hurried slowly off, leaning heavily on his cane, but obviously eager for their evening's adventure.

"Well, okay then," Nora said, and began opening drawers. "Swimming costumes, where are you?" Her jaw dropped immediately as she pulled out a classic Victorian black swimming dress with white trim, a belt, and long—bloomers she thought they must be. "Logan, shall I wear this?" She held it up in front of her.

"You could put two of you in there. And you'd sink, for sure. There must be five yards of fabric in that get-up."

"Now I wish I'd listened to you and packed a swimsuit," she said.

"Let this be a lesson to you, young lady," Logan said. "Always pack a towel and a swimsuit."

"I know, I know, even when the only water you're going to be around is a thousand-foot deep snow-melt lake filled with icy-cold water and fishes." She stuck her tongue out at him. "Well I wasn't going to get in that water, thank you very much. And who could anticipate in-home hot springs?"

Nora quickly folded the Victorian suit and put it back in the drawer. There were two or three suits that had attached the bloomers to the bodice and ditched the over-skirt. Still black. Then a couple of stretchy things that would come to mid-thigh, one black and one in a daring navy blue. In the next drawer she moved into the twentieth century, but didn't find anything newer than maybe 1940's. However, she had several cute one-pieces to choose from, in cheerful colors, or the classic black if she wanted. She held up a red boy-leg suit with a white belt. "Think this will fit me?"

"Looks likely," Logan said.

"Want me to find one for you?"

"I packed some board shorts, remember? But I can't really swim, right? How will I even get a suit on with this rigmarole on my leg?"

"Oh. Good point. Well, I'm interested to see what there is for men anyway." She opened a couple more drawers until she found a stash of striped men's suspender-style one-piece suits, which made her giggle. She held one up for Logan's opinion, but he just shook his head and grinned at her. She kept looking, and found a pair of baggy shorts with an elastic waist. "These might be easier to get on than your board shorts," she said.

Logan shrugged. "Worth a try."

Nora quickly changed into her chosen suit, which fit well enough, and was thrilled to spy a scarf-hanger full of sarongs in the closet. She tied one around herself, then didn't know how to proceed to help Logan. Barnabas hadn't said he could move his leg yet.

"I think we'd better consult our host," Logan said. "Let's take these with us and go meet him." Nora agreed and tossed the shorts in his lap. She slipped on a pair of flip-flops from the semi-tidy collection in one corner, and they left the room, Nora reluctantly, as she would've loved to dig through its offerings more thoroughly.

Barnabas was waiting for them. "Lovely, Nora dear," he said. "Ah yes, Logan, what shall we do with you?" He pondered a moment, and asked, "Have you additional clothing in your pack that you can change into later?"

"Yes, another t-shirt and a pair of jeans, and a pair of boardshorts," Logan said. He was wearing a t-shirt and knit shorts that Barnabas had apparently helped him put on this morning, though Nora hadn't even wondered about that until this moment. He just looked like he looked at home.

"Right." Barnabas nodded. "Let's go," he said, and motioned them deeper into the mountain. They moved off down the corridor. "I think we may have you go in wearing what you have on, sans the shirt. The waters are deeply therapeutic, and in combination with the salve and the herbs you've taken in, by tomorrow the dungarees might be possible."

How would that work? Nora wanted to ask, but kept her mouth shut. She'd seen so many astonishing things today, it seemed foolish to question him now.

"If you say so," Logan said. "I know you'll pardon some skepticism on my part. Not that I'm not completely amazed by how good my leg feels already, but it seems like you're saying I might not need the splint tomorrow."

"It's possible, dear boy," Barnabas said, his tone matter-of-fact, as if he were confirming they'd have roast beef for dinner tomorrow. "Or, we might slip it back on over the dungarees for extra support."

Logan and Nora raised their eyebrows at each other, which she felt like they'd been doing every five minutes all day. They continued in silence, far past where they'd turned around earlier today. The air grew cooler by the second, until Nora had no doubt at all they were deep under a mountain.

Eventually the end of the corridor emerged from the darkness, revealed in a set of heavy double doors, similar to those at the end of the storage hallway. On one of the doors a small brass plaque bore a single engraved word: Springs. Barnabas opened the door and a cloud of sulfury steam billowed out to welcome them.

Glory

What was that noise? Marla worked to control her panicky breathing and concentrated on figuring out where she was. After a moment her whole body relaxed and she smiled to herself. She sat up, glanced at Noelle still sleeping, and then toward the kitchen.

By the light of the bulb over the stove her grandmother worked quietly, obviously trying not to wake anyone. Marla smelled coffee brewing so she got up to go see what was up. Jody was putting together a breakfast casserole. Marla remembered her mom doing this every time there was a crowd at the house.

Marla kissed Jody on the cheek and pulled a coffee mug from the cupboard. "Can I help, Grandma?" she asked. Jody glanced toward Noelle, perhaps not remembering how hard it was to wake her, even when she hadn't been up half the night. "It's okay, Nellie sleeps through anything."

Jody smiled. "Sure, sweetheart, you can help," she said. "I've about got this done, but if you want to empty the dishwasher, that'd be great. Coffee will be ready momentarily."

Marla nodded. She opened the dishwasher and began setting plates and bowls softly onto the cupboard shelves.

Jody cleared her throat. "Did, uh, did your mom ever mention Glory?"

"No, I don't think so. Is that a person?"

"Yes, a person." Jody cleared her throat again and flushed a little. "Marla, she's your aunt."

"My aunt?" Marla stopped, and went from groggy to wide awake in one second. She thought she knew all her aunts, those being Maryland, period. Her dad was an only child.

Jody nodded. "I had a miscarriage between Maryland and Oregon. The children, not the states." She opened the oven and slid the glass 9x13 onto the top rack. "We were in Rwanda, and it had been a difficult pregnancy, and I went into labor at 19 weeks." She set the timer and looked at Marla. "There was no medical care, other than the local midwife, for a hundred miles. The midwife, my dear friend Raissa, did everything she could, but it couldn't be helped.

We named her Glory, and she's buried by the little church there in the village." Jody wiped away a tear with her dishtowel and said with a soft smile, "We're accumulating quite a welcoming committee in Heaven, aren't we?"

Marla didn't know what to say, so she just nodded.

Jody brushed a strand of hair back from Marla's face. "Marla, you don't have to tell me this if you don't want to, but…did you name your little one?"

Marla swallowed hard and fought back tears. "I, uh…." She had, but she'd thought she'd never tell anyone that. But why not? She couldn't remember now. She looked into her grandma's eyes and saw only compassion. *Why not?* "I call her Stephanie in my thoughts," she said, and watched Jody strain to hear her. "Stephanie," she said, a little louder, though her tummy was wobbly and wouldn't push much air for talking.

Jody's entire face smiled, her eyes practically sparkled. "After Stephen. Oh, honey, that's just lovely."

Marla nodded, but her face crumpled and tears pricked her eyes. "Nothing lovely about it, Grandma."

"Oh, honey," Jody said, and gathered Marla into her arms. She patted her back. "You're right, there isn't. Except for one thing, and that's forgiveness."

Marla shook her head. "I don't see how, Grandma. God has to hate me."

Jody drew back and looked her in the eye. "Who told you that? That isn't what your parents taught you, is it?"

"No," she said. "But I don't think they ever expected me to do anything this bad." She swiped at her face. "It doesn't feel forgivable."

"Now you listen to me, young lady." Jody was in her irate bluebird mode again. "You did a horrible, grievous thing. But that one thing, or any of the other things you've done, even all of them together, that's not *who* you are. Those things do not identify you."

Marla sure felt like they did. Where was her grandmother going with this?

"You, my darling girl, are a blood-bought child of God. I know this because you told me so when you were eight years old." She tapped Marla on the arm. "God doesn't hate you, can never hate you, because you belong to him. You can sure break his heart, but you are safe in the palm of his hand, and no one and nothing can change that." Jody tilted her head and frowned. "Did you forget that?"

Marla swallowed hard again, and tried not to squelch the little 'hope' feeling fluttering against her ribs like she usually did. It was bad to entertain hope, she'd learned the hard way and told herself for many years. Hope just made it worse when things crashed and burned again.

But this wasn't like those other times, was it? She was home now, with the people who still loved her, even after everything she'd done. Even after she'd told them about the baby.

"I guess I did forget, Grandma," she said. "I totally did. I can't...I don't know how I could forget that." The truth of that heady promise glowed in her, lighting up all manner of dark corners. Where had that glow been?

Jody took her face in both hands and said, "There is therefore now no condemnation for those who are in Christ Jesus. Right?"

Marla nodded.

"Are you in Christ Jesus?"

Marla closed her eyes and tears squeezed out and ran down her cheeks. She nodded again.

"Okay then. Time to start setting things right between you and him, don't you think?"

"Yeah," Marla whispered, swiping at her eyes again. "Yeah, that'd be good."

"Will you let me help you a little bit?" Jody whisked a tissue from the box on the counter and handed it to Marla.

"Okay," Marla said.

"Good," Jody said. "Then I want you to—do you have a Bible?"

"I just have a little New Testament from the Gideons," she said. "I lost my Bible...somewhere."

"No problem, those Gideon testaments have the Psalms in the back. I want you read Psalm 32, about a hundred times."

Marla laughed. "A hundred times?"

"It's short, you'll see what I mean. You won't be able to stop reading it, I don't think. You do that, and pray through it as much as you need to, and then come talk to me again, okay?"

"Okay," she said. "I can do that."

"'Course you can," Jody said, and squeezed her hand. "Now, let's get our coffee before we're swarmed. Noelle's bound to be at it any second. I never saw such a coffee hound as your daughter!"

Marla laughed. "She comes by it honestly," she said. "Thanks, Grandma."

"I smell coffee," Noelle's voice emerged from her tangle of sleeping bag on the cot. She sat up, her long blond hair mussed, frizzing out of its overnight braid. "Is it ready?"

"Better hurry," Jody stage-whispered to Marla. "Sure, Nellie, come and get some."

Springs

Barnabas led the way through the welcoming steam. They followed him into a cavern whose natural rock walls climbed into the darkness above. The smell of sulfur twitched at their noses, but was not overwhelming.

Logan and Nora gaped at the large natural pool in front of them, its surface intermittently obscured by tendrils of steam rising into the humid air. They stood on a flat floor, surfaced with tiny hexagonal tiles in an intricate floral pattern. Wide, semicircular steps tiled in the same pattern led down into the water, and a polished hand rail stood ready to assist. A ramp sloped gently into the water on the other side of the hand rail.

Logan pointed out the ramp. "Chair and all, I guess," he said.

"Excellent!" Nora said, then clamped her hand over her mouth as the cavern bounced her exclamation around. She spun to look at Barnabas.

He grinned at her. "It's quite a lively echo, eh?" He made a wide sweep with his arm. "Try it out, it's great fun."

Nora 'halloed' experimentally and grinned at the effect. She whooped a bit louder and the men grinned, too. Then, standing in her best singer's pose, she sang out, "Do Re Mi Fa So La Ti Dooooooo!" at the top of her voice. The notes ricocheted around the cavern multiple times before sinking into the pool. "Too cool!" she said. Logan was smiling, shaking his head at her.

"Joy in simple pleasures, Nora-ne-Nelson, I do love that about you."

"An admirable trait," Barnabas agreed.

"Oh, cut it out, you guys, I'm just having fun." She cocked her head at the sound of running water and peered through the steamy mists for the source. "Logan, look!" She pointed off to their right, where a barely visible waterfall, eight or ten feet across, poured into the pool.

"Wow," Logan said. He wheeled in that direction. "That must be cold water coming in, right?"

"It is," Barnabas said. "For which we're grateful, else the pool would be too hot for us." He leaned his cane against the hand rail and shed the terry robe he wore, tossing it onto a long cedar bench along the wall. Nora did a double-take at his red board shorts sprinkled with jaunty yellow pineapples.

Barnabas gripped the rail and dipped one foot in the steaming water. "Nora dear, you can swim over to the falls if you like. Logan will be restricted by the chair, unfortunately." He began descending the steps. "Take your time, children. I find I cannot wait one moment more." He sank into the water and let out a deep groan of pleasure. His eyes closed and a beatific smile wreathed his face as he pushed off through the water and settled on a wide submerged ledge along the wall.

"Are you ready to get in, Logan?" Nora asked. She untied her sarong and tossed it on the bench beside Barnabas' robe.

"I guess so," he said. He pulled his shirt off over his head with Nora's help. "It seems weird to roll the chair right into the water. Can you keep hold of it so I don't roll in too fast?"

"Sure, love, hang on," she said, and kicked off her flip-flops beneath the bench. "Gotcha," she said as she gripped the chair's handles.

They maneuvered the wheelchair to the top of the ramp and worked together to roll it slowly down into the hot water. They both gasped involuntarily—not because of the heat, but in response to the perfect, almost too hot temperature, and the intense sensation of goodness that seemed to permeate their limbs as they sank into the pool.

"This is unreal," Logan said when the intensity backed off a bit. "Is the water the same depth all over?"

"Ah, no, over to the far side it's a bit deeper, and beneath the falls," Barnabas said. "You should be fine in the chair all along here."

The water caressed Logan's shoulders with little wavelets, and he could scrunch down to where his chin touched the surface if he wanted to.

"Are you all set here, sweetheart?" Nora asked. "I want to check out the falls."

"Sure, go ahead."

"Okay, be back in a minute," she said, and kissed his cheek before kicking off to swim to the waterfall.

Logan watched her go. The water had thoroughly relaxed him already. He took a deep breath saturated with sulfury steam. "Barnabas," he said. "Do these waters have medicinal properties?"

"Most certainly, dear boy," he said, his eyes closed, his tone almost sedated. "Hot springs generally are healthful, and these carry unusually high concentrations of the beneficial minerals. The water, year-round, stays at an ideal therapeutic temperature, I've been told, which helps ease transference of the minerals into one's body. I really need to come down here more often."

"What happened to your leg, if it's okay to ask?" Logan said.

"Oh yes, it's okay to ask," he said. "It's an old injury that never has healed properly."

"From before you moved here?"

"Yes, my boy. From a previous life, one might almost say." He looked at Logan with sad eyes. "I used to be a very different person. I caused tremendous suffering."

"You?" Logan said. "That's hard to believe."

"And yet," Barnabas said, and paused. He seemed to be gathering strength to elaborate.

"My son took his own life when he was about your age, Logan," he said. "There followed a harrowing year."

He rubbed his gnarled hand across his eyes. "I lost my business in a scandalous bankruptcy. Then I nearly lost my own life in the motor accident that destroyed my leg and killed a young lady I should not have been with." Barnabas squeezed his eyes shut, the old pain still powerful.

"Finally, the hardest thing of all. My lovely wife, who had stuck with me through thick and very, very thin, suffered a stroke and died a lingering, painful death. And then I was alone with the wreckage I had made of my life."

"Oh man, I'm sorry," Logan said. "That's awful."

They sat in silence, watching Nora splash into and out of the waterfall. "How did you get from there, to here?"

"For that I have to thank my dear friend, Thomas," Barnabas said. "Why he bothered with me...well, I do know why now, but at the time I couldn't see it.

"I nearly succumbed to grief after my wife's death. I woke up in hospital after a very public breakdown. Thomas, my friend since earliest childhood, was there in the room when I woke. He'd become quite wealthy, and quite persuasive, and he strongly suggested a stay at Hart's Burden. At that point I cared little about what happened to me, so I didn't resist his suggestion with much energy.

"He arranged for my private transportation to this hermitage, and stayed here with me for a week until a teacher, Henry, arrived. Henry stayed for three months." Barnabas smiled. "I believe the two of them quite literally saved my life. If they had not intervened, I would most likely be dead by my own hand long before now. Instead, I have a new name and a new life, a hope and a future."

"A teacher?" Logan asked. "What kind of teacher?"

"One who knew the Word, and the One who is the Word. Who knew the Truth, and how to explain it to a benighted wretch like me."

"My uncle Ben was a teacher like that," Logan said. "My dad moved us around, you know, and never really got involved in our lives. But Uncle Ben always found us in the next new place and came to visit, invited or not." Logan grinned. "Mostly *not*. My dad didn't much care for Ben's 'teaching'. But I did, and I gave my life to that Truth when I was ten."

"And what I would give to have done likewise," Barnabas said. "Much pain and destruction could've been avoided."

"You said you have a new name? Isn't Barnabas your real name?"

"It is indeed, but it was not always. I shed the old name with the old life, as people sometimes do."

Logan nodded, some confusion still in his eyes. Nora swam up and splashed him.

"It's weird to swim in hot water!" she said, then took in their serious faces. "Is everything all right?"

"Sure, Nora, Barnabas has just been telling me a bit about himself."

Nora gave him a squinty look to indicate he'd better share that bit with her later. "Okay," she said, and took his hand. "How's your leg? Both of your legs?" She swirled her finger at both men.

"Capital," Barnabas answered. "Just what I needed, and I really should mark it down to visit once a week. It eases off the pain quite dramatically."

"Are you in pain all the time?" Logan asked.

"Oh well, you get used to it. It's the oddest thing, really. When it becomes a permanent part of your everyday life, it can sometimes take a deliberate effort to understand that your body is telling you the pain is bad and you should do something about it. That old 'pain' signal gets fatigued, I think." He shrugged. "So I actually forget to take measures to minimize it. There is much else to be about, you know."

Nora didn't think she'd be able to think of much else if she was hurting all the time, but she nodded as if she agreed with him.

"Barnabas," she said. "I've been meaning to ask you. When we first arrived, you called Logan 'the broken boy'." She paused, not sure how to pry into that. "Were you just being, I don't know, poetic or something?"

"Poetic?" Barnabas chuckled. "I don't believe anyone's ever called me poetic, my dear." He straightened his relaxed posture a bit and said, "No. The truth is, and I can tell you this freely as you've had similar experiences of late, I've been given a message that was opaque to me until you came. I was told, in so many words, that soon after a broken boy arrives, the next sojourner will come, and I will be free to go."

"Free? Aren't you free to leave now?" Logan said.

"Oh yes, surely, whenever I like," Barnabas assured him. "But I am quite content here, you see, and 'tis more as if I'm being told I'm ready to return to the world." He smiled an inward smile. "At some point, a retreat ceases to be a time of healing and becomes an easy escape from life."

He looked up at them. "I am at that point, I believe. Hour by hour, I feel the conviction growing that it's nearly time to go. An eagerness to be gone, even, and that has not been the case at all for these many long years."

"What will you do when you leave? Where will you go?" Nora couldn't picture Barnabas in any other setting.

"Oh, that will come at the proper time. A lamp for our feet usually shows just a step or two ahead, don't you find?" Barnabas' smile shone with peace. "For now, I am glad to know the next adventure is about to begin, and grateful to be here to help you children before my departure."

"Do you mean, we could have arrived to find no one here?" Logan's brow furrowed at that thought.

"The house has been empty for a time now and then. But think of what you're asking. Were you not led here?"

"We were," Nora said, nodding vigorously. "No doubt about that."

"And you needed help. So I think it unlikely Abba would have led you to an empty house when what you needed, Logan, was someone to take up your care when your dear wife had reached the end of her strength."

Logan gazed at Nora, his throat suddenly thick at the fresh realization of what she had done, the amazing feat she had accomplished in getting him here.

She put an arm around his shoulder and kissed his cheek. "It's okay, Logan. It's all good now. I feel great!"

"Yeah, I know," he said, wrapping his arms around her waist. "But tomorrow I'm sending you back out there, Nora." He pulled back, swiped his hand across his eyes and looked up at her. "How can I do that?"

"We talked about this already, right?" she said. She sank into the water next to him. "I don't want to go, I totally don't. But Logan, what choice is there? We have to think about our families. You know Connie called my folks when we didn't show yesterday. My mom is probably headed toward a meltdown right now. And your dad? My mom probably called him, and he's probably worried, too."

"That's a stretch and you know it," Logan said.

"Regardless, I have to do it," she said. She stood straight and stuck her chin out. "'Never give up, never turn back,' Logan."

Logan sighed. "Right, I know."

"An admirable attitude, child," Barnabas said. "Hold tight to that conviction tomorrow. Things don't always go as planned."

Home Alone

Monti sat back and rubbed her eyes. Grimacing, she carefully scratched around the scabs on her palms, which were itching like crazy.

She wondered if she might have leaped into this Scrabble story with a little less caution than was prudent. FE. How was she going to use FE? She'd looked it up on a Scrabble site for ideas, but it made no sense to her why it would qualify as a Scrabble word as an abbreviation for iron, which was the only definition they listed. Anyway, that didn't work, really, because who's going to use that in conversation rather than saying 'iron'?

Her folks' paper Scrabble dictionary described FE as a Hebrew letter. That was still difficult, but since Nora was a young woman of faith, she might be taking Hebrew as one of her college classes. Still, bringing that up in conversation was going to be tricky. Maybe she should look up other Hebrew letters for inspiration.

Wait--the Hebrew alphabet--was there a song for it? Monti dove into her search engines and before she knew it another hour had gone by and she had a shiny idea for the story. She jotted it down so as not to forget it. Time to come up for air.

First, where was everybody? She groaned as she broke out of her writing configuration and went in search of coffee and family. She'd been working on the table in the guest room/office, and couldn't remember having heard any noise for quite a while.

She found a note next to the coffee pot in Kit's handwriting that read, "I told you as we were leaving, but I'm sure it didn't register. Girls are at the mall—for some reason Nellie thinks she needs clothes. Bob's driving me to meet doc at clinic as planned. LYLC. Be back ASAP."

149

I love you like crazy right back, Kit Rising.

She found an inch of coffee slurry in the bottom of the pot, and decided to start fresh. Marla probably needed clothes, too. She wished she'd paid attention and gone with them. Now she felt left out. She wanted to buy pretty new clothes for her daughter. She pouted a bit while she measured out the coffee, then decided that was stupid. They could do a fashion show for her when they got home.

Instead of pouting, she'd better think about that other stinker of a word she had to use: TROPE. Monti didn't think she'd ever used that word in her life. She'd looked it up, but its definition was so slippery it wouldn't stick in her head. She'd look it up again, and not stop working at it until she had it pinned into the story somewhere.

Her tummy growled, and she realized the kitchen smelled delicious. She followed her nose to the crock pot, and lifted the lid to inhale. Yum. Mulligatawny.

Where was the rice cooker? She could start the rice soaking. She found it and the rice and by the time she had it set up, her coffee was ready and she gussied it up with extra calories to carry her through until mulligatawny time.

She'd just sat back down at the laptop, and was carefully scratching around the scab on her chin, when her phone rang. Now where was that thing? She found it in her purse, where it was supposed to be but seldom was. It was Dot!

"Hey girlfriend, everything okay?" Monti listened. "Oh, no I forgot all about that. Can you tell her we won't be back in time? Thanks sweetie, I'm sure your cookies will be a rockstar substitute for...whatever I would have made which I haven't even a clue. How's Jenny doing?"

Monti listened and sipped her coffee, and got all caught up with the news from home. Then Dot wanted to know how things were going with Marla.

"Surprisingly well. And, well, surprising." Monti filled her in on their visit so far, told her they hadn't heard back from the real estate agent yet, assured her Kit was just fine, and was brought to tears when her dear friend prayed for them all before she hung up.

Monti felt a keen desire to fly home tomorrow, dump all her stuff in the hall and go find Dot to get a good hug. Except, she'd forgotten again, she had no hall. *Rats*. That took the edge off her desire to head back.

So many tasks awaited their return. Hard things, like finding a good apartment that would work for all of them. Replacing their household goods. Figuring out how to be a family again, one that included Marla. Trying to get back into the swing of school and church and day to day living, without the refuge of her beloved bungalow.

She could feel herself headed toward pouting again, so she decided to put those thoughts in some order. Turning to a blank page in her journal, she made a list of all the things that had just run through her head, along with a few more that popped up, and even a couple of ideas about one or two of the projects.

Then she firmly shut that door in her brain along with the journal, and returned to her story. She was going to have limited time to write for a while once they got back home. Not to mention she didn't have a computer of her own anymore. Making the most of this gift of free time would be a good idea.

Now, where had she left Logan and Nora?

Fear

Nora's eyes popped open and wouldn't close again. *What time is it?* She fumbled for her watch. 5am.

Today.

The buoyancy she'd felt last night in the hot springs, when the solo hike was in a distant realm called tomorrow, had drained away. A queasy trepidation rolled through her now that the thing was a couple of hours away.

Today she would hike off into the forest. By herself. Voluntarily. She'd never have believed it was possible. But then, she couldn't have imagined the set of circumstances that made it necessary.

Abba, I so can't do this. Will you help me like you did before? Please.

She rolled over to open the *My Utmost for His Highest* app on her phone for a little boost, then remembered her phone was toast. *Sigh.*

She thought for a minute. Was there a Bible in this room? She might as well turn on the lamp and find out, since it wouldn't wake Logan. They hadn't bothered to move a cot into his room for her last night. It had been late and they were all relaxed and sleepy beyond functioning after their extended submersion in the steamy water, so she was still in the pink and green room.

She slid out of bed to scan the titles on the bookshelf. Jane Eyre. The Hobbit. 20,000 Leagues Under the Sea. She could stay in bed and read all day, how about that for a plan.

There, a threadbare KJV. She pulled it down and found Philippians chapter 4. She always found comfort there when she was stressed. The King James was not her usual choice, but the truth still shone brightly through the antique language.

Sitting on the bed she prayed through the passage. *God of peace be with me. I can do all things through Christ who strengthens me. Please, Abba.* She thanked him for his love and mercy over the last couple of days. She laid out her fear before him for the ten-thousandth time, asked him to forgive her for that fear for the ten-thousandth time, begged for the strength he promised in Philippians, and waited.

No miraculous infusion of energy like in the woods. No deep peace like she'd felt when Barnabas had put his hand on her head in the clearing. Nothing. She hung her head with a quavery sigh and fought back tears. How was she going to do this? She had no idea.

Finally she got up and slid the Bible back into the shelf. In the bathroom she splashed cold water on her face. She ignored the dirty laundry still lying there in a stinky heap. Maybe tonight when she got back.

What was she going to wear? Her non-stinky-heap options were limited. Unless she wanted to go raid the costume closet again, which she wasn't even sure she could find on her own, she would have to wear the red "Keep Calm and Sing Solfege" t-shirt she'd slept in. Red was good, right? High visibility. She hoped it didn't, like, enrage bears or anything. She pulled on yesterday's jeans, brushed her hair and pulled it into a ponytail. *Ready as I'll ever be.*

She very quietly opened the connecting door to Logan's room and listened. She couldn't help but smile when she heard the grumbly snore he did when he was deep asleep. She adored that sound.

Okay. Coffee.

She wasn't surprised to see Barnabas already at the table when she got to the kitchen. Even better, he'd made coffee.

"Morning, Barnabas," she said, while heading straight for the coffee pot. The kitchen smelled amazing, and not just of coffee.

"Good morning, child," he said. He pulled off his reading glasses and laid them on his own Bible. "And how is it with you, Nora?"

"Okay, I guess," she said. "I'm not looking forward to the fear factor stunt of the day, but I know I don't have any choice." She brought her coffee over and sat at the table. "Hey, Philippians 4. I was just reading that."

"Excellent choice for today."

"Yeah, it helps. Usually," she said. "Are you already cooking something? It smells great."

"Ah yes, I thought we should send you out with a nourishing breakfast in your belly. And cinnamon rolls."

Nora raised an eyebrow. "Very precisely put. No continental 'coffee and sweet roll' breakfast, huh?"

He smiled. "No. I'll start the bacon and eggs shortly." He closed his Bible and slid it into a shelf before pulling down a folded paper. "Here's the trail map," he said. "I've marked it for you."

"I'm not real good with maps," Nora said, accepting the paper. "I didn't really participate in the parts of Girl Scouts that involved the outdoors."

"No? Isn't that most of it?"

She snorted. "Yeah, kinda. But I...I had a bad thing happen when I was little and I don't like the woods much."

"What happened? That is, if you want to tell me." Barnabas looked at her with such compassion she almost started crying before she got one word of the story out.

"Oh, I got lost," she swallowed hard. "I was at my cousins' out in the country, staying with them while my parents were away on a trip, and I got lost in the woods."

"How old were you?" Barnabas asked.

"Four, almost five," she said. "I loved it there at my cousins'. We played outside all the time." The words began tumbling out. "They had a big garden and lots of animals, and the woods were full of flowers and wild strawberries." She took a deep breath and shivered. "We'd had such a great time that day, playing with baby chicks and a batch of kittens, picking berries, running all over the place like wild things." Nora clasped her hands between her knees and hunched her shoulders.

"We were playing hide and seek after supper, and I was looking for a place to hide when I found this little creek. I started throwing little purple flowers in it, and following them as they floated downstream.

The creek was narrow in some spots and I kept hopping back and forth across it feeling--I can still remember--so powerful at being able to jump across a whole river." She smiled, but tears leaked from her eyes. "But I got turned around and when I got tired and decided to find the others, I didn't know which way to go."

"Oh dear," Barnabas said, never taking his eyes off hers.

Nora nodded. "Then it got dark." She gulped with remembered terror.

"People looked for me. I can remember hearing people call my name, but I didn't recognize the voices. They were strangers shouting at me. I ran, scared to let them catch me. I heard wolves, too, I think, and owls definitely, and all kinds of sounds I couldn't identify. I sobbed hysterically, running and stumbling, falling into the creek at least once, scraping my hands and knees, getting scratched by wild rose bushes, until I was totally exhausted. Finally I crawled into a big rotted out stump and cried myself to sleep."

"Poor child," Barnabas said, and patted her shoulder. "But they found you, after all."

"Yeah. They did. It took them until almost dark the next day. 24 hours. But that's the thing. When they handed me to my aunt and uncle, instead of sympathy I got fury from them, and ridicule and blame."

"What?" Barnabas' face reddened. "You were a tiny child!"

"I know, right?" Nora shook tears out of her eyes. "I remember specifically my aunt said I didn't have the sense God gave a duck, and I had caused them all kinds of trouble."

Barnabas made a sound alarmingly like a growl, and scowled like thunder. "Did they call your parents, at least?"

"They did. But they were away on a boat of some kind, I don't even know what for sure. Maybe a cruise? It took them a couple days to get back." Nora shrugged and sniffed. "By the time they fetched me, I had stuffed it all down. I was ashamed, and humiliated. My aunt and uncle downplayed the whole thing with my parents, almost laughing it off.

Looking back, they must have been afraid my parents would blame them, maybe sue them, even. I don't know." Nora looked at Barnabas with red eyes. "I've thought about this a lot through the years, obviously. And I think the worst thing of all is that my parents didn't talk to me about it. They didn't help me work through my fear and the shame."

She covered her eyes for a moment and took a deep breath. "In fact, and I can still hardly believe this is true, they never mentioned it again."

"Atrocious! I'm sorry, my dear, they are your parents, but that's just atrocious!"

Nora nodded. "I think so, too. A couple of times as I got older, I brought it up, trying to sort memory from imagination, I think. But they claimed they barely remembered it, and they got upset and said I was exaggerating." She shrugged again, folding and unfolding a corner of the trail map. "So I stopped bringing it up. Just kept it stuffed."

"Have you been able to forgive them, Nora?"

She hesitated. "I think so. I've definitely attempted to. But it doesn't always feel like I was successful."

"Oh, no need to worry on that point," Barnabas said, and patted her hand. "The deliberate act of forgiveness is what matters. The feelings to match the action generally take longer for an offense of this magnitude. Sometimes they never come."

"Yeah?" she looked at him. "I keep 'forgiving' them again, when I'm feeling especially—I don't know—damaged."

"It's fine to do that, dear, especially if it helps you. God knows what's in your heart better than you do. You have the Spirit in you, remember? Praying with groanings which cannot be uttered, saying what you don't know how to."

Nora nodded, suddenly tired. She'd only told a couple of people that story in her whole life, and it used up a sizable hunk of energy to get it all out.

"You've shared this with Logan, I assume," Barnabas gave her that 'from under his eyebrows' look. She was glad she had the right answer.

"I have. Before we got married. I wanted him to know what a mess he was getting."

"Very wise," he said. "Marriage should be man and wife against the world, and that's hard to maintain if one or both of you are bearing a dreadful burden the other doesn't know about."

"Right, me and him against the world, that's kinda how we think of it" She paused. "But you know, he still suggested a camping trip in the forest, so I don't know."

"Oh, I think I do, child." He curled his fingers around her hand. "Men must fix things, you know."

Nora rolled her eyes and nodded.

"Well, what better way to fix this—and I'm by no means suggesting he thought it through like this consciously—than to hike into the woods, have a lovely time with no fear or shame, just a happy day or two. Leave the burden beside a forest trail as you leave, go back home and all is well."

"Yeah, when you put it like that I can sorta see how he might think that, at least subconsciously," she said, a little smile curving the right corner of her mouth. "But of course, it didn't turn out that way."

"And there's where we see that God may have had a more...thorough healing in mind. As much as your husband loves you, he doesn't have an infallible ability to heal like our Father does."

"Well, I don't feel healed," Nora said, more sharply than she'd intended.

"No," Barnabas sat back. "I can see that." He hesitated. "But tell me, dear, if you'll examine yourself for a quiet moment, do you still find that debilitating fear? Or perhaps only the memory of it? The habit of it, you might say?"

Nora widened her eyes at him, offended. Did he think she was making it up? Her perfectly reasonable fear of going off into the woods alone?

"Forgive me if I've overstepped, child. But I do hope you'll consider what I've said. It's possible for healing to occur without our being aware of it."

He pushed his chair back and positioned his cane before pushing himself to his feet. He fetched the coffee pot and refilled her cup. "I'll start on the eggs and bacon now, the cinnamon rolls are nearly ready."

Nora got to her feet, her vision blurred by tears, and stumbled back down the hallway to her room.

Shiny

Monti was finding it increasingly difficult not to pout. Where the heck was everybody? She'd been in solitary confinement for hours. Well, okay, she'd mostly been voluntarily sitting this chair, but still, she was going to go bonkers soon.

Did she dare drink another cup of coffee? She pulled herself to her feet. She'd decide when she got to the kitchen.

The front door creaked open and she almost jumped out of her skin.

"Monti?"

Yes! Her favorite person. She grinned and said, "There you are! I thought everybody got lost and forgot where they lived."

"That could happen," her dad said, pecking her on the cheek on the way by. "Your mother forgets where she parks more often than she remembers."

Kit said, "Hey lover," and kissed her, thereby coaxing her several feet back from the edge of bonkerdom.

"Where's everybody else?" she asked.

"Oh, Melissa happened to meet them at the mall," Bob said with his head in the fridge, "and she'll be carrying them home when they've shopped the place out."

Kit set a glossy silver shopping bag with stiff twine handles on the table. "I got you a present." A fancy burst of silver and red ribbons trailed from one handle.

"Well, shall we put it under the tree?" she asked, resisting the urge to tear into the beautiful bag immediately.

"No, no, you should open it now," he said, wonderful man that he was. "Bob helped me pick it out."

Monti hoped it wasn't clothing, as her dad had long been forbidden to buy anyone's clothing, including his own. Even socks. She lifted it experimentally. No, too heavy for clothing. She reached in, past crinkles of glittered red tissue paper, and pulled out a big flat box.

"A new laptop?" Oh, she did love a new computer! "I was going to wait…"

"Why?" Kit said. "I'm sure Bob would like to have his back before you melt it down writing your story."

"Oh no, that's fine," Bob objected, ever the peacemaker. "No worries."

"I don't know why I was waiting," Monti said. "I guess it seemed…self-indulgent when there are so many other things we need worse."

"Be that as it may, I know you, and you need this," he said. He put his arm around her shoulders and she turned her face up to his.

"Thanks, love," she said, "You spoil me rotten."

"I do," he said, "and it yields many benefits." He winked at her and Bob guffawed.

Monti started loosening the adhesive disks sealing the edges of the box. "Hey, what did the doctor say?"

"He said I can go home any time," Kit said, lowering himself onto the chair across from Monti and fiddling with his cane.

She stopped loosening. "Really? I thought it was ten days, written in stone."

"Apparently not. He checked me over thoroughly and seemed surprised by the complete lack of residual symptoms. He was very firm about me seeing Charlie when we get home, but he cleared me to travel. I think we want to stay, though, right?" He glanced up at Monti. "Bob and I talked it over, and we can't imagine telling Jody we're leaving before Christmas."

Monti shut her mouth on the automatic objection she'd been formulating. She loved her own space, even if that space was currently an anonymous apartment in a grimy building crammed with noisy college students.

But no, she couldn't imagine abandoning her mother at this stage of the pre-Christmas build up. "Right. That cannot be done," she agreed. "But the day after Christmas?"

"Absolutely," Kit said. "I already bought the tickets. We have lots to do when we get home."

Monti felt a tick of annoyance that he'd taken that step without consulting her. What if she'd wanted to stay longer? Riiight. What if she was being ridiculous? She'd just said to herself she couldn't wait to get home. "Good," she said. "Um, first class, still?"

Kit nodded and she smiled. He'd decided not to have that fight all over again. "Hey, what's that on your cane?" she asked.

"Bob found this at one of those gadget stores downtown. One of his buddies at church has one." He demonstrated how a flat, stubby black arm folded out from the cane, providing a way to hang it from a table or rest it against a wall. "One minor annoyance alleviated for $6.95," he said.

"Well, I'm sure that'll be worth every penny many times over," Monti said, and refocused on her task. The sticky disks on the edges of the laptop box were terrible. One down, five more to go! "Dot called while you were gone," she said. "Looks like I got out of making cookies for the Christmas pageant after all."

"Any news from home? Besides the cookie-making reprieve?"

"Jenny and the baby checked out fine. Ray has a lump on his head and some bad bruising on his shoulder. She sent me a picture, I'll find it for you later. Purple and green," she grimaced. "What else? Oh, Eddie hit a deer on I-95 and crunched his car pretty bad, but spun into the ditch instead of the other lane, and no one was hurt."

"Except the deer," Kit said. "I wonder if it's totaled?"

"Deer usually are after something like that."

"I think it'd take about fifty bucks to total that car," Kit said. "Maybe I'll call him tomorrow."

Monti had visions of Eddie driving her sweet little Baja while she drove a monster lime green van like her parents', and decided she didn't want to think about that today.

"Thanks for getting the rice started, Monti," Bob said. He rummaged around in the tiny kitchen, pulling out bowls and plates. "Our girls will be ready for soup when they get home."

"Okay, I'll move my shiny new laptop into the office and help you set the table." She hadn't even gotten the box open yet, but she gathered it and the packaging all up and stashed it on the desk in their room.

The door burst open and a flurry of bright giggling preceded the rest of her family into the house. Monti felt another sick twist of resentment at being left out, and quashed it hard. She would *not* pout. But tomorrow she was going to be right in the middle of whatever fun was happening.

Using up substantial reserves of willpower, she re-purposed her pouty lips into a welcoming smile and went out to greet her girls.

Marla was first in, wearing a relaxed smile that did Monti's heart good. She pecked Monti on the cheek and dumped her shopping bags on the sofa.

"Oh, Monti, these girls are so much fun," Jody said. She was loaded down with bags. "I'm absolutely going to come pester you all at least once a month after you leave!" She hauled her purchases on through to her bedroom, exuding a subtle 'nothing to see here, folks' vibe.

"G, we saw the best thrift shop!" Noelle's eyes danced with excitement at the discovery. She kissed Monti on the cheek and pulled her in for a big hug, shopping bags and all. "GG says it's fabulous, but I told her we couldn't go in without you, since you're my treasure-hunting partner. So we have to go back tomorrow and explore."

Monti tightened her arms around Noelle and blinked away the sudden tears, hoping Nellie wouldn't see. She had all the treasure she needed right here.

Jody bustled back through to the kitchen. "We have several good thrift shops nearby. We can hit them all, if you like. But let's go on Monday, so we have the whole day. Oh good, the rice is going. Thanks, whoever did that." She glanced over what Bob had got out, added glasses and napkins and other necessaries. "I'm hungry, what about everybody else?"

"You didn't stop for a snack?" Monti said. It was hard to picture Jody, Marla and Noelle shopping for that long without a treat.

"Oh, we got a foo-foo coffee, but we wanted to get back, since you were here all by yourself. Melissa had to get home, too. We did talk about some possibilities for Monday, though."

Monti felt positively ridiculous about the pity party she'd been throwing five minutes ago. She was grateful no one had witnessed it. Still, she sent up a plea for forgiveness and vowed to grow up and leave self-pity in the rear-view mirror. "That sounds promising," was all she said, not trusting her voice and blinking away more tears.

Dinner was excellent. Mulligatawny had been a family favorite since Monti's childhood and it was seasoned with good memories. The shoppers told about their finds, except for the details that would have to wait until Christmas morning. Monti wondered about Marla's shopping budget, and made a mental note to ask her mother about it later.

Kit told them of his clean bill of health with the doc, which they all hoorahed, and announced their departure date, which doused Jody's exuberance temporarily.

"Ah well," she said, shaking it off. "We already have you for far longer than we expected, so I can't be too grouchy about it." She clapped her hands and declared, "We'll just have to make the most of every day we have left!"

"Good advice for everyone, all the time," Bob said.

The Scrabble board came out after dinner was cleared away, but Jody stopped them as Monti and Bob were setting up to play.

"Let's have a tournament!" Jody said. "It'll keep us off the streets in the evenings until Christmas Eve."

"Your mother can only go so long without organizing something," Bob said, looking at her fondly, "And it's been a couple of weeks so I think we're edging up to the limit."

Everyone agreed, with varying degrees of enthusiasm, that a tournament sounded like fun. Jody drew out some brackets and Noelle wrote up a list and cut it apart so they could draw names for who would square off for the first games. Bob downloaded some official score sheets to keep it…official, and they were off.

The first night's contest matched Marla and Jody. The rest of the family paid intermittent attention as the game progressed, filling the contestants' coffee cups, making appreciative noises when their attention was drawn to a particularly good play, and commiserating when one or the other discretely shared a terrible rack.

In between, they sat and chatted, or puttered. Bob had an aging electric drill that was not working properly, and he and Kit took it apart all over the coffee table to see if it could be made to last another year.

Monti fetched the laptop box from their bedroom and loosened the rest of the adhesive disks. She lifted the flap, pulled aside the foam wrapper and gasped. "Apple green!" she said. This distracted even the Scrabble players, who had to pause the game to *ooh* and *aah* over the shiny machine.

Monti hugged Kit and whispered sweet thank yous in his ear. Then she settled on the sofa, opened the Get Started manual and didn't come up for air until a family consultation was called for, when Marla wanted to play ZOT.

"I'm sorry honey," Jody said, "but it's not in the Official Scrabble Dictionary, and that's the one we agreed to use."

"We inked it into our copy when the kids were little," Monti explained. "Remember the anteater from the B.C comic strip? That was the sound he made when he zapped an ant. We figured it should count as a real word, since we saw it in the newspaper all the time."

"Well, I understand, but..." Jody began, but Bob, who had been refilling his coffee, laid a gentle hand on her shoulder. He gestured for the dictionary at her elbow, took a pen from his pocket and wrote ZOT in the margin of the Z section. Jody watched him. She looked at the faces around her and drew in a deep breath.

"You're right, Bob," Jody said. "I get a little..."

"Intense?" Bob offered.

"All right, you," she said, and smacked him lightly.

Marla hadn't spoken a word during the interchange, but her shoulders were hunched and her cheeks had reddened.

"You okay, sweetie?" Monti said. "Just doing our regular thing, here, no worries."

"Okay," Marla said, still looking a little uneasy.

"Oh, Marla," Jody said. "This is how it goes with family, remember? We have a…disagreement, and a discussion…we work it out, and we're all good."

Marla cleared her throat. "It's been a while," she said, visibly relaxing her shoulders.

"Of course, that's true, it has." Jody touched her arm. "But it won't take long for it to feel comfortable again, don't you think?" She cocked her head in the way that emphasized her 'fluffy bird' look, and smiled at her granddaughter.

"Yes, sure, Grandma, thanks."

Monti hoped against hope that future misunderstandings with Marla could be so easily resolved.

Into the Woods

Nora slammed the bedroom door shut behind her and threw herself onto the bed. The nerve of the old man, telling her she was all healed and not afraid, when obviously she wasn't 'healed' and she was afraid!

She pounded a fist into the bed. He didn't know anything about her! Anything about how hard it was to be afraid of the place you lived in. Afraid to go do what everybody else thought was fun. To be left out, and ridiculed, and punished even, for refusing to do the hike, or the camp out, or the Biology class field expedition.

"Nora?" Logan's voice came through the connecting door. She swiped the tears from her eyes and got up to open the door.

"Hi sweetheart," she said, attempting a smile. She went over to his bed. "How you doing?"

"Doing good," he said. "Um, can you help me with the bedpan?"

"Oh. Sure, hang on."

They took care of that, and when she brought the rinsed pan back in to put it away, she said, "How's your leg?"

"I hadn't really thought about it before you came in. And now that I am thinking about it, I'm mostly noticing that this splint is really annoying."

"Good, I think that's good," she said. "It's not hurting you so much, then."

"Nora, are you okay?"

"Yeah, yeah I'm okay," she said, but her bottom lip trembled and new tears leaked out as she sat on the edge of his bed.

"What's the matter, honey?" Logan's hazel eyes were dark with concern and he laced his fingers through hers. "Are you afraid about today?"

Nora snorted. "It depends who you ask!"

"What?" Logan said. "I don't understand."

Nora told him about her unheard prayers for help, the conversation with Barnabas and her reaction.

"Huh," he said. He didn't say anything else for a bit, and Nora recognized his 'analysis mode' as he thought through what she had said.

"What if," he said slowly, "today, you stay here and I work on your phone some more and try to get it working. And we can ask Barnabas if he remembers where his rice is, and help him look for it if he doesn't. And see if he's thought of where a possible wireless charging setup might be..." he trailed off, because Nora was shaking her head and had put her fingers over his mouth.

"Thank you, Logan," she said, her voice husky.

"For what?" he asked, his forehead corrugated with confusion.

She sighed. "For believing me. For not giving me the ole 'you can do it' pep talk." She pulled their interlocked hands to her mouth and kissed the back of his hand.

"I..." he shook his head abruptly as if to rid it of a perturbing problem. "I don't know what to do, Nora."

"But I do," she said. "Right?" She swallowed hard, and looked away. "Afraid or not, healed or not healed, whatever that means, I really don't have any choice." Her shoulders sagged as she stared into her favorite face. "I just have to suck it up and do it."

Logan pulled their hands to him and kissed hers. He nodded. "I think you do, sweetheart. I'm so sorry." He looked down and she thought she saw his eyes mist up. "I'm sorry for dragging you out in the woods when I knew perfectly well that wouldn't be any fun for you. I'm sorry for showing off on the log and scaring you, and falling in! All of that was so selfish, I can't even believe I did it. This is all my fault."

Nora burst out crying and lay her head on his chest. "It's okay, Logan," she said. "It's okay, really. I could've said no, but I didn't. I *need* to get past this whole 'lost in the forest' thing." She sniffed. "And besides, it's not like you fell in on purpose. Somebody shot at you!"

They confessed and reassured each other for a few more minutes that were a balm to Nora's soul. At last Logan put his finger under her chin and pulled her up to kiss her. "Hey," he said after. "You've already had coffee."

She laughed. "Yep. Time to get you some, huh?"

"Oh yeah. I'm way behind."

"Well, I better get Barnabas to help me move you into the wheelchair," she said, heading for the door. She spun back toward him and said, "Guess what? He made cinnamon rolls."

"Ooh, noo," Logan said. "I'm doomed. Carb coma, here I come. You'll take a hike and I'll gain five pounds."

"Like you've ever gained five pounds in your life," she said, and stuck her tongue out at him. "Wait here."

"Ya think?" he rolled his eyes at her and shooed her out of the room.

Nora popped back in with Barnabas in tow, and he examined Logan's leg, removing the bandage and grunting his approval before tying it all back together. They got him moved into the chair and headed down the hall toward breakfast.

Nora felt awkward with Barnabas, though he didn't say anything about their earlier conversation. Finally, as he and Logan were discussing the relative merits of raisins versus nuts in cinnamon rolls she blurted out, "Barnabas!"

He stopped talking and looked at her. "Yes, child?"

"I'm sorry for walking out on you earlier," she said, her cheeks hot. "That was rude. And I'm sorry for taking offense when you were trying to help me. Please forgive me."

"Certainly, dear, please don't mention it." He paused. "I should say rather, please don't be concerned about it any further. All is well."

"Thank you," she breathed. That was okay, at least.

They ate breakfast. Barnabas made sure Nora ate plenty of everything to carry her through her long hike. He wrapped two more cinnamon rolls in waxed paper and a zipper bag.

Nora jogged back to her room and dumped everything from her

pack onto her bed. She brought the pack, showing some signs of wear now, out to the table and carefully stuffed the rolls in its front zip pocket. She let Barnabas and Logan guide her in what else to take with her. Two soft plastic, wide-mouth water bottles with Expo 86 printed on the side. The first-aid kit. Pocket knife. Her pink hoodie in case it got cool. The trail map, and the message to put in the box. The rest of their power bars, just in case. Flashlight, ditto, though Nora felt a frisson of panic at this.

"What kind of 'just in case,' you guys?" Nora squeaked at them. "You're starting to freak me out!"

"Merely an overabundance of caution, my dear," Barnabas reassured her. "Better to have and not need..." he spiraled his finger in the air to finish the saying. "Now, perhaps you should keep the trail map in your pocket for easy reference."

Nora agreed, dug it out of the pack and stuffed it in her jeans pocket. She tried on the pack, and Logan made precise adjustments of the hip belt until he was satisfied she would be as comfortable as possible.

"Guess I should get going, huh?" The men nodded somberly. "Oh, wait," Nora said. "Gotta pee," she whispered to Logan. She squirmed out of the pack and ran back down the hall. When she returned, Logan helped her put the pack back on and buckled her in.

"May we pray for you, child?" Barnabas asked.

"Sure, I guess," she said with a shrug. God didn't seem too responsive this morning, but whatever. She needed to get going and get back. She held Logan's hand, and Barnabas put a gnarled hand on her shoulder.

"Abba," he said. "We know perfectly well that you love Nora more than we do. Therefore we beg you, please take care of her today, allow her to feel your presence as she goes, and send her safely back to us having accomplished the task she must do. Amen."

"Amen," they echoed. Now there was no way around it. It was time to go. They walked her to the front door. She leaned down and kissed Logan, a long soft kiss. Barnabas opened the door and let in a fresh breeze and a doorway full of bright sunshine.

Nora stepped out of the house onto the flagstones, turned back and gave them a little half-wave, then strode out under the archway and into the clearing. When she reached the trees on the other side she turned to wave again. They were still watching and waved back.

Her jaw set, Nora checked her watch as she turned away and walked into the forest. *Aleph, bet, vet...* Two or three hours, Barnabas had said. Three hours from now was 11 a.m.. *Gimmel dalet hey....* She'd stuff the note in the message box, turn right around and be back by 2pm at the very absolute latest.

Consult

Jody won the Scrabble game, but not by much. Marla's enthusiasm grew as the evening progressed, and she laughed a big old belly laugh that almost made Monti cry when Jody hooked DETOX onto DOOBIES. Noelle would play Kit tomorrow night and then Monti would know who she would play.

The tiles slid down the board into their bag, good-nights were said, and the girls turned the living room back into their bedroom. Bob and Kit sat for a spell on the screened porch, and Monti followed her mother into her bedroom.

"Marla seemed to enjoy that, don't you think?" Monti asked, as Jody quickly stashed a couple of shopping bags in her closet. She dumped out another on the bed.

"Definitely," her mom said. "It was sure good to hear her laugh."

"Definitely," Monti agreed. "Hey Mom, how did the shopping go? I'm curious about..."

"About whether Marla has any money?" Jody snipped the tags off a couple of shirts.

Monti let out a breath. "That's right."

"Well, she told me they gave her a little money when she left rehab, but she didn't say how much," Jody said. "I made her put her wallet away, and insisted that my Christmas present to her would be all the gifts she wanted to buy for her family."

Monti's heart broke all over again with gratitude to her mother, but a big lump in her throat meant she could only nod.

"I couldn't hardly get her to pick out anything to start with, but Noelle got the idea right away, and kept showing her things in a good price range, that she knew you and Kit would like. That helped a lot," Jody said. "After a while, Marla relaxed into it a bit.

That Nellie, she's a keeper."

"She is, indeed," Monti croaked out. "She seemed okay with Marla? She's been really stressed out, anticipating."

"She did fine. Awkward at first, but that's only natural. And she got over it quickly and was very tactful and gentle in guiding her mom. I was proud of her."

"Well, shopping *is* one of her strengths," Monti said, and they both laughed. "Maybe it'll be okay."

"Of course it will, honey," Jody said, and wrapped her arms around her daughter. "I had a talk with Marla, too, about Stephanie. Her baby, I mean. And I told her about Glory."

"She named her baby after Stephen?" The lump in Monti's throat grew to choking proportions.

"Mm-hm. But she's having a hard time feeling like God can forgive her."

Monti pondered this, stricken at the thought of Marla feeling estranged from God. "Mom, that's horrible. Were you able to reassure her at all?"

"We're working on it. It'll take a while. I wanted you to know so you can keep helping her after you head home. I gave her Psalm 32 to work on."

"Oh good, that's a good one." Monti rubbed the tension knots in her eyebrows. "This is going to be really hard, Mom."

"You've done way harder things than this before."

"True. But I was younger then," Monti said, her shoulders sagging.

Jody took hold of Monti's shoulders and looked her in the eyes. "You were, but you're older now and that's good. You're wiser." Monti hacked out a laugh at that.

"You are," Jody insisted. "And you're filled with compassion for your daughter, I can see it. Not judgment, or resentment, but faith and compassion and acceptance and love. That's what your baby girl needs, and I know you'll lavish it on her until she's got her joy back again."

Jody let Monti go and picked up a pair of sheepskin slippers. "Not that her joy is your responsibility, of course it isn't. But your love will help tremendously. It's gonna be okay, daughter."

"Thanks, Mom." Monti sniffed and grabbed a tissue from her mom's nightstand. "I needed a pep talk. It's easy while we're here, but I know it's going to be much harder once we get home." She frowned. "We never did have the easiest relationship, you know."

"I know, honey. It's just your personalities. But I think you're forgetting." She peered at Monti. "Who always eased things between you when it got tough?"

"Kit," Monti said without hesitation.

"Right. And he'll be there, fully involved, making things easier just like he always has, taking good care of all three of you."

"I know. But I worry about him, too, Mom." Monti couldn't swallow that persistent lump in her throat. "I wonder if I'm going to be able to take care of him…"

"Now, you stop it." Jody was fluffing up to furious bluebird mode. "You're not to fret, Montana Eloise. You're supposed to take it…"

"One day at a time, just like I tell Noelle." She blew her nose. "Why do I not seem able to learn that, after all this time?"

"Well, you're a human being, for one thing," Jody said. "I haven't met many people for whom *casting all their cares on Jesus* comes naturally. It's an ongoing struggle. You just have to keep at it. Lie on your bed and cry and ask for help, as often as necessary. Then get up and do the next thing. Even if it's really hard."

"Do you still do that, Mom?"

"Of course!" Jody said. "Are you kidding? Any excuse to lie down for a little while!"

Monti laughed and pulled her mom in for another hug. "You always make me laugh. And I really like your hearing aids. I haven't had to holler at you once since we got here."

"Oh, they're the best investment we've made in a long time," Jody said. "I know people tend to fuss about them all the time, but they've been an unconditional success for me. Great for our marriage, and great for working with the kids."

"So, nobody has to holler at you anymore."

"Well, you know, some people still choose to…" she said, with an impish grin.

"No they don't!" Monti said.

"No, they don't," Jody admitted. "You'd better get to bed, daughter, we have lots to do tomorrow."

"Yep, I'm looking forward to being with everybody all day. I felt kind of left out today."

"I know you did. And Monday will be really good. We'll just leave the guys out this time, they'll like that."

"They will," Monti agreed, and kissed her mother on the cheek. "Goodnight, Mom."

Monti wandered out to the living room. Kit and Bob still sat on the screened porch in the dark, the chirp of crickets punctuating their low conversation. She caught the word 'wheelchair' and 'handicap accessible,' and most of her newly bulwarked confidence drained right back out of her.

She leaned against the wall, squeezed her eyes shut and whispered, "Abba, help!" before she pushed open the door to see if Kit was ready to head for bed. She wanted to tell him about baby Stephanie and Psalm 32.

Alone

The sunshine glowed in bright, slanted bars through every gap in the trees. The gaps grew further apart as she headed into the forest, and the sun mellowed to a dim, golden haze. The birds were busy, swooping across in front of her on their bird business.

The sun occasionally threw a long, sharp shadow out in front of her for a few moments before it blurred back into the shade. She adjusted her pack and fell into an easy pace, covering the ground but not hurrying. She had a long way to go. How far? She couldn't remember if Barnabas had said. Must be at least six miles if he thought it would take her two or three hours. But this was nice. Maybe after she got this under her belt, she'd suggest to Logan they take up hiking.

She snorted. Right. Then maybe after that, parkour, why not? Or boxing, or BASE jumping? Neither of them were real sports enthusiasts, especially outdoor sports.

When they got home they'd probably settle back into their regular neighborhood walks, with occasional forays into national parks for longer treks. That is, after they'd had a nice long spell of cocooning in their own apartment first.

Nora had been cruising for about half an hour, trying to remember the names of the wildflowers nodding into the edges of the path, when she stepped on a stick and startled at the sharp crack when it snapped. *Really, Nora? A wee bit jumpy, are we?* She slowed her breathing and walked while willing her heartbeat to return to normal.

She was calm again by the time she arrived at a fork in the path. She stopped and wriggled the trail map out of her pocket.

Unfolding it, she repeated to herself what Barnabas had said. First fork, bear right. And sure enough, there was a slightly shaky line in blue highlighter, marking the path to the right on the map.

She looked up at the new path. Looked okay, just like the one she was on. She folded and tucked the map back away and headed out on her altered vector.

She was warming up, and couldn't imagine wanting the sweat jacket wadded in the bottom of her pack, cushioning the two water bottles. A fresh breeze pushed through the thickening woods and cooled her forehead. *Thank you, Abba, that was nice.* She smiled.

The breeze picked up and swirled the forest litter into a tiny twister in front of her. She hesitated and her smile faded. *Now you're just letting yourself get freaked out. It's just a little dust devil. Stop it.*

She started walking again and picked up the pace. The next landmark was supposed to be a little creek, and Nora kept a lookout for it. She heard the delicate, musical warbling of water over round rocks up ahead, and was charmed as always. Even though a creek had featured significantly in her childhood trauma, she had never lost her love for running water. It wasn't the lovely creek's fault, after all.

She caught her breath as the steam came into view. The forest canopy had bowed politely and stepped back to make way for the creek, and in the open space sunlight dappled the water and mossy low banks. Clear water rilled around sizable lichen-splotched boulders crouched in the creek. Pine needles swirled and raced downstream. Rings of ripples spread as little fishes snatched tidbits from the surface.

It was mesmerizing, but Nora didn't let herself get drawn in. She spotted the bridge Barnabas had told her to watch for, and walked toward the flat wooden crossing built of wide planks. Her tennies made little noise on the sturdy boards, and she was across in a moment. She followed the path on the other side, which wandered off into the woods again. The trees closed back in.

She jumped at a faint boom. *What was that?* A fat drop splatted on a serviceberry leaf to her right. Another boom a minute later sounded closer. She walked faster as a quickening breeze pushed at her from behind. The light flattened, and as the air temperature dropped, she glanced up and realized with a sinking heart that heavy clouds had rolled in.

There was no weather report available at Barnabas' house. *Thunder*. That's what she had heard. She didn't even have a rain jacket, only her hoodie, which would be soaked instantly if it started raining. She hurried, jogging for a few steps whenever the path looked smooth enough. Should she stop and put her hoodie on anyway? No, she should just hurry up and get there. A little rain wouldn't hurt her.

The instant she thought this, a brilliant blaze of lightning and its rifle-crack chaser knocked her to the ground. She curled into a ball and covered her head instinctively.

Get up!

She jerked her head up and looked around.

Get up!

Nora scrambled to her feet, gasping for breath, her heart hammering at her ribs.

Run!

She took off, running down the path with adrenaline-fueled speed. She was in a forest of tall trees during a thunderstorm, and that was bad! That was very, very bad.

The rain let loose, pouring down in rivers so thick she felt she was running underwater. Wet leaves made the path instantly slick and she slipped repeatedly. She tripped on a log fallen across the path, caught herself on her hands and reopened the healing gouges. She cried out and wanted desperately to turn aside and huddle under a tree, even knowing how stupid that would be.

But adrenaline pushed at her, propelled her forward even as the rain half blinded her. Thunder cracked and boomed at terrifyingly brief intervals, the concurrent lightning capturing instants of time in bleached-out white like a strobe light from hell.

Nora ran, and stumbled, and ran. The path dog-legged to the left and a gigantic boulder loomed into sight about twenty feet off to her right.

The ancient rock hulked hugely among the tree trunks, a monster shaggy with lichens and moss, with shrubs growing on it at crazy angles. As big as a hill all by itself, a deep overhang on the near side created a dark shelter she could just make out.

She stopped. She could get to it, maybe, and wait out the storm. A wide tangle of thick brush and thorny brambles sprawled between her and the rock, too wide to get around.

But another bone-rattling boom decided her. She stepped off the path and began picking her way into the thicket, wincing as wild blackberry canes tore at her jeans and her bare arms. She had to keep wiping the rain out of her eyes, and pulling loose from thorns snagging her shirt.

Thunder cracked again and in the thick, wet silence that followed Nora heard a sound that froze her in place, one foot lifted off the ground.

She was not alone.

Dawn Walk

Monti dandled baby Stephanie on her knee, making her giggle and telling her they'd meet her soon.

Kit nudged her gently. "Hmm?" she murmured, still smiling.

"Hey lover, it's almost six. Want to go for an early walk?" Kit said.

Monti frowned, resisting. *How far from six*? Kit had been known to claim that 5:15 was almost six. She rolled over, opened one eye and looked at her scrumptious husband sitting on the edge of the bed, holding her hand. How could she resist?

"Okay," she said. "But you're already dressed. And I'll need coffee."

"I know, it's brewing. I'll go check on it while you get dressed." He leaned down and kissed her, then used his cane to get to his feet. He was relying on it more and more, but seemed to have accepted it. She hadn't heard him angry about it since they got here.

By the time she was ready, Kit had filled two travel mugs with coffee. He handed her one as Bob emerged from the bedroom. "Hey kids, where you off to?"

"Thought we'd take a turn around the pond," Kit said. "Back in plenty of time for breakfast."

"Okey doke," Bob said, and turned in to the bathroom.

Kit led Monti through to the screened porch and out to the grassy park. Night still hung richly in the air, but pillowy clouds in the east were promising a show coming soon. They picked their way carefully over the wet grass until they reached the gravel path that followed the edge of the pond. Lamp posts lit their way, but they wouldn't need them for long.

They crunched along the path in silence for a while, listening to the crickets winding down and the birds tuning up. A cat bounded across the path in front of them, an undefined breakfast dangling from its teeth. Foxtail palms rustled in the soft pre-dawn breeze.

Monti scratched her scabbed chin with one careful fingernail, then looped her arm through Kit's, careful not to spill his coffee. She noticed she automatically walked on his left now, as he usually held the cane in his right hand.

"I was dreaming of baby Stephanie when you woke me," Monti said.

Kit grunted. "Marla's doing all right, don't you think?" he asked.

"Really well, all things considered," Monti said. "It's still scary, but not like I feared it might be."

"It's possible that most things are not like you fear they might be, Monti."

Monti opened her mouth to retort, but closed it again. Why did he always zero right into her worst character flaws? "You might be right, love."

He squeezed her arm to his side. "I've been pleasantly surprised, too. And she and Nellie seem to be getting to know each other."

"And getting to like each other," Monti added. "But, we're still in the honeymoon phase, I think. It's going to be harder at home. In that little apartment, with Noelle in school and me working and you arranging for everything in our lives to be replaced and rebuilt."

"Yep, that's gonna kick the stress level up a few notches," Kit said. "Look there." They stopped to watch a mama duck waddle down to the water's edge in the pre-dawn light, leading a short, wobbly queue of tiny ducklings. "It's early for ducklings, I think."

"Why do you know when ducklings should be out and about?" Monti shook her head. "Where do you learn all this stuff?" She froze. "Wait, aren't there alligators in the ponds in Florida?"

"There can be, yes," he said slowly. "But this is a senior citizen community, and it's a man-made pond that's well-maintained. I think we're pretty safe as long as we don't go wading."

"Oh, the ducklings, silly," she said, though she knew he was teasing her. She almost nudged him sideways, but didn't want to knock him off balance. There were going to be a thousand tiny adjustments, she realized. As well as the gigantic ones that would happen when a wheelchair became a real thing in their lives, and not just a new word in quiet conversations.

They fell back into silence, and walked along watching the horizon pink up and get fancy, decorating the piled-up clouds.

"Thanks for the laptop, Kit, it's beautiful."

"You're welcome. I know you generally like to pick gadgets out for yourself, but this seemed like a pretty safe bet."

"Oh, you nailed it," she said. "It's exactly what I would have chosen. I guess you know me pretty well by now, huh?"

"If I don't, I can't have been paying attention for the last 40-odd years."

"Well you must have been paying close attention, because I sometimes think you know me better than I know myself." Kit smiled at her and they walked on, keeping an intermittent eye on the developing glory in the eastern sky.

"Mike Rutherford texted me yesterday," Kit said.

"He texted you? Is he out of jail?"

"Temporarily," he said. "He asked if we could meet when I get back. It sounds like they're going to hit him hard with the sentencing." Kit used his cane to flick a fallen palm frond off the path.

"And they should!" Monti said. "Driving drunk, without a license, and crashing into a little old lady. Poor Mrs. Millard."

"That's part of the reason. She's going to survive, apparently, but she'll be in a wheelchair for the rest of her life."

Monti shot Kit a sideways glance and hugged his arm, but decided not to go there. "Another of the messy situations we'll be dealing with when we get back home," Monti said. Kit nodded his agreement. "And the fire," Monti said. "Do you think they're ever going to charge anyone with that?"

"Well, Monti, you might want to loosen your grip on that idea. I think we can be fairly certain it was some associate of Blaine and Stevie Jakes, but proving arson is difficult, and proving who did it even more so. You know this."

"Yes, I do," she said, heaving a sigh. "But it doesn't feel safe not knowing who—not having the person held accountable."

Kit stopped walking, put an arm around Monti, and pulled her close. "It isn't particularly safe, Monti," he said. "But that's where we are." He crooked a finger under her chin and made her look at him. "If at all possible, I think it would help Marla and Noelle if we could not stress about that too much."

She looked into his eyes, feeling her jaw tighten, but wanting to be with him on this. She closed her eyes and deliberately relaxed into him. "Yeah," she said. "That'd be good, huh? They have enough to think about and figure out, without me adding 'fret about arsonists' as an ingredient to every conversation."

"That would be one way to put it," he said, a smile tugging at one corner of his mouth. He rested his cheek on her head. "You and me against the world, lover, right? Just like always. You can fret about arsonists to me privately if you need to," he said, "although—"

"I know, fretting is specifically forbidden." She sighed. "I'll do my best, love."

They walked on in silence for a little while. "I'm looking forward to hearing the Lost Boys sing," Monti said. "Mom says they're doing a quartet today."

"From what Bob says, they aren't lost anymore. He and Jody have a great discipleship group going with them, and he tells me they have a terrific hunger to know God and understand what it means that he loves them, what he wants from them individually. He says they challenge him more deeply than any group he's worked with in years."

"Wow. My parents found the front lines again," Monti said. "They have an uncanny knack for that."

"And they don't hesitate to jump right in when they find it, that's what I admire," Kit added. "Although it does make me feel like a slacker."

"I don't know, Kit. It feels like we've been in the line of fire for a couple of months now."

"True," Kit agreed. "Different kind of battle, but just as challenging." They walked up the gentle slope of the lawn to Housels' back door and wiped their feet on the mat. "And no signs of a general ceasefire anytime soon," he muttered as they stepped inside.

Not Alone

Nora squeezed her eyes shut in the pouring rain and listened with her entire being. Someone was crying. A woman—no, a child!

Her eyes flew open. Hysterical, heartbreaking, throat-tearing sobs and panicky wails—the unbearable sounds choked Nora, and involuntary empathetic tears trickled down and disappeared into the rain pelting her face.

Nora turned slowly, focused on determining which direction the sound was coming from. She glanced back at the overhang and the safe shelter beneath it. Felt herself physically pulled toward it.

No.

She closed her eyes again, cocked her head, focusing. The heavy rain intermittently drowned the sound, but the sobs tore painfully into her, keeping her from breathing properly. She held her breath and stood poised on the balls of her feet, searching for the sound, swiveling, turning, there!

She took one tentative step, two, then three, and opened her eyes. She was looking into the woods opposite the shelter of the huge rock. She hesitated, checked behind her to anchor the rock's location in her mind, then stepped out toward the terrible sounds.

The rain and trees made it hard to see more than a couple of steps in front of her, but at least the underbrush was, for whatever reason, less dense over here. She strained to see ahead, scanning right and left, pushing wet hair back from her eyes, remembering to keep checking around her feet too, lest she fall for real this time and crack her head.

She felt like her head was already cracked. This was not the mission. And this was not safe.

But before her resolve could waver, she found what she was looking for. She stepped around a truly huge cedar to find, not ten feet from her, a girl of seven or eight slumped in a miserable heap on the ground, cradling a man's head on her lap and crying her little heart out. She was drenched with rain, and wilted pink ribbon barrettes hung crookedly above her long, dark, tangled ponytail.

The man lay very, very still. He made no attempt to wipe the rain out of his eyes, even though they were open. A shudder rocked Nora. Rain had rinsed away the shocking red that should have shouted the fact, but there was a terrible wound, a mortal wound in the man's chest.

He had been shot, she was pretty sure, and he was quite dead, she was absolutely sure. *Exit wound. Shot in the back.* Even she could see that.

Nora's skin prickled. She turned slowly, trying to see into the woods around her, and beyond the girl and the dead man. Nothing. She forced her eyes back to the piteous tableau, and made herself think of the next hard thing she had to do.

"Hello," Nora said, taking a step toward the girl, but a fierce crack of thunder obliterated her choked greeting. She cleared her throat and tried again. "Hello!"

The startled girl threw her hands up and stared at Nora, her face a contortion of pain and terror.

"It's okay," Nora made calming motions as she closed the distance between them. "I won't hurt you."

"My daddy," the girl said, and succumbed to sobbing again. "My daddy is hurt."

"Oh sweetheart," Nora said, and her heart convulsed in her chest and bent her over with excruciating empathy. "He's not..." she stopped herself. *How can I do this, Abba?* She knelt by the girl and put an arm around her narrow shoulders.

"Can you help me?" the girl choked out between sobs, pleading with her eyes.

"I...it's not safe to stay right here, sweetheart, because of the lightning." She paused—was the girl understanding her? "We need to get you to shelter. I found a little cave..."

"I can help you carry Daddy," she said. "I'm very strong." The girl made a half-hearted attempt to flex her bicep to prove her strength, but she couldn't stop crying.

"Baby, we can't—" this was too, too hard. She took a deep breath. "My name's Nora. What's your name, sweetheart?"

"L-Lydia," the girl said.

"Lydia, honey, I don't think we can help your daddy."

"Yes we can," she insisted. "I can carry his legs, because they're lighter, and you—"

"Lydia." Nora put a gentle finger on the girl's lips, and lifted her quivering little chin until Lydia was looking at her. "Lydia, my poor sweet girl, your daddy is gone."

Confusion in her eyes, Lydia gestured to her father, not understanding how Nora couldn't see him right there. But then her face slowly changed, and she looked down at her daddy again with devastating comprehension, seeming to see for the first time the evidence of his rain-drowned eyes, his mangled torso.

"Noooo," she wailed, "no, no, no, Daddy!" She put her little hands on his cold cheeks and pleaded with him. "Daddy, please...please wake up!" Brutal sobs wracked her drenched little body. She was oblivious to the rain and the thunder. Nora held her, sobbing with her, smoothing her sodden hair.

When Lydia took a shuddering breath, Nora squeezed her shoulder. "Lydia, we have to get under shelter. Your daddy would want you to be safe, right?" Lydia nodded tentatively. "It's not safe to stay out in the trees in a thunderstorm. We could get hit by lightning." The girl's eyes widened, and she nodded, fear fighting with grief on her white, splotched face.

"Can we take Daddy?"

"No baby, we have to hurry." Nora stood and tried to pull Lydia up, but she resisted.

"I can't leave him here all by himself!" Lydia cried, fiercely clutching fistfuls of her father's shirt.

"Just for a little while," Nora said, soothing. "We need to go to that big rock over there," she pointed it out. "We'll be safe from the lightning there, and we'll be able to see this big tree from there, right? It's a really big tree." She demonstrated how she couldn't get her arms around it.

A terrifying crack of thunder and blinding burst of lightning made both of them cower. The rain poured down with violence, hating them.

"Then when the thunderstorm is over," Nora had to shout, "we'll come back to your daddy and figure out how to move him." She pulled at Lydia's arm again, meeting less resistance this time. "Come on, baby, we have to go right now!"

The girl, sniffling, reluctantly moved out from under her father, careful to lay his head gently on the ground, and got to her feet. Nora grabbed her hand, then decided carrying her would be faster.

"Come on Lydia, here we go. Hang on, now!" She scooped the feather-light girl into her arms, and the child wrapped her arms and legs tightly around Nora. Nora could feel her trembling, poor thing.

She took off at a careful jog, back to the path, blinking the rain out of her eyes, terrified she'd lose her way. But here was the path, and there was the thicket, and the boulder on the other side, right where she'd left it.

Nora's eyes went wide. A narrow game trail cut through the thicket. She'd come back onto the path at a different angle, and this trail had been invisible from where she'd stood before. *Thank you, Abba!*

"Almost there, Lydia," Nora said, and took them quickly through the thicket. A few thorns still tore at her wet jeans, but it was a paved highway compared to her first attempt.

The boulder towered over them. "Get down, baby, I don't want you to bump your head." Lydia slithered down Nora's body and they ducked under the overhang.

Nora couldn't quite stand up straight, and the ceiling lowered unevenly until it went vertical and met the ground about fifteen feet in. But it was enough. A large flat floor carpeted in dry pine needles provided plenty of space for them to ride out the storm.

They stood dripping, looking at each other for a moment. Then Lydia wrapped her arms around herself and turned back look out into the rain, making sure she could see the tree where her father lay. Nora quickly checked the perimeter of their little refuge. No critters that she could see, no holes large enough to house one. She relaxed a fraction. Safe for now.

She let her pack slide off her knotted shoulders, wincing as the straps scraped her bleeding palms. She opened it, and suddenly she recognized all the 'just in case' items as supremely valuable. Nora took out the two bottles of water, and remembered the cinnamon rolls in the front pocket. She unzipped the front pocket. They were a bit squished, but who cared?

"Lydia, are you hungry?" The girl turned to Nora, and the ancient sadness on her face nearly did Nora in. But there was an reluctant interest, too. She was hungry.

"Barnabas made these cinnamon rolls this morning," Nora said. "They're really good. Here, sit down. There's one for each of us."

"Who's Barnabas?" Lydia asked, walking over and sitting cross-legged across from Nora.

"Um, he's a friend of mine who lives in a house back that way," Nora gestured vaguely back the way she'd come.

"Do you live there, too?"

"No, no. My husband, Logan, and I were hiking and he got hurt..." She hesitated, but Lydia didn't react to this. "And you know what? A big beautiful deer helped us to find Barnabas' house. My husband, Logan, is there now, and he's getting better."

"A deer helped you?" A childish skepticism scrunched Lydia's forehead. "Why didn't a deer help me and Daddy?"

"Well, that's a good question, Lydia," Nora said as she unwrapped the cinnamon rolls. *I don't know why,* she thought. But she said, "The deer, I think, God sent as a helper for Logan and me," she said slowly. "To show us the way to Barnabas' house, so Barnabas could help Logan get better." She paused.

"Maybe," she looked at the bedraggled child before her, now shivering with cold. "Maybe God sent me to be a helper for you, because you need help that a deer can't give."

Lydia nodded, seeming to accept this as logical. "A deer couldn't carry cinnamon rolls," she said, bolstering Nora's hypothesis.

"That's right," Nora said, stifling a laugh. "And, I have a hoodie you can wear, because it looks like you're getting cold."

"I am," Lydia agreed, hugging herself. Nora set down her roll and dug down to the bottom of her pack. When she pulled out the hoodie, a shiny packet fell out onto the pine needles. "Hey, a mylar blanket! Woohoo!" Nora cheered, and squeezed her eyes shut and said a brief *Thank You*. She knew they hadn't packed this, she would have noticed. "With this and the hoodie, you'll be warm as toast."

"That doesn't look like a blanket!" Lydia said through chattering teeth.

"I'll show you in a minute, Lydia. You'd better take off that wet shirt, and we can zip you into this nice dry hoodie. It's my favorite one, it's really warm."

Lydia tried, but her sopping wet, long-sleeved t-shirt suctioned itself to her tummy and twiggy arms, so Nora peeled her out of it.

"You like pink?" Lydia asked.

"I do," Nora nodded at the girl's shirt. "Looks like you do, too."

"Uh-huh," the girl said, sliding her goosebumped arms into the soft sleeves of Nora's neon-pink fleece hoodie and letting Nora zip her in. "It's my favorite color. Daddy calls me Princess Pink..." the horrible truth broke over her again and crumpled her into herself. A dreadful keening came out of her mouth, like an injured animal might make.

Nora collected the little one into her arms again and sat rocking her, dripping tears into her hair, until she quieted again. "My daddy's gone," she whispered. "I have to tell Mommy. She'll be mad..."

"Mad? You mean sad?" Nora said.

"No, she'll be mad, because even though it was Daddy's weekend she didn't want him to take me camping. But I begged her please..." Now Lydia gripped Nora's arm and gave into crying again, but weakly. She had very little energy left, Nora could see.

"Oh baby, it's not your fault!" Nora assured her. "Your daddy was the grown-up, right? It was his job to decide. And this storm blew in all of a sudden, he probably didn't expect that."

"And he probably didn't expect the bad men, either," Lydia said, sending a frozen chill down Nora's spine.

"Bad men?" she barely managed to croak out.

"They were shooting guns, and Daddy said we should go a different way because of all the lines of fires, but I didn't see any fires..." she frowned in remembered confusion. "Then it thundered real loud and Daddy fell down and couldn't get back up, and then it started raining." Lydia's voice trailed off.

Nora had to think. She slipped the cinnamon roll into the girl's grimy little hands. Lydia automatically pulled off a curl of raisin-studded sweet bread and stuffed it in her mouth while staring out into the rain, tears sliding unchecked down her cheeks.

What should I do? They couldn't stay here if people were still shooting. That was even more dangerous than a thunderstorm! Although, who would stay out hunting, or whatever they were doing, in this weather? Surely they had headed back to their hotel. Or their camper, or their evil lair.

Nora rubbed the back of her aching hand over her bleary eyes and shivered. She was feeling the cold too. Regardless of the rain or the cold, she had to get Lydia back to Barnabas' house. She couldn't drag her along the rest of the way to the message box, then all the way back.

Wait! She sat up straight. Maybe she should do exactly that!

She would add to the note from Barnabas, and tell them about Lydia's father. When the storm was over they'd hurry to the post box, put the message in, then hightail it back to Barnabas and Logan. It was...Nora checked her watch and was shocked to see it was after ten already! How far was she from the box?

She gently pulled the map from her back pocket. The paper was saturated and softening. She carefully peeled it open, hissing in through her teeth when it separated wetly down one long fold.

She spread the paper on the dry pine needles and looked for Barnabas' markings. The rain had nearly erased them, but a faint blue line still traced from the house into the woods and along the path. A blurry X marked the post box.

But big boulders and fat cedar trees weren't marked on the map. How many of these squiggles in the path had she already traveled, and how many were ahead of her? There was no way to know.

Lydia appeared at Nora's shoulder, licking her sticky hands. "Nora? I'm thirsty." The girl could barely keep her eyes open.

Nora twisted around to grab the water bottles from where she'd set them. "Here's some water, sweetie." Lydia opened her bottle and took a long drink. "You want to lie down for a little while? I'll show you the mylar blanket,"

Nora said. Lydia just nodded, and followed Nora to the rear of the shelter. Nora chucked a couple of rocks out of the way, and patted a relatively flat place in the pine needles. The girl sank to the ground, her eyes closing as she lay down. She roused a little as Nora made interesting crinkly noises with the emergency blanket and spread the shiny foil over her. "It's like a happy birthday balloon," she said, fingering the mylar.

"It is exactly like a happy birthday balloon," Nora said, and tucked it under the little girl's shoulder and hip.

"Nora?"

"Hmm?"

"What if the bad men come back and shoot us, too?"

Nora gulped. "They won't, baby. Bad men don't stay out in the rain. I'm sure they're long gone, back to their bad-guy house."

Lydia gave a little nod, heaved a deep breath, tucked her sticky hands under head and slept instantly.

Nora put her head in her hands, hoping with all her might that what she'd said was true.

It is Well

Marla was pouring ladles of pancake batter onto an electric griddle when Kit and Monti returned. She glanced at them but immediately returned her focus to her task. "Have a nice walk?" she asked.

"Yep," Monti said. We saw one duck, seven ducklings and zero alligators."

Marla laughed. "Well, that sounds like good stats for any walk." She flipped a couple of pancakes, revealing their perfectly golden undersides.

"You're pretty good at that, Marla," Monti said, coming over to examine her work. "I never could make pancakes."

"I remember," Marla said, a smile pulling up one corner of her mouth, just like Kit's did.

"Hey!" Monti said. "Waffles. I make good waffles."

"And BCC muffins," Kit added.

"Mm, yes," Marla said. "I miss those. Will you make them tomorrow, Mom?"

"Oh sure, if we can get hold of some ripe bananas and some chocolate chips."

"I have dead bananas in the freezer." Jody appeared, wearing a pink kimono sprinkled with dainty Chinese maidens carrying parasols, and joined the conversation. She hugged Monti. "I'll have to look and see if I have chocolate chips. Wouldn't it be a scandal if I was out of such an essential item!"

Kit leaned down and kissed her on the cheek. "I'm gonna hate it when you all leave," she said. "I miss you already." She started opening cupboard doors, looking for the CC's.

"Refill on your coffee, Dad?"

"Thank you, daughter." He slid onto one of the stools at the counter. "Where'd you learn to make pancakes?"

"Oh, necessity, I guess. They're pretty cheap eats. Good with hamburger gravy, too. If you have hamburger money."

Monti's eyes and nose hurt as she fought the sudden need to cry. She couldn't think about it. Couldn't bear to think of Marla in desperate straits. Hungry. Homeless? She'd probably need to hear all the stories eventually, and maybe it would get easier. But right now it felt like every new detail was going to kill her, even though Marla didn't bat an eye in the telling of them.

"Refill, Mom?" Monti nodded, not trusting her voice, and unscrewed the lid on her travel mug.

"You okay?" Marla asked as she poured, a frown deepening all the lines on her face that were just starting eight years ago.

"Sure," Monti said. "It's uh…it's hard to think about you being hungry, Marla." She tried to smile. "I want you to tell me everything, I do. But it's hard to hear." She shook her head and buried her face in Kit's shoulder. He put an arm around her and squeezed. No one spoke as Marla flipped two more pancakes.

"I know it's hard, Mom, I'm sorry," she finally said. "It wasn't all bad, though, okay? There were some bright spots, too. I saw some beautiful places, met some good people, learned some things…"

"It'll be okay, Marla," Kit assured her. "It'll take a little time to put it in perspective. You tell her pancakes are cheap eats, and she's instantly got a whole story written in her head about you starving and homeless, and embellished it with gory details I can't even imagine."

"Not gory," Monti protested into Kit's shoulder.

"Whatever," Kit said, squeezing her again. "Be sure to tell us the bright spots, too, that will help."

Noelle emerged from the bathroom groomed and dressed, though still a couple of coffees this side of awake. "Hey, everybody," she said, and gave out hugs and kisses all around.

"Maybe you all could go home and we could keep Nellie," Jody said.

"I'd love to stay, GG," Noelle said. "But school…" She made her way to the coffee pot and emptied it into a big mug.

"I know, sweetheart," Jody said. "I'm just dreaming. I can't think how we got settled so far apart from each other."

"You're not far from Maryland and her gang," Monti reminded her. "If you were closer to us you'd be further from them."

"And just try to keep up with wherever Oregon is," Kit said. "You'd be moving every year or so."

"Just like in the old days," she said. "But no, I wouldn't want to do that now." She sighed.

Marla opened the oven, letting out the sizzle of bacon. She pulled the pan out and set it on the stove, careful not to let the hot grease slosh over the short rim. Bob came in the front door carrying a bulging paper bag.

"Hey, it smells good in here!" he said, and plopped the bag onto the counter. "Fresh oranges. Guy down the street has a big tree, gave these to us when he heard we had family in town."

Monti plucked one from the bag and held it to her nose, inhaling.

"We can juice them if you want, but I like to eat them out of hand," Bob said.

"Let's just eat them," Noelle said. "Way better for you that way. Shall I wash 'em?" She took the bag to the sink, washed several big oranges and piled them in a brightly painted wooden bowl Jody handed her.

"Time to eat, it looks like to me," Jody said. They had their buffet style dishing down pat by now, and everyone filled their plates and their coffee cups, and found a place to sit. Kit asked the blessing and they got to work emptying their plates.

Church was in an hour and a half so Bob, Noelle and Kit took kitchen cleanup while the rest of the ladies took turns at the bathroom mirror getting beautiful.

***

The Housels' church met in a storefront on a tired side street in downtown DeLand. A young man with asymmetrically spiked hair, a beard, and a plaid flannel shirt met them at the door with a bulletin and a brilliant white smile. "Welcome back!" he said. He was the worship leader, if Monti remembered right, and played a mean keyboard.

A lovely woman in a wheelchair rolled over to greet them. "Hello again!" she said, and grasped Monti's hand. "It's so good you can spend some time with your parents. They're such dear people."

"Oh, Melissa, you're the dear and you know it," Jody said, reaching down to kiss her on the cheek. Melissa patted her on the back. "Thank you for the meals last week," she said in a low voice. "It was a rough few days and that really helped."

"Don't mention it," Jody said, and squeezed her friend's hand. They walked on in to find a place to sit.

"That's the pastor's wife, right?" Monti asked.

"Mm-hm," Jody said. "Melissa Blalock. She's fighting MS. It's a terrible disease. But the thing I hate the most," she said near Monti's ear, "is that Ron had a hard time finding a congregation to pastor when they retired from the mission field, because the search committees thought Melissa would be a burden. It still steams me." She pressed her lips together and squinted her eyes. "And they don't know what they let get away, either! She works as hard as any of us when she can. And the sweetest spirit...Oh, don't get me started!"

Monti smiled to herself as they found their seats. She knew how little it took to get her mother started when she thought someone was being mistreated. Playing fair and fighting fair had been foundational absolutes at the Housel home. No picking on the little guy, no leaving anyone out, no saying unkind things, no being selfish or greedy. Jody had a zero-tolerance policy for anything mean-spirited and she enforced it with fierce impartiality.

Jody's zero-tolerance policy met significantly more resistance in the world outside their home, but injustices large or small still got her fluffed up and furious. If she could set things right, she didn't hesitate to do so. If she couldn't, she stood with the underdog and did her best to help them fight their fight while making sure they had meals and transportation and whatever else she could provide.

Her dad sometimes had to run interference between Jody and the world. Often, Monti thought, to protect clueless offending parties from being blindsided by Jody's genuinely righteous indignation. But once in a while he reeled her in and sat her down for a quiet chat, after which she would back down from whatever had her hackles up at the moment. They made a good team.

The keyboard and a couple of guitars started up a lively praise song, rousing Monti from her musing, and church was on. The extended worship time included hymns and old favorites along with the trendy songs, which Monti appreciated. Then the Lost Boys sang a spine-tingling, a Capella rendition of *It is Well with My Soul* that had Monti's handkerchief out of her bag before the end of the first stanza.

Ron, the pastor, working from Ephesians 2, reminded them that salvation was a free gift, not something that can be earned. He didn't let his listeners camp there, but forged ahead to the part where the church is told to roll up its individual sleeves and get to doing the good works prepared for it beforehand.

Why it was hard to keep those two concepts in balance Monti didn't know, but it was. She needed the reminder and his ideas for making it happen as much as anyone.

Bob and Jody invited Ron and Melissa to lunch at DeLand Fish House, and they all had a good long visit over their shrimp tacos and crab patties. Eventually Monti noticed how tight Kit's jaw was, and how frequently he shifted in his seat. She whispered in her mom's ear and they said their goodbyes soon after.

On their way home Jody pointed out several of the thrift shops they would explore tomorrow. Monti was looking forward to replenishing her nearly nonexistent wardrobe, with Noelle along as her personal shopper. That girl would soon have them all looking like a million bucks on a nickel and dime budget.

When they reached the Housels', Kit immediately excused himself and retreated to their bedroom. Monti poured a glass of water and took it in to him. He sat on the edge of the bed slipping off his shoes. His jaw was rigid.

"Anything else I can do for you, Kit?" she asked as she handed him the water.

"No, lover, but thanks for this." He set the glass on the table and moved carefully to get out his pain medication. "I'll be out after a bit, okay?"

"Sure, no problem, sweetheart." She leaned down and kissed him. "See you in a while." Monti returned to the living room, where this evening's Scrabble round was under discussion.

"Hey Monti, is Kit okay?" Jody asked. "He's on the chart to play Noelle tonight."

"Oh, I think he'll be fine for that. Just too many long stretches in chairs this morning." She glanced at the bedroom door. "He'll be feeling better in half an hour or so."

"Well, good. I hope he is. We could put this round off until tomorrow…"

"No, no, Mom. Trust me, it'll be fine."

And it was fine. Kit and Noelle started with stately bows to each other before they sat down at the board. But Kit got a triple word score early on, and Noelle threw a piece of popcorn at him. He returned the favor when she got triple points for the Z, and they kept this up back and forth, amidst much kibitzing.

When Kit got a 50-point bonus, a wildly undignified popcorn fight ensued, with significant audience participation. Eventually, Kit trounced Noelle by nearly a hundred points. That meant tomorrow night Bob would play Jody, and the following night, Kit and Monti would square off.

"The battle of the ancients, parts one and two," Marla said, a wicked gleam in her eye.

"Oh, I see. You haven't even played yet and already you heckle?" Monti said, and pulled Marla in for a hug. "You'd better behave yourself, you young whippersnapper," she added in her best ancient crone voice.

Marla wrapped her arms around Monti's neck and whispered, "Love you, Mom." Monti hugged her tighter and wondered if tears would ever stop smarting at the back of her eyes when Marla was around.

"Love you too, baby girl."

The Plan

Nora sat watching Lydia. Her grief temporarily trumped by exhaustion, the girl slept peacefully while the tracks of her tears dried on her cheeks.

The respite would be brief enough. Nora sighed and wished she could take a nap, too, but she knew that wouldn't work for a hundred reasons. For one thing, she was wet and cold. And for another, when she closed her eyes she saw Lydia's father, his dead eyes, his chest blown apart. By comparison, Logan's broken leg seemed quite the minor injury. But then, he had come so close to dying in just the same way as Lydia's dad.

Nora shuddered and returned to the pressing problem at hand. Problems. One, her hands. She dug the first aid kit out of her pack and after giving them a good rinse in the rain, tended to her newly raw wounds. She was going to have scars if she kept ripping them open again.

The time. She glanced at her watch again. The summer days were still long. It would be light until at around eight, she thought. At least, on a sunny day out in the open it would be. Here in the dense forest, and if the clouds stuck around, who knew? She might only have seven hours of usable light. But that should be way plenty, right?

She balled up the first aid detritus and shoved it in the pack, then squat-walked over to study the map. Even if she'd only come one mile so far, two more miles shouldn't take more than an hour, even on rough ground. Though...with a small child in tow...but surely that distance wasn't more than Lydia could handle. Her dad had felt comfortable taking her camping, after all, so she wasn't a couch potato softy.

Nora would help Lydia, and they could do it together. If the lightning ever stopped. She gazed out at the rain still pouring down. Thunder boomed, but not quite so close. Maybe the storm would move on soon.

Meanwhile, she had to amend the note they'd leave in the post box, to let the authorities know about the shooters, about Lydia's father, and that the girl was safe. She'd have to ask Lydia her last name.

Nora found the note Barnabas had written in the pack, protected in a zippered plastic bag, and pinned it under her knee while she rummaged for a pen. A frisson of panic fluttered in her stomach — why couldn't she find a pen? They had to have packed one. She took a deep breath and let it out slowly.

She deliberately removed every item from the backpack and laid it all out neatly on the ground. A fat roll of orange engineer's tape surfaced, which she knew for certain hadn't been in there when she left the house. Miraculous emergency blankets and engineers' tape, but no pen? She didn't understand. She checked every pocket. She turned the pack upside down and shook it.

There was no pen. No pencil, no crayon or marker or lipstick, even. Nothing to write with. Her shoulders sagged. A wild plan to prick her finger and write in blood skittered through her brain. Could she make ink?

She rubbed her eyes. Maybe Lydia had a pencil in her pants pocket. That seemed unlikely. She looked over her shoulder at the sleeping girl. She was so grimy, poor little thing. Nora wished she had a washcloth, or a miracle brush she hadn't packed so she could untangle her long hair and put her pink barrettes back in straight.

Pink barrettes. *I'm brilliant!* She would put Barnabas' note in the box with Lydia's two beribboned barrettes clipped onto it. That should be weird enough to make his courier — Roland, was it? — ask around a little. Maybe if he saw a Ranger or a police officer he could ask if there was a little girl gone missing.

Even if the oblique message didn't trigger any immediate alarms, at least the man would be bringing help back to Barnabas' house for

Logan, and they could help Lydia then, too.

The cinnamon roll caught Nora's eye. She may as well eat it, there was nothing else she could do until Lydia woke, or it stopped raining. She brushed off a couple of ants and bit into it, relishing every bite, grateful Barnabas was in the raisins camp, not the nuts camp.

When she finished, she thrust her hands and face out in the rain to rinse off the sticky. The icy water was a shock, and she would have to redo her wet band-aids, but it refreshed her.

She should probably rest for a few minutes, too, wet and cold as she was. She snuggled down against the wall at Lydia's head, rested her arms on her knees and her head on her arms. That felt good. *Abba, thank you for this shelter from the storm. Thank you for cinnamon rolls, and pink ribbons...*

Nora snapped at her brother to stop jiggling her arm, he was making her mess up the picture. Then she woke to find Lydia gently pulling at her. "Nora?"

"Hey, sweetie. I guess I fell asleep." She straightened her back and rolled her head to get a crick out of her neck.

"I have to pee," Lydia said, "and it's still raining."

"Oh, of course." Nora looked around their abode and shrugged. "Anywhere you like, kiddo. Maybe over there, you could lean on the wall to balance your squat."

Lydia nodded and went about her business.

"Need any help?" Nora ventured, and was rewarded with a cute little eye roll.

"I'm not a baby," Lydia said. "I know how to pee in the woods."

"Well, all right then," Nora said, hiding a smile, and impressed by how tidily Lydia took care of matters. "How old are you, Lydia?"

"Seven and three-quarters," she answered promptly. "See? I already have my grown-up central incisors," she said with precision, flopping down in front of Nora and pointing out the blocky permanent teeth flanked by gaps on either side, top and bottom.

"You do, indeed," Nora agreed. She was going to fall completely in love with her little charge.

"I need to wash my hands," Lydia said, holding them out in front of her.

Nora nodded toward the rain. "Cold water wash okay?" Lydia didn't bother to answer but pushed up the too-long hoodie sleeves and stuck her hands out into the deluge, wiping each with the other until she was satisfied they were 'washed', and shook them vigorously as she returned to Nora.

"What happened to your hands, Nora?"

"Oh," Nora said. "I hurt them on some rope. After Logan got hurt, I had to pull him up a steep bank, out of a creek." Lydia nodded and made a darling little sympathy face.

"Where do you live, sweetie?" Nora asked.

"I live with Mommy in Redmond, except on Daddy's weekends, then I stay with him in Port Angeles..." Her voice faded away and her face crumpled again. She buried it in her wet hands. "My daddy's dead," she sobbed into her hands.

Nora gathered her up again and rocked her gently, gazing at the wall of rain, a veil between them and the rest of the world. Lydia's grief filled the small space as a palpable presence. Their refuge from the storm provided no escape from her pain. The girl needed her mother. Nora rocked her and listened to the storm.

She hadn't heard thunder for a while, had she? She looked at her watch, trying not to panic at how late it was getting. After a few minutes, Lydia's crying subsided. Nora squeezed her and said, "Do you want to know the plan?"

"What plan?" Lydia said, her voice still thick with tears.

"Well, when I found you, I was on my way to put a note in a post box, to send someone a message."

"A message to who?"

"To our families, to let them know Logan and I are okay, since they didn't expect us to be gone this long. And to someone who could come to Barnabas' house and help us get home, because we don't know the way from there, and my husband has a broken leg."

Lydia considered this. "What's a post box?"

"I don't know, exactly," Nora answered. "I picture it as a wooden box on a post, though it wouldn't be called a post box *because* of the po—well, never mind about that. A box on a post, I think, that holds messages on pieces of paper until someone comes to collect them."

"That's kind of weird," Lydia said, cocking an eye at Nora.

"I agree," she said, "But we couldn't think of a better plan. And now we need to let people know that you need help, too."

"And Daddy," Lydia said.

"Yes, and your daddy, too, sweetheart." She checked the time. "I haven't heard any thunder for at least 15 minutes," she said. "If we don't hear any for another 15, we should probably head out."

"In the rain?"

"Uh-huh," Nora said. "It might not stop raining for hours, and we can't take the chance of waiting. We have to get to the post box and back to Barnabas' house before dark."

Lydia chewed her lip, thinking this over. "I understand," she said. "As soon as it's safe, we'll move Daddy in here so he'll be nice and dry, then hurry really fast to the post box." She looked up at Nora. "That's a good plan, Nora."

Nora's stomach sank. "I don't know about moving your daddy, sweetheart."

Lydia straight-armed her like a tiny traffic cop, halting any further discussion. "You said 'only for a little while' before. We have to move him in the cave before we go." Her little chin jutted out with a stubbornness Nora recognized from her own personality. Arguing the point would not accomplish anything. And anyway, she'd pretty much promised. She sighed.

"Okay, Lydia, we'll move him first." That shouldn't take too long, it wasn't far. And really, they were probably almost to the post box anyway, with plenty of daylight left. Not a huge deal.

Treasure Hunt

"Might as well start here," Jody said as she turned the van into the Goodwill parking lot. "It's just like Goodwill everywhere else, so the day will only get more interesting as we go on."

"Besides, you never know where you'll find a real treasure," Noelle said, speaking from years of experience.

They took their time, skimming through the racks and trying on a few things. Jody scoped out the kitchen shelves. She always needed sealable boxes and bowls for giving meals or cookies.

Noelle nabbed two pairs of jeans that fit her perfectly, and Monti found a lavender silk blouse with a 50% off tag. Step one toward rebuilding her fabulous wardrobe.

Marla spent most of the time in the book racks, and when Monti went to check on her, she had three recent novels tucked under one arm. Monti bumped hips with her. "You still like to read?"

"Yeah, I think so. It's been a while. I don't recognize most of these authors."

"Well, neither do I, daughter. It's impossible to keep up anymore, there are so many."

"Come on, girls," Jody said from behind them. "Let's pay for this stuff and move on down the road. Lots of territory to cover today!"

"Marla," Monti said in her daughter's ear as they got in the checkout line behind Jody and Noelle. "How are you set for funds? I want you to enjoy today, and be able to buy what you want."

Marla pressed her lips together and forced herself out of what looked like a habitual hunch, pushing back her shoulders and straightening her posture. "I don't have a lot, Mom," she said quietly. "Around fifty bucks to my name. I don't know what I can do about that, until I can get a job."

Monti squeezed her daughter's arm. "Listen. We're not going to worry about that until we get back home, okay? I haven't gotten to spend any money on you for eight years, and I'd really like to do that now." She turned to face her girl and cupped one roughened cheek in her hand. "Will you let me buy you 'all the things', at least while we're here? We can make a more sustainable plan when we get back to Idaho."

Marla nodded and pressed her cheek into her mother's hand. "Thanks, Mom," she whispered, her eyes wet. "Love you."

"Love you right back, baby girl." She patted Marla's cheek. "At our next stop, you pick out something pretty."

When they'd climbed back in the van and dumped their bags in the back, Jody said, "This next place is a great consignment shop. It's a little pricey, but they're particular about what they stock."

The mound of bags in the back of the van slowly grew as they worked their way down Woodland Boulevard. Some shops were crammed with racks without any discernible organizational scheme, requiring muscle power to shove apart the tightly packed hanging clothes, and an eagle eye to spy out the good stuff. Other shops obviously benefited from more space and the hand of a born organizer, making the hunt easier.

One place smelled of rodents and mildew, and after a cursory glance over the inventory, they quickly made eye contact with each other and headed back to the van. "That one's gone downhill," Jody said apologetically.

Monti made some good headway toward replacing the basics of the working wardrobe she needed, and found some good pieces for Kit, too.

Jody mostly browsed, but did find a unique coral and silver chunky necklace and earrings that suited her bright personality. The girls had a blast. They were both starting from near-empty wardrobes, and had similar quirky taste, so once Marla relaxed into the idea, they laughed a lot and got a little giddy.

They refueled with foo foo coffee at a drive-through place, and kept on shopping. Monti's energy and enthusiasm were flagging by the time Jody said, "It's getting late, how about lunch? There are two more shops I'd really like to hit, but they're a bit further down the road, and I'm ready for a break."

"Sure, GG," Noelle said. "I'm hungry!" Monti and Marla chimed their agreement and Jody looped around into the parking lot of the Hackle House Cafe.

"Ooh," Noelle breathed as they mounted the creaky steps to the deep enclosed porch of the house-turned-restaurant. Heavy antique tables with classy mix and match chairs filled the space and hinted at more delights to come. When they stepped into the house itself, Noelle squealed with delight. "It's like the cutest thrift shop there ever was!"

This dining room, and another they could see through a doorway, overflowed with miscellaneous treasures. Books, mirrors, baskets, knick knacks, and more tea pots than would fit in anyone's kitchen sat on mantles, windowsills, and shelves, and hung from hooks and pegs on every available inch of wall space. Some items bore price tags, but most constituted the eclectic and evolving decor of the place.

"It is cute" Jody said, "but fortunately this shop focuses on delicious food." She stood on tiptoe scanning for an open table. "And we have to save room for dessert."

They settled at a round oak table in the corner, and eagerly took the menus handed them by a smiling young lady in a Daytona State College t-shirt. After serious consideration, Noelle chose the Chicken Fandango salad, Jody picked Seafood Crepes, and Marla and Monti opted for the soup and salad special of the day.

"Peach bread pudding with bourbon sauce," Monti said. "Is that what we're saving room for? It sounds yummy."

"Yes, that or the key lime pie," Jody said.

"Or both," Marla said, surprising them all. They looked at her and she shrugged. "Why not?"

"Exactly," Jody said, "Why not. We'll share." They did share. Samples of crepes and chicken and salads were offered across the table throughout the meal. The server brought them extra-large servings of the two desserts, so they all had a good taste of both to go with their final coffee refill.

Monti soaked up the sight of her most favorite women eating and laughing together, and stored it away for cherishing later. When they'd finished their lunch, she asked their waitress to take a picture of them all, to make the cherishing even better. They piled back into the van re-energized for the last round of treasure hunting.

At their very last stop, a huge Hospice resale shop, Marla and Noelle hit the jackpot. The store had a good all-around selection, and their 50% off rack offered a plethora of scrumptious clothes in both their sizes.

Monti and Jody sat in chairs just outside the dressing rooms, and the girls kept popping out wearing one adorable thing after another, with a wide grin accessorizing each outfit. Noelle practically floated out of the store, and Monti watched Marla watching her daughter, a quiet happiness radiating from her weathered face.

"That's good to see, isn't it?" Jody asked, looping her arm through Monti's as they followed their girls out to the van.

Monti nodded. "Balm for a mother's heart, not to be too schmaltzy about it."

"Oh, that was pretty schmaltzy," Jody teased. "Ready to head home?"

"Definitely," Monti said. "That was enough shopping by anyone's measure."

"Even Noelle's, I think," Jody said. "She sure had a good time."

"Well, even having all your belongings go up in smoke has a silver lining or two. Replacing your entire wardrobe is one of them." She paused. "Can't really think of what another might be, but that one's enough for today."

"Yes, indeed."

They drove back to the Housels' tiny home and relived their greatest treasure-hunting triumphs of the day by recounting them to Bob and Kit, and displaying their fabulous finds.

The guys nodded politely, smiling at how happy the girls were. Bob had a pot of chili simmering on the stove. Just he and Kit ate some at supper time, the women still being full from lunch. But they all eventually succumbed to the mouthwatering aroma after the day's treasures were packed away, the board was brought out, and

Bob and Jody sat to play their round of the tournament.

As day sank into evening, the little house shone in the dark, brimming with laughter and conversation, the soft click of Scrabble tiles and one family's fragile happiness. Monti let it wash over her with a deliberate effort, stuffing down her habitual 'waiting for the other shoe to drop' feeling as hard as she could.

But it did feel too good to be true. Or at least too good to last. And it couldn't last, of course. Even barring further disasters, life for this family was going to be difficult going forward.

She didn't let herself start writing a mental list of all the ways it was going to be difficult, but instead turned her focus out to the love and joy happening around her at this moment. This was a gift. A good and perfect gift. *Thank you*, she breathed, and picked up the empty popcorn bowl. She'd go make another batch.

Waiting

Rain cascaded down the sloped roof and splatted unendingly on the flagstones. Logan wheeled around and rolled across the porch again. Staring hard at the other side of the clearing where the trail disappeared into the forest, Logan searched for any movement, for a glimpse of shiny brown hair or a pink hoodie.

Nothing.

Barnabas stepped out of the house and joined him, leaning on his cane. "The rain, son, will no doubt slow her journey."

"Still, it's three o'clock. She should have been home by two at the latest." He scrubbed his hands through his hair and gripped it by handfuls. He was so helpless! "Even allowing another hour for the rain, she should be back by now."

"As Mr. Eliot said, 'The faith and the love and the hope are all in the waiting.'" Barnabas lay a hand on Logan's shoulder. "It's very difficult to wait when every fiber of your being wants to take action. But child, there is no action we can take."

"This blasted leg!" Logan slammed his fist on the arm of his wheelchair. "This is my fault. I shouldn't have been screwing around—I got us into this mess and now she's out there alone." He glared up at the older man. "Do you have any idea how terrifying that must be for her?"

"I do have some idea, yes. However, I also understand the concept of the id, and am familiar with how fear works, and how our Sovereign works through these complex frailties under which we all labor."

"Huh?" Philosophy class notwithstanding, Logan was having a hard time following Barnabas' train of thought.

"I am merely saying, child, that we may rest in the knowledge that Nora is a willing bondslave of the King. And therefore we can trust him to care for her as will bring him the greatest glory."

Logan pondered this. It was not comforting in a 'please say everything will be okay' way. "Caring for her that way won't necessarily be all sunshine and roses."

"No." Barnabas ran a veiny hand over his eyes. "Likely not. More often thunderstorms and mud," he gestured to the soggy world beyond the porch. The two men fell silent, thinking their own thoughts, staring through the rain into the dark and empty trail entrance on the other side of the clearing.

What would he do if she didn't return? Logan squeezed his eyes shut. He...he couldn't even go down that path. It would break him. Barnabas turned to go back in the house.

"Barnabas," Logan said. The old man turned with his hand on the doorknob. "Have you remembered if there's any rice in the house? And maybe...would there be a recharging device?"

Barnabas nodded. "Good thoughts both, my boy. I will conduct a thorough search. We can petition the king whilst we take what meager actions we can take."

Logan followed Barnabas into the house and watched as he limped around ransacking cupboards and closets. *Take care of Nora. And by that I mean bring her back to me. Today.*

Please.

Intersection

On Tuesday the imminence of Christmas was palpable, most vividly in the aroma of cinnamon and vanilla. Monti's mother always launched into a flurry of baking right before Christmas, cranking out batches of cookies to distribute to a long list of friends and neighbors, and any fortunate strangers who happened to cross her path while she had a plate of cookies in her hand.

Jody and Noelle were pink cheeked and dusted with flour. The tiny kitchen was full to capacity.

Marla sat at the bar, cutting glossy magazine pages into long strips.

Monti kissed her cheek. "Paper chain duty, huh?"

"Well there's no room for more help in here," Jody said. "And there's lots else to do. I usually don't have enough time to help decorate for the church Christmas party, but this year I will! Many hands…" she beamed at her expanded workforce.

Monti wove her way through her family to the coffee pot, kissing each of them en route. "I was going to offer my help, but it looks like you have everything well in hand. Well in *many* hands," she said, weaving carefully back out of the kitchen with her full cup. "Unless there's something you need me to do, I'd like to finish getting my beautiful new computer set up, and transfer my story off of Dad's machine."

"Oh sure, you do that, sweetheart," Jody said, sliding another batch of snickerdoodles off a cookie sheet onto a cooling rack.

"Where are the guys?"

"I'm not sure," Jody said. "They left…when did they leave?"

"About an hour ago," Noelle said. "They didn't say where, but I think it was eldering."

Monti pouted for a second at not being kissed goodbye, then decided that was stupid and disappeared back into her room to finesse her computer setup. She was almost ready to dive into her story again. She knew she'd never get any writing done if she set up out at the table, but she left the door open so she wouldn't miss out completely. If it sounded like too much fun happening, she'd just go out for a refill and get in on it.

She opened the laptop box, slid the beautiful apple-green machine out of its foam sleeve, and swam again into the delightful world of brand-new-computer.

When she came up for air and coffee a couple of hours later, the kitchen was empty and the table was buried under a heap of multi-colored paper chain. The ladies sat shoulder to shoulder on Jody's small sofa, heads down, studying a photo album on Jody's lap. The Rwanda volume, by the look of it. Monti refilled her cup and wandered over to sit in the recliner.

"Hi G," Noelle said. "How's your story coming?"

"Pretty good. I got it all transferred to my new machine. And I've started with a disaster at the beginning, so who knows where it will go from there."

Marla scrunched her eyebrows. "You don't know?"

"Oh heavens, no," Monti said. "I have a vague idea. Or in this case, a specific word list. But really, anything could happen." She sipped her fresh coffee. "Hey, you'll never guess what my new laptop has."

"A cup holder?" Noelle instantly suggested.

"Ha ha." Monti made a face at her.

"A pad of paper where you can write down all your dang-blasted passwords?" Jody said.

"No," Monti said. "A fingerprint reader."

"Really?" Marla said. "Like in the movies?"

"I don't know about in the movies, but it's right there below the keyboard," Monti said. "So I guess I won't need my password. At least the one to get into my computer."

"One down, 4,968 to go," Jody muttered.

***

Kit collapsed his cane, opened the van door, and hauled himself in. He buckled up while Bob watched for an opening in the traffic.

"It's eerie how similar our eldering scenarios are," he said to Bob. "We have a cat lady of our own in Coeur d'Alene. Not quite so many animals, but almost."

Bob shook his head. "It's a tough situation," he said, smoothly joining the flow of traffic. "Betty's a longtime widow. Her kids are out west, except for the middle son, who died on the streets in Tampa a couple years back. That about killed her."

"Similar story with our Agnes," Kit said, then stomped on imaginary brakes as he caught a silvery flash barreling into the intersection from his right.

Bob stood on the real brakes simultaneously, but the silver flash slammed into the front corner of the van with a horrifying squeal of rending metal and shattering glass, before careening on past to smash into another truck.

The seatbelt viciously wrenched Kit's shoulder and pain shot down his spine. A momentary dread immobilized him, until he forced himself to remember that there were no IEDs on these Florida streets, and no one would be shooting at their disabled vehicle from the buildings lining the street.

He winced with pain as he turned to his father-in-law. "Bob, you okay?"

"Yeah, think so," Bob said. But a tremor in his voice said otherwise. He rolled down his window a few inches and tried to catch his breath. The open window cranked the volume on the barrage of shouts and honking horns that had erupted in the intersection.

"Don't move," Kit said. He pulled out his cell phone and was dialing 911 when a burly man startled him with a brisk knock on his window. The man motioned for him to roll it down. Kit hesitated.

"Hey, it's Lenny," Bob said, his voice so weak Kit could barely hear him.

Kit rolled down the window. "Lenny?" A first siren sounded in the distance. Thin clouds of steam rose from under the van's hood, a haze between them and the mess in front of them.

"Yeah? Do I know you?" Lenny's thick eyebrows signaled his confusion as he felt for the radio on his shoulder.

"No sir, but I think you know Bob," Kit gestured toward Bob, sitting paper-white and sweaty in the driver's seat.

"Oh Lord, Bob, are you okay, man? I was parked there at the cafe and heard the crash..." Lenny's voice faded as he jogged quickly around the van to open Bob's door.

"Are you hurt?"

Bye, Daddy

Thirty minutes. It had been at least half an hour since Nora had heard thunder, though the rain hadn't let up appreciably. "Time to pack up, Lydia," she said. They had sat quietly after agreeing on the plan. Nora had watched the girl out of the corner of her eye. Her chin quivered intermittently, and a fresh flood of tears wet her cheeks now and then as she sat with her arms wrapped around her legs, swathed in Nora's over-sized hoodie.

Lydia roused and stood slowly, pushing the long sleeves up again.

"Here, let's roll those," Nora said, and helped her. "Let's make sure we don't leave any trash in here," she said, folding up the mylar blanket with a long crash of metallic rustling. "Can you get the bag from the cinnamon rolls?" In short order they crammed the trash, the mylar blanket and Lydia's wet shirt into Nora's pack. Nora carefully refolded the disintegrating map, and laid it gingerly on top.

"Let me have your barrettes, sweetie," Nora said. "I couldn't find a pen, so I want to clip them on the note. That way the person who finds the note will know you're with me."

Lydia unclipped the barrettes, having some difficulty freeing them from her long, tangled hair. "That's a good idea," she said, and handed them to Nora. "Smart thinking."

"Why thank you," Nora said with a smile. She slipped the note out of its zipper bag, clipped the barrettes onto it, and zipped it up again.

She placed the note into the very top of the pack with the map, anchoring both with the roll of orange engineer tape. She knew better by now than to bury that inexplicable gift in the bottom of the pack, even if she had no clue why she had it.

"We still have two energy bars," she said. "Are you hungry?"

Lydia shook her head, so Nora stuffed them in the front pocket where they could get at them easily. She shrugged on her pack, clipped the hip belt, and looked around their little shelter. "I guess that's it," she said. "You ready?"

Lydia nodded, but the prospect of returning to her dead father was visibly weighing down her little shoulders. Her chin wobbled, and an apparently endless supply of tears kept her cheeks wet.

"Come here," Nora pulled her in for a hug. "Abba, please help us. We have to go out in the rain and do some hard things now. Please help us and protect us." She squeezed Lydia. "Let's go." Hand in hand, they plunged out into the rain and hurried back to the giant cedar.

Lydia stopped in her tracks when they moved around it. Her father's body was ghastly. His limbs lay splayed where he'd fallen, eyes still staring at the socked-in sky, skin blanched and pruning from the rain. Nora was horrified. Why hadn't she at least closed the poor man's eyes? Arranged his limbs? She knelt at his side, and was shocked to discover his eyes would not close. She quickly gave it up and moved on to draping his arms across his chest and straightening his legs, hoping to minimize the horror Lydia must be experiencing.

She turned to the girl. "Are you okay, sweetheart?"

"No," Lydia said in a quavery voice, but moved to her father's feet. "I'll carry his legs, okay?" She stationed herself between her father's boots and waited for Nora to get into position at his head. A heavier torrent of rain plastered their hair to their heads and chilled them as they bent to grip the leaden body.

"Right, I'll lift his shoulders," Nora said, raising her voice over the noise of the rain. "Ready? One, two, three, lift!"

Lydia was able to lift his feet, but Nora could hardly budge his torso. She looked at him more closely. He had to be well over six feet tall, bulky with muscle and heavy with rain-soaked clothing and hiking boots. Her spirits sank. This wasn't going to work. But for Lydia's sake, she wasn't going to give up right away.

"Okay, let's try again. We'll try to move him just a foot or two the first time, okay?" Lydia set her jaw and nodded. "One, two, three, lift!"

They both grunted with effort, their faces purpling. They did succeed in moving him—about four inches. Nora stumbled and sat down suddenly. Lydia sat, too. They caught their breath for a moment.

"Another go?" Nora asked. Lydia nodded. They gave it five or six hard-as-they-could tries, and Nora could see Lydia slowly giving in to reality. There was no way they could move her daddy all the way to the shelter.

"We can't do it," Lydia finally said, her spirit and her shoulders sagging. "He's too big."

"I think you're right," Nora agreed, wiping rain from her eyes and crawling down to the man's feet to hug Lydia. After a pause, she said, "What about this—we'll get out the mylar blanket and put it over your dad. It'll be like a little shelter, and it's shiny, so it will help whoever comes to help us find him easily.

"Can we hold down the edges with pretty rocks?" Lydia asked.

"Uh, sure, we can look for some good rocks, that's a great idea, Lydia." She checked her watch again. She closed her eyes and vowed again to stop looking at the thing. It wasn't going to change anything, and it only stressed her out. She took it off, shrugged off her pack, and stuffed the watch into a side pocket.

"What did you do that for?" Lydia said.

"Oh, I don't need to keep looking at my watch so much," Nora said. "It's just making me worry, so I decided not to wear it."

"What are you worried about, Nora?"

"Um, mostly daylight," she said, unwilling to lie to the girl. "But we still have plenty, so let's not even think about that, let's just find a half-dozen pretty rocks and get the shelter in place for your dad, okay?"

Lydia pressed her lips together, got to her feet and started searching the ground. There were not many rocks of the size Nora thought would work to anchor the emergency blanket. They'd have to be flexible in their definition of 'pretty.' But Lydia immediately surprised her with a football-sized dark gray rock, speckled throughout with reddish bits, shiny with rain.

"Wow, that is pretty," she said, and set the rock next to the man's foot. Nora found one with a thick stripe of bright white quartz running through it. Lydia found an orange-striped chunk of sandstone and Nora found two more like it.

"Look, it's a bunch of little rocks all stuck together in a big rock." Lydia presented a hunk of what Nora would've identified as concrete, if they'd been anywhere near a human-built object.

"Huh, that's cool," she said. "That makes six, right? That's probably enough." She gently drew the mylar out of the pack with a prolonged rustle, taking care not to tear it on the zipper. Raindrops pattered over the material and ran in rivulets off the shiny surface as she opened it up.

Lydia took the edge Nora held out to her, and they spread it over the body, pausing for a moment to let Lydia kiss her daddy's forehead before covering it. They anchored the sheet with their pretty rocks, then stood side by side examining their handiwork.

"That'll work until we get back," Lydia said. "It's pretty." She slipped her hand into Nora's and rested her head against Nora's arm. "I could wait here, to keep him company," she said.

Nora was so horrified at the thought she had to stifle a gasp. She squeezed Lydia's hand. "I couldn't leave you out here in the woods all by yourself. I mean, with only—"

"I know what you mean," Lydia said. "My daddy's dead. So he can't help me anymore if something bad happens."

"Yeah, baby, that's what I mean," Nora said, astonished at the girl's occasional precocious insights. "I can't let you stay, you know?"

Lydia nodded. "I know."

Nora squeezed her hand briefly and said, "Now, help me with one last thing." She'd thought of a use for the inexplicable tape. She retrieved the orange roll from the pack and worked the end loose with her thumb. "Here, take this," she said, handing the roll to Lydia and holding the loose end firmly. She stepped up to their fat cedar. "Now walk all the way around the tree two or three times. Then we'll tie a big bow."

"Cool idea," Lydia said. "Then we can find our way back to Daddy super easy." She circumnavigated the tree five times for good measure, only tripping twice on roots and rocks. She handed the roll, much diminished, back to Nora.

"Perfect," Nora said. She tore the tape loose from the roll and commenced knotting and bowing the ends. "How's that?" she asked when she'd finished.

"Perfect," Lydia echoed, with the same nod and emphatic tone Nora had used.

Nora smiled and stashed the tape back in the pack. "I guess we'd better get going, then," she said.

Lydia gazed at her father's silver shroud, fought off another round of tears and nodded with a trembling chin. Nora squeezed her hand once more, then struggled to pull her wet pack on over her wet clothing.

"Oh!" she had a sudden inspiration. "Lydia, we should take your daddy's wallet with us, if he has one. Then we can put his driver's license in the post box with the note." *Thank you, Abba, for putting that in my head before we left!*

"Is it in his back pocket, do you think?" Nora was reluctant to rummage through the man's clothing. She glanced at Lydia, who was clearly thinking through Nora's idea, figuring out why it made sense.

"No," Lydia said. "He keeps it in the side pocket when he wears those cargo pants. On this side." She knelt by her father's side, moved a striped rock out of the way, and extricated a worn leather wallet from the pleated side pocket of his pants. She handed it up to Nora and replaced the rock.

Nora opened the wallet and stared into the face of Elliot Bingham, who had a dimple in one cheek when he smiled. "Is your name Lydia Bingham?" Nora asked.

"Uh huh," she said. "Mommy's new last name is Camacho, but mine's still Bingham."

"I see," Nora said. She thought the chances of Lydia's name

changing to Camacho were pretty good now, but she kept that to herself. She slid his driver's license out and added it to the bag with the note before dropping it all back into her pack and working again to pull the straps on over her wet shirt. She snapped the hip belt.

"Ready?"

Lydia nodded. She knelt and put her hand on the shiny foil over her father's head and whispered, "'Bye, Daddy." Then she accompanied Nora back around the fat cedar and onto the trail.

After a delay she couldn't have conjured up in a nightmare, Nora was finally continuing on her way to the post box, with a newly fatherless, seven and three-quarters-year-old girl holding her hand.

Aftermath

"I don't feel too good," Bob said. "But I—"

"Okay, stay put, I'm calling a rescue." Lenny peered back through the van at Kit. "Are you injured, sir?" Kit shook his head carefully and Lenny turned away to make his call.

"Lenny's a great guy," Bob said, fumbling in his pocket for a pill tin. "Veteran—medic in the Army. Fifteen years on the police force." His voice was hoarse and a bit shaky. "Leads a young men's discovery group at a church down the road." He placed a small tablet under his tongue.

Kit nodded. He noted what Bob was doing, but didn't ask about the tablet. He turned to survey the chaos in front of the van. He unbuckled his seatbelt, taking care with his movements, unwilling to send another lightning bolt of pain down his spine.

Every synapse firing in his brain ordered him to exit the vehicle and run to the Land Cruiser, which is what the silver flash had turned into, and which now lay on its side on the middle of the intersection, its engine still rumbling. He needed to calm the two men shouting at each other in the far lane. He wanted to keep back the growing crowd of gawkers, and aid emergency personnel as they arrived.

His hands tightened into fists. He couldn't do any of that. He might not even manage to get out of the van without help. He dropped his head to his chest, got a grip on the impotent anger surging through him, and did his best to hand it over to God. Then he inhaled deeply and turned to the one person he could help.

"Bob? Tell me what's going on," he said.

"Oh, not too much," Bob said. "It's just my heart…"

"Your heart?" Kit's eyebrows shot up. "What do you mean?"

219

Bob waved down his concern. "Not that big of a deal, son," he said. "The doc told me last year I had a little heart trouble. Gave me some meds, told me to drop a few pounds." He stopped to catch his breath. "We didn't want to worry you all, we're just dealing with it."

Kit bit back the rebuke on the tip of his tongue. "I understand. I'm not sure Monti will."

"You're probably right. I knew from the beginning it was unwise to keep it from our kids." He turned to Kit, pleading for his understanding. "But I didn't want people to make a fuss." His shoulders sagged. "And honestly, it's not easy to admit you're failing. That you're getting old and frail for Pete's sake." He grimaced. "It's humiliating."

"Don't I know it," Kit said. "Believe me, Bob, I know that story from once upon a time to the bitter end."

"Bob?" Lenny reappeared in Bob's window. "The rescue will be here momentarily. But hey, there's a big fire on the other side of town and there's limited personnel heading this way." He pursed his lips. "Let me check you over? If you're stable and feeling okay, we can route the EMTs to the other injured folks. Whaddaya think?"

"Sure, sure," Bob said. "I took a nitro and I'm starting to feel better already, Lenny. You give me the okay and I'll head home as soon as we can get extricated here."

Lenny helped Bob out of the van and checked his friend over. Kit watched the familiar military medic routine from his seat. Lenny agreed Bob was stable and cleared him to leave, but they obviously wouldn't be extricated from the jammed-up intersection anytime soon.

Kit decided to survey the broader situation in the intersection from ground level. His door was jammed and he coaxed it open with an elbow shot that sent electric jolts into his neck. He waited for that to back off, then carefully climbed down, popped open his cane, and made sure of his balance before walking slowly around the front of the van.

He grimaced at the pain radiating from his spine, and at the smashed headlight and grill he glanced at on his way by. When he arrived at the driver's side, he was shocked to see a tiny red Geo in the left lane, a few feet behind the van.

"Bob, I'm gonna go check out the Geo," he said. "You okay?" Bob nodded, his eyes closed.

Kit went over and stooped to look inside the little car. A trembling boy sat with one hand still clamped to the steering wheel, a phone in the other.

"You all right, son?" Kit asked, resting one arm on the open window.

The boy started. He couldn't have been more than 17. "Uh...n-...yeah, I'm okay," he managed. He swallowed and implored Kit. "I don't know what to do," he said. "I've never been in an accident before. Well, not that I was exactly in this one, cuz you guys' van..." here he made a careening gesture describing how the Land Cruise had pin-balled off the van away from the Geo.

"But, I'm late for work, and I have to tell my dad—" he swallowed hard again but he was going to lose the fight against crying if he talked much more.

"Son, I know dads can be pretty strict, but I don't see that you had any control over what happened here. You think he's going to be upset with you anyway?"

"I—dunno. Maybe." He gulped. "My sister was supposed to drop me off and," he squeezed his eyes shut. "I talked her into letting me drop her instead."

"Okay, that was out of line, but you haven't damaged the car, so that might count for something." Kit tilted his head and thought for a second. "You want to get out of the car and take a couple of good breaths maybe? Calm down a bit, before you call him?"

The boy nodded tentatively. He fumbled around with the not-yet-familiar steps of putting the car in park and removing the key, then climbed out of the car.

"It's my mom's car," he said as Kit walked around to his side. "I don't really have permission to drive it by myself yet."

"Haven't had your license long?"

He shook his head. "I had to get my grades up first."

221

"Sounds like your parents have their heads on straight," Kit said. "They must love you a lot to set the bar high for you."

The boy tucked his chin and peered up at Kit, doubt written across his reddening face. "I guess."

"My name's Kit Rising," Kit stuck out his hand. The boy switched his keys to the other hand and shook Kit's awkwardly.

"Rafael Jackson," he said.

"Good to meet you, Rafael." Kit cleared his throat. "It's not my business, but a word of advice?" Rafael shrugged his consent.

"Tell your dad exactly what happened. Not that you won't get in trouble if you tell it straight; you probably will. But you're on a short leash, you want more freedom, more privileges, so you're building a foundation of trust, right?" The boy frowned, but nodded thoughtfully. "That's delicate work. You can screw it up easy. Sticking to the unvarnished truth might help minimize the damage you did today."

"Yeah?"

Kit nodded in his best 'wise father' manner. He glanced at the mess all around them. "Looks like it'll be a while before they get this cleared away. You have plenty of time to call and get things figured out with your dad and your boss. And if you need help of any kind, give a holler." He pointed out Bob, who was walking in their direction. "Mr. Housel here is local, and he knows that officer over there, so between them they can probably help with anything that comes up."

"Thanks, Mr. Rising," Rafael said. He leaned on his mom's car, and Kit could see the wheels turning as the boy started rethinking what to say to his dad.

Bob had his phone to his ear when Kit returned. "I'm calling Jody," he said. *Don't sit under the apple tree, with anyone else but me…* warbled in four-part harmony until she answered. He told her an understated version of the story, wincing at her exclamations in response, while Kit set off to tour the rest of the intersection.

Light bars flashed and stuttered. Sirens still sounded in the distance, but those on site had been silenced. Shards of plastic and broken safety glass spilled across the intersection like a nightmare

Milky Way, crunching under the boots of emergency personnel. Someone had shut the Land Cruiser's engine off. The Cruiser lay angled across both lanes, completely blocking traffic in both directions.

The other truck's hood had crumpled at an angle, and the front wheel on this side sat cocked oddly. Someone with reflective stripes on her vest was questioning its occupants. Uninvolved motorists hung out their car windows taking pictures and passersby stood with arms crossed watching the scene.

Kit turned in a slow circle. He narrowed his eyes as he looked at the angles. It took a minute to process, but when it did a shiver coursed down his tortured spine.

If Bob's old van had not been traveling three feet ahead of Rafael's Geo in the flow of traffic, the Land Cruiser would have obliterated the tiny car. He rested both hands on the top of his cane as his knees weakened. *Thank you, Lord, for your gentle mercies.*

He made his way back toward the van, weary and hurting. When he reached the Geo he slid one of his elder contact cards out of his wallet and offered it to Rafael. The boy was deep into an intense phone conversation, and barely glanced at Kit as he automatically accepted it and stuffed it in his pocket.

Bob was crouched in front of the van. The two of them examined the damage closely and concluded it wasn't drivable.

"We just have the one rig." Bob's normally cheery face was solemn and a bit gray. Kit wondered how they could possibly replace it on their meager retired missionary pension.

Bob called a tow truck but it would have to wait until the intersection was cleared before it could get to the van. Kit climbed back in, swallowed a pain pill, and called Monti while they waited, giving her his own brief outline of events so far. The girls would no doubt compare notes. Bob got in shortly after and sagged into his seat. They were too old for this crap, that was certain.

Another officer in reflective gear stopped by, and Bob and Kit both gave statements about what happened, although it had to all be on film from the intersection cameras and probably at least a couple of dash cams.

All told, it was over two hours before they climbed, sore and exhausted, into the extended cab of a rusty tow truck for the ride to Bob's mechanic. Bob texted Jody as they got underway and when they arrived at the shop she and Monti were waiting for them in a borrowed sedan.

The repair shop bore a striking resemblance to a small house, with worn toys strewn across the scraggly lawn and a side yard full of cars and parts. Kit recognized the signs of Bob helping a guy out.

While Bob and Jody spoke to the mechanic and his wife in fluent Spanish, Kit shifted to the sedan, where Monti had moved from shotgun to the back seat. He got in beside her and folded up his cane. She touched his cheek but didn't say anything, for which he was grateful. He wanted all this tedious business to be over, and to rest.

"Remind me to tell you about the Geo later," he said, his eyes closed, head leaned back.

"Okay," she answered, and rested her hand on his knee.

"And about Bob," he added.

"Okay," she said again, anxiety creeping into her voice. They waited in silence until Bob and Jody joined them and drove home.

Message Posted

Nora pictured the blurry blue line in her mind. She didn't want to expose the map to the rain again unless she had to, and there was little chance of getting lost if they stuck to the trail. There were two more forks in the path, but Nora had them memorized: right on the next fork, then left on the last one. She could always check the map if she forgot.

Nora shivered with cold and wondered if the girl felt it as badly as she did. "Doing okay?" she looked down at Lydia, still clutching her hand. This made it tricky on the narrow trail, but she didn't have the heart to make her let go.

"Yeah." Lydia's voice dripped with misery. The fleece hoodie was sopping wet, and Nora thought she heard Lydia's teeth chatter. Nothing she could do about that.

They plodded on. Intermittently one or the other of them remembered they were hurrying and picked up the pace. But it was hard to keep from reverting to a tired trudging, especially since the ground was uneven and did not reward speed.

They rounded a bend and Lydia gasped as she tightened her grip on Nora's hand. Nora looked up sharply. The girl pointed at a sleek doe and her spotted fawn, staring at them through the rain with big chocolate eyes, chewing nonchalantly.

"Ooh," Nora breathed. "They're beautiful, aren't they?"

"How come they don't run away?" Lydia whispered.

"I don't know, sweetie. Maybe they're used to seeing hikers."

"Do you think we could pet them?"

"Um, no, Lydia, I'm pretty sure they *would* run away if you tried that." Nora frowned. "I'm kind of surprised they're out in this rain.

I guess it's been raining for hours and hours now, though, so they probably got hungry."

"Look, they're right in a triangle," Lydia said.

"What?" Nora squinted. What was she talking about? "Oh! Oh my gosh, the next fork in the path!" The right fork, which they were meant to follow, was not as well-trod as the main trail that veered left. "I might have missed it," she said. She closed her eyes. *Again with the deer, Abba, thank you. And out of the mouths of babes...*

"Nora?"

"Yes, sweetie?"

"Why are you smiling like that?"

"Oh, I was just thanking God for putting the deer right in that triangle, so you'd notice them and then I'd notice the fork in the path. We're supposed to take this smaller trail here, see? But it's kind of overgrown, so I might not have seen it if we hadn't stopped to look at the deer."

The doe calmly turned away, her fawn high stepping it to follow her off into the brush and disappear into the trees as the girls watched.

"So a big beautiful deer did come to help me," Lydia said.

"She sure did," Nora agreed. "Come on, let's get going on our new path."

Lydia let go of Nora's hand and took the lead, peering ahead as if this new trail might reveal more treasures around the next bend. And well it might, Nora thought.

Despite the overgrown nature of the trail, they made good progress. Lydia seemed to have got a second wind, and was moving right along. Nora followed, keeping an eye out for the next fork. Once they got there, they couldn't be far from the post box. And the exertion of walking was keeping the cold at bay, just. They could make it.

The final fork was more obvious, and Nora stopped them for a moment at the Y.

"Hungry?" Lydia shook her head. "Want a drink of water?" No.

"Okay, let's keep going, then." She steered them to the left. Now the ground sloped gradually but steadily downward in front of them. The trail had dissolved into mud long ago, so they had to slow down and step carefully. Even so, they slipped and slid their way down the slope and landed on their rear ends a couple of times. They got muddy, but they weren't hurt beyond a little bruising.

"We're almost there, sweetie," Nora said. Lydia just nodded and kept watching where to put her feet. She was a trooper, that was for sure. They trudged on in silence, seeing no more deer or even pretty rocks, just wet trees, mud, and more wet trees. Eventually the ground leveled off, and Nora glanced ahead. Her heart skipped. That had to be the post box!

About fifty yards ahead, their trail appeared to end where it intersected with a deeply rutted dirt track. At the T, right in the middle of the trail, stood a wooden box mounted on a pole.

"Look, Lydia, there it is!" she said, pointing down the trail. Lydia looked up, and without a word picked up her pace. Nora scrambled to keep up with her, and before she knew it they had reached the destination Nora had been trying to get to since early this morning.

"We did it!" Nora said. She squatted down to hug Lydia, who wrapped her little arms around Nora's neck and kissed her on the cheek. Then, hand in hand, they took a moment to gaze at the long-looked-for post box. It was built like a big birdhouse, painted a fading yellow, with a steeply gabled black plywood roof, shiny with rain. But there was no hole in the side of the box to make any big birds feel welcome.

Lydia let go of Nora to walk clear around the box. "How do you get the message in?" she asked, pushing her sopping bangs back out of her eyes.

Nora took a closer look. "Here we go," she said. "See the roof? It's hinged in the middle." Nora raised one half of the roof, and they peered into the box.

A Motel 6 notepad, its paper all wavy and a bit mildewed from long exposure to damp, sat forlornly in the bottom. There was also a length of ball-chain secured to the inside wall, the other end of which was duct-taped to a pen cap. But no pen. Oh well, they'd be sticking with plan A, then.

Nora undid her hip belt and eased the pack to the wet grass at the side of the muddy trail. After this trip, she didn't care if she ever wore a backpack again. She unzipped it and pulled out the zipper bag.

"Ready?" she asked Lydia. For some reason, it felt like a ceremonial moment. Lydia nodded and held the lid open for her. Nora set the bag in the bottom of the box, and Lydia dropped the hinged roof.

They looked at each other and Lydia shrugged. "What now?"

Nora caught sight of the orange tape in her pack and grabbed it. "Let's make it unmistakable that there's a message in the box!" she said. She wrapped the tape around the box twice, tore it loose and made a floppy bow.

"Just like around the big tree," Lydia said.

"Yep. We have our own style going here, don't we?" She dropped the tape back in the pack. "How about a celebratory power bar?"

"What's sellabastory?"

"Um, like a little celebration. That we made it to the post box." Nora's cheeks got hot. She felt silly about it now.

"Okay," Lydia said. Nora handed her a bar and unwrapped another for herself. She handed Lydia a bottle of water too, and took several long drinks from her own. She wanted to sit down, but there wasn't anywhere remotely dry to sit, not that she wasn't completely wet already, and she was afraid she wouldn't get back up again if she did sit, anyway.

"I guess we should get going," she said, pulling on her backpack again.

Lydia nodded, and Nora could see she was crying again, in between bites of her power bar. Nora hugged her. "Sweet girl," she said. "You've been so brave, Lydia. The hardest parts are over, I think. Let's get you back to Barnabas' house, where you can have a good supper, and a bath, and settle in to wait for your Mom."

"My mom's coming?"

"Well," Nora said, taken aback by the intense yearning in the girl's voice, "She will, I'm sure, once whoever picks up the message reads it, sees your barrettes and your father's license, and figures out how to notify her. It might take a little while, though. Barnabas said his friend checks the box every two or three days, and then he'd have to make a bunch of phone calls probably." She smoothed Lydia's tangled hair away from her eyes. "But don't worry about all that, the grownups totally know how to do all that stuff. And when your mom is notified, I'm sure she'll come right away. You'll be safe with us at Barnabas' house until she gets there."

"Okay," Lydia said. She sniffed and wiped her eyes. "Let's go, then."

They turned their backs to the post box and started back up the trail. Nora glanced back once, noting with satisfaction the orange bow, a bright beacon in the dark, wet woods. She sent up a prayer, asking God to send Roland around sooner than later, and for him to understand what she was not able to explain in words, and that he or the Rangers or the police or whoever, would have no trouble finding Lydia's mom and getting her to Barnabas' house.

Then she concentrated on setting one foot in front of the other, because the hill was slippery, the day was waning, the rain fell as heavily as ever, and they had miles to go before they slept.

Subdued

Dinner was subdued. Monti did her best not to fuss overmuch, because Kit hated that. But her mom was in total mother hen mode, and her dad was not allowed to lift a finger for the rest of the evening. He did not protest. He didn't look well and Jody bustled him off to bed early.

Kit was obviously exhausted, and in more pain than usual. Though he graciously answered Jody's myriad questions, Monti could see it was taking a toll. Finally, she said, "Mom, I think maybe we can talk about it more tomorrow, if you need to, okay?"

Jody closed her mouth and folded her hands in her lap, her posture rigid. But she soon softened and said, "You're right, I'm sorry Kit. You need to rest, too." She stood and glanced toward their bedroom. "And actually, I think I'll turn in."

She was worried about Dad, Monti realized, but just as she opened her mouth to ask, Kit laid a gentle hand on hers and she reconsidered. Instead, she kissed her mother and hugged her soft shoulders. "Good night, Mom. Love you."

That left the four of them. Monti felt she should be thrilled at this little advance opportunity to practice their new nuclear family dynamics. But another look at Kit told her otherwise.

"Well kids, it's Kit and me up next for Scrabble, but I think we want to postpone that until tomorrow, don't you love?"

Kit just nodded, not even enough juice left for a witty reply. Noelle frowned at that but didn't say anything.

They kissed their girls goodnight and retired to their room. As they changed into their PJ's, Monti reminded Kit he was going to give her some news about her dad. When he told her about Bob's heart trouble, Monti took a minute to decide how upset to be.

She couldn't say she was shocked. Watching her dad and mom this evening, it was obvious there was a pre-existing 'something' going on. And she wasn't too surprised they hadn't told her.

Her father, especially, did not like the focus to be on him. He was the guy in the back row near the edge of every group photo. Probably worked harder than anyone else in the group, whatever it was, but he didn't care if no one knew that, and would certainly never blow his own horn. Even a horn of warning to his family that his health was deteriorating. And he'd ask Jody to keep it mum, too.

"Okay, I've decided not to fuss about that," she said. "I guess he is 85, so heart trouble isn't a huge shock. I think I would've been more shocked if they'd made a big family announcement, or even mentioned it casually. Not like them."

"Good girl," was all Kit said.

"But what about this Geo?" Monti asked.

"Oh, yes, Rafael," Kit said. He told her the story of the lime green monster van giving its life to protect the tiny Geo and its disobedient occupant.

Monti covered her mouth, cringing, thinking of what could have happened. "Do his parents know? How close he came?"

"No idea," Kit said. "I can't imagine him volunteering that information. I'm not even sure he realizes it at this point, but it may sink in later." He carefully arranged himself on the bed, adjusting spine and pillow. "I gave him my card," he said. "Probably won't hear from him again, but you never know. Seemed like a promising kid."

"You think all kids are promising," she said.

He nodded his agreement. "They generally are. With a an exception here and there."

"Yeah, like the ones who burn threatening words in your lawn, for example." Monti slid into the sheets beside him. "Well, no one was badly hurt, right? That's the main thing."

"Maybe. Maybe the main thing is that a few people were shaken up, and now have an opportunity to pause and think about what their lives are about."

"True," Monti said, rolling toward Kit to kiss him good night.

"You've always been great at seeing the big picture."

***

They had a family pow wow the next day. The Housels apologized for keeping them in the dark about Bob's heart condition. They rehashed the accident, incorporating added details from the morning paper. No serious injuries. Unlicensed, impaired driver in the Land Cruiser. "That sounds disturbingly familiar," Monti said. "How many Mike Rutherfords are out there wreaking havoc in our streets?"

"More than you want to know about, Mom," Marla assured her. They took a few minutes to thank God for sparing Kit and Bob and everyone else involved from grievous harm.

Bob and Kit took the borrowed sedan to go consult with the mechanic. Were they going to pay a huge repair bill or find a new van? That question was weighing on Bob, and he needed more information.

Jody continued churning out cookies and nut breads, and then recruited the girls to help her deliver them through the neighborhood while Monti burned up her spanking new laptop keyboard, building chapter after chapter.

The men returned with tentative good news about the van. It was going to take a while and a pile of money, but Jorge thought he could put it back on the road for them one more time. They also brought steaks for the grill, and the holiday spirit began regathering its lost steam.

After the steak dinner, Kit and Monti played their first game against each other since the house burned down. Back in Idaho their new, mysteriously delivered Scrabble board sat in their apartment still wearing its cellophane shrink wrap.

Her girls cheered her on, but Monti found herself distracted and unable to string together more than a twenty-point word the whole game, even though she drew the J, the Z, the K, two S's and both blanks.

"I don't think that was your best game, lover," Kit said as they slid the tiles back into the bag.

"No. I guess not. That's all right though, it means you get to play Mom tomorrow. You'll enjoy that."

"You can demand a rematch when we get back home," Noelle said. "Then we'll see." She kissed Monti on the cheek, then her phone chirped. She peeked at the screen and skipped outside to take the call.

Jody raised her eyebrows at Monti. "Nick," Monti guessed. She was proved right a few minutes later when Noelle floated, pink cheeked, back into the house.

"Was that Nick?" she asked.

Noelle gazed at her, uncomprehending.

"Who was on the phone, sweetie?" she tried again.

"Uh huh," Noelle replied. "Sorry, did you need me?"

"Is this normal?" Marla asked Monti, a divot of concern between her eyes.

"Not really," Monti replied. "But we haven't had a lot of…romance…events so far, so I'm not intimately familiar with the symptoms."

Kit waved Noelle over to his chair and indicated she should sit. "Nellie."

"Yes, Grandpa?"

"Are you with us?" His eyes twinkled as he strove to keep a straight face.

"Sure, what do you mean?"

"We were just wondering who might've been on the other end of the line, during your most recent outdoor phone conversation."

That cut through her haze, and she blushed furiously. "Nick," she said.

"We figured," Kit said, sproinging one of her long curls. "But you don't normally go far, far away after a chat with Nick, so what's up?"

"Well," she began. "Well, there's a fancy party. Or a dance, I'm not sure what they call it, something at his parents' club."

Monti and Marla perched quietly nearby, not wanting to spook the shy creature.

"Yes?" Kit prompted.

"Uh huh," she said. "And Nick says he misses me tons and doesn't want to be pals anymore and will I go with him." She looked at Marla. "Mom? Will you help me pick out a dress? I need a ball gown." Her voice squeaked on the last word and she clasped her hands tightly, grinning from ear to ear.

A needle of jealousy pricked Monti's heart. She shut her eyes and gave internal orders to stop that nonsense immediately. Marla *should* help her daughter pick a dress, and Monti was truly, deeply grateful she was home now so she could do that.

"Uh...sure, honey," Marla said. "I'd love to help you pick a dress." She slid her eyes sideways to Monti for help.

"When is the party?" Monti asked, smiling at her girls.

"New Year's Eve," Noelle said. "Eek! That's only nine days away!" She jumped up. "Rats! I saw the most gorgeous, floaty, ocean green gown at that little consignment shop Monday. GG, which one was that?"

Marla raised a finger. "Do you still like pink? I remember one at the Hospice shop."

"Of course," Noelle said. "Pink rules! But green is lovely, too. Ooh, can we go back tomorrow?" She clasped her hands again and implored Jody with big eyes.

"Oh yes, of course we can!" Jody said. "One of them is bound to still be available. Or we'll find another one. We'll go first--" She stopped abruptly. "Rather, you girls should go first thing in the morning. I think I'd better stay home with Bob this time."

"No, no, no," Bob said. "I'm fine. You drop us off at the rent-a-dent place, Jody. We need to find some temporary wheels while the van's in the shop. Lucy's gonna need her car back."

"But Bob, maybe you should rest a couple—"

"Jody." Bob looked at her with a scowl somewhere between stern and sad. "Please don't. I'm fine, and you know I'll *be* fine. Unless I'm not, and then that's fine, too!"

What could she say to that? Monti couldn't wait to hear, but her mom didn't object further. It was apparently case dismissed. She did get up and go kiss him on the cheek. "As you wish, love."

Marla, meanwhile, was on task. "You'll need shoes, too. And a little purse, maybe?"

"What about a flower for your updo?" Jody asked, and with this the strategy session was off and running. Bob and Kit escaped to the screen porch.

Pain

Rain. Mud. Trees. Rain. Mud. Trees.

Nora was sure she'd never done anything in her life but slog up and down this miserable trail in the pouring rain.

Wasn't it ever going to stop? Even the terror of Logan's injury and their night in the forest seemed like a memory from the distant dry past, slightly improbable.

Lydia's pace had slowed after her initial spurt of energy after the post box. Nora kept checking behind her as they climbed the slope, scared to let her get too far behind. She'd make sure Lydia was in front for the next section.

Finally they made it to the top of the slope, and were on level ground again. Then she had to keep an eye out for the forks in the trail, which would look different from this direction, and she wasn't good at that.

Logan had been shocked one time when they'd wandered through a city park for an hour and she got completely turned around. All the way back to their car, she never knew which way they should turn every time there was a choice. Logan had some kind of compass in his head, apparently, but she sure didn't.

She turned her head to check on Lydia again, and caught her foot over a root. She went flying and a lightning bolt of pain shot up her leg as she fell. She stifled a howl of pain as well as she could as she lay writhing on the muddy ground, holding her leg, gritting her teeth.

"Nora! What's wrong, Nora?" Lydia scrambled, tripping herself and reaching Nora on hands and feet. "Are you hurt?"

"Yes," Nora answered through clenched teeth, tears leaking from eyes squeezed shut. "Twisted my ankle." She tried to catch her breath. "I'll be okay, baby, but it huuurts."

She rocked back and forth, keening and waiting for the first intense agony to back off. Lydia patted Nora's head whenever it came her way and made soothing noises. Then it was too much and the girl cried too.

"Oh, honey, don't cry," Nora said, trying to stop writhing. "I'm okay, really. It just hurts." She held Lydia's hand and focused on breathing. She mustn't send her into a panic. Relax. Breathe.

After an eternity the pain became bearable and she sat up in the mud. She forced herself to pull up her jeans leg and look at the ankle. It was already swelling. She dropped her head to her knees. What was she going to do now? Rest, Ice, Compression and Elevation, right? She grunted out a laugh.

"Nora?" Lydia's eyes were round, and her lip trembled.

"It's okay, baby," Nora said, and cupped the little girl's cheek. "I have to think for a minute, okay?" She struggled to get out of her backpack straps. "Can you find the first aid kit for me?"

Lydia hurried to open the pack, and found the kit right away. She handed it to Nora and waited for further direction.

"Thank you." Nora opened the kit, hoping for painkillers and an ACE bandage. Thank God, she scored on both counts. "Hand me one of the water bottles?" Nora tore open the packet of tablets and swallowed them down with a gulp of tepid water. "You want the rest?" she offered the bottle to Lydia, who shook her head, so she closed it up and tossed it back in the backpack.

Nora gingerly touched her throbbing and now very puffy ankle. "Okay, now I have to wrap this, then we can keep going." She extracted the bandage from the kit and handed that back to her helper.

To distract herself from the pain, she went into teacher mode. "I learned in school that if you sprain your ankle, you should remember RICE."

"Rice?" Lydia scrunched up her nose.

Nora wound the bandage around her ankle and shoe, not daring to take the shoe off for fear she'd never get it back on. "It's an acronym. It stands for Rest, Ice, Compression, and Elevation."

"We haven't got any ice," Lydia said.

Nora laughed. "Right. Plenty of water but no ice. Also, I can't exactly rest until we get back to Barnabas' house."

"I don't know the other words you said."

"Compression," she gasped, having unwisely flexed her foot while wrapping. "Means to compress, to wrap it tightly, like I'm doing right now."

"And your shoe, too?"

Nora explained why she was doing that. "And elevation means to keep it lifted up, like on a footstool or something."

"No footstool either," Lydia said. "One out of four."

"Right. We're not doing too well on RICE, huh?" Nora said. Lydia shook her head. Nora finished the wrap and secured it with the little metal hook thingy, wincing as she pulled it sideways to anchor it.

She sat back and examined her somewhat muddy handiwork, the bandage already darkening with rain. "So, I've done the one thing I can do. We'll just have to go slow, and I'll take care of the other three when we get home."

"And I can help you, Nora. I can carry the backpack."

Nora thought about it for a second. It wasn't heavy with its daytrip-only load. "Sure, sweetie, that'd be great. That'll be a big help." She zipped up the pockets and shortened the shoulder straps, then motioned for Lydia to turn around. They got her buckled in, no problem.

"Now, I need to stand up. Can I lean on you for that?"

Lydia nodded, stood up and leaned a shoulder down for Nora to grab. Nora got her right foot under her, gripped Lydia's shoulder, and hauled herself up. She tentatively set her left foot on the ground but changed her mind instantly when searing pain shot up her leg. She swallowed back tears and said, "Um, I think I'm gonna need a stick or something, to use like a cane or a crutch."

She let go of Lydia's shoulder and gripped a wet sapling leaning into the path. "I can't put any weight on the hurt leg."

"Okay, I'll find you one," Lydia said, and immediately started scouting for a stick. Nora marveled at her. She was cool under pressure. She'd make a great nurse. Or firefighter. Or senator.

"Don't go too far, sweetie. Stay where you can see me."

"Okay," Lydia called, stomping fearlessly through the undergrowth off the side of the muddy trail. "How about this?" She strained to heft one end of a downed sapling.

"Maybe a bit smaller," Nora hid a smile. "So I can lift it easier."

"This one?" She held aloft a tall, skinny doghair pine that had been dead for a while. She was afraid it might be brittle, but she didn't have a lot of choices. Or a lot of time to find the perfect staff.

"Good, Lydia, let's try that one."

Lydia stomped back over to her and presented her ten-foot-long treasure. The bark was sloughing off in big hunks, and it looked like it would shred the rest of the skin from Nora's palms in short order. She winced in anticipation and wished she had her hoodie back. Oh! "Hey Lydia, would you mind if I wrapped your shirt around this rough wood to protect my hands?" She held out her gouged hands to her.

"Ow! Sure, Nora, I'll...I mean here, you can get it." She turned her back to Nora and Nora dug the wet shirt out of the pack. She was going to have to buy the girl a new pink shirt after this. It was going to be destroyed.

"Thanks, that'll be just right," Nora said, and tossed it over her shoulder. "Now, If I can break off some of this length, please Abba," she breathed as she exerted all her meager strength to bend and break the pole. A loud crack of success astonished them both.

"You did it!" Lydia said. "You're really strong!"

"Well, not usually," Nora said. "I think God helped me."

"I heard you ask Abby..." Lydia said, confusion in her voice.

"No," Nora giggled. "I said *Abba*. That's a name for God that means Father, or Daddy."

Lydia's face sagged, then crumpled into tears as her new daddy-less reality punched her in the heart again.

"Oh sweetheart, come here," Nora beckoned to her, and gathered her into her arms, working hard not to topple over and drop them both back into the muck of the trail. "I'm so sorry, baby." Nora held her while she cried it out again. After a couple of minutes Lydia sniffed hard and swiped a muddy hand across her grimy face.

"We better go," she said in a small voice. "I'm cold."

A spasm of dread shivered through Nora and made her knees wobbly. She glanced around and noticed the changing light. They might not have a lot of light left.

"You're right, we'd better go," Nora agreed. She quickly wrapped Lydia's shirt around the broken tree and knotted the sleeves to secure it. Better than nothing. "Ready?" She lay her hand on Lydia's head, took a deep breath, and set about learning how to walk with her makeshift staff.

Instantly it became clear this was going to be much, much harder than she'd thought. First, the end of the stick sank into the mud each time she leaned on it. It was impossible to avoid touching her hurt foot to the ground, and each time she did pain shot up her leg. She found she had to grip the top of the staff with both hands, putting as much weight as possible on it as she hopped forward one short step on her good foot.

When she accidentally kicked the staff with her left foot she choked on a scream and almost blacked out. After twenty feet she was exhausted.

No. I can't be exhausted. They had far too much trail ahead of them, and far too little daylight. She had to do this. And anyway, what other option was there? Lie down in the mud and give up? She had a couple of ideas, though.

"Lydia, we're going to have to fix up the stick a little. Turn round again."

The girl faced away from her and Nora fetched out a water bottle and the orange tape. "Want a drink? I have to dump this water out."

Lydia took a drink and handed the bottle back to her. Nora took a sip too, and poured the last swallow out. She leaned on a tree, brought up the bottom end of the stick, and crammed it into the bottle. Then she crumpled the bottle, smashing it up against the wood, and secured it with most of the rest of the engineer tape. She pushed it heavily to the ground and it didn't sink at all. "Okay, that works. Now, can you do something really important for me?"

Lydia stepped close to examine her handiwork. "Yeah?" she looked up at Nora with red eyes.

"I really need you to count my steps for me. If you'll tell me when I've gone ten steps, then I'll rest for just a second. Then we'll go another ten and rest, like that, again and again. Okay?"

"Sure, Nora. I'll count and you walk, poor baby." She hugged Nora's waist and patted her wet back. Tears pricked at the back of Nora's eyes.

"Thank you," she whispered.

They set off. The next fifty steps were excruciating as Nora learned what not to do, figured out her balance and how best to use the stick.

It gradually got easier, and she noticed when the medicine, whatever it was, kicked in. The shocks of pain were not quite so brutal after that. She considered letting Lydia off counting, but any measure of progress was precious at this point, and keeping their focus there would help them not to dwell on worse things.

"I'm starting to get used to it," Nora said. "How about every fifty steps for a rest? You can count to fifty, right?"

"Of course I can!" Lydia was offended. "I can count to a thousand. Even by twos. Or fives."

"Wow, that's amazing," Nora said. "But I don't think I can walk a thousand steps without a rest yet."

"Okay, I'll count to fifty then," she said, and they settled into the new rhythm. The drone of Lydia's voice counting aloud, the effort required for each step, the long, long day...Nora felt her eyelids getting heavy.

That was ridiculous! She couldn't fall asleep standing up. Her dad used to talk about soldiers falling asleep on the march, but she'd bet they didn't have sprained ankles. Why couldn't she keep her eyes open? Maybe the medicine?

"Nora?"

Lydia's voice startled her. "Yes, sweetie?" She turned her head to look at the girl. She had stopped walking. "What's wrong?"

"Isn't that where we were supposed to turn? On the fork?" She gestured off to the side.

"Is it?" Nora's heart thumped with adrenaline. She maneuvered to face back the way they'd come. Yes, facing this way, it did look like where they'd taken the left fork. They should've turned right there. "I think you're right, Lydia, thank you for being so observant. I missed it completely."

"That's okay," she said with a shrug, and led the way on to the correct path.

The light was fading by the minute. *I'm going to get us lost in the woods. In the dark.* Fear twisted her stomach and weakened her grip on the staff. But she looked at the little girl trudging on ahead of her.

Soaking wet, her hair tangled, Nora's filthy and over-sized hoodie sagging off her tiny limbs, her daddy lying shot to death in the forest. If Lydia could keep going and not dissolve into a puddle of blubbering fear, then so could she.

"This way," Lydia said with confidence and angled them left at the next fork, which Nora again had not seen.

"Good job, kiddo! Only a little creek to cross and one more fork now, then just follow the path to the clearing and we'll be home."

Tapping at the back of Nora's mind though, was the knowledge that their next landmark was really a giant cedar wrapped with orange engineer tape.

Floating

"You know, your daughter is an amazing young woman," Monti said, slipping her arm through Marla's. "She's had three old ladies grilling her all day about Nick and the party and the dress code and the venue and everything else, and she just keeps answering. And smiling."

"And floating a couple inches off the ground," Marla added. "She told me about Nick the other day, but she didn't mention she was head over heels."

"She may have only recently discovered that," Monti suggested. "There's that moment, you know, when you suddenly realize that this is what everybody means when they talk about being in love."

Marla nodded thoughtfully as they strolled back to the car. Noelle glided ahead of them, an exquisite, filmy pink gown in a dry cleaner's bag draped daintily over her arms. Jody carried a sack with a matching pink satin clutch and neon-orange sequined sandals that Noelle assured them were perfect with the dress.

Monti thought of the fox stole Kit had given her on their tenth anniversary. How she longed to bring it out of her closet, drape it around Noelle's shoulders and watch her rub her cheek on the soft fur. Monti had rarely worn it, but it would've been perfect with this gown. Her heart ached to think of it burnt up and gone.

Monti wiped her eyes. Marla's eyes were damp too, as she watched her daughter, and Monti hugged her arm. "Nick's a very nice boy," she said. "I'm glad they're taking it to the next level."

"Nellie told me he sings in the chorale with her at school."

"Mm-hm. And helps her with her AP math. And generally manages to be wherever she is a great deal of the time, without ever being obnoxious about it." Monti smiled. "Your dad likes him."

"That's good," Marla said. "Because he's bound to be around even more now, and if Dad didn't approve then *he* would get obnoxious…"

"He has that capacity, true," Monti agreed. Before they climbed into the car, Marla touched her elbow.

"Actually, Mom,' she said so quietly Monti had to strain to hear. "I *don't* know that moment. The one about being in love." She glanced at Monti, her cheeks aflame.

Once again Monti's heart twisted with grief for her daughter. She had missed so much that Monti took for granted. "Oh baby girl," she choked out, and gave her a quick squeeze. "It's not too late. Maybe God will send someone your way yet."

Marla shook her head, her multi-colored hair falling across her face. "I doubt it," she said. "But, I'm very, very happy that Noelle is experiencing it."

"Me too," Monti whispered, and kissed Marla on the cheek before climbing into her seat. She decided not to pursue the subject with her, but she mentally added 'true love for Marla' to her prayer list. You never knew what delightful gifts God might see fit to give. And in her experience, asking for them was quite effective.

Monti pondered. The time might be approaching to share with her daughter the circumstances surrounding their own family's beginning. Maybe. They'd never lied to Marla about anything, but they also had never gone into any detail regarding Kit's out-of-the-blue proposal. She'd talk it over with Kit. No sense opening that rusty old can of worms if it would do more harm than good.

When the ladies arrived home, satisfied by their successful quest, a worn maroon minivan sat in the driveway. Dented, as advertised. Jody peeked through the window and shrugged her acceptance before following the others into the house.

After they took off their shoes and downed tall glasses of sweet tea in the mercifully cool air conditioning—the AC in the borrowed car functioned only sporadically and they were all sweating—the gown had to be tried on and shown to the G's.

The men oohed and aahed with genuine appreciation, though they looked as if they could not quite believe that the dazzling vision in pink chiffon was the same little curly-haired girl they knew and loved.

Noelle handed her phone to Marla, requesting pics. Her friends had to see her dress sooner than later, and she wanted to show Nick to be sure it was appropriate for the occasion. She giggled at his immediate response, but wasn't inclined to share any details.

"Two more days," Jody said after the gown had been carefully packed away. "I can't believe it's gone by so fast."

"Now, Jody," Bob said. "It's a week more than you were supposed to get, remember? Don't be greedy." Then he sighed and added, "but another week would be good."

"You know, Dad," Monti said. "It just popped into my head that you told us you had plans for Christmas. That first day, remember, in the hospital?"

"Oh well, that's water under the bridge now," he said, waving it away.

"It was just dinner with the Blalocks," Jody said. "Absolutely no big deal. Melissa has already replaced us with a single mom and her three teenage kids. Bless her heart, she'll need ten times as much food. Those boys are on the football team." She looked around for her notebook, muttering, "I'd better take her a few dozen more cookies tomorrow."

That evening Jody made a big show of the set up for her moment-of-truth game against Kit. He won handily, but the defeat rolled right off her feathers.

"I think Kit should play Marla on Christmas Day," she said. "Full circle back to the beginning. She came close to beating me, and she should get chance to defeat the champion."

Marla and Kit squinted at each other in their best Wild West gunslinger imitations, and it was a plan.

Prince

Nora saw the tree when it was some distance ahead but didn't say anything. Lydia's gait faltered when she saw it. Was this going to be too much for her?

Lydia turned to face Nora. "Can we stop and say goodnight to Daddy? And let him know some people are going to come help us?"

Nora swallowed hard and said, "Sure, sweetie. Let's do that." Lydia high stepped her way over to the tree. If they hadn't previously stomped down the path somewhat, Nora couldn't have managed it with her injured ankle. As it was, by the time she caught up Lydia was kneeling in the mud beside the mylar-shrouded form of her father.

Some wise instinct in the little girl had kept her from uncovering his face, for which Nora was grateful. She couldn't imagine the shock his increasingly-dead face would have inflicted in Lydia's fragile state.

"Abba, please take good care of my daddy until the people come to help him," she was saying. Praying, Nora realized. "And help Nora walk on her poor hurt leg all the way to Barney's house." Nora smiled in spite of it all, leaning on the tree, resting her tortured hands. Lydia was such a little darling. How horrible that such a dreadful thing should happen to such a sweet child. *To any child.* No child should have to experience grief or pain. But every single one did.

She shook the thought out of her head. She couldn't dwell on that today. *Someday, Abba, you're going to set it all right. Please do that soon. And meanwhile, help us get through this.*

By the time Lydia got to her feet, eyes brimming with tears, the light was failing. They made it back to the trail, but then Nora stopped them. "We need the flashlight, sweetheart," she said, and motioned for Lydia to turn round. Nora dug it out of the pack. "You'll have to carry it, okay? Just keep pointing it at the trail in front of us."

She switched it on and handed it to Lydia, who took it without comment. She dutifully pointed it ahead of them, and they set off again. Lydia didn't resume counting and Nora didn't remind her.

The rain shooting through the beam of light was surreal. The light bounced around dizzyingly as Lydia negotiated the rough trail. The combination made Nora a bit woozy. She really needed to concentrate on where she was putting the staff and her foot, which she could now barely see. She didn't want to endure the agonizing pain that would result from a fall.

She kept at it. Carefully place the staff. Lean her weight on it. Hop forward. Repeat. Repeat. Repeat forever.

"Nora!" Lydia squeaked, and the beam of light abruptly swung around and hit Nora in the eyes. She threw up an arm and closed her eyes, heart suddenly hammering.

"What? What's wrong?" she asked.

Lydia stood practically on Nora's feet and gripped her shirt. "I saw eyes," she whispered, her own as big as an owl's.

"You did?" Nora gulped. "What kind of eyes?"

"I don't know," she said, her voice trembling. "They were shiny. Greeeen."

"Okay, don't worry," Nora said, her own voice just as trembly. *Wolf?* She took the flashlight from Lydia and aimed it at the path ahead of them.

"No," Lydia whispered. "Higher."

"Higher?" Nora shot her a glance, alarm tightening her chest. Lydia nodded.

Nora gulped again and moved the beam of the flashlight back onto the path, then slowly raised it until two emerald green orbs shone back at her through the rain, from above her own eye level.

She suffered a brief spasm of panic, and then peace flooded through her. Peace that she recognized from just a few days and a lifetime ago. She angled the light higher, revealing a majestic rack of wet, velvety antlers.

"It's all right, baby," she said. "It's the beautiful deer."

"It is?" Lydia stood beside her, gazing at the green eyes. "Did he come to help us?"

"I guess so," Nora said. "I think we should follow him."

As if he understood them, the buck chuffed and stamped a hoof. He flicked one large ear, then made his trademark turning leap and set off walking away from them.

Nora handed the flashlight back to Lydia and motioned for her to follow him. Nora found it wasn't difficult to keep up with them. Her ankle hurt fiercely, but the deer's presence energized her as it had before. Still, she thought he must be walking very slowly. And why not? Why would Abba send a magical guide she couldn't follow? But why had he sent him at all? They were doing okay on their own, weren't they?

She glanced up and saw that Lydia had the light trained on the buck's rump, a black tipped tail in a blazing white oval shining in the complete darkness.

"How come the mama deer didn't come?" Lydia asked. Nora blinked and frowned in thought.

"I don't know. Maybe it was time for her baby to go to sleep, and she had to stay with him."

There was no reply to this. *Do all children ask such wondrous questions?* Perhaps Lydia was exceptional. Well, clearly she was exceptionally brave and tenacious, anyway. Lydia stumbled and recovered ahead of her.

"Are you okay, sweetie?"

"Uh huh, I'm all good," the girl said, not turning around. "What do you think his name is?"

"The deer? Um, I don't know if he has a name."

"Do you think it's okay if I call him Prince?"

"Like Bambi's dad? Sure, sweetie, I think that's a good name for him."

"Yeah, since we don't know what his real one is." She trudged on, following the magical wild deer, Prince.

Nora smiled and shook her head. She wanted to take Lydia home with her, give her a bath, comb out her long hair, read her stories and watch her grow up.

But first she wanted to sit down. Or lie down. Oh, to soak in Barnabas' hot springs! Then have a cup of his healing tea. Then sleep for twelve hours. That was good motivation to pick up her pace.

She glanced upward. Was the rain slackening at last? But just as she thought that the sound of rain through the trees pulsed louder, and fat drops splatted on her upturned face. She sighed. It was never going to stop.

After an eternity of slogging silently through the mud, following a small, grimy girl, a wildly bouncing light beam and an inexplicable deer, she was startled when Lydia stopped abruptly in front of her. Nora nearly lost her balance and had to grab the girl's shoulder to keep from falling.

"Sorry, baby, why did you stop?" Nora said.

"Prince is gone," Lydia said.

"What? Weren't you looking at him the whole time?"

"Uh huh," she said. "But then he was just...gone," By the sound of her voice, Lydia was about to burst into tears. Nora patted her shoulder and gently took the flashlight from her.

"Let me look," she said. She maneuvered past the girl and labored on down the trail, scanning with the flashlight to the right and left, back to—she froze. "Lydia, look!" she called back over her shoulder. Lydia hurried to join her, and Nora shone the light straight ahead. The trees opened up into the clearing. She had an irrational desire to shout, 'the meadow!' and go prancing out.

But...wait, shouldn't the house be directly in front of them on the other side of the clearing?

Where was Barnabas' house?

Christmas

Twin girls holding heaping baskets of white candles greeted them at the door. The girls, wearing matching red taffeta dresses and dimpled smiles, gave a candle in a paper collar to each person coming into the softly lit sanctuary. A rail-thin teen boy handed out songbooks. Carols played softly in the background as the Risings and Housels found their seats for the Christmas Eve service.

In one front corner a satin and sequined banner proclaimed, "Christ is Born!" In the other corner stood a fragrant fir aglow with white and gold Chrismon ornaments. Monti drew in a long breath, drawing the wild forest scent deep into her lungs. It smelled like home.

She looked around, admiring the transforming effect of thousands of tiny white lights twinkling in graceful swoops throughout the little storefront church. Jody and the Lost Boys had hung them just today.

Monti and her family smiled and nodded, murmuring "Merry Christmas" to those arriving and filling the seats around them. The room was at capacity by ten minutes to seven, but people kept filing in. By the time the pastor stepped behind his pulpit the walls were lined with people willing to stand through the service.

For Monti, the goosebumps started immediately after the pastor's welcome, with the opening a Capella notes of *Let All Mortal Flesh Keep Silence*. *O Come, O Come Emmanuel*, one of her favorites, intensified the solemn but exalted mood of anticipation.

They sat back down while a small Chinese woman walked to the front. She filled the room with a glorious *O Holy Night*, and Monti wasn't the only one to pull out a handkerchief.

The children's choir brought them smiling back to earth by

singing *Away in a Manger*, directed by the young worship leader. Then the congregation got to sing all the best carols from the two millennia since Jesus' birth, interspersed with Scripture readings.

Monti's heart leaped when the Lost Boys quartet moved to the front. They sang *I Heard the Bells on Christmas Day*, and she had to retrieve the handkerchief she'd stashed earlier.

Finally, Pastor Blalock encouraged them to take Christmas seriously and to pray without ceasing for the troubled world around them, but to never forget that the true King has come, and though there will likely be some hard times before he comes again to put all things right, we can know the wonders of his love right now.

They stood one last time and belted out *Joy to the World* with everything they had left.

As everyone waited for the youth group to shift the configuration of the chairs from "church" to "fellowship and refreshments", Kit said in Monti's ear, "I don't believe I remember a finer Christmas Eve service anywhere."

Monti nodded. She and Kit had been to, oh, probably forty Christmas Eve services since they were married, but she had to agree. This was the best. Her parents were part of a live-wire little church all right.

They ate peppermint fudge and Chex mix and drank cider. They thanked the children for their lovely singing, and congratulated the Lost Boys on their great song. The Chinese woman was nowhere to be seen, and when Monti asked her mother, Jody told her she'd had to rush out to start her night shift in the ER. "But I sent a box of goodies with her for her crew," she said.

Of course she had.

***

Christmas morning required more tissues than Monti had anticipated, but most of it was just delightful.

Her mother had picked out earrings for all of her girls, "Because a pretty bauble does a woman's heart good sometimes, you lost all of your baubles."

"I always thought they'd lost their marbles," Kit said. Noelle and Marla threw pillows at him.

Monti had stuck to consumables for her folks, as there was not room for a single permanent addition to any shelf or cupboard in their tiny house. But mango chutney and ghost pepper hot sauce would perk up her parents' suppers for weeks.

The tissues came out when Bob presented Marla and Noelle each with a leather-bound study Bible. "Better than any flashlight for lighting your way," he quipped. The girls kissed him and hugged each other.

"We could do a study together, Mom…if you want," Noelle said, blushing.

Marla swallowed hard and wrapped her arms around her daughter again. "Sure, baby, that'd be great. Let's do it."

Then the girls opened Kit and Monti's gifts to them. A Kindle for each, and a gift card to put some books on the digital shelves. "You'll need to pick out a laptop when we get home," Kit said, "but this is for fun. And so we won't have to draw in quite so many bookshelves on the new house plans."

"And those new Kindles have Wi-Fi," Monti said. The girls oohed their appreciation and that took care of entertainment for the rest of the day, as mother and daughter explored their e-readers, showed each other each new discovery, and shopped for books to load.

The grands and great-grands smiled on, not without some device envy, but joyously soaking up the giggles and the growing camaraderie evident between Marla and Noelle. Monti passed the day in a state of near euphoria, and her usual 'waiting for the other shoe to drop' unease was almost completely absent.

They ate Christmas dinner pretty early, and then Kit and Monti decided they'd better start packing, as their flight left early the next morning.

The hauling out of suitcases put long faces on Bob and Jody, but Monti found herself looking forward to getting back home and picking up the threads of their lives. And to weaving in a bright new thread named Marla. Her stomach fluttered at the thought.

She'd imagined it so often, and had tried to disentangle the dream from her heart so many times. She could scarcely make herself believe that they were actually going to do it.

The fantasies had all been set in her dear bungalow, but that detail didn't matter now. Marla was coming home with them. Tomorrow.

At sunset the board was set up with some ceremony, for who knew when there would be a similar occasion.

Marla drew an E to win first draw, and with an admirable poker face showed her opening rack to Monti. Monti did her best, but she did not have an admirable poker face at her disposal, and the sight of QENSS and both blanks on Marla's rack was hard to absorb in a neutral manner.

Kit eyed her suspiciously. "No kibitzing," he growled.

"I don't think that's going to be necessary, Dad," Marla said, shuffling her tiles around.

"Though kibitzing certainly has been allowed up to now," Monti said, trying not to laugh while pretending to be offended. "It's just a game, right love?"

Kit grunted, hiding his one-corner smile that was so like Marla's, and Monti knew it was going to be a great game. Marla snapped all seven tiles onto the board and said, "That's a U and an I for the blanks. My dad always told me that if you have an S and both blanks, you should be able to get a 50-point bonus," Marla said, her eyes sparkling. "So *two* esses and both blanks practically played itself. SEQUINS for 98 points."

"And the Q didn't hurt," Kit grumbled, but the corner of his mouth kept twitching and he gave up trying to hide the smile. "Great play, daughter."

"And what a great word, SEQUINS!" Jody said. "Hey you two, you should do all Christmas words."

Marla and Kit snorted in unison, which set everyone off. It took a few minutes (and a delicate blotting of the board) before play could resume.

Kit reused Marla's Q. The lead shifted back and forth. Kit got a 50-point bonus and Marla another. Monti had forgotten the competitive streak the two of them brought out in each other. The friendly tension grew thicker and thicker until Kit played his last three tiles at once. He won by a hair, only because Marla still held the K at the end. Added to her rack on her very last draw, she had only one chance to play it, and it refused to fit anywhere on the board. Kit added an extra five and she lost five, and that was that.

"Wow," Noelle said. "You guys are intense."

"You should've seen them play Candyland when she was five," Monti said. "It was scary."

"It'll be scary tomorrow morning if we don't have ourselves put together and ready tonight," Kit said. "We'd better get a handle on that now."

Jody and Bob visited with everyone while they finished their packing, but it had to be an early night. Goodnight hugs were heartfelt and sniffly. Their 5am departure time in the morning would not allow much beyond a quick cup of coffee and brief goodbyes.

Message Received

Roland slowed his old Jeep and pulled over at the turnoff. He used his bottom lip to smooth his walrus mustache. Time to make a decision.

In his headlights, rain shone silver against a pre-dawn black background. The weather was still crappy today and didn't look like letting up anytime soon. The dirt road out to Barnabas' post box was a five-mile detour off his route to work. Even from here he could see the deep ruts in the road were brimming with brown water, and rain still splashed into them in big drops. The whole loop would be a mud slog. He'd be lucky not to get stuck and have to radio for help.

But it had been three days already, and he had committed in his contract to check the box every two to three days. And though he hadn't always been a man who honored his commitments, he was now, come wind or rain or dark of night, or however that old postal slogan went.

Besides, he wouldn't be able to live with himself if Barnabas needed help and Roland's own laziness made it all go south for the old man. Barnabas was a good friend, and Roland owed him. He didn't even want to think about where he'd be now if Barnabas hadn't talked bare, brutal truth to him a couple of years ago, when he'd been hell-bent on destroying his life like he had his marriage. He sighed, fought the Jeep back into first gear, and cranked the steering wheel.

His ex had got the Camry in the divorce, but this old heep was the right rig for this road. It was every bit as bad as he'd figured it would be, and water kept geysering up through that hole in the floorboard whenever he hit an especially deep hole. He glanced heavenward in silent gratitude for the hole being on the passenger side.

He jolted and bounced the three winding miles out to the box, wincing as the ride jammed his spine repeatedly. His eyes widened when the box appeared in his headlights.

What the hell? Someone had wrapped orange engineer tape around the box and tied it in a bow. Was it a joke? He put the brake on and left the headlights shining at the box. He fiddled with the sticky door latch, gave up and popped the door open with the heel of his hand.

Hunched against the rain, he jogged over to the box and opened the lid. He squinted down into the dark interior, catching a glint of…what? He reached in, retrieved the zippered bag, and hightailed it back to his Jeep.

Back inside he turned the heater down a click and examined the bag before opening it. A folded piece of paper had two girl's barrettes clipped to it. A driver's license slid around as he turned the bag over. He unzipped it and pulled out the note, fumbling for a moment with the barrettes to get them off the paper so he could unfold it. It was from Barnabas, so that at least made sense.

Roland,

At your earliest convenience, please send someone to Hart's Burden. I have Logan and Nora Longfire here, who met with a serious mishap in the woods. Logan broke his leg quite badly. I've set the bone, so it's not extremely urgent, but they will need transportation back to their car at the Storm Ridge trail head. If you could also contact Nora's parents at this number, she assures me her mother will let other concerned parties know they are safe.

Thank you so much for all you do to help me, and for all you will do to help these dear children, it is deeply appreciated.

Barnabas

Roland turned the paper over. He glanced in the bag at the other items. There was nothing in the note to explain the barrettes. He pulled out the driver's license. Elliot Bingham. He looked back at the note. Not Logan Longfire. Roland's mouth scrunched into a knot to one side. Who was Elliot Bingham?

He lay the note in his lap, sat back and scratched his neck, trying to make sense of it. Nothing rose to the surface, and he glanced at his watch. He'd better radio in. He was going to be late for work no matter what, now. He lifted the mic from its cradle.

"AB7F, AB7F, this is KZ7RD. Billy, you at the radio, over?"

"Where else would I be, Davis?" came a whiny tenor from the speaker.

"Great radio etiquette, Billy. Hey, let Pressman know I'll be late today. I stopped at Barnabas' box and there's some kinda emergency situation. I ain't got it all figured, but I'm gonna have to make some calls, contact the Ranger and such, over."

"Roger that, Davis. We'll do our best to manage until you drag your sorry ass in."

"Thanks Billy, you dipstick. Out."

That done, Roland returned to the mystery items in Barnabas' message bag. Except—Barnabas wouldn't have left him any mystery items. He did talk about mysterious things, but he wouldn't do this. He would have explained everything, like he did in the note.

Which meant someone else must have added to the original contents of the bag. But why hadn't they just written on the back of the note? He pondered that for minute and then grinned his lopsided grin. They must not have had anything to write with. *Pretty good thinkin', Mr. Davis, if I do say so myself.*

His grin faded quickly, though. If someone else was having an emergency, and they couldn't write it down, or stick around to explain it either, that meant he had to figure out what these additional items meant. And/or get help to do that. He'd better call Hank pretty quick, anyway, so they could get word to the Longfires' people. He retrieved the mic again.

"W7NP, W7NP, this is KZ7RD, over."

"This is W7NP, go ahead, over."

"Hey Hank, I found a weird message in Barnabas' post box. Not sure what's up, entirely, but possibly someone's needing urgent help, over."

"Roger that, Roland. What's your location, over?"

"At the post box now, Hank, but headin' out to finish the loop in a minute here. Wanna meet at Lyle's? I got a driver's license for ya, and a note from Barnabas, over."

"Affirmative, Roland. ETA 10 minutes to Lyle's. Gimme the license number, over."

Roland read him Elliot Bingham's driver's license number and signed off. He resealed the bag and tucked it under the edge of his lunch box on the passenger seat and braced himself to jolt down the rest of the muddy track to meet the Ranger. He could use another cup of java, anyhow.

Home

It started to snow as they pulled into the parking lot of their apartment complex. Austin and Warren jogged out through the fat wet flakes to help them haul their luggage in, and Gulliver did his ecstatic best to impede and obstruct the whole arrival project, but no injuries were incurred.

Kit wiped his feet and took his and Monti's bags through to their bedroom, and Monti cringed at the hunch in his shoulders as he closed the door behind him.

"It's quite a change to escape the cold into the warm, instead of the other way round!" Monti said, joining in the general stomping off of snow just inside the door. She turned to hug both boys.

"Austin and Warren, this is our daughter, Marla. Marla, Austin and Warren Woodlow." Austin shook Marla's hand, and Warren gave her a shy wave. "Thank you so much for taking care of Gulliver for us," Monti said. "And I'm sorry that it ended up being such a long time."

"Oh, no worries, Mrs. R," Austin said. "It was great to have a place to ourselves. You know, away from all the drama."

"How is the situation now, Austin? Everything resolved?" Monti kicked her wet shoes off and padded over to sink into the creaky sofa. Marla came and curled up beside her.

Austin snorted. "Not hardly," he said, running his hand back through his shaggy hair. "No disrespect to my family, but they're like a bunch of four-year-olds. 'He called me a name, did not, did too.'" He waved a frustrated hand. "All that kind of crap and worse. In front of lawyers and judges!"

"Oh, dear," Monti said. "Are you okay to go back home, then?"

"Yeah, yeah, that's no problem," he assured her, sitting across from her. "My dad's actually being the most grownup of the bunch now, even though he sorta started the whole thing. I mean he did start it, he punched Brad. But Brad was being a real—" he stopped and groped for an acceptable replacement word.

"Well, uh, Brad was in my dad's face about us," he indicated himself and Warren. "About me, really. About how Dad must be a bad influence or I wouldn't have ended up in jail, and like that." Austin's shoulders sagged. "Dad's trying to get everybody to calm down, but..." he shook his head and shrugged. Monti had no easy wisdom for a mess of that magnitude.

"Gulliver was fun," Warren said, changing the subject. "He'll eat right out of my hand."

"Gulliver will eat, period," Kit said, returning in his slippers to sit carefully in the wobbly recliner. "Out of your hand, out of a dish, off the floor...I think he'd eat out of the fridge if he could figure out how."

"He didn't stalk off and ignore you when you got home," Marla said. "I always thought cats got ticked when you went away, and punished you when you came back."

"Normal cats do," Kit agreed. "But I don't think Gulliver has ever read the manual of normal cat behavior."

"Well I'm glad," Noelle said, "I like him this way." She nuzzled his neck and his purring ramped up another notch. She had hardly put him down since they arrived.

"Did you notice he smells like smoke?" Warren asked, his cheeks flaming from talking to the cute older girl.

"He does, doesn't he?" Noelle said. "I've given him three or four baths, and the smell doesn't go away."

"Weird," Warren said.

"Yeah, especially since he apparently wasn't even in the house during the fire."

"What?" Warren's eyebrows met his hairline. "What do you mean?"

Noelle told him the story of Gulliver's return, delivered via motorcycle by an unknown...benefactor.

"That's wild," he said.

"You boys stay for dinner and catch us up on everything else we missed," Monti said.

Austin protested, "Oh, no, you don't have to do that."

"I'm not doing anything," she said. "We'll have way too much pizza if you don't stay. Did you see those fat puppies in the kitchen? They can be ready in…" she got up and glanced at the directions tucked under the plastic wrap. "About half an hour. Do you like Papa Murphy's stuffed pizza?"

"Oh man, yeah!" Warren said with enthusiasm, then blushed again when everyone smiled at him.

"That's my favorite, too," Kit said. "That and the barbecue chicken they have in the summer."

"I remember that!" Marla said. "Man, I haven't had that in years."

"It's a plan then," Monti said. She turned the oven on, finished peeling off the plastic wrap, and slid a pizza onto the rack.

Everyone ate as much pizza as they wanted. Monti was astonished at how much their guests put away, her experience with feeding teenage boys being limited and long ago, before Papa Murphy's was a thing.

After dinner, Austin and Warren scratched Gulliver under his chin and said goodbye, were admonished to drive carefully in the snow, and then it was just the Risings.

Can you get jet lag flying just from Florida to Spokane? Monti wouldn't have thought so, but she was exhausted and ready for bed, even though the clock said it wasn't even seven. She sat on the sofa and watched her girls tidy away the dinner things without feeling the least urge to help them.

Her chin itched. The scabs had finally peeled off her palms and knees, but the deep one on her chin was taking a little longer.

Monti startled awake. Noelle was nudging her knee. "Hey G, Mom and I are going to stay up for a while, but do you want to head to bed? You look pretty uncomfortable there."

"Oh, right, thanks honey." She straightened up. "I guess I should. I don't know why I'm so tired. Where's your Grandpa?"

"He's in the shower, I think," Marla said. "Come on, we'll pull you up."

"Do you have everything you need for tonight, Marla?" Monti asked as her girls hauled her out of the sofa.

"Yep. Nellie gave me the tour and helped me unpack. I'm all set."

"Okay, great." Monti felt disoriented. And old. "All right then, we can talk in the morning. My synapses are firely baring tonight." Both girls giggled, but Monti didn't get the joke. She pulled them in for a hug. "Love you both like crazy," she said into their necks.

"I love you right back, G," Noelle said, and kissed her cheek.

"Love you too, Mom," Marla said. "It's good to be home."

Monti felt tears threatening and decided bed was definitely the best place for her. She just nodded and shuffled to the master bedroom.

Steam billowed invitingly from their bathroom. She couldn't make herself open her suitcase to find her robe, so she just dropped her clothes on the floor and went to see if Kit had saved her any hot water.

***

Marla adapted easily to their routine over the next few days. Monti guessed she'd had to adapt quite a bit over the last eight years, to far worse situations than living in a cramped apartment with your parents and your daughter. She did tend to sleep in. And her taciturn nature was more pronounced than Monti remembered, but who could blame her? She probably didn't have a stock of light-hearted stories to share.

Too, she must have some anxiety about how her life was going to go now. How long would she be stuck living with her parents? Would Noelle go with her if she moved out? Monti's heart spasmed at that thought. She vowed to do everything in her power to make Marla feel welcome and loved and valued.

"What's the matter?" Kit asked. "You're white as a sheet."

"Oh, nothing," she said. "I was just thinking..." She waved it away, but then couldn't help herself. "Kit, what if Marla moves out and gets her own place, and takes Noelle with her? I couldn't stand it!"

"Wow, Monti. It might be a tiny bit premature to worry about that at this point." he sat at the table with her. "She hasn't even started looking for a job yet. She's light years from living on her own."

"Oh, I know it," Monti put her head in her hand.

"And besides, Nellie is going to light out of here sooner or later anyway. One more year of school, and she'll be transferring to Seattle, or Michigan. Boise, at least."

"That's not really helping, Kit."

He put his hand over hers. "Monti. Have you really not thought about this at all?"

"Not too much. My mind wanders in that direction and I distract it with…distractions."

"You distract your own mind with distractions?" He cocked an eyebrow at her.

"Oh hush," she said. "Never mind."

"Hey, do you want to go with me? I need to hit the hardware store for a few basics," he said. "I know we're hoping to find a better apartment shortly, but a couple of things need attention around here."

"What things?" Monti asked, envisioning Kit contorted into a pretzel under the kitchen sink. "Can't we call the super, or whatever he's called, and ask for a repair?"

"That would be an option," Kit agreed. "But we're going to need allen wrenches and screwdrivers anyway, and I don't really think tightening a couple of chairs is worth calling for help."

"Oh, the recliner? I did notice it was pretty wobbly."

"Not sure if I can fix that, but these chairs are loose, too." He demonstrated the wiggle in one of the four worn wooden chairs that constituted the dining room seating. "And the lamp in our room is about to fall apart."

Monti sighed. "You have to be fixing something, don't you, love?"

"There's always something that needs fixed," he countered.

"True. You go. You'll have lots more fun stocking your toolkit from scratch without me looking over your shoulder. And then I can stock the kitchen drawers without you, and we'll both be happy."

"Wise woman," he said.

"Besides, I'm almost done with my story. I want to finish before school starts. I won't have any time at all then."

The door opened, sucking in a swirl of snowflakes and a blast of cold air with their girls. "Do you miss Florida yet?" Kit asked Monti.

"Not really. I like the snow," she said, but felt less certain about this than she had a decade or so ago.

"Hey G & G," Noelle said. "Is it okay if Nick comes over after supper? Tomorrow's the party, you know, and I guess there's all this fancy etiquette they do, and I want him to do a tutorial." Her cheeks, pink from the cold, deepened to red. "I don't want to embarrass myself."

"Sure, Nellie. Why not invite him for supper? Then we could all do the tutorial?"

"Aren't we having pizza again?" Marla asked, holding two pizzas.

"Oh. Right. We hardly ever use butter knives and oyster forks when we serve pizza."

"Oyster forks?" Noelle looked panicked.

"Never mind, dear. And don't worry. You can always learn about oyster forks in the unlikely event you ever need to, but I doubt you'll need to know that for this party."

"He's welcome to share the pizza though," Kit said. "We haven't seen him since we got back."

"I already tried that," Noelle said. "He can't tonight, his mom is paying him and his buddies to serve at a bridge party today and they won't be done until at least seven."

"My," Monti said. She turned to Kit. "When's the last time we threw a bridge party, love?"

"You don't play bridge," Marla pointed out. "Do you?"

"Not that I recall," Monti said. "Possibly that would be a prerequisite."

Marla rolled her eyes. "You really haven't changed a bit, Mom," she said.

"Why thank you, dear." Monti said. "Well, Nellie, if you're a quick study on the etiquette tutorial, maybe he can stay for some Scrabble."

"It won't be too late?" Noelle asked. "That actually might tempt him. He's been curious..."

"About Scrabble?" Monti said.

"Well...about Scrabble as the Risings play it." She looked unwilling to elaborate further.

"Brave man," Kit said.

Hart's Burden

"Is this the clearing? At Barnabas' house?" Lydia asked.

"I think so. I don't know...his house should be right there," she said, pointing to the empty forest across the clearing from them.

"Where is it?" Lydia's voice squeaked with panic. Oddly, Nora felt none. Had God sent the deer to guide them? She had no doubt. Had they followed the deer where it led them? Yes, they had. Well then, they would be okay. She just had to figure out why the flashlight beam wasn't showing them Barnabas' house right now.

"Don't worry, baby, it'll be all right," Nora said. "Stick with me and we'll figure this out, okay?"

"I want Prince," Lydia said, a whine creeping into her tone. She was just about done, Nora could tell. She took a step out into the pitch-black clearing, and methodically swung the light slowly to the right, then to the left of where she thought the house should be.

Nothing.

She laboriously limped clear out to the middle of the clearing, Lydia clinging to her shirt, and began searching the tree line to their right.

"Nora?"

She jumped and nearly dropped the flashlight. "Logan?" She automatically tried to swivel toward his voice, kicked a hummock of dirt and went down in a hissing heap of pain.

"Nora!" Lydia yelled. "Help us, Logan!" She scrambled to find the flashlight where Nora had dropped it in the tall grass.

"Who is that?" Logan shouted from the porch. A door opened and Logan's voice was less clear. "Barnabas, someone is out there with Nora."

Barnabas appeared in the bright doorway a moment later, and wasted no time as he took his lantern down from the wall.

"Which way, my boy?"

Logan said, "The middle of the clearing, I think."

Lydia by this time had recovered the flashlight and was swinging it wildly about. She finally caught sight of Barnabas' lantern and steadied the light in that direction.

"One moment," Barnabas called out. "Lower the light a bit, please, child," he said. He slowly made his way over the saturated, uneven ground, the tip of his cane sinking into the mud with each step, to where Nora lay groaning with pain. Lydia stood staring at him with round eyes.

"Hello, dear," he said, and lay a gentle hand on her head. "All shall be well, never fear." He patted her a couple of times and moved to tend to Nora. "Nora, how are you hurt?"

Through gritted teeth she managed, "Sprained ankle." She took a deep breath and tried to lie still. "I just now kicked the hurt leg into a rock or something. I'm okay, really."

Barnabas and his lantern moved down to her ankle, where he tentatively lifted the hem of her jeans. "Oh dear," he said. "That's dreadful. You can walk though, obviously." She nodded confirmation. "Very well, can you make it the rest of the way to the house? Or do you need to rest a bit more first?"

"I can do it," Nora said. "Where's my stick?" Lydia leaped to return it to her. "Barnabas, this is Lydia. She's had a very, very bad day and has been a terrific help to me."

"How do you do?" Barnabas said with a slight bow. "Let's complete our introductions once we're in out of the rain, shall we? Here, dear, you take the lantern." He handed it to Lydia, trading her for the flashlight. "Lead the way, Lydia, we'll be right behind you."

Barnabas helped Nora get to her feet, and put a shoulder under her arm. He shone the flashlight on the ground immediately in front of them, and they made their way at long, long last to the porch of Barnabas' home.

Nora fell awkwardly into Logan's arms and wept. All the fear, all the shock of finding Lydia's father and the girl's grief, and her own pain and exhaustion, heaved out of her in gut wrenching sobs. Logan held her tightly, rubbed her back, shushed in her ear, and waited until her tears were spent.

Barnabas had brought a chair for her, and Logan held her hand as she sank into it. She didn't let go of his hand. Lydia hovered, switching anxiously from foot to foot, and Nora gripped her hand, too.

"What happened?" Logan said, which nearly set her sobbing again, but instead she choked out a humorless laugh.

"What *didn't* happen?" she said.

"Please tell us all about it," Barnabas said, "But let's go in, shall we? It's quite cold out here." So they moved indoors and dripped all over the bright, warm, dry kitchen.

While Barnabas made tea, set out a plate of shortbread, fetched a hot washcloth to wipe Lydia's face and hands, propped Nora's foot on a stool, and generally made everyone as comfortable as possible, Nora poured out the story of the simple hike gone horrifically awry.

Lydia filled in a small detail here and there, especially about the doe and fawn, and Prince, but said little else.

"But what I don't understand," Nora said, "is how we came out of the woods clear around there, instead of across from your house."

"You must've gotten off the trail in the dark without knowing it," Logan suggested.

"And," Barnabas added, "were immediately provided a guide, named Prince, to keep you from losing your way entirely." he smiled at Lydia. Lydia nodded sleepily and took another bite of shortbread.

"You have been mightily used, child," Barnabas said to Nora, who made a disparaging sound.

"Yes, you rescued this little one from the storm, and from being alone in the dark in her grief," Barnabas paused. "Think if you had not gone, Nora."

Nora's eyes filled for the hundredth time that day, and she swallowed back the lump in her throat. She nodded, and gazed at the grimy, grief-blasted girl. She was so sleepy she could hardly chew.

"We need to get Lydia to bed," Nora said. She reached for her makeshift crutch but Barnabas lay a hand on her arm.

"Let me, my dear. My wife and I raised four children, including three daughters," he said. "She did most of the work of course, and it was a long while ago now, but things can't have changed much." He thought for a moment. "Logan, if I might lay her in your lap for the journey to her room, then I can take it from there."

Logan nodded, and Barnabas leaned his cane against the table. He scooped the girl up and deposited her on Logan's lap, trailing shortbread crumbs along the way. "Why, she's light as a feather," he said. "Even soaking wet. I'd forgotten how very small they are." He straightened and retrieved his cane. "Off we go, then."

Nora watched the little band disappear into the corridor, each person in it broken in one way or another, and each unbearably dear to her. Logan soon rejoined her at the kitchen table. He leaned over and kissed her cheek.

"You about ready to give it up, too?"

"Soon," she agreed. "Maybe one more cup of tea first. The heat is finally starting to thaw my bones."

"So you posted Barnabas' message," Logan said after a companionable silence. "And when someone picks it up they'll also know that Lydia's family needs help. That's amazing too, Nora, that you thought of a way to include that information. And really, how would she have got out of the woods without you? Even if she did get out somehow, she'd have had no idea how to direct authorities back to her father's body."

Nora smiled. "Prince would probably have shown up, and she'd have followed him anywhere." She rubbed her eyes. "Her father was shot in the back, Logan. And she mentioned 'bad *men*', so there's more than one maniac out there shooting at people. I hope whoever shows up to help us doesn't get caught unaware. I didn't have any way to tell them about the shooting."

"If it's the same people we…almost encountered, then it's been going on for a few days now. Maybe someone else has heard shots and reported it."

"Yeah, that'd be good," she said. She rolled her head and arched her back. "I'm gonna have to hit the hay. After I twisted my ankle, I started fantasizing about the hot springs, but I think I'm too tired tonight."

Barnabas, a little grubbier than he had been, turned the corner into the open kitchen in time to hear her last statement. "A soak in the waters will do wonders for your ankle," he said. "If you can at all stay awake, I encourage you to soak tonight. The sooner you start the leg healing, the shorter your recovery. And you'll sleep very well afterward!"

That made sense to Nora. She nodded. "Okay, but not by myself, right? Are you guys coming?"

"Absolutely, at least I am," Logan said.

Barnabas said, "I believe I'll remain available should Miss Lydia be in any distress while you're out of earshot. I've put her directly across from your rooms, so you'll hear her in the night, but until then I shouldn't want her to cry out and no one answer."

"No." Nora said with a shudder. "Poor thing, we need to make sure that doesn't happen, thank you Barnabas."

"Not at all," he said, collecting cups from the table. "I'll just tidy the kitchen and think things over until you return." He frowned. "I don't like it. When the seamy elements of Seattle slither into our woods, I want them to slither right back out, or be helped to do so."

Nora looked at him, speechless. She hadn't seen him quite this hot under the collar. The gentle gentleman had been replaced by a firebrand with a thundery brow.

"Have you had this kind of trouble out here before?" Logan asked.

"Once in a great while," Barnabas said. "We're fairly remote, and few of the seamier sort venture so far from civilization. But now and then..." he shook his head in disgust.

"So your friend Roland might realize something bad's happening, right?" Nora said. "When he sees the driver's license and Lydia's barrettes?"

"I think he will suspect, yes," Barnabas agreed. "He's survived many dangerous situations, and has keen instincts. You needn't worry about him. Moreover, he knows who to call to get real help in attending to the matter." He smiled in an unsettling way, then brought his attention back to Logan and Nora.

"Now you two, off to the hot springs. Do you need my help? Remember where it is?"

"We'll manage, thanks Barnabas," Logan assured him. "Thanks for taking first watch over Lydia." He took Nora's hand. "Ready, love?"

She nodded, and winced as she gripped her stick and pulled herself up.

"In the morning I'll find you a better stick. Or crutches...I think we have some crutches..." Barnabas limped to the sink with a handful of teacups, muttering about crutches, and Logan and Nora made their slow way to their rooms to change. Anticipation of the blissful soak to come put a little bit of pep into Nora's laborious steps.

Dad

Nora hummed as she washed the breakfast dishes, her foot resting on a little stool. She adored the tiny villagers with their cows and their egg baskets and their ponies. She vowed to get her own wedding dishes out and use them every day when they got home, and to banish the 'practical' melamine set to the top shelf of the cupboard.

A bell rang, startling her, nearly making her drop a teacup. A bell? She listened, and it rang again. It came from outside…a doorbell?

Who could be ringing the doorbell? It was way too soon for help to have got here. She dried her hands, awkwardly positioned the crutches Barnabas had found for her, and made her way to the front door. She opened it and gasped.

"Daddy!" She threw her arms around his neck, allowing the crutches to clatter to the floor. "How did you get here so fast? I can't believe it! I thought Mom would come."

"Nora?" Her father pulled her arms from his neck. "What are you doing here?"

"Just doing the dishes, I…what do you mean?" She frowned, taking in his shocked face. "Dad, didn't you come to take us home?"

"N-no," he said. "I don't understand why you're here. Are you hurt?" He looked past her to where Logan was wheeling his way to meet them, a book in his lap. "Logan? Will someone explain what's going on?"

"Hi, Mr. Nelson," Logan said, and put out his hand. The man shook it automatically. "Come on in. We didn't expect you so soon. Or you at all, really, Nora thought you were…" he looked at Nora with eyebrows raised. "We weren't sure you would get the message," he finished.

"What message?" They stood staring at each other, incomprehension written across all three faces.

Barnabas and Lydia appeared, Lydia clutching a stuffed panda nearly as big as she was.

"Bruce Nelson?" Barnabas put out his hand to shake the visitor's hand. "Welcome to Hart's Burden." He paused and looked around at the three dazed faces. "Is there a problem?" No one answered him. "Come in, come in, bring your luggage." He gestured at the carry-on duffel sitting on the flagstones. "What seems to be the trouble?"

"Barnabas, this is my dad," Nora said, accepting the crutches he'd picked up from the floor. "But he doesn't know about the message." She paused, waiting for an explanation.

"Well, I say," Barnabas said, drawing out the words and looking back and forth between Nora and her father. "Isn't that something."

"Barnabas, I don't understand. How do you know my dad?" Nora's confusion was rapidly changing to frustration.

"I don't at all, my dear," he said. "But when Roland last brought my mail I had a letter…which said that I might, at some point in the near future, expect the hermitage's next tenant. The director was not certain it would be Bruce, but his name was at the top of the list." Barnabas stopped. "Curious. I would say astonishing, if I didn't know Who was arranging this coincidence."

"I don't know how my name could be on any list," Mr. Nelson said. "I only decided to come a couple of days ago." His brows drew together. "And that doesn't explain why my daughter is out here in the middle of the godforsaken woods."

"Quite the opposite, sir," Barnabas said, nearly under his breath. "Your boy here met with an accident, and they've taken refuge with me until they can be taken home." He took Nora's elbow. "You should put your foot up now, my dear."

"We were going camping, Daddy," she said as she let Barnabas guide her to a chair and slide the footstool under her leg.

"For our anniversary, sir," Logan put in.

"And Logan fell into the creek—"

"You don't camp, Nora," her father interrupted. "This is nonsense."

Barnabas motioned for everyone to be still. "Now, now. Just, take a moment. It's all quite explicable, but let's take a breath. Mr. Nelson, if you'll follow me, you can put your bag in your temporary quarters. You'll have my rooms after I go."

"Where are you going, Barnabas?" Lydia piped up, her face stricken with anticipated grief.

"There, there," he said, placing a gentle hand on her head. "I'm not going anywhere, little one, until you've been reunited with your mother. All right?" She nodded uncertainly. "Logan will put the kettle on, won't you my boy, and Mr. Nelson and I will be back shortly. Then we can sort it all out." With that, he turned and began walking down the hall, his cane thudding dully on the wood flooring with each step. After a moment, Nora's father started out of his daze, grabbed his duffel, and followed.

"That was weird," Logan said, after they'd watched the men disappear around the corner.

"I don't get it," Nora said.

"Your dad looks...I don't know. Haggard."

Nora's lip trembled. "He looks awful," she whispered. "Mom said she was worried about him, and I can see why. I wonder what's the matter with him?"

"Maybe he's sad," Lydia offered. "Sometimes my daddy gets really..." she gulped, clutched the panda and buried her face in its soft plush.

Nora held her arms out and Lydia came to sniffle on her shoulder. "It's okay, baby girl," she said, and waited for Lydia to get control, stroking her hair and cooing. With sad eyes she looked over the girl's head at Logan. He moved his wheelchair closer and took her hand.

When Lydia's shoulders had relaxed, Nora said, "Logan's supposed to make us some tea, but I don't think he really knows how. Do you want to help him?" Lydia sniffed and nodded. "Good girl. Maybe I could hold your Panda?" Lydia solemnly handed the damp panda to Nora, who accepted it in like manner.

Logan put the kettle on and Nora, from her chair, suggested little tasks for Lydia to do to help the project along. As Lydia set the table she told them all about the panda, who was called Rupert, apparently, and who had lived a most adventurous life. The tea was nearly ready when the two older men returned.

Nora's father had shed his jacket, and looked a hair less irritated. He sat at the table and accepted a cup of tea, though Nora had never seen him drink tea in her life. He even made appreciative noises about Barnabas' shortbread as he picked up a second piece.

"Now children, I've sketched out for your father how you ended up at my door, and you can fill in all the details later." He refilled Lydia's cup and handed her the sugar. "Perhaps, Bruce, you'd like to tell the children the story of your journey here." He gazed at Bruce with his piercing eyes, and Bruce seemed disinclined to deny his request.

He cleared his throat. "Yeah, I guess so." He shifted in his chair. He peered at Nora from under his bushy eyebrows. "Your mom and me...after the..." He rubbed his eyes. "Hang on. I'd better start at the beginning, I guess."

He turned to Barnabas. "About six years ago, we sold our farm to a developer. They dumped more money in our lap than we'd ever imagined having. Way more." He clasped his fingers together on the table and rubbed one thumb with the other. "I uh, didn't handle it well. It wasn't too bad while Nora was still at home," he looked at her and she shrugged.

"But after she left for college, I went off the deep end. Bought a lot of crap we didn't need. Made some stupid, risky investments. And..." he glanced at Lydia feeding shortbread to Rupert. "And then I...I...betrayed your mother...," his face crumpled and he covered his eyes as a sob tore through him.

Nora blanched as she sat ramrod straight. Then her face reddened with a fury Logan had seen only two or three times. She swallowed hard but didn't move or say anything. Her father quickly regained control and pulled a handkerchief from his pocket.

"A good friend of mine from church, Fred," he looked to see if

Nora remembered Fred. She gave him a curt nod. "He—they've been through some rough spots, and he sat me down one day and told me to quit being an imbecile. And that if I didn't think I could keep from destroying my life and my marriage without help, he knew of a place I could go for a while to get my head straight."

His cheeks flaming, he looked at Barnabas. "He offered to pay for my stay, but of course I didn't need his help for that, at least." He fell silent, then slowly slid his gaze to Nora. "I'm sorry, sweetheart."

An awkward silence stretched out until Nora said, "Does Mom know?"

Her father's entire body sagged. "She knows everything. She knows where I am and why." He narrowed his eyes and pointed at his daughter. "But she doesn't know where you are, Nora."

"I told her we were going camping," Nora's hackles rose. "And even after Logan got hurt I managed to send a message to her that we were stranded. Not that either one of you cares what happens to anybody in the woods."

"What?" Her father's confusion was plain.

"Nora," Logan said, and stroked the back of her arm. "Come on, honey."

"I begin to see," Barnabas said, and straightened in his chair. "Pardon me, but perhaps if you both would step back and consider the larger picture..."

Bruce flung up his hands. "What picture?" His jaw tightened. "What are you talking about, Nora, and why is everybody talking in riddles?"

"Riddles," she choked out. "It wouldn't matter If I wrote it out for you step by step. If you don't care, you don't care." Nora scraped her chair back, grabbed her crutches and limped with surprising speed down the hall to her room, slamming the door behind her.

Lydia began to whimper and Barnabas pulled her onto his lap. "Now, now, little one," he said. Logan handed her the panda and she clutched it tightly. "Please don't fret. Nora's quite upset just now, but it will soon be set right, I'm sure of it." He hugged her gently. "Can you and Rupert play on the sofa for a bit? We'll be right here, we're not going anywhere."

Lydia sniffed and wiped her eyes on a plush panda ear. "I think there are some story books on on those shelves." Barnabas pointed. "Go and see what you can find, and choose one or two for Nora to read to you later on."

She nodded and slid off his lap, the picture of reluctance, and shuffled across the great room to the wide bookshelves on the far wall. All three men watched in silence until she had settled Rupert on the sofa and become absorbed in exploring the books.

Barnabas cleared his throat. "Now. I have learned, rather late in life, I'm afraid, that sunshine is a great disinfectant. Logan, I believe it may help Nora if we bring to Mr. Nelson's remembrance her childhood trouble."

"What childhood trouble?" Bruce broke in, indignant.

Barnabas continued as if he hadn't spoken. "Will she mind if I recount the story she told me, I assumed, in confidence?"

"She won't mind, Barnabas." Logan said. "It's not...she doesn't think of it as a secret. It's just a pretty traumatic memory so she doesn't share it with many people." He shrugged his bony shoulders and heaved a sigh. "If you think it'll help, please, give it a try."

"I have no earthly idea what you guys are talking about," Bruce said, folding his arms across his chest. "Nora had a good childhood. There was no 'trauma,'" he emphasized with air quotes.

"I don't think that's entirely for you to say, Bruce," Barnabas said, "and I believe you are quite mistaken."

He folded his hands on the table and repeated the story Nora had told him of her terrified night in the woods when she was four. Of how her aunt had humiliated her afterward. Of her repeated attempts to talk to her parents about it and her heartbroken realization that they were never going to comfort her about it or help her in any way to get past it. "Was that accurate, Logan?" Barnabas asked when he had finished.

Logan nodded, trying to swallow the lump in his throat. "Yes, sir. That's it all right." He relaxed the fists his hands had formed of their own accord.

"I honestly don't remember any of that. At all," Bruce said, running his hands through his hair and sagging into his chair.

"Regardless. Loathe though you may be to accept it, you did your daughter harm all those years ago, Bruce," he insisted, "and her grief and fear did not heal. But we serve a God who brings healing and joy out of pain. He saw fit to orchestrate another traumatic time in the forest for Nora these past few days. She has revisited her fear, though unwillingly, and found strength and the beginning of healing, I believe." He looked to Logan for confirmation, and he nodded.

"But forgiveness is also part of healing," Barnabas added. "And though the presence of the offending party is not absolutely required for forgiveness to happen, our astonishing Sovereign has arranged for your and Nora's paths to cross at this crucial juncture." Barnabas sat back. "I can't recall the last time I encountered such brilliant evidence that 'the very hairs of your head are numbered."

The men fell silent as they considered how unlikely was the coincidence of Bruce and the Longfires meeting in this remote spot. If coincidences ever actually did happen.

"I'm gonna go talk to Nora," Logan said, and wheeled off down the hall.

"So when Fred said this wasn't going to be easy…"

Barnabas chuckled. "He spoke truth, my friend. But I very much doubt if you will require a 27-year sojourn at Hart's Burden to set your life straight and help your daughter to mend."

"Twenty-seven years?" Bruce blanched at the number, and Barnabas chuckled again.

"Another day, Bruce. We've plenty of time."

Nick

Marla held out her hand and shook the hand of the nervous young man, then stood on tiptoes to pull him in for a hug. He visibly relaxed. Monti smiled to herself, approving.

"So you're the hot date, huh?" Marla said, shocking Monti with her effortless one-two punch of 'put him at ease' and 'keep him off balance.' Almost if she'd grown up at Kit's knee. Which, of course, she had.

"Yes, ma'am," Nick said with only the slightest hesitation in his voice. Noelle squeezed closer to his side for moral support.

"Well, I'm looking forward to your etiquette tutorial," Marla said, taking his coat. "We never got too formal with our manners when I was growing up. Although, you could sure get in hot water if you were rude at the table." She considered. "Or sang too much."

"Sang too much?" Nick cocked his head.

Marla nodded, one corner of her mouth tweaked up in her trademark smile. "We actually had a 'no singing at the table' rule."

"Huh?" Nick said, and glanced down at Noelle seeking enlightenment.

"Don't look at me, that wasn't still a thing by the time I was around," she said. She tugged on his arm to get him to sit down.

"We had to make that rule when they were both in musicals in high school," Monti said. "Spontaneous harmonizing and improvised percussion instruments are all very well in their place..."

"Just not at their place at the table," Kit said from the recliner. "Conversation was impossible and the food got cold. Would you like a soda, young man? I know you've had a long day already, so sit down and relax while you're showing Nellie the niceties."

"Thanks, Mr. Rising," Nick said, and sat on one of their newly tightened dining room chairs.

Noelle got him a Fresca—she'd made sure they had his marginally eccentric favorite on hand—and Monti showed him the motley place setting she'd come up with from their 'furnished' kitchen.

"Will you need anything else? I'll see what we can improvise."

Nick scanned the mismatched plates, silverware, and glasses arranged in front of them, and said, "No, this is great. I don't want you to stress, Noelle, you'll do fine. There's just a couple of things to remember to make it easier."

He told Noelle about the things that tripped him up when formal waiters hovered closely, serving and taking things away. After he finished his soda he got up and demonstrated, playing the part of the waiter with practiced skill.

Eventually Noelle looked a little more confident. "Okay, thanks Nick. I know I'm still going to be nervous tomorrow, but not as much."

"They won't care," he said. "They'll adore you." His ears reddened and he glanced around covertly to see if he'd been overheard.

Marla asked him, "Do your parents do a lot of entertaining?"

"Yeah, kind of. Mostly at the country club, but sometimes at our house, too." He shook his head. "It gets boring. Mostly older people, no offense."

"None taken," she said, the corner smile tweaking again. "I sometimes find older people to be pretty boring, too."

"I'm not hearing that, are you hearing that?" Monti said to Kit. "It must be time for Scrabble. Can you stay, Nick?"

Nick could stay, and after some negotiations—Kit agreed not to sit this one out—Nick and Noelle teamed up on one side of the board. They clued him in on The Rising Variations, which he absorbed admirably, and he and Noelle beat the 'older people.'

Noelle came back in pink cheeked and shivering and giddy after saying goodbye on the front steps. Monti wrapped her in a hug. "Did you have fun?"

"Uh huh," she giggled. "I can't wait for the party!"

Monti couldn't imagine how Noelle was going to sleep, but a cup of hot cocoa did the trick for all of them.

Mom

Nora had thought that fear was her biggest problem. But as it turned out, anger fought hard for the title. Barnabas, sweet, infuriating, inexplicable man, had knocked on her door and presented her with a thick stack of folded handkerchiefs on the night of her father's arrival.

She soon recognized his wisdom, as she and her father had intense conversation after intense conversation over the next couple of days. She cried more than she thought possible.

Gradually she felt something loosening in her, and eventually found that where the fear and anger had been braced so rigidly in her heart, there was now a soft, exhausted peace.

Logan hovered around the edges while she and her dad worked through the thing. He helped Barnabas and read and kept Lydia entertained. Nora barely noticed when he started practicing with crutches. But the day after that Barnabas examined his leg thoroughly again and removed the splint.

Nora's father looked on during the examination, listening to Nora's description of Logan's injury with some skepticism. "An infected compound fracture? How could it have healed this fast?" he asked, fingering the pot of Barnabas' salve she had handed him. "Is this available on the market?"

Barnabas' brow went thundery. "Do not think along those lines, Bruce. It will not do." He gathered up the remains of the bandages and splint. "And in any case, the salve would not be so efficacious away from Hart's Burden."

"Why not?" Bruce asked.

"The effect is—what is the word? Synergistic. The salve and the hot springs work together. And, I believe, the blessing on this place plays its part in the healing that happens here."

***

That evening they all soaked in the synergistic springs. Nora swore she could feel her ankle improving every moment, and Logan, freed from the wheelchair, got to wade around cautiously and swim in the pool for the first time, wearing a big grin the entire time.

While Barnabas and Bruce chatted on the steps and Lydia splashed around, Logan and Nora sat under the waterfall together, their pleasure tempered with regret.

"They're bound to show up soon. Tomorrow, maybe," Logan said.

"I know," Nora said, pouting. She leaned on his shoulder. "Then we'll have to go home and be grownups again."

"I think you've been pretty grown up, Nora-ne-Nelson," he said, lifting her hand to his lips and kissing it.

"Yeah, I guess you're right. But still, it's been like a dream. A magical adventure in a different dimension or something. Now it'll be work and school, work and school." She sat up. "I changed my mind."

"About what?" Logan asked, concern creasing his forehead.

"No, wait. I changed it again." She flashed him a smile, looking sideways at him.

"Gonna tell me what you're talking about?"

"I was thinking about the List of Worsts, and how this adventure shouldn't go on it after all. But that first day and night? They totally need to stay on it."

"You got that right!"

"But I think we should start a List of Bests, too," she added, turning to face him. "Then our first anniversary can go on both lists."

***

When the doorbell rang again, no one answered it.

Nora and Lydia were having a blast in the costume room, laughing at the odd clothes and taking pictures with a vintage

Polaroid camera Barnabas had produced at breakfast. Barnabas and Logan were giving Bruce a thorough tour of Hart's Burden, and Nora hadn't seen them for a couple of hours.

So when a woman's voice said, "Lydia?" Nora about jumped out of her skin.

Lydia, decked out in an ancient flower-trimmed hat and feather boa, spun around at the sound and shouted, "Mommy!" She tripped out of the heeled pumps she was wearing and barreled into her mother. Then she burst into tears. Her mother knelt and enveloped the girl in her arms, tears streaming down her own face.

"I got here as fast as I could, baby," she said, covering Lydia's head with kisses.

Nora, feeling she was intruding on this private grief, quietly began putting away the scattered garments and accessories. She happened to glance at the doorway and was startled to see a thin, rough looking man staring in at them. His walrus mustache, deeply lined face and raggedy ponytail made her think of the Vietnam vet who lived in the woods near her school. But he smiled and gave her a shy wave.

"Barnabas around?" he said.

"Um, yes he is. I'm not sure exactly where, though." Nora grabbed the single crutch she was still using and stepped carefully over the shoes and bonnets still strewn about the floor, making her way to the door. "Are you Roland?"

"Oh, yes, sorry," Roland said, and stuck out his hand. "Roland Davis, nice to meet you."

"I'm Nora Longfire," she said, shaking his hand.

"Oh, Longfire, from the note. Good."

"So you got the message, great," she said. "And you must have figured out the barrettes and everything." She gestured at Lydia's mom.

"Sure did. And on the way back here, I put half a dozen pens and a new notepad in the post box."

Nora laughed. "Thank you! I'm sure the next damsel in distress will appreciate that."

He nodded at Lydia and his face grew serious. "This little damsel is in some serious distress."

"Yes, poor thing." Nora turned toward the mother and daughter. Lydia had calmed down and her mom stood, though Lydia clung to her waist as soon as she was upright. "Mrs. Camacho? I'm Nora Longfire," Nora said, and offered her hand again.

"Please, call me Tammi," the woman said with a tear-stained smile, and shook Nora's hand. "Can you tell me what happened?"

"Yes...some of it," Nora said. "Let's go out to the kitchen. Would you like a cup of tea, Tammi? Or coffee maybe?" She glanced at Roland, who mouthed 'coffee' and gave her a silent thumbs up.

"Either, I don't care, thanks," Tammi said, stroking Lydia's hair as Nora had done so many times. But it was clean and tangle-free now, and Nora was grateful Tammi hadn't had to see her little girl soaking wet, filthy, and shivering in the cold rain.

They walked back down the hall and the new arrivals sat at the table while Nora started a pot of coffee. Lydia climbed immediately into Tammi's lap and wound her arms around her mother's neck.

"Where's Elliot? Is he hurt?" Tammi asked. "Lydia said he's gone...to the hospital? And something about bad men?"

Nora blanched and glanced at Roland. Of course, there was no way either of them could know what had happened to Tammi's husband. Her ex-husband.

"Tammi," she said leaning her crutch on the table and moving to sit facing the woman. "I'm so sorry to have to tell you this, but he's dead."

"What? Are you sure?" Her words morphed into sobs and she clutched Lydia tightly as the girl began crying again, too. Nora exchanged looks with Roland, and covered her own wet eyes with one hand. Roland got up and went to finish the coffee set up, appearing to be no stranger to this kitchen and its accoutrements.

Tammi got herself marginally under control and said, "Tell me."

Into the World

Nora told Tammi how she'd met Lydia, what had happened through that long, dreadful day, and where Elliot Bingham's body was at this moment.

Barnabas, Logan and Nora's father returned at some point during the telling. Barnabas and Roland silently shook hands and all three men listened intently while Nora finished the harrowing story.

When she was done, tears streamed unceasing down Tammi's face and Lydia sniffled into her mom's shirt.

Barnabas motioned for the four of them to move to the living area, giving Tammi and her daughter some privacy.

"You and Tammi hiked in from the post box?" Barnabas asked.

Roland nodded. "We went the alternate route, because that low area near the box is still pretty boggy after all that rain. It takes a little longer, but I think we should go back the same way. Hank loaned me a park van and it's sittin' at the box so we can carry everyone out in one trip from there. Hank'll meet us at the station to take statements and see what else needs to be done." He shifted in his seat.

"Where exactly is Mr. Bingham's body? I'll need to give Hank an idea where to look."

Barnabas fetched another map from his wide drawer—the one Nora had used hadn't survived the wet walk back. This one was incredibly detailed, and after Nora located the huge boulder she was able to point out with fair confidence where to look for orange engineer tape wrapped around a giant cedar, and a mylar shroud anchored with pretty rocks. Roland seemed satisfied as he folded the map and tucked it into his pocket.

"I seriously hate to rush anybody," he said in a low voice, "but I gotta report for work tomorrow bright and early, and it's gonna take the rest of the day to get these folks taken care of."

"Quite right," Barnabas said, and immediately pulled himself back up. "How soon can you children be ready to go?" he asked Logan and Nora.

"Oh, in a few minutes," Logan said. "We just have to stuff everything back in our packs."

Barnabas nodded. "Very good." He pointed at the crutches strewn around the sofa. "You'll need a sturdy stick or cane, each of you, to replace those for this hike," he said. "Crutches will never do in the woods. You pack and I'll find them." He limped away shaking his head. "It's impossible to predict what one will need in this place."

The Longfires headed down the hall and Barnabas stopped at the table where Tammi sat rocking Lydia on her lap. "Pardon me, ladies, but I'm afraid you'll need to prepare to go shortly. Roland must be to work early tomorrow, so there's no time to spare for a longer visit."

"Oh...oh sure, thank you," Tammi said. "Come on, baby girl, we have to get ready to go home." She kissed Lydia's forehead and nudged her to slide off her lap. "What do you have to take with, Lydia?"

Lydia shrugged. "I lost my backpack. Oh!" She dashed down the hall to her room and came back with Rupert the Panda. "Barnabas, can I take Rupert?"

"Certainly, young lady, please do," he said, laying a gentle hand on her head. "I'd be very pleased to think of him living with you."

"Are you sure?" Tammi asked.

He waved away her objection. "Please don't give it another thought. If it brings her some comfort, I'm deeply grateful for her to have it. I don't even know how it came to be here, honestly. Children don't generally stay here."

There followed a quarter hour or so of bustling activity while packs were filled, canes found and tried, packets of shortbread and bottles of water distributed, and hugs given all around. Then suddenly everyone was ready, and they stood in a group in the foyer, looking at one another.

Barnabas broke the awkward silence. "Well, children, let me pray for you, will you?" They all agreed.

He raised one hand and looked through the open door toward the late afternoon sky. "Abba, Father. I send these children back into the world with a heavy heart, having come to love them. But of course, you love them so very much more than I do, and I know you'll watch over them. Give them comfort, and peace, and the healing for their bodies and hearts that only you can work. Light for them the next steps on the path ahead. Teach them, as you've taught me, to know and love you, to love one another, and to be sure of your presence and your love for them, even when more difficult days come, as I know they must until you call us home and we can finally leave grief and pain behind forever. In the name of Jesus, amen."

"Amen," echoed several of them.

Lydia wrapped herself around Barnabas' legs and he stroked her shiny hair. "There, dear," he said. "Time to go for now." He smiled at her mother, who peeled Lydia away and picked her up.

The girl stiffened in her arms and stage-whispered, "Mommy! Look!"

Tammi turned around and inhaled sharply. The rest of them stepped out onto the flagstones. In the center of the clearing, the gigantic buck stood gazing at them with his shining chocolate eyes, his many-tined antlers a magnificent crown upon his head.

"It's Prince!"

"It sure is," Nora breathed. Logan stepped close behind her and put an arm around her waist.

"Wow," he said.

Lydia wriggled down from her mother's arms in an instant, and before anyone could stop her she ran out to the deer and stopped inches from him.

"Lydia!" Tammi called, panic in her voice. The girl reached out her small hand and the buck dipped his head to allow her to stroke his velvety nose.

"Hi Prince," she said softly. "Did Abba send you to say goodbye? We're gonna go home now." She stepped closer, lay her head on his broad neck and smoothed her hand over his twitching flank.

"Are you all seein' what I'm seein'?" Roland said.

"Quite," said Barnabas. "Astonishing."

Tammi stepped tentatively out into the clearing, panic and protectiveness plainly fighting for control. She walked slowly until she could reach forward and hook one finger in Lydia's sweatshirt hood. She tugged gently. "Lydia," she said in a trembling voice. "Come away, honey."

"He won't hurt us, Mommy," Lydia said, "He's for helping." But she allowed herself to be drawn back. "'Bye, Prince," she said, and waved.

The buck lifted his gaze to the awestruck group for a moment, then did that marvelous leaping turn and stalked majestically into the forest.

"He didn't go on the path," Lydia noticed.

"I guess he knows we have Roland to guide us today," Nora said. "He just came to say goodbye, like you said."

"Mommy, can I have french fries and a 'nilla milkshake when we get back to civilization?"

That broke the spell, and everyone laughed. The people departing shook hands with the two remaining, and hugged again, and some of them blinked back a few tears.

Nora whispered, "Thank you," into Barnabas' ear.

"Not at all, my dear. I'm naught but—"

"I know. Naught but a bondslave," Nora said, smiling. "Like me. All the same, I'm very grateful for everything, and I hope we meet again."

"Well of course we shall, child. Perhaps not until the next chapter of the Story, but then! Then we'll have plenty of time for tea and shortbread and walks in the woods, if we still want such things. And no calamities at all."

"Ready, Nora?" Logan switched his cane to the other side and shook Barnabas' hand. "Goodbye, sir."

"I'm ready," Nora said. Then she got a good grip on the gnarled, polished walking stick Barnabas had given her, grabbed Logan's hand and followed the others back out into the world.

New Year's Eve

Marla and Noelle declared Friday to be Spa Day, dashing out into the winter wonderland first thing to get supplies. Queen Esther would've been proud to participate in their beautifying, though Noelle had 12 hours rather than 12 months to get gorgeous.

Monti joined in on the treatments intermittently, ending up with exfoliated skin on her face and sparkly polish on her toenails. But she mostly wrote, coming out to take a picture or two on her coffee breaks and whenever the giggling was irresistible. Kit had been gone much of the day working on several of the thousand details of the rebuilding project, so Monti took advantage of the time, everyone else being occupied, to try and finish her story.

Next week she had to return to her teaching schedule and Noelle would be back in classes. That would leave Marla and Kit home together, and Monti thought that was going to work out fine. Every so often, one of them would bounce an idea off the other regarding Marla's slowly developing bicycle repair and rental business idea. Marla knew she'd have to find work in the meantime, but they were increasingly confident that with Kit's help, Marla could make that project work.

Their daughter still looked rough, even after Spa Day. The hard years had taken their toll. Lines of pain and sorrow were etched deeply into her face, and the damage to her hair would have to grow out.

Already since they'd reunited with her, though, Monti could see a softening beginning, an overall easing of tension. And though Marla was as taciturn as ever, she was becoming more open. Yesterday she'd called Jody and talked with her for quite a while about the Psalm 32 study. An idea for a family Bible study in the new year kept banging around in Monti's head and she needed to remember to talk to Kit about it.

But today was all about Noelle. Kit finally returned, depositing a box in their bedroom before coming out to catch up with his girls. Then before Monti knew it her granddaughter, holding Marla's hand, emerged from her bedroom to twirl for them in her lovely pink ball gown, gossamer layers of silk and tulle swirling in a soft cloud around her. Her updo was perfect. Her nails and makeup were perfect. Her eyes and her shoes sparkled.

Kit excused himself and disappeared again into their bedroom, returning a moment later with a stole draped across his arm. Monti gasped and he winked at her.

"Nellie, this is for you." He shook it open. It looked like fox, almost. A rich scattering of ultra-fine opalescent glitter in the faux fur made the stole shimmer as Kit held it up. Noelle gasped and clasped her hands.

"I know your grandmother would have loved for you to wear her fox tonight but it was, of course, lost in the fire." He draped the stole across Noelle's shoulders, just as Monti had imagined doing. "I hope this will do in its place."

"Oh Grandpa," Noelle sighed, fighting tears.

"Don't cry!" Marla said, "We'll have to redo your eyes if you cry!" But Marla's voice was choked with tears, and Monti's eyes filled, remembering Marla at ten and eleven, begging to wear the fox just for a few minutes. She had had her own long blond curls in those days, and had looked like a miniature princess swathed in the rich fur.

Marla had to be remembering that, too. She didn't know Noelle had worn it too, when she was a girl, looking just like her mother at that age.

"Thank you," Noelle said, and stood on tiptoe to kiss his cheek.

The doorbell made its quirky ring/squelch sound, and Monti welcomed Nick in. The smile on his face turned to shock and awe when he caught sight of Noelle. Whatever polite greeting had been on his lips was gone forever. Monti thought he'd be lucky to put a coherent sentence together for the rest of the evening, which made her grin.

She decided to take pity on him and help him out. She looped her arm through his and said, "Is this for Noelle?" pointing out the corsage in his hand.

"Uh...yes! Yes, um, this is for you, Noelle," he stammered, handing it over. "You look...oh my gosh." He gulped, poor thing.

Noelle was melting into his gaze. She reached blindly for the corsage box, but since she wasn't looking at it, her aim was off. Without a word, Marla took it from Nick's hand, opened it and slid the corsage's wristband onto Noelle's wrist.

After several more moments of stunned silence, Kit said, "How are the roads, Nick?" This brought the boy back to earth.

"Oh, they're fine, sir. They're plowed and sanded, good traction all the way."

"Good to hear. Nevertheless, drive with care, will you? Speaking for all of us, you have our very favorite person in your charge."

"Yes, sir, I will," he said, tearing his eyes away from Noelle to look at Kit. "She's my favorite person, too, sir." He flushed red from neck to ears with that, and Monti and Marla exchanged wide eyed glances.

"Very good," Kit said, trying to keep a straight face. "Midnight or so, do you think?"

"How about one, G?" Noelle put in. "Just in case, you know, we need to drive slow to be safe." She blushed too, and looked to her mother for a supporting opinion. Marla just nodded.

Monti kissed Noelle on the cheek and hugged Nick. "Have fun, you two," she said.

Marla kissed her daughter, too, and shook Nick's hand. "Take good care of my baby girl."

"Yes ma'am," he said. "I'll have her home safe and sound by one o'clock."

Then they were gone, into the starry moonlight sparkling on fresh fallen snow, into the magical realm of brand-new love. The very finest kind, where you discover that you've fallen in love with your best friend.

Monti, Kit and Marla stared after the disappearing tail lights of

Nick's Supra.

"You're sneaky," Monti said.

"Not on purpose. I was on my appointed rounds, and happened to drive by a shop with that stole in the window. It reminded me, and I couldn't leave it there."

"It's perfect," Monti said. Winding her arm around his waist, she tilted her head up for a kiss.

"Thanks, Dad," Marla said, and wrapped her arm around him from the other side.

"You're welcome, daughter. And if this isn't the perfect way to end a year, I don't know what is," he said, his arms around their shoulders.

"Well," Monti said, "there's Scrabble..."

Epilogue

Roland wiped his feet on the mat outside Hart's Burden. A rich swirl of cinnamon-scented air drifted out when Bruce opened the door, and Roland inhaled deeply.

"Hey Bruce," he said, and stepped inside. "Smells good in here, Barnabas. It's making me drool." He set Barnabas' mail on the table as usual, and helped himself to a cup of coffee.

"Good to see you again, Roland," Bruce said. The two shook hands.

"Ah! A letter from Nora, how lovely," Barnabas said, glancing at the top envelope before donning an oven mitt. The cinnamon rolls were ready to come out of the oven.

"There's one from Nora for you too, Bruce," Roland said, "and Lydia sent a card." He stirred sugar into his coffee.

"Got some news." He cleared his throat. "Hank told me this morning they got the ballistics report back the other day on the bullets in little Lydia's dad." He shook his head with disgust. "They had no problem tracing the rounds to a known poacher, some rich mover-and-shaker dude outta Seattle who don't think the hunting regs apply to him. He got dinged for it last year, and before that skated two or three times after a word in the right ear."

"Really." Barnabas frowned. "I think he'll find that the manslaughter laws do apply to him regardless of his friends' ears."

"I sure hope so. There's lots of ways to be stupid in this life, and I'm especially against the ones that hurt other people. I hope they put him away for a long time. But I ain't holdin' my breath."

Barnabas lifted out three steaming hot cinnamon rolls onto plates and brought them to the table. "Roland," he said as he sat, "justice is occasionally served in this country."

"Yeah, I guess."

"It might actually be quite a promising scenario."

"How do you mean?" Roland said.

"Well if this convicted poacher is a mover and shaker and has powerful ears at his disposal, I suppose that also means he's wealthy."

"I would assume."

"Then consider this. I believe he's committed a Class C felony, since he was convicted of the same offense less than five years ago."

"The poaching?" Bruce asked.

"Yes. And in many places manslaughter, even involuntary manslaughter, is handled like first degree murder when it happens in the course of a felony."

"He'd have a hard time skating on that," Bruce said.

"Indeed. Not only that, Lydia's mother can sue the man for wrongful death. If they have any kind of decent lawyer, you can be sure that path will be thoroughly explored and doubtless recommended once the criminal verdicts have been handed down. I would predict sizable compensatory and punitive damages could be won."

"Are you a lawyer, Barnabas?" Roland said.

"Oh, I may have been," he said, waving any further questions away as he sipped his coffee. "You know, even Logan could bring suit against the man."

Bruce took a guess. "For pain and suffering?"

"Personal injury. Perhaps pain and suffering, too. Medical costs, lost wages, his young age, the life-threatening nature of his dreadful injury occurring in a remote wilderness…he'd have quite a strong case."

Barnabas picked up Nora's letter, loosened the unglued corner of the flap and then neatly tore down one end of the back of the envelope, an unusual method Roland had copied and adopted as his own. Barnabas read for a moment and then chuckled. "Roland, my boy, we've been invited to a surprise birthday party."

"Let me guess. Lydia."

"Yes, her 8th birthday is next week." He looked at Bruce. "I believe that will dovetail nicely with the conclusion of our shared time here." He paused. "Do you think you're ready to be on your own?"

"Yes," Bruce said, drawing the word out. "I think so. I have a lot of work to do still, obviously, but yeah, I think it'll be fine."

"Excellent. Let's plan on that, then. I'll be happy to take any letters for your daughter with me."

"I'll come by early that day and help you lug your bags out, Barnabas. Then you can ride with me to the party," Roland said.

The men ate their cinnamon rolls and drank their coffee, reading aloud bits of the letters from the young people they all cared deeply about. They laughed at Lydia's description of Rupert the Panda's adventures, and prayed together for the healing still needed for the girl and for Logan and Nora. Then they pushed the plates away and helped Barnabas begin to plan his own journey back into the world.

About the Author

LeeAnn Bonds is the author of Montana Rising: Wordplay. The people she writes about persevere through unusual difficulties to live abundant, faithful lives, inspiring her to do likewise.

LeeAnn currently lives with her husband in Saipan, where they have the same beautiful weather all the time, except when they have typhoons instead.

Connect with LeeAnn at www.leeannbonds.com

Also by LeeAnn Bonds

Montana Rising: Wordplay

Available at Amazon.com